The Lake

The Lubetkin Legacy

By the same author

A Short History of Tractors in Ukrainian
Two Caravans
We Are All Made of Glue
Various Pets Alive and Dead

The Lubetkin Legacy

MARINA LEWYCKA

FIG TREE
an imprint of
PENGUIN BOOKS

FIG TREE

UK | USA | Canada | Ireland | Australia
India | New Zealand | South Africa

Fig Tree is part of the Penguin Random House group of companies
whose addresses can be found at global.penguinrandomhouse.com.

First published 2016
001

Copyright © Marina Lewycka, 2016

The moral right of the author has been asserted

Set in 12/14.75 pt Dante MT Std
Typeset by Jouve (UK), Milton Keynes
Printed in Great Britain by Clays Ltd, St Ives plc

A CIP catalogue record for this book is available from the British Library

HARDBACK ISBN: 978–1–905–49056–1
TRADE PAPERBACK ISBN: 978–0–241–24921–5

www.greenpenguin.co.uk

For Kira, Maya and Yanja

'Nothing is too good for ordinary people.'

Berthold Lubetkin, architect of the
Finsbury Health Centre, 1938

BERTHOLD: *Sweet sherry*

'Don't let them get the flat, Bertie!' gasped my mother as they carried her away on the stretcher, clutching my hand as though she was clinging on to dear life itself. Through a haze of grief, regret and Lidl own-brand sweet sherry, I played the ghastly scene over and over in my head, sifting my memory for details.

It had started out like any other day, with an early morning walk to pick up the newspaper and a pint of milk. I stopped for a latte at Luigi's on the way back, one of my small indulgences – one of the very few, I should add – the intense aroma of coffee a blast of pleasure in my unexciting world. I finished, paid and stepped out on to the pavement when suddenly a white van sped up out of nowhere. A pigeon that was foraging for scraps on the road a few feet away couldn't lift off fast enough. I heard the thud of impact. The bird fell, stunned, then it started desperately batting with one wing. I could see that the next passing vehicle would make it roadkill so I bent to pick it up. It flapped and struggled in my hands but I gripped it tight and carried it to the garden at the front of our block of flats, where I set it down on the grass under a cherry tree. As it fluttered away, I noticed it only had one leg; a raw pink stump protruded from the grubby under-feathers where the other should have been. One of life's little casualties – like me.

As soon as I entered the flat, I sensed that something was wrong. Flossie, our African grey parrot, was hopping from foot to foot in her cage squawking in her strange dalek voice.

'God is dead! First of March, 1932!'

Mum had still been in bed when I went out, but now she

was sprawled on the carpet in the living room, her eyes closed, a thin sour-smelling drool leaking from her mouth. The sherry bottle on the table was half empty. I felt a twinge of anxiety, sharpened by irritation. Oh fuck, it was only nine o'clock and she'd been at the bottle already.

'Mum? Are you okay?'

'You're on your own now, son.' As I leaned to button a cardigan around her shoulders, she grasped my hand.

'Don't let them get the flat, Bertie!'

'Who, Mum, who?'

She sighed and closed her eyes. Most likely she'd overdosed on sherry – it had happened before – but I called the doctor just in case.

Dr Brandeskievich, a whiskery old cove who I suspect had once been Mother's lover, applied the stethoscope to her chest with more diligence than seemed strictly necessary, all the while making tutting noises that got trapped like the morsels of breakfast in the thicket of his moustache.

'Poor little Lily. Better send you off to hospital.'

While he called an ambulance, I packed an overnight bag for her.

'Don't forget my make-up, Bertie!'

Mother's vanity was endearing. Yesterday you'd have said she looked good for her eighty-two years, but today everything about her was altered – her cheeks and lips had lost their colour and her eyes seemed to have shrunk deeper into her skull, so she didn't look like my mother at all but a tired stranger acting out an impersonation. How had this sudden change come about? It had crept up on her so gradually that I had not noticed the point at which my indomitable mother had become a frail old lady.

Then the ambulance arrived and two guys lifted her on to a stretcher. I watched them out of the window walking the stretcher down the winding path through the cherry grove. A gust of wind lifted the blanket, and Mother's white nightdress fluttered like a moth. I felt a sob rising in my throat.

Dr Brandeskievich laid a steadying hand on my shoulder. 'Let me know if you need something to help you sleep.'

As the sound of the siren faded in the street outside, a sinister silence of bottled-up anxiety settled over the flat; even Flossie was quiet as if listening for her mistress's voice. They have a strange Dom–sub relationship, those two. In her bedroom, the lingering scent of L'Heure Bleue and a trail of discarded clothing on the floor accentuated her absence: fluffy high-heeled mules; a white cashmere shawl with visible moth-holes; a cream silk slip with a mysterious brown stain; a pair of creased satin French camiknickers. There was something queasy about this wanton display of my mother's undergarments. I left them where they were and went and made myself a tinned tuna and lettuce sandwich in the kitchen.

Later that day I phoned the hospital – it was the same hospital she had retired from more than twenty years ago – to be told that Mother was asleep and comfortable now; I could visit her on the ward tomorrow. After I'd put the phone down, the silence in the flat jangled in my ears. I wished I had taken up the doctor's offer of sleeping tablets, but I had to make do with half a bottle of Mother's sweet sherry, which made me feel nauseous without sending me to sleep.

'Goodnight, Flossie.'

I tucked her in under a tablecloth to keep her quiet during the night, as Mother used to do.

'Goodnight, Flossie!' she replied.

VIOLET: *Curtains*

The morning sunlight pouring in through the window wakes Violet much too early. The previous tenants seem to have taken everything – even the curtains. She dives back down under the duvet which Jessie lent her. It's warm in bed but the flat is cold, and she needs a pee. The carpet under her bare feet feels sticky and the smell from the bathroom is disgusting.

Still, it feels good to have her own place after a month of sleeping on Jessie's sofa, and the daily commute from Croydon was a grind. This ex-council flat in Madeley Court is fifteen minutes by bus from her office. It'll do for now.

She cleans her teeth, then splashes cold water on her face, pats it dry on her T-shirt – her towel is still in her suitcase – and smiles at her reflection in the smeared mirror screwed to the wall. Despite the dishevelled hair and the zombie-like smudges of mascara around her eyes, she likes what she sees: a young woman with a quick smile, white teeth and healthy skin; a young black woman, twenty-three today, who has just started a good job at a respected City firm, a job she has trained for and worked for; a job she thinks she deserves, but can hardly believe she has got. What she really needs now is a coffee.

There's no coffee and not even a kettle in the kitchen, but a chaos of takeaway boxes with mouldy remnants of food and broken plastic cutlery sticking out, jumbled together with half-empty drinks bottles, fag ends, scratch cards, socks, trainers, a pair of underpants, opened tins, packets of crisps, pizza crusts . . . her eyes glaze over. The people before her were students. Boys. Typical. Back in the bedroom, which turns out to be not a bedroom at all but the flat's living room with three beds in it, she pulls on her clothes, locks the door behind her, and goes downstairs in search of coffee.

A block away on the main road is a small brown-painted café with a striped awning called Luigi's. She orders a double cappuccino with a croissant and gets out her laptop to check her emails. There is a flurry of messages from her friends, some with ecards attached, and one from her mother wishing her 'Happy Birthday' and good luck in her new job.

Thanks, she writes back, I'll need it. Her role is trainee account manager in the International Insurance Department of Global Resource Management where her boss is the formidable Gillian Chalmers, a small steely woman with a quiet voice and a tough reputation, who grilled her during her interview and seemed displeased at all her answers. The other interviewer was Marc Bonnier who heads up the Wealth Preservation Unit, who was almost as intimidating as Gillian, despite his chin dimple and a twinkling smile that reminds her of Jude Law. Her friend Jessie once told her that a chin dimple is a sign of sensitivity in a male. It would be nice to work for him, she thinks.

At the next table in the café, an elderly man is nursing a latte in a glass cup and reading the *Guardian*. He has a baldish head and a morose expression on his face. Jessie's mum once said that reading the *Guardian* makes you morose compared with the *Telegraph*. Maybe he does not know this. Apart from him the café is empty. On the main road, buses and lorries are thundering past, but Luigi's is calm and cosy, with soul music playing quietly in the background, the gentle hiss of the coffee machine and the rustle of the old man's newspaper. She finishes her coffee, and is about to go in search of some rubber gloves and a load of bin liners to start clearing the flat, but instead she gets out her phone and calls the agency in a cool assertive voice that matches her new status as a City worker.

'The flat has been left in a disgusting condition. Please send someone round to clear up and make it fit for habitation. Thank you so much.' Ha! That feels good.

Then she sits down and orders another coffee.

BERTHOLD: *A blue butterfly*

Next day I cycled over to the hospital, locked up my bike against the railings and stowed my cycle clips in my anorak pocket. The ward was on the first floor, at the end of a long corridor that smelled of antiseptic and had branches named for unpleasant-sounding procedures like Spectroscopy, Oral Surgery, Trauma. In my experience hospitals are like condemned cells, best avoided, but sometimes you have no choice.

It took me a moment to recognise the frail, dishevelled old woman propped up in bed as my mother. Her appearance shocked me. Dishcloth-grey hair, limp and uncombed, pink lipstick that overshot the edges of her mouth, a dab of bright blue eye shadow on one eyelid but not the other. Dear Mum: even in extremis, she was still trying to look her best.

'Bertie! Get me out of here!'

'How are you, Mum?'

I handed over my bag of grapes and kissed her, continental style, on both cheeks. The ritual of gallantry perked her up.

'There's nothing wrong with me, Berthold.' She swivelled her eyes around the ward. 'I want to go in an NHS hospital.'

'This is an NHS hospital. You used to work here, remember?'

'No, I used to work up Homerton.' Her blue-shadowed eyelid fluttered like a lost butterfly. 'They're trying to kill me, Bertie. To get the flat.' The spark of conspiracy brightened her eyes.

'Nonsense. They wouldn't . . .'

But maybe they would. A stab of panic caught me between the ribs. Mum had always promised that after she died the flat she had rented from the Council, ever since it was built in the 1950s, would pass to me. But lately she had started muttering darkly that there was a plot to take it away from us.

'It's global capitalism that done this to me, son.'

'It's probably just sherry, Mum.'

'I didn't touch a drop, Bertie. Nor any food.' She sat up, hitching up her nightie with agitated hands. 'They're starving me to death. All you get in here is a few lettuce leaves and a pot of yoghurt. And bloody fresh fruit. In the NHS you get tinned peaches in syrup.' She glanced dismissively at my grapes. 'Did you bring my ciggies, son?'

'I don't think you're allowed to smoke in hospital.'

'That's what I mean. They're killing me. It would never happen in the NHS.'

At that moment, a violent spasm of coughing from the next bed made us both turn around. An ancient crone with grey, wrinkled skin was clearing her throat with a horrible outpouring of phlegm into a cardboard receptacle on her bedside table.

'Shut up, Inna,' said Mother. 'That sound is disgusting. This is my son, Berthold, come to see me. Say hello.'

'Nuh, Mister Berthold.' The crone peered at me between drapes of long silver hair and held out a hand as bony as a bunch of twigs. 'You lucky you ev lovely son, Lily. Nobody come visiting to me.'

'Stop moaning. Don't be a Moaning Minnie,' said Mum. 'Keep on the sunny side!' Her voice quavered into her favourite song, which I remembered from childhood. 'Always on the sunny side!'

'Sunny side! Ha ha! No sunny side round here, Lily.' The crone struck out defiantly on her highway of negativity. 'Too many bleddy foreigners. Every day somebody get dead.'

'They're dying because it's private.' Mother pursed her lips severely. 'It's wrong to be racist, Inna. We should be grateful to all those coloured people leaving their own sunny climes to come and work for us.'

'Aha! Good you tell me is privat.' Inna smoothed her sheet with her twiggy hands. 'I was think we in Any Cheese.'

'No,' asserted Mum. 'There's less death in the NHS.'

'That doctor got pink tie.' The old lady pointed at a young doctor leaning over an elderly cardiac arrest at the far end of the ward, and whispered, 'Pink mean homosexy?'

'It don't make no difference what he is,' replied Mum. 'Being queer don't harm nobody.'

'You always right, Lily.' Inna cleared her throat and spat again. 'Good you tell me. I know nothing. In my country everybody normal.'

Then her eyes rested curiously on me and on the crimson T-shirt I was wearing, now faded to a dusky pink from years of washing.

'Take no notice,' Mother murmured to me, 'she's from Ukraine, like my Lucky. Got beetroots on the brain. Emphasism. She gets everything mixed up. Don't you, Inna?'

The crone's wrinkles realigned themselves merrily like an obscure script on her aged face. 'Better mix it up than dead!'

'We're all dead in the end.' Suddenly, Mother reached for my hand, and pulled me down close to whisper in my ear. 'Are you thinking of getting married again, son? You might need someone to look after you, if I don't come out of here alive.'

'Ssh. Don't talk like that, Mum. You're going to get better.'

This talk about marrying again had me worried, for Mother had always been hostile towards any woman I brought home – especially Stephanie, my acerbically beautiful ex-wife, on whom I had doted beyond the normal call of husbandly duty. Stephanie had realised right from the start that Mother was her only serious rival and the two had regarded each other with mutual loathing scarcely concealed under a mask of kiss-kissy politeness. When we had finally divorced, Stephanie handed me over into the care of my mother like a recycled mattress whose springs have gone: 'You can have him back, Lily. All yours. He's completely fucked.' Now it sounded as though Mother was preparing to pass me on again.

'The doctor said . . .' she pointed in Dr Pink-tie's direction, 'he said I've got . . .' she rummaged in her memory for the right phrase, 'a fibreglass atrium.' The words sailed out with an air of adventure like a galleon with sails puffed by the wind. 'Atrium! Who'd have guessed it? In Madeley Court! My Berthold always said he wanted to put an atrium in there. Or a skylight.'

There was no atrium in Madeley Court, the block of council flats where we lived, though there was a grimy skylight over the stairwell. And Mother's claim that she'd had a passionate affair with Berthold Lubetkin, the architect who designed the block after the war, probably had as much substance as the atrium.

'It's there somewhere, Bert. Under the sofa, I think,' she insisted. Poor Mum, I thought, she's really losing it. Who ever heard of a skylight under a sofa?

I squeezed her hand and murmured, 'Light, seeking light, doth light of light beguile.'

'Ah! You can't go wrong with Shakespeare! Did you hear that, Inna? Shakespeare, the Immortal Bard? Say some more, Bertie!'

'Why, all delights are vain; but that most vain, which with pain purchased doth inherit pain . . .' I repeated Biron's speech.

The crone looked baffled. 'Is Pushkin, no?'

'See what I mean?' said Mother. 'Emphasism. Now, Inna, sing us one of your foreign songs.'

The old woman cleared her throat, spat and started to drone: '*Povee veetre na-a Ukrainou* . . . Is beautiful song of love from my country. *De zalishil yah-ah-ah* . . .'

The other patients were craning in their beds to see what the racket was. Then the pink-tie doctor came up to the bedside consulting his notes. He looked hardly out of his teens, with tousled hair and long pointed shoes that needed a polish.

'Are you Mr . . . er . . . Lukashenko?'

This was not the time to go into the complexities of Mother's marital history.

'No. I'm her son. Berthold Sidebottom.'

For some ignorant people, the name Sidebottom is a cause of mirth. The teen-doctor was one of those. In fact Sidebottom is an ancient Anglo-Saxon location name meaning 'broad valley', originating, it is believed, from a village in Cheshire.

The doctor smirked behind his hand, straightened his tie and explained that my mother had atrial fibrillation. 'I asked her how many she smokes. Her heart isn't in good shape,' he said in a low voice.

'What did she say?'

'She said first of March, 1932.'

'That's her birthday. She was eighty-two recently. I'm not sure how many she smokes, she keeps it secret – doesn't want to set me a bad example.'

The teen-doctor scratched behind his ear. 'We'd better keep her in for a few days, Mr . . . er . . . Lukashenko.' He glanced down at his notes.

'Sidebottom. Lukashenko was her husband.'

'Mr Sidebottom. Hum. Have you noticed any variation in her behaviour recently? Any forgetfulness, for example?'

'Variation? Forgetfulness? I couldn't say.' I myself have found that a bit of selective amnesia can be helpful in coping with the vicissitudes of life. 'Age cannot wither her, nor custom stale her infinite variety,' I said.

To my embarrassment, my eyes filled with tears. I thought back over the years I'd lived in the flat at the top of Madeley Court with my mother, assorted husbands and lovers, the politics, the sweet sherry, the parrot. In my recollection, she'd rambled a bit at the best of times, but the core of her had been steadfast as a rock. 'Shakespeare,' I said. The teen-doctor looked miffed, as if I'd been trying to get one up on him, so I added, 'When you live with someone, you don't always notice the changes. They hap-pen so gradually.'

'You still live with your mother?'

I detected a note of derision in his callow voice. Probably he was too wet behind the ears to understand how suddenly everything you take for granted can fall apart. You can reach half a century in age, you can have some modest success in your profession, you can go through life with all its ups and downs – mainly the latter, in my case – and still end up living with your mother. One day it could even happen to you, clever Dr Pointy-toes. People come and go in your life but your mother's always there – until one day she isn't any more. I was filled with regret for all the times I'd been irritated with her or taken her for granted.

'Yes. We sup-port each other.' My old stutter was spluttering into life. Must be the stress.

Mum had slipped further down the bed. Her breathing was laboured. A frail filament of saliva glimmered between her open lips like a reminder of the transience of life. She let out a shuddering moan, 'First of March, 1932!' The filament snapped.

The doctor dropped his voice to a murmur. 'Of course we'll do all we can, but I think she may not be with us very long.'

Panic seized me. Big questions raced into my mind and took

up fisticuffs with each other. How long was very long? Why did this have to happen to her just now? Why did it have to happen to me? Had I been a satisfactory son? How would I manage without her? What would happen to the parrot? What would happen to the flat?

The teen-doctor moved away and the ward sister sailed up, shapely and black, a starched white cap riding like a clipper on the dark sea of her curls. 'We need to change her catheter now. Can you give us a minute, Mr Lukashenko?'

'Side-b-bottom.'

'Sidebottom?'

Our eyes met, and I was struck by how beautiful hers were, large and almond-shaped, with sweeping lashes. The beast in my pants stirred. Oh God, not now. I withdrew outside the drapes, thinking I'd better find the canteen and have a calming cup of tea, when from the next bed the old woman hissed, 'Hsss! Stay. Sit. Talk. Nobody visit me. I am all alone.'

As a penance for my unruly thoughts, I pulled up my chair closer to her bed and cleared my throat. It's hard to know how to strike up conversation with a total stranger who thinks you are gay. Maybe I should put her right?

'You think people who wear pink are homosexual. Well, there's absolutely nothing wrong with being homosexual, but –'

'Aha! No problem, Mister Bertie,' the old woman interrupted. 'No problem wit me. Everyone is children of God. Even Lenin has permitted it.'

'Yes of course, but –' I really needed that cup of tea.

'You mama, Lily, say we must treat all people like own family. She like good Soviet woman. Always look at sunny side, Inna, she say.'

'Yes, Mother's a very special person.' I glanced at the curtain around her bed, my heart pinched between anxiety and

13

tenderness. There seemed to be a lot of whispering and clattering going on. 'What about your family, Inna?'

'Not homosexy. My husband, Dovik, Soviet citizen,' Inna declared. 'But dead.' She leaned over and spat into her bowl.

'Oh, I'm sorry!' I put on a faux-sympathetic voice, like Gertrude in *Hamlet*, trying to avert my eyes from the revolting greenish fluid that was lapping at the cardboard edges of her bowl.

'Why for you sorry? You not killed him.'

'No, indeed not, but –'

'Killed by olihark wit poison! I living alone. Olihark knocking at door. Oy-oy-oy!' This sounded delusional. She fixed me with dark agitated eyes. 'Every day cooking golabki kobaski slatki, but nobody it wit since Dovik got dead.' She wiped her nose on the sheet. 'Husband Dovik always too much smoking. I got emphaseema. Heating expensive. My flat too much cold.' She reached for my hand with her dry twiggy fingers and gave it a flirtatious squeeze. 'You mama tell me she got nice flat from boyfriend. Now she worry if she will die they take away flat for under-bed tax and you will live homeless on street.' Behind the silver curtain of hair, her eyes were watching me, dark and beady. What Mother been telling her?

Mother had lived in the flat since it was built in 1952, and she used to tell me with misty eyes that Berthold Lubetkin, the architect who designed it, had promised it would be a home for ever for her and her children. But since then the buggers hadn't built enough new homes to keep up with the demand, she fumed, and the ones instigated by the council leader, Alderman Harold Riley, and built by Lubetkin's firm Tecton had been flogged off to private landlords – like the flat next door, which had once belonged to a dustman called Eric Perkins and now belonged to a property company who filled it with foreign students who played music all night and littered the lift with takeaway boxes.

'Under-bed tax?' Could they make me move out because of that?

'Is new tax for under-bed occupant.'

I kept mainly dog-eared scripts, odd socks and back copies of *The Stage* under my bed. Nothing you could call an occupant.

'You mama very much worrying about break-up of post-war sensors. She say it make her sick in heart to think they take away her apartment and put you into street. This tax is work of Satan, she say. Mister Indunky Smeet. You know this devil-man?'

'Not personally.'

I'd heard of course of something called a bedroom tax, which Mother described variously as an affront to human decency, the final death-blow to the post-war consensus, and a pretext for squeezing more money out of poor people who happened to have a spare bedroom. But it never occurred to me that it might apply to me, so I hadn't taken much notice. I did recall Mum and Flossie swearing at some minister on the television news recently; though, to be fair, this was not an uncommon occurrence. I sympathised with her righteous anger, of course, but I had my own problems to contend with, and you can't just live in a permanent stew of rage, can you?

'But I tell her no worry, Lily, this under-bed tax for lazies scrounging in bed all day. You hard-working decent, Mister Bertie?' She eyed me sideways.

'Oh yes. Absolutely.'

'What work you working, Mister Bertie?'

'Actually, I'm an actor.'

I always dread this question. It raises such expectations.

'Aha! Like George Clooney!' Inna cooed. 'You mekking film?'

'I'm mainly a stage actor. Best known for my Shakespearean roles. And some television.' If you can count a stint as a proud football dad in a washing-powder advert back in 1999. 'But I'm not working at present.'

The old woman was still impressed. 'I never met actor before. I would like met wit George Clooney. He got nice eyes. Nice smile. Nice teeth. Everything nice.' She pursed her lips and discharged some more green phlegm. I looked away.

Bloody George Clooney. If he and I didn't happen to share a common birthday, I probably wouldn't care; in fact I probably wouldn't even notice him. As it was, I couldn't help comparing his success with mine (lack of). Of course someone who has dedicated his life to Art, as I have, cannot expect to wallow in the excesses of materialism. We have our spiritual consolations. But still, it would be nice to have more than an occasional latte at Luigi's to look forward to.

Take the case in point: it was George bloody Clooney with his affected smile and clean-cut chin that this old crone lusted after; yet it was I, Sidebottom, who sat here at her wretched bedside watching her phlegm-bowl fill to overflowing. How could that be fair?

The beautiful nurse was still making busy sounds behind Mum's curtain. It seemed to have been going on a very long time.

Inna's hands fiddled with the sheet. She gave me a sly look. 'You got good apartment. Your mother tell me about her.'

'Yes, it's a nice flat. Top floor.'

'Aha! Top floor, good flat, bad lift. She say lift always broken, nobody repair her because she got hysterity.'

'Hysterity?' It's true the lift was getting cranky but I personally would have described it as unreliable rather than hysterical.

'She say banks made creases we give money. Now banks got all our money we get hysterity.'

'Ah, you mean austerity! There's a lot of it around nowadays.'

'Yes. Hysterity. You mama explain to me. Very clever lady. Almost like Soviet economist.'

'Well, I wouldn't go so far –'

'She love this flat, you mama. It is so beautiful, she say, she got it from arshitek boyfriend.'

Why was she going on about the flat? What had Mother been saying? Suddenly she crossed herself and fell silent, listening. I listened too. Behind the curtains around Mother's bed a machine had been beeping constantly. Now in the silence I became aware that the sound was becoming intermittent. There was a flurry of scurrying and scuffling and low voices talking in urgent whispers.

Suddenly the nurse drew back the curtains, and murmured, 'Mr Lukashenko, your mother has taken a turn for the worse.'

I leaned over her and peered into her dear old face, so familiar yet so mysterious, already sealed behind the glass wall of the departure lounge, checked in for the one-way journey to the undiscovered country.

'Mum. Mum, it's me, Bertie. I'm with you.' I took her hand.

Mum let out a long rattling sigh. A single blue butterfly fluttered on the withered garden of her face. Pulling herself up in bed with immense effort, she gripped my arm and drew me down towards her, to whisper into my ear, 'Don't let them get the flat, Berthold!' Then she fell back on the pillows with a groan.

VIOLET: Mary Atiemo

Violet doesn't plan on staying in the flat for long. When she's saved up some money from her amazing salary, she'll find something better – not a council flat. This place is convenient for work, and she was lucky to get it at short notice, but she viewed it in a hurry and didn't notice how tatty the decor was and how rough the neighbourhood. On the day she arrived she watched someone being carried out on a stretcher. And there are those strange alarming shrieks from the flat next door, which sound like someone possessed by a shetani. Besides, it's too big for one person. The smooth-talking estate agent had persuaded her it would be easy to find some room-mates, but now she isn't sure she's ready for another flat share after her last disastrous experience.

When she first came to London, she'd done casual office work and waitressing to fund her internship with an NGO and shared a zero-housework flat in Hammersmith with a girl from Singapore and two boys from uni, one of whom was her boyfriend, Nick. The Singaporean girl, who used to borrow her clothes, eventually borrowed Nick too. She came home early one day to find them having a shower together.

Her friend Jessie, who had just moved into a flat in Croydon with her boyfriend, let her sleep on the sofa in the sitting room. But a month on a sofa is a long time.

The agency that found her this flat in Madeley Court specialises in student lettings, and it is furnished with seven narrow beds, seven desks, seven wooden chairs, seven small chests of drawers, and a small round table in the kitchen. How did seven people squeeze into here? Maybe they were dwarves? She smiles, remembering the movie she saw with Jessie, when they were both at primary school in Bakewell.

When she got the flat, Jessie lent her a spare duvet, pillows, a set of yellow crockery and a frying pan. She texts Jessie a 'Thank You', with a picture of yellow crockery on the kitchen shelf.

She opens another door off the sitting room/bedroom, and finds it leads out on to a balcony with a view – she hadn't expected that. Leaning on the parapet, looking down on the flowering tops of the cherry trees and the splashes of yellow from the daffodils in the verges, she breathes deeply and closes her eyes. The sunlight on her skin touches her memory with the view from her grandmother's veranda in Langata, Nairobi, the Nandi Flame trees and the dazzling blood lilies. It's been a long while since she remembered that time in her childhood. A man with a bald head is pushing his bicycle across the green. Looks like the same old guy she saw in Luigi's. Maybe he lives nearby.

She's only been in her new job for a month – thinking of it still makes her stomach flip with excitement. Tonight she's meeting up with her friends at the Lazy Lounge to celebrate her birthday. So now is her only chance to sort out her flat and explore her new neighbourhood. She puts on her trainers and decides to go out for a run while the weather holds.

It's a mixed sort of area, where old-fashioned terraces rub shoulders with scruffy council estates, little artsy shops, galleries and studios tucked up the side streets, and further away a lively street market. She passes several building sites bristling with cranes where modern offices and apartments are shooting up, and from time to time she catches the dark gleam of a river or canal threading its way between the streets.

In terms of clothes shops the area is disappointing, but there are plenty of cafés and eateries with cheap and interesting menus, two supermarkets – Lidl close by and Waitrose a bit further away. She stocks up in both places, spending freely, especially on treats for herself. She buys a kettle in a quaint little hardware store halfway up a side street, where she also splurges on a cafetière. As an afterthought she buys a blue plastic bucket with a mop, a dustpan and brush, some rubber gloves and detergent, just in case the agency cleaner never shows up.

By the time she's unpacked her shopping there's still no sign of the cleaner, and she is resigned to doing it herself. But first she plugs in the kettle to try it out, and spoons coffee – Kenya AA of course – into the cafetière.

Just as she pours on the water and breathes in the dark aroma, the doorbell rings. A young black girl is standing there, so young and skinny she looks like only a kid, wearing a blue overall and carrying a mop and bucket, a brush and some rubber gloves. Violet peers at her name badge: Homeshine Sanitary Contractors. Mary Atiemo. That's a Kenyan name.

'Cleaning contractor,' says the girl with a broad smile. Her front tooth is chipped. Violet's grandmother Njoki used to say that dental deficiency is a sign of untrustworthiness. She was full of funny ideas like that.

'You're late,' says Violet. 'I was just going to do it myself.'

'Sorry, please,' says the girl. 'No bus. Please, let me clean it for you. No clean, no pay today.'

Tears well into her eyes. Violet hesitates. She looks a bit useless, lost in her too-big uniform, twig thin, smaller than the mop she's carrying, this scrap of a girl standing on the grey concrete walkway, with a grey thundery sky looming behind her.

'Where are you from?'

'Kenya. Nairobi,' Mary Atiemo says. 'Kibera. You know Kenya?'

'I was born in Nairobi,' she replies. She remembers Kibera; it's a slum not far from her grandmother's house. Once or twice she glimpsed its dirty twisted alleys from the back seat of the car and shuddered. How has this slum girl from that wretched insanitary place got to be a 'sanitary contractor' in London, standing here on her doorstep just as she's standing on the doorstep of her exciting new life? It seems a bad omen, as if the past won't let her go.

'My mother is Kenyan,' she adds, to put the girl at ease.

The girl's smile widens till it takes up half her face. '*Shikamoo.*'

'*Marahaba,*' Violet replies, cringing at the deference in the girl's voice.

Suddenly a clap of thunder rattles the rooftops, and rain sheets down like a monsoon.

'You'd better come in. I've just made some coffee. Would you like some? It's from Kenya.'

Mary Atiemo nods. 'That would be fine. In my home we only used to drink tea.'

Despite her small size, Mary Atiemo is a wizard of a cleaner. She sweeps the floors, bags the garbage, then fills up the bucket at the sink, squirts in some detergent, sloshes it around the floor, and chases it furiously with the mop. Scraps of food, shreds of grime, cigarette butts, every type of filth, all float up on the frothy water to be captured in the strands of the mop, swirled into the bucket and flushed down the loo. She cleans the grey fingerprints off the woodwork, the grime off the cooker, the yellow stains off the toilet, and the black ring around the bath. Just watching makes Violet feel exhausted and she thinks, with her new salary, it would be nice to have a cleaner to come in once in a while.

'Do you have a phone number?' she asks the girl. 'Maybe you can come and clean another time.'

The girl looks embarrassed. 'We're not allowed to have a phone. Mr Nzangu doesn't let us work for somebody else. But give me your number, please, and I'll get in touch when I can.'

She writes down her name and number on a bit of paper. The girl slips it into the pocket of her overall, gathers up her cleaning things and disappears out into the rain.

BERTHOLD: *Mrs Penny*

Mrs Penny, the Council's housing officer, was twenty minutes late. I'd tried to telephone to cancel her visit of course, feeling too devastated to do battle with the tentacles of bureaucracy so soon after Mother's sudden death, but the Town Hall phone was constantly engaged and I gave up in the end. Well, it was probably best to get the tenancy business out of the way sooner rather than later. At last the doorbell rang. *Ding dong!*

'Ding dong! First of March, 1932! Ding dong!' Flossie chimed, to make absolutely bloody sure I'd heard.

Mrs Penny stood on the doorstep, reaching out her hand.

'Mr Madeley?'

Should I correct her? I let it pass, and took her pale manicured hand. It was like shaking a lettuce leaf out of the fridge – cold and limp, not what you'd expect from such a warm solid-looking woman.

'Come in. Come in. I appreciate your . . .' What exactly did I appreciate? 'Your hair.'

Her hair was shiny and a slightly unnatural copper colour, swept up in a curled ponytail with a deep fringe and long curled sideburns, sort of country-and-western singer meets rabbi. She ignored my comment and advanced into the entrance hall, releasing a powerful floral perfume in her wake. Was she my type? She was in her fifties, I guessed, not unattractive for her age, but way too old for me. She was a bit plump, too, though her high-heeled shoes made her legs look shapely. A saucy pink silk scarf was tucked into the lapels of her municipal-colour raincoat.

'It's ages since I've been in one of these big old family flats.' Her voice was pleasant and low, with a slight hesitation, not quite a stutter, that at once disarmed me. 'There's not many left with the Council now. They've mostly been bought up and sold on under Right to Buy. I'm surprised this one wasn't. It would have been quite an –' she stopped, aware she was committing a faux pas.

'Investment. Mum didn't agree with it.'

Mother could have bought the flat for £8,000 back in 1981, after the Right to Buy came in, but she had refused. 'I told them to stick their offer where the sun don't shine,' she'd told me. 'I said it belongs to the people of this borough and it ain't yours to sell.'

I'd already left home by then, and it never occurred to me that I would return one day, let alone seek to inherit the tenancy, so I was mildly amused at Mum's fury. Needless to say, when Eric Perkins next door – now resident in the South of France – resold his for £38,000 a few years later, she was regretful and envious. But by then she had divorced Lev Lukashenko, and he'd disappeared with all her cash.

Mrs Penny peered in through the open door to my mother's bedroom, where the assortment of crumpled lingerie was still strewn on the floor.

'You do sometimes wonder,' she said cryptically, making a note.

She also noted down that my mother had lived in the flat since it was built, and that I had lived there from birth until I went to university, and then again for the last eight years. She didn't ask why I had come back eight years ago, and I wondered whether, if she had, I would have told her the truth. She asked about siblings, and I explained that my half-brother from my father's previous marriage had moved out many years ago.

'Mmm. I always longed to live in one of these big modern flats. I grew up in a poky terrace in Hackney. It's nice that you can support Mum, and help her keep her independence in today's challenging environment.'

There was something so sympathetic in her manner that I was on the point of pouring my heart out, telling her about my daughter Meredith's death and the bear pit of depression, the split-up with Stephanie, the stutter, the dead end of my career, the eviction from my bedsit, the hospitalisation, the valiant way I had fought back with Mother's help against the bloody injustice of life.

A sudden squawk from Flossie interrupted my train of thought. 'Shut up, Flossie!'

Yes, Flossie was right – I must shut up. Despite her niceness, she was the local agent of 'Them' – the shadowy bureaucracy that Mother had warned me about – probably on a reconnaissance mission.

'She sup-ports me too,' I replied. 'We look after each other.'

'I've got this tenancy registered to a Mr and Mrs Madeley,' she said. 'Is that right?'

'She remarried. She's now Mrs Lukashenko.'

'Luckychinko? That's a pretty name. Chinese, is it?'

'Ukrainian, actually. Her last husband was Ukrainian.'

'Mm.' She scribbled something in her file.

Mrs Penny was impressed, as most people are, by the sitting room with its rooftop view over London towards the City. My father, Wicked Sid Sidebottom, Mum's second husband, who'd been a bit of a handyman when he wasn't being wicked, had put up the bookshelves in the living room, giving the flat a genteelly bohemian air, though the books were mostly his thrillers and Mum's romances, interspersed with a few leather-bound classics for gravitas. The floor was carpeted with Persian rugs, rescued by Lev 'Lucky' Lukashenko, her last husband, from a fire-damaged warehouse – they still retained a faint whiff of their smoky odour. The walls were cluttered with pictures and photographs which had fascinated me as a child, though now I barely noticed them. Without wanting to appear snobbish, I would guess it was a notch above your average council flat.

'My, it's spacious! May I?'

Without waiting for a reply, she opened the door to my bedroom and stepped inside. There was something so presumptuous, so rudely intrusive, in this action it was as if she had yanked down my underpants to examine my private parts. Worse, in fact, because at least I can confirm that my privates are clean. My room was as untidy as Mum's but in a different way. Dead coffee cups, stacks of newspapers and theatre magazines, sports shoes, T-shirts and cycling gear instead of soiled silk.

'I'm afraid it's a bit of a mess.' Why the hell was I apologising to her?

'Don't worry. You should see some of the places I visit, Mr Luckyshtonko. Is that another bedroom you've got through there?'

Alarm bells started ringing in my head and Mother's last words rang in my ears. I remembered the beep . . . beep . . . beep and the terrible groan when it stopped.

'It's just a small study.'

What I didn't say was that when Howard lived with us – he was my father's son by a previous marriage – that little study had been my bedroom. What was it Inna had said about the under-bed tax? My heart thumped. While Mrs Penny was taking notes, I decided to make a pre-emptive move.

'I would like to register the tenancy in my name. Would

there be any p-problem with me taking it over from my mother?'

'Hm.' Mrs Penny sucked the end of her biro nervously. 'No, not normally a problem, Mr Lucky-s-stinker. You need to satisfy certain conditions. For example, you would need to demonstrate your relationship with the tenant, and you would need to provide evidence that you have actually lived here as your main abode for the last two years.'

'Fine. No problem.'

'But in the challenging currently prevailing climate of acute multi-causal public sector housing defectiveness, I mean deficiency, and a major increase in the number of deserving qualified decent hard-working local families on local authority waiting lists, the Council is spearheading a multi-fanged, I mean -pranged. No, sorry, I mean a multi-pronged initiative. To counteract incidence of under-occupancy in the borough.' She spoke too fast, mangling the words between her teeth. 'It means that a tenant in receipt of housing benefit might incur an under-occupancy charge. According to the Council's newly formulated criteria, this flat could be classed as having too many rooms.'

'Too many rooms?' She should see where George bloody Clooney lives.

'I'm just doing my job,' she murmured, blushing rather sweetly and lowering her head to flick through her file. 'But don't worry, the rule doesn't apply to pensioners. Your mother is still living here, isn't she?'

'Yes.' As I said it, a spasm tightened my jaw. But it was too late. The word had bolted. 'She's just popped out to the shops,' I added, for realism.

Mrs Penny smiled. Her face was pretty, her features delicate and doll-like, despite her age. 'Oh, where does she go for her shopping?'

'Er . . . just around the corner.'

'I live locally myself. The area has improved so much, hasn't it? There's even a Waitrose not far away.'

'Mm.' I made a mental note to avoid Waitrose from now on. 'She goes out quite a lot.'

'Important to keep active at her age. How old is she, by the way?'

'Eighty-two.'

Mrs Penny made another note.

'Well, the easiest thing would be for her just to sign a little form to put the tenancy jointly in your names, in the event of her death or mental disability. But no rush. Just keep us informed of any change of circumstances, won't you, Mr Looka-skansko?'

'Of course.'

She stowed her notebook in her handbag.

I watched through the window as she crossed the grove and squeezed herself into a small red car parked on the far side. Then I flopped down on the sofa. The whole encounter had been far more stressful than I had imagined. Fortunately the sherry bottle was not quite empty.

'God is dead!' Flossie called.

'Shut up, Flossie.'

'Shut up, Flossie,' Flossie retorted. The Dom–sub relationship only applied with Mum. She and I would have to fight it out now.

'Shut up, Flossie. I need to think!'

What I was thinking, as with a trembling hand I poured the last drops of sweet sherry into a chipped crystal glass, is that frankly, when you think about it, one dotty old lady is pretty much like another, isn't she? If a substitute were to appear in Mum's place, who would know the difference?

BERTHOLD: *Daffodils*

One thing you can say about the English weather – it keeps you on your toes; it toughens you up to face the general spite-fulness of life. Although it was almost mid-April, black clouds were bunched above the church spire as I cycled back to the hospital later that day, and a sudden cannonade of hailstones forced me to seek shelter under a greengrocer's awning. Bunches of bright daffodils winking from a bucket caught my eye. Good idea. She'd appreciate them.

In the bed where Mother had died yesterday, a new occu-pant was already installed, a slight grey shape on the freshly laundered palimpsest. But where was the old woman Inna?

'Sss! Mister Bertie! Come here!'

She'd been moved to a bed by the window. The card-board bowl had less than a centimetre of mucus. I realised she must be on the mend. Her hair was pulled back into two neat silver plaits coiled around her head and she was wearing elaborate cat's-eye spectacles whose frames sparkled at the corners with diamanté. Behind them her eyes were bright and alert. Even her skin had plumped out so the wrinkles appeared less deep. I guessed that at one time she must have been an attractive woman, with bold dark eyebrows and high cheekbones. Even now, as she turned away from the light, traces of beauty lingered in the curves and hollows of her face.

'Hello, Inna. I came to see you.'

She accepted the daffodils with a gracious nod, and patted my hand. 'Aha, you already missing you mama, poor Mister

Bertie. She was great lady. Almost like saint.' Her eyes rolled heavenward.

Although I loved my mother, I couldn't help feeling that Inna was exaggerating a bit. She can't have known her for much more than a day.

'I've been thinking about our conversation yesterday, Inna. How you don't like living alone.'

Inna cocked her head to one side expectantly but said nothing.

'I've been thinking . . . I have a problem . . . I have a nice flat but . . . I need . . .'

'Aha?'

Did a small smile steal across her face, before she composed it into a look of concern? Some words from our previous conversation popped into my head: gobalki kosabki solatki. I had no idea what they were, but they sounded rather tasty – a step up from a lukewarm takeaway curry from Shazaad's. In stage drama, this is the point at which the gent falls to one knee and kisses the hand of the lady before slipping a ring on to it, but now I simply grabbed her hand and said, 'Why don't you move in with me, Inna?'

Her lips pursed flirtatiously. 'You want to make sex wit me, Mister Bertie?'

I wondered for one ghastly moment whether she really meant it. Although I had not given up hope that someday I would once again become an object of desire, this was not at all what I had in mind.

'No, Inna, no. Truly, nothing could be further from my thoughts. I just want you to make globalki sobachki and slutki for me.'

'Aha! I understand, Mister Bertie.' She winked. 'You homo-sexy no problem for me, okay.'

'No, it's not that, Inna. I'm not denying that I am homosexual.' I was not going to be outshone in political correctness by George bloody Clooney. 'But I'm not confirming it either. Man delights not me; no, nor woman neither. Though by the bloody grin on your face you seem to say so. That's Shakespeare for you.' I have long been intrigued by the question of the Immortal Bard's sexuality, but this did not seem to be the best time to discuss it. 'All I want is for you to act like my mother. That's not too difficult, is it?' Then a sudden prudence seized me: usually motherhood is for life. 'Just on a trial basis,' I added.

She may not have heard that last bit, for she was already crossing herself and declaring, 'Aha, you poor mama! No one can be like her! God save her soul, she is already wit Lenin and Khrushchev and all Soviet saints in heaven!'

I felt a prick of apprehension. Maybe all old ladies are not so alike after all. Inna did seem to lurch wildly between conflicting ideologies, whereas Mother had been unshakeable in her beliefs. Then again, did it matter what she believed, so long as she was still cool with the gabolki kasobki and salotki? And would say the right things to Mrs Penny?

'I know, Inna. But if you could just pretend . . .'

Inna arched her eyebrows. Dimples puckered her cheeks. The thought of being desired again, even if for the wrong reasons, had brought out the flirt in her.

'If you say so, Mister Bertie.'

Curious about what I had let myself in for, I asked, 'Tell me about yourself, Inna. Where are you from? When did you come to England?'

'We come in 1992. Husband got research job. Bacteriophage. Wit Doctor Soothill. Very good man. You know him?'

'I can't say I do. And you . . . ?'

'In Ukraina I was nurse. But to work in here I got to learn English.'

'Thank heavens for that, then. I said, 'Mother's last husband, Lucky Lukashenko, was from Ukraine. From Lviv, right in the west. She probably told you.'

'Hah! Lviv is Galicia, not real Ukraina.' She spat into her phlegm receptacle. 'Galicia only 1939 got in Ukraina. Before was wit Hungary, Poland, Lithuania, Ruthenia, Avstria. All Catholiki. Real Ukraina Orthodox true faith.'

She crossed herself. Behind the diamanté glasses, her fire-coal eyes blazed with ardour. I had heard Lucky Lukashenko going on in a similar vein about the non-Ukrainianness of the population of the east who, he claimed, were all transplanted Russians, people of low culture and criminal tendencies. So I already had some inkling of how touchy these Slavs could be.

'I born Moldova, but live Odessa,' she added.

'Odessa? Really?'

All of a sudden she took on a more exotic air, redolent of champagne and caviar, of grand bougainvillea-draped villas and leafy boulevards haunted by Pushkin and Eisenstein.

'Ah! Odessa. Most beautiful city in world. Beautiful street. Beautiful monument. Beautiful harbour. Beautiful sea. Beautiful moon. Beautiful people all time laughing, making joke, eating slatki, drinking shampanskoye, falling in love.' She narrowed her eyes. 'You ever been in love, Mister Bertie? Wit lady, I mean, not wit man?'

'Actually, I was married once.' Okay, so I was letting the side down by not sticking up for gay love, but frankly her obsession was getting tiresome.

'You mama ev told me. Very bad woman. Ectress.' She wrinkled her nose, as though the very idea carried a noxious whiff. 'No wonder you gone homosexy.'

Stephanie, my ex, had sniffily described Mother as an inter-fering over-protective drama queen, and Mother always referred to her in a voice loaded with sarcasm as 'your darling wife'. Stephanie had never forgiven me for Meredith's death, and I had never forgiven myself. After my divorce and break-down, Mother and I had settled into a companionable domesticity, a bit like marriage without the sex, which took place, if at all, off piste. I was the man in her life, and she was the woman in mine. When I had relationships with other women, I didn't bring them home. And by then I think she was past bringing men home – or if she did, she was discreet. I wondered about Inna's love life.

'So you lived with Dovik in Odessa?'

'Odessa, Georgia, Krim, Kharkiv. All one great Soviet Union. But in Great Patriotic War many Jews killed in Odessa.' She crossed herself again. 'Only my Dovik got away. Now I living Hempstead. One day I will tell you my story.'

The beautiful ward sister, coming up to change Inna's phlegm bowl, recognised me and offered condolences. 'She was a lovely lady, your mother. And a perfect patient. No fuss.'

No fuss. I remembered Mother's last words and the terrible whisperings behind the curtain before I was admitted to witness her death. Tears stung my eyes.

'I don't know how I'll get on without her.'

'Still, it's nice you've made a new friend. Mrs Alfandari doesn't get many visitors. Do you, sweetheart?'

Alfandari – what kind of a name was that? It sounded Italian or Middle Eastern, not Ukrainian. Who was this woman I had just invited into my life?

'Yes, Mister Bertie has invited me go live wit him. I will mekkit golabki kobaski slatki.'

Inna smiled, and for the first time I noticed the black edges of her teeth. Mother's were even and pearly white – though of course they were not her own. I was already having second thoughts about my invitation when the beautiful nurse beamed, 'Oh, that's so lovely. You'll have to give us the details for our discharge procedure.'

She smiled, and my doubts vanished as it struck me that in all my fifty-two years I had never been out with a black woman. Now they suddenly seemed to be cropping up everywhere. There was that astonishingly pretty girl in Luigi's the other morning, and now this beautiful nurse. Without Mother's officious appraisal to greet them at the door, I could even invite them to the flat. A cloud shifted and a shaft of sunlight struck my heart. Before me a whole new world of possibilities was opening up.

The storm clouds had completely disappeared by the time I cycled home. The sky was borage blue with scraps of cirrus driven along by a blustery wind that set the daffodils in all the window boxes and forecourts dancing.

'When daffodils begin to peer,' I sang as my wheels spun along merrily, 'With heigh! The doxy over the dale . . .'

It was Autolycus's song in *The Winter's Tale*, which I'd sung at the New Vic in Newcastle, directed by the great Peter Cheeseman. That was back in 1997. Before the Prozac. Before Meredith's death and the break-up with Stephanie. In those days, I still had hair. I wasn't quite George Clooney, but I was on my way.

I crossed the cherry grove and hit the lift button to carry me up to my home on the fifth floor, before spotting the *Lift Out of Order* notice. Again. Madeley Court, the 1952 local authority housing block where I lived with Mum, had definitely seen better days. The paintwork was shabby and the concrete surfaces were discoloured. Even the name-sign had been vandalised many years ago by a friend of my half-brother Howard, a kid called Nige, who had an exceptional head for heights and a long rope he had filched from the tarpaulin of a lorry he was robbing. He had prised away some of the ornate terracotta tiles, and the missing letters had never been replaced, leaving just: MAD   Y   URT. Mad Yurt. The name seemed apt.

'One day he'll fall! Splat! Brains spread all over the pavement. If he's got any brains!' raved Mrs Crazy from the balcony of her flat directly below ours, who had narrowly missed being hit by the falling L.

'Shut up! Stop your shouting!' Mother shouted down at full volume from our balcony. 'You're lowering the tone around here. It used to be decent before you moved in, Crazy! You think wearing a big cross on your neck makes you holy. Well, it don't! It makes you a bigot!'

Mrs Crazy, whose real name was Mrs Cracey, was the widow of a former East End evangelical minister undone by gambling and alcohol. She and Mum enjoyed that particularly venomous enmity reserved for people who have once been close friends. As the oldest resident, in both senses, Mum felt her status entitled her to respect. Mrs Cracey, a retired dental secretary some ten years younger than Mother, flaunted godliness and social superiority, which after her husband's death from liver failure gradually drifted away from the evangelical and towards the High Church, as evidenced by her purple coat, mitre-like hairstyle conserved under a shower cap, and her penchant for jewellery, including the inevitable flashy gold cross on a chain around her neck. She patronised Lily as a lower-class upstart and a godforsaken communist.

'I've had more communists than you've had hot dinners!' was Mum's oblique retort as she flicked a long finger of ash over the balcony, the gold and diamonds on her fingers glinting in the sun. She too was not averse to a bit of bling.

That was my first inkling that the community spirit of our block was provisional and mutable, despite the revolutionary intention of the architect Berthold Lubetkin to design solidarity into the structure of the estate.

Berthold Lubetkin, after whom I was named, was either an old flame of Mother's or a celebrated Russian modernist architect, depending on whom you chose to believe. According to her, Lubetkin's company Tecton had been responsible for the finest post-war public housing in London, and it was a sodding shame that he was best known for the penguin pool at London Zoo. When the sherry sweetened her memory she would sometimes drop hints about a secret love affair with Lubetkin, and weepily confess that it was thanks to him that she came to occupy this prime penthouse flat in the flagship Tecton development.

In an alternative version of the story, Lubetkin was born in Georgia, and Mother got her flat thanks to Ted Madeley, who sat on the Council's Housing Committee alongside the legendary Alderman Harold Riley, who had first commissioned Lubetkin. Riley was a passionate socialist but not much of a looker. Lily admired him, but fell for handsome already-married Ted Madeley. She lived with Ted out of wedlock at first, a shocking enough deed at the time, then she married him, thereby acquiring the tenancy of this desirable flat. After Ted died, she had married twice more and raised two children here (though only I was hers by birth – the other was my half-brother, Howard, my father's son from a previous marriage, of whom more later).

'So it serves them right!' she would declare. 'They' and 'Them' were shape-shifters who featured large in Mother's demonology.

The spacious and sunny top-floor flat in Madeley Court which had been my childhood home later became my sanctuary, when my life fell apart and I needed somewhere to go to ground. As a child I'd taken for granted the two generous-sized bedrooms and small study, the comfortable old-fashioned kitchen and the square book-lined living room; but its special surprise, which even as a kid I had appreciated, was the south-facing balcony where Flossie the parrot was put out in her cage on summer mornings to sun herself, and where the impulse-bought barbecue rusted drowsily under the red dome of its lid. In front of the flats was a fenced area of communal garden which we called the grove, where cherry blossom flowered, toddlers played on swings, old folks cultivated dahlias in raised beds, and where Howard, my louche half-brother, snogged the local schoolgirls, weather permitting. Idyllic would be too strong a word, but it was all perfectly pleasant. Even the vandalism was minimal.

Neighbours had come and gone; the flats which had been built to rehouse the poor from the slums of the East End now housed a global community who lived together in relative harmony, though without the same intimacy as the original East Enders. I had never got to know the seven foreign students crammed into the flat next door where the dustman Eric Perkins had once lived – they changed every year. But there were people who still recognised me and greeted me when I went out, which made it feel like home.

Now some swivel-eyed politician, of whom Mrs Penny was the local instrument, wanted to take it all away, and cast me out into the unknown. A bedsit in Balham? Or Bradford? I'd already experienced the transience and insecurity of the private rented sector. It nearly did for me. Why couldn't they just leave me alone? What I'd almost forgotten, before Mrs Penny reminded me, was that for several years, while Howard had lived with us, I had slept in the tiny study off the sitting room. Technically, it could be a three-bedroom flat – to which I, having dedicated my life to the Immortal Bard instead of to

Mammon, was not entitled. The monstrous unfairness of it gnawed at my guts.

Watching the sun go down from the balcony, I tried to imagine what it would be like living here without Mother. I was on the opening page of a new chapter in my life. Had I been foolhardy to invite the phlegmy old woman Inna Alfandari into my life, or had I stumbled upon the only possible way to secure my home?

The more I thought about her sighs, smiles and glances, the more I wondered whether I'd been had.

Or did my dear protective mother, deliberately or unwittingly, plant the idea in Inna's head? And what about the beautiful ward sister, whose presence had sealed the arrangement? In retrospect, there was something rather sinister about the way her elaborate white headgear perched on her dark curls without any apparent tether, and the secretive ticking of the little gold watch pinned to her bosom. Had they plotted this peculiar ménage, no doubt from the best of motives: mutual support, friendship, to keep depression at bay?

From the balcony, I watched a boy wandering down the winding path through the grove towards the road, his head bent down over a phone in his hands. As he stepped off the pavement, a speeding white van, using the street as a short cut, appeared out of nowhere.

'Careful!' I shouted, but I was too far away and my voice did not carry. The driver swerved just in time, the white van of destiny sped by, and the boy escaped.

'Careful!' Flossie screeched from inside the flat.

'Hello, old girl. It's just you and me, now.'

I topped up Flossie's feeder, grateful for her chattering which cut through the stifling silence in the flat. As I filled the water bottle, I noticed that her cage needed cleaning out. It was getting disgusting. Hopefully, this was a little job that Inna, grateful to be rescued from loneliness, would be glad to take on. Pleased at my good deed, I turned on the computer in the study and tried googling various spellings of gobalki, kos-abki and solatki but I drew a complete blank.

VIOLET: *Karen*

International wealth preservation sounds much more glamorous than international insurance. Violet has started googling for information, should the possibility of a transfer ever arise. Her first taste of her new job has been a bit disappointing. She'd imagined a succession of high-level business meetings, negotiating with billionaire clients and steely underwriters, involving complex calculations using new software packages she'd learned at uni. Instead, she seemed to spend her first weeks mainly at the photocopier or making very weak organic ashwagandha tea for Gillian Chalmers, the head of the International Insurance Department at GRM, who spent her whole time in meetings, apparently ignoring her new assistant.

So it has fallen to Laura, Marc Bonnier's assistant, to induct her into the culture of the firm. Laura is a brisk cheerful girl about her age – with a rather fat stomach, which she conceals under loose draped tops, lively eyes and shiny dark hair – who came into the Wealth Preservation Unit three years ago as a graduate trainee. Since international insurance is not her field, she briefs Violet on the office gossip instead: who is going out with whom, who is due for a million-pound bonus, and who is in or out of favour with the CEO.

'It must be great working for Marc Bonnier,' Violet ventured one day, 'he's so –' She bit her tongue. To talk of a male colleague as hot was just too girly. 'So impressive.'

'You're lucky to be working for Gillian Chalmers,' Laura said. 'She's the rising star around here, and she's had to fight hard to get where she is. It's still a male-dominated environment.'

'Mmm. I had noticed.' Though being dominated by Marc Bonnier seemed quite appealing.

'Don't be fooled by Gillian's traditional style. She thinks to get on in a man's world women have to look professional – you know, suits, heels, all that.' She glanced at Violet's short skirt, black tights and cardigan. 'She can be quite a dragon, but don't be put off.'

In the kitchen corner off the open-plan office where the juniors work, which still houses an ancient photocopier as well as a fridge, kettle and a selection of personal mugs, to which Violet's yellow one has now been added, Laura informs her that Gillian Chalmers and Marc Bonnier, the two principals who interviewed her for her job, used to be an item for years, but split up acrimoniously about six months ago, and that Marc is on the prowl for a replacement.

She doesn't tell Laura that she'd found herself standing next to Marc Bonnier in the lunch queue in the staff restaurant yesterday, and while she was fumbling in her bag he whipped out his swipe card and paid for her lunch. He himself only had a black coffee and a bowl of salad.

'Tell me about yourself, Violet. I didn't have a chance to get to know you during the interview.'

He sat down opposite her while she tucked into a prawn curry (prawns are supposed to make you brainy) and told him she was fascinated by international insurance.

He raised one eyebrow and grinned. 'Really?'

'Really.' She laughed. 'Well, I'm interested in other things too.'

'Tell me.'

So she talked about backpacking around Brazil, without mentioning Nick, with whom she'd travelled. The way he watched her as she talked made her cheeks flush. It seemed far too informal for a boss–worker relationship.

Why, she wondered, did Marc Bonnier and Gillian Chalmers

41

split up? Maybe it's because of Gillian's dominating personality – but she doesn't say this to Laura, who seems to rather hero-worship Gillian.

Then this morning, without warning, Gillian summons her to her office.

'I'm sorry I've been a bit busy these past few weeks, Violet. I've had a couple of deadlines. I hope you've settled in.' Without waiting for an answer, she hands her a thick black slip case. 'We want to develop our reputation as a global company. That's one of the reasons we appointed you, Violet. We were impressed by your language skills. I'd like you to take a look at this proposal, and prepare a risk assessment so that we can match our client to a suitable underwriter.'

Their client, who goes by the initials HN Holdings, is seeking to build a shopping mall in Nairobi's downtown district. She takes the slip case with a tremor of panic. At her interview she'd managed to sound knowledgeable and confident, but being faced with a real-life situation with millions of dollars at stake is different.

'Er . . . which risks . . . ?'

'That's up to you to discover. There are known terrorist risks in Nairobi, which you need to quantify and put in perspective, alongside other potential risks in that environment. You know Nairobi, don't you?'

'Oh yes, I was born there.' She doesn't add that she was eight years old when she left.

'Excellent. I'm sure you'll do a good job.' Gillian smiles briefly and turns her gaze back to her computer monitor, indicating that the meeting is over.

Back at her desk, Violet opens the slip case to pore through the papers and photographs. The figures involved are astronomical, the language is bristling with jargon, yet through all the abstraction a rush of memories flood in on her of Nairobi's hot bustling streets, seedy shopping parades, and the chaotic building sites where new developments spring up apparently unplanned on any corner or patch of land. And in their wake another cooler memory tiptoes in, of the quiet sunny bungalow in a suburb called Karen where she lived until she was eight. Her mind wanders through the cool rooms out on to the veranda and down to the wide securely fenced garden where hummingbirds glimmer in the flower beds and Mfumu, her dog, lazes in the shade all afternoon, moving around to keep out of the sun. That was a happy time.

She can't exactly remember when she realised she was different from the ragged children who crowded around the car that picked her up from school each day. Her father was a newly qualified doctor from Edinburgh doing a stint of VSO before settling down to a well-paid consultant's job in a teaching hospital in England. Her mother was a nurse at the Mbagathi District Hospital on an HIV-prevention team. They met over a suspect blood sample, and soon realised that they shared a love of benga music and mandazi. They married in the Presbyterian Church on Mai Mahiu Road six months later, and in less than a year Violet was born. When her father's VSO term ended, he took a post at the same hospital.

While her parents were at work, her grandmother Njoki looked after her at her home in Langata. It was a two-storey wooden house that smelled of spice and black soap, with a front-facing veranda that had a view over the garden towards the mountains and a back window looking down towards the river where the Kibera slum festered like an open sore and skinny Maasai cattle grazed on any parched patch of grass.

She smiles as she remembers her grandmother's flowery pinafores, the scent of coconut oil on her hair, and the way her face wrinkled like an expressive prune when she told her funny stories about the naughty monkeys that lived in the forest; but of her grandfather Josaphat she has no memory at all. He died when she was three. She tries to recall what her grandmother said about his death; the circumstances had been hushed up in a fog of sighs, murmurs and downcast glances.

Once her cousin Lynette, in a rage after losing half her garden in a corrupt land deal, muttered down the phone, '*Mnyamaa kadumbu.*' Those who keep quiet survive. By the time she started her geography degree at Warwick, it had become a catchphrase in Kenya; troublesome people were getting bumped off regularly. Yes, if she is to assess the hazards of investing in Nairobi, corruption will be high in her league of risks.

'Wake up. You look miles away.' Laura lays a hand on her shoulder as she passes by her desk on her way to the Wealth Preservation office.

'I'm just daydreaming,' Violet laughs. 'About Kenya. About what it was like coming over here.'

'I bet it was a shock.'

'It really was!'

Leaving Karen when she was eight to settle in damp chilly Bakewell was like being expelled from paradise. In fact for a long time, she had believed it was her fault, a punishment for some naughtiness. Her infant antennae picked up her parents' grave looks and silences, but it wasn't until her teens that she learned that the move was not about her but about her parents' hopes for another baby. However, the longed-for sibling never arrived, and she grew up a lonely and over-protected only child with a rose-tinted memory of immense warmth and lushness, of a half-forgotten language and a vast sky that was blue or dramatically red, but seldom grey like this.

Grey – that's the colour of England. As she watches from

the window, a bank of cloud rolls over the sun and settles on the tall buildings around her office. A fine rain, hardly more than a mist, draws a fine veil through which she can see in the distance the outlines of the familiar City skyscrapers – the Gherkin, the Shard, the Cheese Grater – all poking their ugly stumps at the sky. Their numbers seem to increase all the time. Where do they find room for them all?

'Listen,' Laura taps her shoulder again. 'I've just reminded Marc that I'm starting my maternity leave next month.'

'You never even told me you were pregnant, Laura!'

'Isn't it rather obvious?'

'Well, I didn't like to ask, in case you weren't.'

They both burst out laughing.

'I told him you might be interested in a secondment to Wealth Preservation.'

'Laura, you didn't! What did he say?'

To work in Wealth Preservation, she thinks, would be like entering an exotic secret world of glamour and high finance, an exclusive community peopled by handsome bachelor billionaires with London mansions, private jets and Caribbean islands.

'He said it was an interesting possibility.'

BERTHOLD: Silk

I'd seldom been inside Mother's bedroom for more than a few minutes at a time while she was alive. It had seemed an exotic secret place, a private shrine with long-dead faces transfixed in sepia, crystal glasses with sticky residues, strewn jewellery, spilled powder, dried-out nail varnish, faded silk, intimate odours, mothballs and stale perfume. As a child I had found it both repellent and fascinating. Sometimes at night it had echoed with strange and fearsome cries which, despite the pillow over my head, had leeched into my nightmares. Now it was time to empty it out and to prepare it for another resident.

Like a trespasser I picked my way through the scattered clothing, paperback romances and crumpled lingerie with a bundle of carrier bags in my hands, steeling myself to start disposing of her belongings. I threw open the window and set to work, grabbing the creased peach-coloured silk and stuffing it roughly inside the plastic bags.

I thought I was coping well by keeping myself busy but I'd barely filled two bags when a tidal wave of grief crashed over me, knocking me totally off balance. I slumped down on the bed, feeling my head and my limbs suddenly adrift like seaweed, and I let myself weep, my shoulders heaving helplessly with the rhythm of my sobs, snot dribbling into my mouth, my eyes blinded with salt.

The weeping must have exhausted me, or perhaps the sudden overwhelming fatigue was a symptom of the crushing depression that dogged me ever since . . . no. Stop. Don't go there. Not now. Always on the sunny side. I slammed my mind shut to memories and tried to focus on the moment, keeping the taste of salt at the front of my consciousness. I must have fallen asleep like that on Mother's bed, because when I opened my eyes again the sun had disappeared and a strange mottled twilight was pouring in through the window. In the far distance, I could see the sinister glint of the Shard, and in the next room Flossie was rattling the bars of her cage, calling, 'God is dead! Ding dong! God is dead!'

She had been jumpy and unsettled ever since Mother had been stretchered out of the flat.

'Hold on, old girl!'

I hunted in the kitchen cupboards for the bird food. The packet of seed was almost empty. Where the fuck did Mum buy it? I seemed to recall that hemp seed is mildly hallucinogenic. Maybe I should try some. I crunched one or two between my teeth then spat them out. While Flossie pecked busily, the silence in the flat flooded over me once more. I realised how utterly alone I was: alone to the bone. No one would come and put an arm around my shoulder, and say, 'Sorry about your mum.' No one at all. The thought was so chilling that it seemed to freeze up my tear ducts. If I let myself cry again, who would ever tell me to stop?

Keep a grip, Bertie. Food. That's what you need. I peered into the fridge. Lettuce. Milk. Sliced bread. No butter. No tuna.

A takeaway from Shazaad's was my only hope.

'Curry sauce or balti, mate? Did you see Ramsey's goal? Incredible.'

'Curry, please, Shaz. No chillies, thanks.'

It was those few sentences of banal conversation that I was hungry for, I realised.

Apart from Flossie, I hadn't spoken to another soul all day.

On my way back to my flat, I encountered Legless Len

down in the grove. He was in a jubilant mood, wearing his Arsenal cap and spinning around in his wheelchair with a bottle of beer in his hand.

'Did you see Ramsey's goal?' he whooped. 'I wonder who'll kick the bucket this time?'

'What d'you mean?'

'Don't you know? Every time Aaron Ramsey scores a goal, somebody famous dies. Obama bin Laden. Colonel Gaddafti. Robin Williams. That Apple Jobsy bloke. You name it. The Grim Reaper, he's called. Heh heh.' He chuckled grimly.

'That sounds like a load of bollocks, Len, if I may say so. I mean, statistically, the chances of somebody famous dying once a week are pretty high.'

One of the problems with Len is that he is drawn towards the irrational. That's how he ended up with a UKIP poster in his window at the last election, much to Mum's chagrin. 'Len, you are supporting the forces of reaction. Stick to budgies,' she said.

'You just see, Bert, some celeb'll die by tomorrow, for sure.'

'Actually, Len, my mum just died.' I hadn't meant to embarrass him; it just slithered out, and ended on a sniffle.

'Lily? Oh God, I'm sorry, mate. I didn't mean nothing. About Ramsey's curse and all that. It's just a joke, an Arsenal superstition. I'm really sorry. She was a lovely lady, your mum, one of the greatest. Never mind her bolshie politics, she always meant well to everybody, like she radiated sunshine wherever she went.' He was beside himself with apologies.

'It's all right, Len. You weren't to know. Just don't spread it about.'

I was worried that the whiff of gossip would reach the council offices. One of the problems with the traditional East End communities that architects like Lubetkin had rebuilt as 'streets in the sky' is that everyone knows everybody's business.

'Listen, Bert, she would have liked this.' He spun around in his wheelchair once more, brandishing a crumpled brown envelope like a magician who has produced a rabbit out of a hat. 'I just got a letter from the DSS saying I'm going to have my claim for disability allowance reassessed.'

'Reassessed? That doesn't sound good. I don't know why you say Mum would have liked it. She was all for the welfare state.'

'Lily was all for welfare, God bless her, but she couldn't stand no scroungers.'

'But you're not a scrounger, are you, Len?'

'Nah, that's what I mean. They're going to help me find employment, so I won't be a drain on the economy. Anyway, I'm sick of being on the dole. They want to rescue me from the scrap heap of existence. Give me pride in myself. Why are you always so negative, Bert? They're trying to do some good.'

This did indeed sound very positive, but once again the cynic in me would out.

'Look, I'm sorry, Len, but you're not exactly going to grow new legs, are you?'

'Legs ain't everything they're cracked up to be. Ramsey managed without a leg for six months.'

'Good luck with it, pal.'

He trundled away, leaving me with a guilty aftertaste. Had I been a bit blunt?

The lift was out of order so I climbed the stairs – see, Len, legs can come in handy at these moments? – and sat down in front of the TV to tackle my meal: rubbery chunks of reconstituted chicken floating like styrofoam in a fluorescent orange sea. I ate it straight from the box, staring at the television that was playing some pulpy sitcom punctuated by bursts of synthetic laughter. But my mind was already engaged elsewhere: I was planning Mother's funeral.

Because she'd died in hospital of an unknown cause, I'd been told Mother would have to undergo an autopsy. This would give me time to make suitable funeral arrangements. I thought about giving her a grand East End-style send-off: a big funeral procession with a jazz band, dancing, former lovers and husbands meeting at her graveside to exchange tearful embraces and anecdotes. She'd have liked that. But I found myself lacking in energy, too exhausted even to clear her room. Besides, I reckoned if I was going to keep up the pretence that Inna Alfandari was, in fact, my mother, then the fewer people who knew about the real Lily's demise the better. I logged on and googled 'burial rituals'.

I wasn't sure what religion Mother had embraced at the end, if any. She'd certainly been through a few changes. Born into a radical East End family in 1932, she related with pride that her father, Grandad Robert, was a religious pacifist: 'Religion was like opium to him. He was addicted to it.' Her mother, my Granny Gladys, aka Gobby Gladys, had been a strident supporter of George Lansbury, the Labour Party leader in the 1930s, and his mild vision of Christian socialism. Ted Madeley, Mother's first husband, had been a Methodist lay preacher, but apparently none of the sobriety and self-restraint associated with Methodism had rubbed off on her – or even on him, as it turned out. For a while, when I was young, she'd championed High Church of England like my dad, Wicked Sid Sidebottom, a lapsed Anglican. In her later years, she turned to the Catholic faith like her last husband, the Ukrainian Lev 'Lucky' Lukashenko, who had swept her off her unsteady feet in a blaze of candlelit romance; but after their bitter divorce, she was drawn to the peaceful Buddhism of the Dalai Lama.

Maybe she would have liked a Buddhist sky burial. That would be discreet enough, since our flat is on the top floor and Tecton had installed a communal drying area on the roof, which is now unused. I glanced out of the window. The sky above Hackney was overcast. A couple of grubby pigeons flapped by, but alas no vultures. Cremation or burial seemed rather run of the mill for Mother, and would be easily discoverable, but burial at sea left few traces. Brighton Pier would be a good location – Brighton was the scene of her honeymoon with Ted Madeley, her first real love, and maybe her last. These thoughts brought on a new bout of melancholia, and I cheered myself up by googling the protocols involved.

Next day, fortified with a breakfast of two Shredded Wheats, I cycled over to Islington to drop off my bulging carrier bags full of Mother's stuff at the Oxfam shop. It was a Saturday and the shop was heaving. I pushed my way through towards the back door where you leave donations. On the left was the changing cubicle, beneath the drawn curtains of which a woman's bare feet were visible. The toenails were painted mauve, the ankles were swollen with matching mauve-coloured scabs that looked like flea bites. Oh horror! Suddenly the curtain was yanked aside, and a plump woman in a baggy sweater and too-tight black leggings emerged. It was Mrs Penny.

I wasn't quick enough to look away. We couldn't pretend we hadn't seen each other.

'Hello,' I said.

She looked utterly mortified to be discovered in such a downmarket setting.

'Fancy seeing you here, Mr L . . . L . . .'

Then with a self-conscious gesture she held up the bright green dress, under her chin, in front of the mirror and asked with a giggle, 'Does this colour suit me, d'you think?'

'It's too . . . green.' It looked way too small; she would never get into it.

'You think so?'

Our eyes met in the mirror. She blushed. Then she glanced down at the two carrier bags in my hand as I deposited them by the donations door.

'Having a clear-out?'

'Yes, just . . .'

As I let go of the handles the bulging bags opened up. A peachy silk lace-trimmed camisole slid out on to the floor. I picked it up quickly and stuffed it back in the bag. She was watching curiously.

'. . . freeing up a bit of space.'

'Oh, you have to, don't you? When you live in a small flat?' I thought I detected a touch of malice in her voice. She turned her back for a moment to hang the green dress back on the rail and I made a dash for the door.

'Bye-ee!' Her voice trilled after me. I responded with a quick backward wave as I exited on to the street, to find my bicycle had been stolen.

BERTHOLD: *George Clooney*

After two hours at the police station, during which every detail of my ex-bike's spec was minutely noted down, the bored woman in uniform gave me a crime number and told me that it was very unlikely that it would ever be recovered, and she hoped it was insured.

'Thanks for that,' I replied.

Waiting at the bus stop, fatigue overcame me once more and tears started prickling my eyes and nose – sniff, sniff. I recognised the warning signs. Depression. Thief of delight. Cries in the night – Stop. Always look on the – Meredith. Not my fault. The childhood stutter. Immortal Bard can help. 'What a p-p-piece of work is a man.' Say it again. Slowly. Again. 'What a piece of work is a man. Noble. Infinite.' But without Mother's cheerful cajoling, which had saved my sanity as well as my diction, how would I ever get back on track?

A fine rain had started and the bus shelter was jammed with people chatting or absorbed in their cell phones. I ached with aloneness. The 394 bus, when it arrived, had a banner advert across its side for the latest film starring George Clooney. He looked so fucking pleased with himself. We can't all be George bloody Clooney but, God knows, I've tried. In fact some people might say that I've followed Clooney's career with a mildly obsessive interest. Look, I've got nothing against the guy personally. He always seemed a perfectly decent type, and not a bad actor. It's the unfairness of life that was bugging me. While the bus juddered and swayed homewards between the long featureless streets and squares of local authority housing that comprise this area of London, I drew up a mental balance sheet.

Similarities between Berthold Sidebottom and George Clooney

Profession: Actor. Eyes deep brown, with interesting wrinkles.

Smile: Clooney, self-deprecatingly lopsided. Sidebottom, passable imitation.

Date of birth: 6 May 1961. Yes, we share a birthday, and that's what made the comparison so pointed.

Differences between Berthold Sidebottom and George Clooney

Hair: Clooney's is dark, lightly streaked with grey, and waves elegantly around his rugged forehead. Sidebottom's is largely absent – the hair, that is. The forehead is still there, thank God.

Height: Clooney, 5 feet 11 inches. Sidebottom, 6 feet. Ha ha.

Transport: Clooney (according to Google) owns a Piaggio scooter, a Harley-Davidson motorbike, a vintage Chevrolet Corvette convertible and a high-spec Tesla Roadster. Sidebottom until recently owned a bicycle. Now he is reliant on public transport.

Women: Clooney twice voted 'Sexiest Man Alive', twice married. Sidebottom? Well, you'd better ask his ex, Stephanie. There were of course persistent rumours that Clooney was gay, which he coolly batted away, refusing to confirm or to deny out of respect for his gay friends, he said. How PC can you get?

Residences: Clooney lives in a thirty-roomed villa overlooking Lake Como, and he also owns a luxurious 700-square-metre villa in Los Angeles. Sidebottom lives in a two-bedroom-plus-study council flat in Mad Yurt, Hackney, shared until recently with his elderly mother.

IMDb: We can come back to that later.

At the moment it was the question of residences that dominated my mind – or, to be precise, the questions raised by that nosy Penny woman. Now I'd shamed her by gawping at her naked ankles, would she seek revenge by getting me removed from the flat on the grounds of 'under-occupancy', if she discovered that Mother was not living there? Would my wheeze to move Inna Alfandari into the flat succeed in keeping those homeless hard-working families at bay? Was Mrs Penny under orders to sniff out instances of under-occupancy and send the undeserving sub-occupants packing? Did she already suspect me? Frankly, I'd done her a favour by saving her from that too-tight, too-green dress. She could return the favour by leaving me alone.

I got off outside Madeley Court and the bus pulled away with George Clooney, darkly dimpled, smirking his lopsided farewell. I gave him the finger. Let's face it, I was thinking as I trudged homewards, living with his aged mum would have cramped even Clooney's sexual style. As for his professional success, it was surely just the fleeting and shallow glamour of celluloid that gave George Clooney an unfair leg-up in his acting career. While I was playing a cool, moody Hamlet in the school production during my A-level year, George Clooney was just an extra in a crowd scene in *Centennial*, which, let's be frank, was about as crap a TV show as you could get. At Highbury Grove School I'd been the star of the drama society, thanks to my mastery of all those Shakespeare soliloquies that

Mother had drilled into me to conquer my stammer, first with a pencil in my mouth to keep my teeth apart, then a matchstick, then an imaginary matchstick. Daring to stand up and spout in front of an audience was exhilarating. Girls started to notice me. I developed a hunger for attention. My stammer melted away. At university I acted more than I studied, and then went on to drama school, while Clooney was still working his way through the ranks of film extras.

At twenty-one I was on the stage, under the name of Burt Side, in a succession of provincial reps, gradually progressing into leading roles. I didn't mind the long hours and the grind – I had found my vocation, I worshipped the Immortal Bard, and I had dedicated my life to Art. George Clooney, meanwhile, played a supporting role in *The Return of the Killer Tomatoes*. In the same year that Clooney landed his first big role as Dr Doug Ross in *ER*, I was an acclaimed Antony at the Blackfriars Theatre in Boston (Lincs), recently married to beautiful actress Stephanie Morgan and new father of Meredith Louise, our baby daughter. I auditioned for the RSC and was offered a three-year contract.

Then in 2001 Meredith died, and everything went into free fall. In 2002 I split up with Stephanie and had a breakdown. While George Clooney moved on from *O Brother, Where Art Thou?* to *Ocean's Eleven*, I underwent my first course of Prozac treatment. Four years later, when George Clooney won an Oscar for *Syriana*, I came out of the Friern Hospital and moved in with my mother on the top floor of Mad Yurt.

The sun peeped out briefly from behind the clouds as I walked across the grove, daffodils nodded all around me and white blossom was drifting from the cherry trees. For a moment my spirits lifted again. It wasn't paradise, there were rats and graffiti. But even Lake Como must have its downside.

*

Some white A4 notices were stuck with sticky-tape to the lamp posts. Someone had lost a cat. It happened regularly. The residents of Madeley Court weren't supposed to keep pets, so unfortunate animals were hidden away indoors, always on the lookout for a chance to break free. *'Answers to the name of Wonder Boy.'* The black and white cat in the picture looked cross and confused. I peered into the shrubby area where the feral moggies dwelled, but I knew the cat, like my bike, would never reappear.

'Hello, Bertie!' called Mrs Crazy from her balcony. 'How's your mum?'

'Fine!' I shouted back.

'I saw her took away in an ambulance.'

'Just a twisted ankle. Nothing serious.' The lie sprang easily to my lips – too easily, as it turned out.

Mother and Mrs Crazy had once been friends, but the latter had bought her flat from the Council in 1985 with some small savings from her late husband's gambling proceeds, and Mother had never forgiven her. She claimed that all the troubles in Madeley Court dated from the break-up of public ownership when private speculators had got their claws into the estate and started it on a downhill spiral, for which grasping coiffure-obsessed fruitcakes like Mrs Crazy and Mrs Thatcher were personally to blame.

Mrs Crazy's pretensions once she became an owner-occupier were particularly annoying to Mother, the wrought-iron window guards, the hanging baskets, the royal-blue front door and ostentatious brass knocker an affront to Lubetkin's purity of line. The final blow came when Mrs Crazy, with support from Legless Len, mounted a coup that ousted her from the Chair of the Tenants Association. She'd always regarded Madeley Court as her personal fiefdom because it was named after her first husband, Ted Madeley, who'd wooed her and married her in 1952. Or 1953. She was vague about the dates, but his photo, framed in walnut, still hung on her bedroom wall. He was a big good-looking, dark-eyed man, who bore an eerie resemblance to moustachioed George Clooney in *The Monuments Men*. In fact he was only a few years younger than her father when she'd first met him at a Labour Party rally in Finsbury Town Hall in 1951. She was nineteen years old, sitting in the audience with her dad, and Ted was up on the platform smiling darkly alongside Harold Riley, Aneurin Bevan and Berthold Lubetkin, who was firing off on all cylinders about the right of working-class people to a decent home for life. Labour lost the election in 1951, but Ted Madeley won Lily's heart.

'It was love at first sight,' Mum reminisced, sherry glass in hand, half a century later. 'Only problem was, he was married with two girls, twins they were, Jenny and Margaret, dark haired like gypsies. You'd have guessed he had a bit of gypsy in him.'

They had moved into Madeley Court together soon after. 'Berthold got the flat for me,' said Mum. Later I read that the block was not completed until 1953. There were other inconsistencies in her stories, but as a boy, I was swept along by the glamour of it all, and never stopped to question the details.

I took the photographs down from the walls one by one and stowed them in a cardboard box with her papers in the boiler cupboard. There were bright squares on the faded wallpaper to mark where they'd been. Inna Alfandari, I supposed, would have her own photos to bring.

VIOLET: Pictures

At the weekend, Violet sorts out the photos she has brought from home: her parents wind-blown and smiling on High Low above Hathersage; her dad with Grandma Alison in front of Edinburgh Castle; her Nyanya Njoki surrounded by all her seven grandchildren; their garden in Karen with Mfumu, her dog that she'd left behind; Kinder Scout purple with heather; her and her friend Jessie wearing stupid hats on a school trip.

As she Blu-tacks them on to the wall, she thinks about the two sides of her family, black and white, far and near, poor and comfortable. Her two cousins on her father's side are tall, blonde, willowy girls a few years older than her who read Music and Art History at Oxford. They work in the arts, shop at Zara, laugh toothily over lunch, and are generous with invitations and free tickets. On her mother's side, her seven cousins are thin, dark and wiry, with respectable but ill-paid office jobs and ready smiles, who shop at Jumia and never have quite enough money. She gets on with all of them; in fact she loves the feeling of sprinting like a runner along a high ridge looking down on each side into two completely different valleys. It's exhilarating up there, but it's scary too. There's always the danger that she will lose her footing and slip down into the wrong valley, the poor side, the dark side.

She steps down from the chair, and stands back to admire her handiwork. At once, the place feels more like home.

From the flat next door, she can hear that weird tinny voice repeating the same incoherent phrase over and over again.

She shudders; she definitely won't be staying here long. She goes into the kitchen to put the kettle on, then takes her mug of Kenya roast coffee out on to the balcony to survey the scene down below. At the far end of the communal garden, a taxi has drawn up, and an old lady dressed in black is getting out.

As she watches, a pigeon lands beside her on the parapet and turns its head to fix her with its round beady eye. It is a tatty-looking bird, with scruffy feathers and only one leg. What has happened to the other one? She scatters some bread crusts for it on the balcony and it hops down to devour them, throwing its head back as they work their way down its blue-green throat. Then it puffs out its feathers and starts to coo in a sweet warbling voice, its whole pathetic body vibrating with the sound. Cooo-coo. Cooo-coo.

BERTHOLD: *Luxury modern skyscrounger*

Inna Alfandari arrived in a taxi. I'd been expecting something more formal – forms to be filled in, a home inspection visit from the shapely nurse, at least a phone call – but I looked out of the window one afternoon and there she was, a diminutive figure dressed all in black, struggling across the grove with her enormous bags, as the taxi pulled away. I ran down to help her. Thank God Mrs Crazy wasn't watching.

'Hello, Inna. Welcome to Madeley Court.'

'Oy! Is council house!' She put her bags down and clasped her hands in an attitude of despair. She didn't seem at all pleased to see me.

'Yes. Didn't my mother tell you?'

'The way she was talk talk talk about this boyfriend flat, I was expect luxury modern skyscrounger.'

'Modernist. She probably said modernist, Inna. It's very nice inside. Wait till you see it.'

I don't know why I was being so apologetic. I'd expected a bit of gratitude and deference from her, but obviously she was under the impression that she was the one who was doing me a favour. I pressed the button for the lift, and while I waited a thought crossed my mind. 'How did you know the address?'

'Nurse told me. She got all informations from you mama file. But she never told me is council flat. Never!'

She crossed herself and stepped into the lift reluctantly. At once, her nose wrinkled up.

'Stinking piss in here.'

What was it Mum used to say? 'Don't be a Moaning Minnie, Inna.'

'Aha! Always keep on sunny side! Ha ha ha!' She brightened up instantly. 'You good man, Mister Bertie, good like you mama.'

It was the first time she had smiled.

When you live in a place you forget how it looks to a newcomer. The communal walkway from the lift to the flats might have been built to a sleek modernist design, but now it was cluttered with dead plants in cracked pots, threadbare mats, a three-legged chair, a discarded Christmas tree four months old, and a mystery object shrouded in black plastic that had been there ever since the seven foreign students had moved out from next door. Inna walked with her head stiff, staring in front of her like a doomed man walking to his death. Wisps of white hair were sticking out from under her scarf.

'Here we are. Home.'

'God is dead!' Flossie screeched, when she heard the door open, and rattled the bars of her cage.

'Aaargh!' Inna let out a shriek and crossed herself. 'Is voice of devil! Mr Indunky Smeet!'

'It's just a parrot, Inna. Don't be afraid. Come on in and say hello. See, she's in a cage.'

'Lily tell me he stealing her flat!'

Inna advanced cautiously into the room, looking around her, sniffing the air. I sniffed too. Flossie's cage urgently needed cleaning.

'Hello, Mister Indunky Smeet,' Inna said. 'Devil-bird.'

'Shut up, Flossie!'

Inna looked nonplussed. 'I am not Floozie.'

'No, it's her name. Flossie.'

'Not Floozie!' chimed Flossie.

'He talk wit himself?'

'It's a girl. Female. Flossie.'

'Is not girl, is bird.'

'Forget it.' I sighed. 'Here, Inna – here's your room. Make yourself at home.'

I pushed open the door of Mother's room, taking in a poignant breath of the heavy powdery air that still carried the smell of her, maybe for the last time. Inna had a different unfamiliar smell, soapy and faintly spicy. She followed behind me, as I set down her bags in front of the ornate walnut dressing table, and sat down on the stool staring at her reflection in the mirror. She took out the pins holding her silver plaits in place, and flicked her head to let them fall. Then she worked the plaits loose with her fingers until her hair cascaded like a sheet of crinkled silver on to her shoulders.

'Oy, I am too old.'

I shook my head but couldn't bring myself to deny it. 'Would you like something to eat? You must be hungry.'

She didn't reply so I brought her a tuna and lettuce sandwich and a cup of tea. She made no move to help, but sat on the stool looking around her.

'I'll leave you to make yourself at home. Let me know if you need anything.'

I closed the door of her room with relief. Feeling somewhat agitated, I went and hunted in the larder, the hall wardrobe and the back of the meter-cupboard to see whether Mum had a spare bottle of sherry secretly stashed away, but I drew a blank. I did, however, find an ancient ten-pack of Players No. 6 wrapped in a tea towel.

Next morning I was woken by Flossie's voice – not her usual repertoire of greetings, she seemed to be squawking randomly. I went into the sitting room to investigate, and there was Inna, looking more ladylike than crone-like in a pale silky blouse and pleated black skirt; her diamanté-framed glasses sat square on her nose, and her long plaits were neatly coiled up behind her ears, on which two of Mother's clip-on earrings glistened. She was trying to teach the bird to sing a folk song – *'povee veetre'* she wailed – rewarding her with pieces of toast.

'Aha! Good morning, Mister Bertie! I mekkit toast. Coffee still hot. But first we drink vodka for good luck.' There was a small bottle of vodka on the table, and two glasses. *'Na zdorovye!'* She tipped back a glass. 'Lack nothing! Be merry!' I tipped back the other, and we both laughed.

'This Mister Indunky Smeet is not too intelligent. He not understand nothing.' She put her face up to the cage. 'Nuh, say "Hello, Inna".'

The bird wailed, *'Povee! Vee!'* Then she hopped about on her perch and reverted to her usual repertoire. 'Say hello, Flinna! First of March, 1932!'

We both laughed again. This arrangement isn't going to be so bad, I thought. It's nice to have someone cheerful in the flat. It'll stop me getting on to that downhill spiral. At least until I get through this gloomy phase and square things with Mrs Penny. After that, Inna could go home – wherever that was. I realised how little I knew about her and her life before I met her in the hospital, but I guessed we would have time enough to find out.

The hospital had phoned to apologise for the delay in the autopsy, which was due to staff shortages, they said. I felt that until the funeral and mourning period were over I couldn't really move on in my life. But the parrot lesson had given me an idea: before I could let Inna loose in the neighbourhood I must teach her to play the part of my mother. This would be a challenge. I poured us both some coffee. She drank hers black with four heaped spoons of sugar.

'Inna, sit down. There's something we have to discuss.'

'You want to make sex wit me, Mister Bertie?' Her eyes twinkled behind her cat's-eye glasses.

I wondered for a moment whether she was having me on. 'No, I want you to play the part of my mother. When you go out. When you meet people. Remember we discussed it in the hospital?'

'Aha! You want I mekkit golabki kobaski slatki? I mekkit delicious wit yushka.'

'Yes, that too. But the main thing is, you have to say you're my mother. You have to say your name is Mrs Lily Lukashenko, and your date of birth is the first of March, 1932. Can you remember all that?'

'First of March, 1932!' squawked Flossie. 'Shut up Flinna!'

'Inna!' said Inna.

'Shut up, Inna!'

'But my birthday is the twentieth of April.'

'Shut up, Inna!'

'I know, but you have to pretend, remember?'

'Oy! Pretend remember not my birthday?'

'Shut up, Inna!'

'Shut up, Flossie! Yes, that's it. Don't worry, Flossie will remind you.'

'Who is Flossie?'

'Flossie the parrot.'

'No, parrot name Mister Indunky Smeet. Your mother has told me.'

'Listen. Listen carefully. The parrot is Flossie and you are Mrs Lily Lukashenko.'

'Oy! Why for such ridiculous name? Alfandari is better.'

'I know, but it's my mother's name.'

Inna sighed deeply. 'If you say so.'

★

Inna went out that afternoon to Hampstead, saying she needed to retrieve some of her belongings and to pick up her mail. I gave her a key, and pointed out the bus stop, but five minutes later she was back, saying, 'I forgot papers.' She tucked a large brown envelope into her handbag. Why does she need papers to go back to her old flat? I wondered. But it wasn't until later that I became suspicious of her comings and goings.

Around five o'clock, I spotted her walking back through the cherry grove with a couple of carrier bags. I could see from my window that her bearing already seemed sprightlier, more optimistic, as if buoyed up by my small act of kindness that nature's fragile vessel doth sustain in life's uncertain voyage. The thought made me feel rather pleased with myself. She paused to rest near the playground, where the boy who had nearly been hit by the van was idling on the swings, toying with his phone. I wondered who he was. Suddenly Mrs Crazy appeared, heading towards the community garden. She and Inna greeted each other, then to my alarm they began to chat, leaning together as if exchanging confidences. This could be dangerous. If Inna tried to pass herself off as Lily Lukashenko, Mrs Crazy would smell a rat. She knew Mother well, and I had told her she had twisted her ankle.

A few minutes later Inna's key turned in the lock.

'Hello, Mister Bertie. Look! I got cabbage for mekkit dish from my country, best in world.'

That evening, we dined on mashed potatoes with yuksha, a type of gravy, and globokli. These turned out to be boiled cabbage leaves stuffed with a mixture of minced meat and rice. Inna had picked up the ingredients in the market at Hoxton and spent an hour in the kitchen preparing them. It would be an exaggeration to say they were delicious, but they were more edible than the fluorescent styrofoam chunks from Sha-zaad that had become my staple diet. This arrangement was working out just as I'd hoped.

'Lovely, Inna,' I said. 'You're an excellent cook.' Which was perhaps a slight overstatement, but I thought she'd be pleased.

Instead she burst into tears and buried her face in her apron. 'Oy! Oy! My good husband, he was saying same exactly thing!'

I laid a hand on her wrist. 'Hush. I'm sure he is in heaven looking down on you.'

Sometimes a white lie can mend matters, but this one clearly opened up a wound.

'Not in heaven! Dovik is Jew of Sephardim, I am Christian of True Believer! Oy! We will never be together in heaven wit Lily and Lenin and Khrushchev!'

'I don't think Lenin and Khrushchev will make it to heaven, Inna. Religion and politics have slightly different rules.'

'Not so different. In my country first we have religion, everybody dead, then we get communism, everybody dead, then we get religion again, still everybody dead. Always every-body dead!'

She crossed herself in a display of fervour which culminated in a violent coughing fit. Not wanting to risk another green phlegm eruption, I quickly changed the subject.

'Never mind, Inna. What's past is prologue. I saw you met one of the neighbours today – the lady in the purple coat. Her name is Mrs Cracey, but we call her Mrs Crazy.'

'Aha. Yes, very nice lady, she told me husband was bishop. But dead. I say why for bishop living in council flat?' Her nose wrinkled up. 'She said he come from East London lost all money at poking. I said my husband come from East Ukraina lost all money at smoking. Ha ha. Men always good for losing money.'

So Mrs Crazy was now claiming her late husband had been a bishop, was she? The old fibber. Hence the jewellery and showy headgear, no doubt.

'So what else did you tell her, Inna, about . . . you know . . . about us?'

'Don't worry, Bertie, I tell her I am your mother.'

VIOLET: Risk

Risk. Violet has never thought about it much before, except when it affects her directly. But now the world seems to be full of it. The CIA *World Factbook*, for example, paints a frightening picture of corruption and terrorism in Kenya which is at odds with her own idyllic memories.

The Nairobi shopping mall project is turning out to be more challenging than she imagined. The land the mall will be built on is to the east of the city, not a part she is familiar with, uncomfortably close to the Nairobi River where flooding or landslip could be a hazard, not far from Eastleigh with its Al Shabaab influences, and the Gikomba Market, a vast emporium of clothing from UK charity shops where fires are a regular occurrence. So many risks. If she had been setting up a major development, she would not have chosen this place. She wonders who owns the development company HN Holdings. Buried in the paperwork she finds the name Horace Nzangu. It rings a bell. Where has she heard it before? Has there been a proper survey or planning permission granted for this development, or did money change hands to get it approved?

Out of curiosity, she finds the Nairobi City Planning Department online, and telephones with her questions, slipping in a few friendly words of Swahili that she remembers, but after an hour of being transferred from one department to another, asked for details, and kept on hold, she finds she has gone around in a full circle and learned absolutely nothing – except that there is no apparent record of a planning application, nor anyone available to talk to her who is responsible for planning in that area. She's fizzing with frustration when Gillian Chalmers emerges from her office with a pile of slip cases, clack-clacking on her high heels as she heads towards the lifts.

'How's it going, Violet?'

She sighs, and before she can think of a suitably upbeat comment, Gillian reads her expression and asks, 'Would you like to come out to Lloyd's with me this afternoon, and meet some underwriters?'

The Lloyd's Building, which is the hub of the UK insurance industry, is one of those too-tall, too-modern buildings the City of London is full of. It is designed by some architect guy called Richard Rogers, whom Gillian raves over. And sure, the view from the glass elevators is nice. But all that steel is too shiny and cold.

'It's one of the great modernist buildings in the City of London!' Gillian's tone could be interpreted as either instructive or condescending. 'Like the Pompidou Centre in Paris. See how all the essential services are located on the outside? It increases the space for business inside.'

'Cool.' She pretends to share Gillian's enthusiasm, but she's thinking, for heaven's sake, it's only insurance, not a temple to some new religion.

But Gillian seems to come to life in that environment, cutting and thrusting as she puts her clients' needs to a series of slick young men in sharp suits, who melt under her offensive. While at GRM Gillian often seems severe and distant, in this setting she has a tigerish magnetism that fills Violet with reluctant admiration. Will she ever be able to perform like that?

'It's all in the research,' Gillian says as they ride down in the elevator. 'You have to be confident of your ground, Violet, before you can win the best deal for your client.' Her eyes are sparkling, her cheeks flushed with her successes.

Suddenly Violet sees why Marc Bonnier was attracted to her. But is he still?

Turning this thought over again in her mind, she brews up a jug of coffee in her kitchen after work. Her friends have messaged to say they're meeting up at the Lazy Lounge, but she texts back that she's too done in. It's a relief to escape from the high-rise City echoing with the rush of traffic on to her quiet balcony. The stillness of the early evening washes over her like a wave of cool water. Her friendly pigeon flutters up and she crumbles up a chocolate biscuit for him. He gobbles it down, then thanks her with two minutes of chest-puffing and cooing before flying away. Cooo-coo, cooo-coo.

She's surprised how little she misses Nick. Sometimes she struggles to remember what it was she'd liked about him. His smile? His cheesy socks? His weird ideas about astral projection? He was just another messy immature male who shattered her heart as casually as dropping a beer glass. She's ready for someone more grown-up now, someone sensitive and intelligent, who will take her seriously. Someone with a good sense of humour. A bit like Marc Bonnier, perhaps. Until then, she's happy living on her own.

Far below in the garden, where fallen cherry blossom dusts the ground like snow, a man in a wheelchair is rolling along the winding path between the trees, turning the wheels with his hands. Now here comes the baldie from Luigi's making his way towards the flats. Their paths cross and they stop to talk. A lady in a purple coat comes along and joins in. What's that weird thing on her head? The old lady dressed in black, the one she saw arriving in a taxi the other day, has appeared on the scene too. They're all talking and shouting, but she can't make out what they're saying. It reminds her of her grandmother's neighbourhood in Langata, when the air begins to cool in the early evening and the street comes alive with people hanging out. She decides to go down to the garden and see what's going on, but by the time she gets there the little group of neighbours has dispersed. The purple-coat lady is heading towards a raised vegetable garden that has been fenced off for the residents. The weird thing on her head that looked like a plastic bag turns out to be a shower cap made of clear polythene protecting a stiff arrangement of curled bleached hair, even though it isn't raining. The ladies in Nairobi wore hats like that in the rainy season when they'd had their hair straightened, chattering on the pavement like go-away-birds with their distinctive headgear, waiting for the taxi-vans to take them home. She says hello, and the shower-cap lady mutters something inaudible as she hurries off to the communal vegetable beds, letting herself in through a high mesh gate and disappearing like a *kivuli* into a wooden shed.

There are notices stuck on the lamp posts in the garden. She's seen them before: they're for a lost cat called Wonder Boy. Or are they? She looks again and sees they are not appeals for the lost cat but announcements of an application for planning permission. Town and Country Planning Act. Residential development. Area bounded by . . . All the street signs around here are missing, so she doesn't know exactly where it refers to, but it must be somewhere nearby. Remembering her frustrating morning trying to phone the Planning Department in Nairobi, she decides to let this one pass. But – fourteen storeys – why does everything need to be so high? Why can't they leave the sky alone for everyone to enjoy?

A familiar crooning sound above her head makes her look up. There is her friend the one-legged pigeon perched up in the branches of a cherry tree.

'Hello, Pidgie.'

The pigeon lets fall a large glob of poop, which lands by her feet. A sign of luck!

She takes the bird's picture as it perches up among the blossom and posts it on her Facebook page with a joke about her new boyfriend, the one-legged pigeon.

She is just about to go back up to her flat when a large shiny black car draws up by the pavement. It's like the limos that Government officials in Nairobi drive around in. Everybody knows that nobody who just lives on their salary can afford to buy one, but they do it anyway. She expects the chauffeur to now get out and hold open the door for some big-shot, but instead the back door opens from inside and a schoolboy gets out, pink-faced and slightly plump, wearing a grey school uniform that is too tight in some places, and a bit baggy in others. He waves to the driver of the limo and steps out into the road, his head bent over his phone. An approaching car slams its brakes on. Oblivious, he ambles into the Madeley Court garden and sits on a bench by the path. The black car glides away into the traffic. As she gets closer, she can see the boy is still hunched over his phone, texting.

There are a few other kids in the garden, some are kicking a ball around, but no one comes and sits next to him or asks him to join in. It's easy to see why: all the other kids are wearing a navy-blue school uniform, whereas his is grey. But that isn't the main thing: all the other boys, even the little ones, are wearing long trousers. His are short. He looks ridiculous, poor kid.

A memory like a sudden wind whisks her back in time, whisks her up and sets her down in the playground of her primary school in Bakewell, where she is standing alone by the railings, painfully conscious of her wrong colour, her wrong hair, her wrong clothes, her wrong family, all her general can't-put-your-finger-on-it wrongness, watching the groups of children playing together, pretending she doesn't care. Then Jessie, the same Jessie whose duvet she's been sleeping under this past week, comes up without a word and shoves the end of a skipping rope into her hand. And she turns it, turns with full concentration, while Jessie jumps over the spinning rope chanting, 'My brother Billie had a ten-foot willy . . .' She thought a willy must be some kind of a boat.

While she is wondering whether to say something friendly to the boy, a man appears at the end of the path, a tall good-looking man in a high-end suit with a briefcase under his arm.

'Come along, Arthur,' he says to the boy, and the boy, still without looking up from his phone, gets up and follows him towards the flats.

BERTHOLD: *Unaccommodated man*

It was as I feared. Letting Inna go out in the cherry grove on her own was risky. Although she had obeyed my instructions to the letter by telling Mrs Crazy she was my mother, Mrs Crazy of course smelled a rat, and she was just the vindictive type to go telling tales to the authorities. She stopped me in the grove on my way to Luigi's.

'Berthold, who is this foreigner impersonating your mother?' She pulled herself up stiffly; the polythene shower cap protecting her platinum bouffant sweated in the sun. 'Your mother has gone through many changes, Berthold, and not all for the better. She may have embraced communism, but she never came from Odessa. I know, because Pastor Cracey and me went there on a deluxe cruise for our honeymoon.'

Bloody hell. Why did Inna have to mention Odessa? It took me a full twenty minutes of RADA-schooled performance with tearful eyes and quavers in my throat to persuade her that Lily was still in hospital and the twisted ankle had turned out to be a multiple-fractured leg – yes, with complications, Multi-Antibiotic-Resistant-Whatsit – and that Inna was, in fact, her sister, tragically struck with dementia, who had forgotten who she was. Yes, dementia made her talk funny. No, they didn't look alike, that's because they had different fathers. Yes, I do believe her father was actually of Ukrainian origin – really? Did Inna say she's from Odessa? Ha ha – I expect she's been watching travel programmes on TV. What she means is Ossett. Ossett in Yorkshire.

Ossett was a town lodged in my memory as the birthplace of my father, Sidney Sidebottom, Lily's ex-husband, but I doubted Mrs Crazy knew this. She eyed me with suspicion. Legless Len came to my rescue with a meandering account of his late wife's illness, which involved dementia, aphasia, amnesia, with a bit of mistaken identity and inappropriate behaviour thrown in, all of which he had endured with wisdom, wit and the occasional whisky. Len can vex the dull ear of a drowsy man, but sometimes it's useful.

'Are you sure you're not getting just a little bit confused yourself, Mrs Cracey?' I adeptly turned the tables on her, and she flounced off to the communal potting shed.

Still, it was a bad omen.

When Inna came in later with her shopping bags from one of her long afternoon outings, I sat her down and told her we must practise some techniques to enable her to perform the part of my mother better.

'You see, my mother was often confused,' I explained. 'She didn't know who she was. That's what we must aim for.'

She looked at me acutely. 'Lily like Soviet pioneer, Mister Bertie. No confused. I tell this crazy lady I am you mama, she tell me she seen you mother tooken in hospital wit ambulance.'

Bloody Mrs Crazy. She's the consummate curtain-twitcher. 'So what did you say, Inna?'

'I said I seen her in hospital.'

'That's good, Inna, that's very good. I told Mrs Crazy you are my mother's sister, so naturally you would visit her in hospital.'

'Aha! So I am mother or sister?'

'Sometimes my mother, sometimes her sister. I tell you what, Inna, the best thing is to pretend that you are totally confused. Pretend you don't know who you are. That should cover all eventualities.'

'Oy, Mister Bertie! You are actor, I am not actor!'

She was beginning to cough and I could see a green phlegm moment coming on, so I grasped her hand.

'You just have to talk about philosophy, while cultivating an absent expression. Like this.' I rolled my eyes upwards, revealing the blank whites. I have played many fools and madmen in my time, but my favourite is Lear's Fool, where the wisdom is concealed inside the madness. 'Unaccommodated man is no more but such a poor, bare, forked animal as thou art.'

And unless Inna learned her part, I was in danger of becoming unaccommodated.

'What is mean un-commandant?'

'It means homeless. But it also means that we derive our station and our place in society from where we live. Underneath our finery, we are all naked.'

She looked alarmed. 'You want I be naked?'

'No, Inna. Shakespeare is full of double meanings. Just pretend to be a homeless madman.' I flapped my arms and swivelled my eyes. '*With hey, ho, the wind and the rain!* Like you're listening to the sound of an approaching storm on the blasted heath.'

She listened, cocking her head. 'I can hear no storm.'

'The storm is not there. It's in your mind.'

'Aha!' She looked at me beadily. 'You are too clever for me, Mister Bertie. Better I not pretend nothing, better I just cooking golabki kobaski slatki.'

'Don't lose heart.' I patted her arm. 'You can do it. Just say anything that comes into your head, and listen for the coming storm.'

'Like this?' She slid her eyes upwards and sideways, Kinski-style. I was impressed.

'God is dead!' Flossie squawked from her perch.

'Shut up, Indunky Smeet! Devil-bird! God is not dead, he is risen!' cried Inna.

It was perfect.

'Let's take a break for dinner,' I suggested. 'Bring on the globalki!'

VIOLET: *Gillian*

Global Resource Management: even the name makes Violet feel overwhelmed by the extent of her new responsibilities. The job is both more challenging and more interesting than she'd thought at first, and she starts to imagine herself growing into it until she too will be storming like a tiger into the Lloyd's Building and winning contracts by the sheer power of her research.

After her afternoon out with Gillian, she feels a new respect for her boss's talent. So when Gillian hints one morning over a cup of organic ashwagandha that in a man's world it's important for women to dress in a feminine but businesslike style, her heart sinks. Does that mean turning up for work in tailored suits and pussycat bows? Please! She thought her straight skirts and opaque tights were businesslike enough, but apparently Gillian thinks otherwise.

When she mentions her difficulties with the shopping mall proposal, Gillian replies in her schoolmistressy voice, 'Every risk is insurable at a price, Violet. You have to match the underwriter to the risk. Some of the people we met at Lloyd's specialise in problem risks.' Then she gives what is probably meant to be a reassuring smile.

Violet returns to her dossier trying not to show her dejection. She had gone into her new job bouncing with confidence. Now at the end of her first month she is wondering whether she has chosen the wrong career.

Then on the Friday afternoon something miraculous happens.

She is summoned into Gillian's office to be told that Laura

has gone into labour prematurely and has been taken into hospital – and as the Wealth Preservation Unit is under a lot of pressure, would she mind very much taking a temporary secondment to that department starting next week?

Would she mind very much? She struggles to control the grin that tugs at the corners of her mouth.

BERTHOLD: *Slatki*

Something miraculous has happened.

The beautiful black girl from Luigi's has moved in next door. I saw her catching the lift, poised behind the closing doors as I approached, like a goddess about to ascend to Elysium. I raced up the stairs and was in time to see her letting herself into the next-door flat with her key. (Since losing my bike, I do sometimes climb the stairs in a fruitless attempt to stay svelte – I hadn't realised how pissy they were.) Since then, I have been thinking of ways of introducing myself. I must stock up on sugar, in case she decides to borrow a cup. Or coffee. Ah! 'I'm sorry to trouble you, I'm having a dinner party, and I've run out of coffee'. One little-known fact about that iconic 1980s Nescafé Gold Blend ad is that I, Berthold Sidebottom, actually auditioned for the part. Okay, smarmy Tony Head got it, but that doesn't mean I'm barred from using the lines. Then of course George bloody Clooney got in on the act with that fussy coffee machine and its overpriced capsules. Ristretto! A woman would have to be unbelievably shallow to fall for that.

'Bertie!' Inna called from the next room. 'Come drink vodka, it slatki. I make it special for you!'

Actually, I have developed quite a taste for slatkis, which is a generic term for small delicious pastries with honey, almonds, pistachio or other nuts, and an unspeakable calorie count, best consumed with vodka, though mint tea is an acceptable substitute. Unfortunately, these sweet delights don't always seem to agree with me. Once or twice, I had noticed a feeling of nausea after eating them, which I put down to the accompanying vodka or just unaccustomed overindulgence, but now there was something about Inna's beady-eyed insistence that sent a shiver through me. I suddenly remembered. Almonds. Prussic acid. The murderer's poison of choice. In my first year at drama school we'd done an improvisation on an Agatha Christie novel in which the victim was murdered by small regular doses of prussic acid, whose distinguishing characteristic was the odour of almonds. As a nurse, she must know about poisons.

I stared at the pastries in horror. I knew of course that Inna liked our flat, but would she go so far as to kill for it?

'Ittit!' Inna insisted. She popped one into her mouth and washed it down with a good slug of vodka.

That convinced me I was being paranoid. A murderess would not deliberately take poison herself. Even in low doses. Would she? I ate a couple more, letting them melt on my tongue with a sip of vodka, which I had come to prefer over Mother's sweet sherry.

'Delicious, Inna!' My heart thudded weirdly.

'Aha, Mister Bertie! My good husband always used to said way to men heart is veeya stomach.'

I paused for thought as I savoured another mouthful, trying to remember how she said her husband had died. Then I observed that all the slatkis had little halves of glacé cherry on top of them. Except the one she had eaten. I started to feel an unpleasant tightness in my throat. My pulse began to race. What was Inna's motive to poison me? A moral objection to my supposed gay lifestyle? Or was her real purpose to gain possession of Mother's flat? Then she popped another slatki in her mouth – this one definitely had a glacé cherry on top. I relaxed.

'It! It!' she urged. 'I make sweet special for you because you lady-man like it everything sweety.'

I resisted the temptation to slap her, for her words kicked off a new train of thought in me. Femininity and sweetness often go together. Women have a weakness for pastries and chocolate. I had stumbled on the perfect way to woo my delectable next-door neighbour. Then I had a moment of pure inspiration which I felt in my loins would be life-transforming. Call it the Gold Blend Gambit. Call it the Clooney Clemency. Call it the Berthold Breakfast Breakthrough. It would be an opportunity to put Inna through her acting paces, and at the same time to get my delightful neighbour hooked on these honey-loaded morsels.

'Inna,' I said. 'There is a new neighbour next door. Is it not customary in your part of the world to call round with a welcoming gift?'

'I seen it,' grumped Inna. 'Is blackie.'

'Now, Inna . . .' I remembered the firm but kind way my mother had squashed a similarly unacceptable outburst in the hospital. 'It's wrong to be racist. Black people can be very . . . nice.'

It hadn't come out quite as forcefully as I intended, but she backed down at once.

'Aha! You are right, Mister Bertie. Your mama told me is bad to think such thoughts. In my country everybody whitey, everybody normal, we not meet another type of person. She say we must be good to everybody. Same like Lenin say all nationalities equal. Same like Jesus say everybody is negbur.' She clasped her hands together in an attitude of prayer. 'She was like saint in heaven, your mama.'

Funnily enough, I think she meant it.

VIOLET: *Cherry blossom*

Violet posts a card to Laura congratulating her and thanking her for putting in a good word for her. She feels like a small ship buoyed on a high tide of hope embarking on the journey of her life. Of which the first port of call was landing the job at GRM. Now she is set to travel deeper into the mysterious channel of Wealth Preservation, the domain of handsome and enigmatic Marc Bonnier.

But – first things first – what should she wear for the voyage? Gillian's remark about looking businesslike has stuck in her mind; she wants to look the part. But Gillian's style of severe suits and high heels doesn't appeal – if she had her way, she'd spend her life in jeans and trainers. Her cousin Lucy, who works at a gallery in Bond Street, suggests Fenwick's, so they agree to meet there for lunch on Saturday. Two hours later and £600 poorer, she comes away with a tailored dress in a dove grey with a matching jacket, a suit in a soft lilac colour like one she's seen Amal Clooney photographed in, and a pair of high-heeled suede shoes that she can wear with either. See it as an investment, she tells herself, as she hands over her credit card. She also splashes out on a little baby suit in sea green from the baby section that would suit a girl or a boy, and goes to visit Laura in hospital.

Laura is sitting up in bed looking dreamy and blissful, surrounded by flowers. The baby – it is a boy – is fast asleep in a cradle at the foot of the bed, a tiny mite with dark wisps of hair like Laura's and a red squashed face.

'Oh, Laura, he's gorgeous!' she exclaims, though she suspects that newborns only look gorgeous to their mothers.

Laura laughs. 'He's not exactly George Clooney. But I hope he will be one day!'

The baby opens one bright eye, sucks his thumb, and falls asleep again.

'Talking about gorgeous, Violet, did you hear anything from Wealth Preservation?'

'Yes. Thanks for putting in a good word for me. They've seconded me to the WPU while you're away.'

'Be careful with Marc Bonnier. He's got a reputation.'

A reputation. What exactly does that mean? Her stomach flutters with anticipation.

On Sunday morning she wakes early again and lies in bed, watching the daylight filter through the flimsy sari curtain, listening to African music on her iPod, as she waits for the tap-tap of the one-legged pigeon on her window. He's late. Maybe he's at church, ha ha. She remembers Sunday mornings in Kenya when her grandmother took all the cousins to church while their parents had a lie-in. They all stood together in a pew and sang at the tops of their voices – *Fight the good fight with all thy might!* – while an old man in a blue smock thumped at the piano.

At last the pigeon arrives and they eat their toast together on the balcony, the pigeon cooing in a chatty sort of way and trying to strut, which isn't easy with one leg. After he's flown off to his cherry tree, she stands for a while gazing down at the garden. She watches the woman in the purple coat emerge from the garden shed, still wearing her shower cap, as the wheelchair man passes on the footpath. They stop to talk. The woman starts waving a carrier bag, tossing chunks of something on the ground. A grey shadow emerges from the bushes like a *kivuli*, grabs one of the chunks in its jaws, and disappears. Other shadowy creatures creep up like giant rats. The wheelchair man waves his crutches at them, but they dart around and under his wheelchair, sneaking out between the wheels. He tries to grab the bag. Then he tries to bat away the white stuff with his crutches. The woman takes a swing at him with the carrier bag and knocks his baseball cap off his head.

Uh-oh! It's time to intervene.

She races down the stairs and out into the cool freshness of the garden. Blossom is drifting down from the trees. As she approaches she sees that the man in the wheelchair is trying to shoo away half a dozen skinny cats fighting over raw chicken wings, snarling and hissing and batting each other with their claws.

The woman is egging them on. 'Pss, pss! Come on, my love-lies! Eat up!'

The wheelchair man has fake legs – metal posts are fitted into his shoes where his legs have been amputated below the knees. He is not effective at shooing the cats away – they are literally running rings around him. Then the schoolboy she saw before, the one with the grey uniform and short trousers, appears from the other end of the path.

'What's up, Len?' he asks the wheelchair man.

'Bloody cats, innit?' the man exclaims. 'It's against local authority regulations feeding vermin!' His cheeks are red with rage, and his brow below his red football-supporter hat is shiny with sweat.

'They're not vermin, they're God's creatures!' shrieks the lady in purple. Beneath the shower cap, her hair looks stiff with lacquer like a warrior's helmet. It reminds Violet of another song they used to sing at church in Nairobi: *Onward, Christian soldiers!* A pair of arched pencilled-on eyebrows give her a look of permanent alarm.

The boy starts to run around, chasing the cats away. They scamper for the bushes, but then his phone sounds, he pulls it out of his pocket and wanders off down the path, busily texting with his thumbs. The cats slink back.

Violet asks the wheelchair man, 'Why don't you like them?'

At once, the old lady launches her counter-attack. 'Don't you go sticking your nose in here, young madam. I'm just doing the Lord's work, feeding the hungry.'

'They come in my flat, steal my food and piss in the corner!' shouts the man. 'And she bloody encourages them!'

They both seem mad with rage. When she was little, her Grandma Njoki used a trick of distraction whenever there was a fight among the cousins.

'Have you seen these notices?' She points to where the notices have been fixed to the lamp posts and tree trunks. Now she sees they have mostly disappeared; only a couple are still hanging by a shred of sticky tape.

'More stray bloody cats. I'd poison 'em if I had my way! Or shoot 'em all!' The man in the wheelchair is warming himself up for another eruption.

'No,' she says. 'Not the lost cat. An application for planning permission. They want to build a block of private flats here. On the garden. Where the cherry trees are.'

'Get rid of all the bloody cats, wouldn' it?' mutters the wheelchair man, deflated.

'Private flats is better,' says the shower-cap lady. 'No scroungers.' She looks daggers at the wheelchair man.

'But what about the cherry trees? They'd have to cut down all the trees,' says Violet.

'They make a bloody mess, don't they?' he mutters. 'All that white stuff. Blows everywhere. Gets stuck on my wheels and ends up on the carpet. They don't think about that, do they, when they plant them?'

From being at loggerheads moments before, they are now united – against her.

'But don't you think they're beautiful? Uplifting?'

'Uplifting?' The shower-cap lady studies her through narrow eyes. 'You don't live around here, do you?'

'I live up there.' She points up at her window.

'There's a mad old woman lives up there. Potty as a whacker.' Her look implies it is contagious.

'Living in a natural environment is good for us. It's an established fact.' Her mother was always going on about trees.

'Huh!' snorts the wheelchair man.

'Mm. But it could affect property values.' The woman stiffens. 'You!' She jabs a finger at Violet. 'You talk posh. Why don't you ring up the Council and find out what's going on?'

'I can't. I'm too busy.'

The woman has a cheek, insulting her and then bossing her about. She has more important things to do right now than get involved in some local squabble.

'No you're not!' snaps the woman. 'Nobody round here is busy.' Then she adds in a softer tone, 'Where I come from, round Thanet, there's no end of cherry trees. God's gift. Look proper at this time of year, don't they?'

'Well, all right, if I find time I'll give the Council a ring. But don't count on me to do anything else.'

By Monday morning the cherry trees and the planning application have vanished from her thoughts as she flaps around deciding which outfit to wear for her first day in Wealth Preservation.

She runs to the bus stop in her trainers, carrying her high heels in her bag. Crossing the cherry garden, she sees the boy again, dragging his feet as he crawls along a few metres behind his dad while she sprints towards the bus stop, and she feels how lucky she is to have an interesting job with good prospects – if only she could tell him it is worth putting in the effort at school.

Breathless and wind-blown, she changes her shoes in the lift. Marc looks up from his computer as she taps on the door and enters his office.

'Welcome to Wealth Preservation, Violet.' He raises an eyebrow. 'That colour suits you. Matches your name.'

She blushes and wishes she'd worn the dove grey.

His office is small and hot, cluttered with papers and dead coffee cups. A fancy black and chrome coffee machine gleams on a side bench beside the copier. There is a subtle smell of coffee, expensive aftershave and something else – how would she describe that smell? Male. The smell of maleness.

'Sit down. Coffee? Now, Violet, what do you know about Wealth Preservation?'

'I've had a look on –' She stops herself. To admit to looking things up on Google sounds naff.

'It's not as technical as it sounds.' He presses a capsule into the coffee machine and hands her a thick slip case. 'Here, have a look through these files. It'll give you an idea of what we do. A lot of it is just about moving client money around to low-tax jurisdictions. How do you like your coffee?'

'White with one sugar.'

It turns out Marc has no milk or sugar. She finds some in the fridge in the kitchen corner. Back at her desk in the outer office she sips her coffee, which is very strong and too highly roasted for her taste.

She misses having Laura to chat to. Most of her new colleagues are several years older than her and although they are perfectly pleasant towards her seem to be mainly interested in property prices, stock indices and other such fascinating topics. She sends off a text to Laura with an emoji kiss for the baby. Then she opens the slip case and starts to read through the papers.

At first, nothing seems to make much sense. The wealthy clients seem to be mainly from poor places – Ukraine, Russia, Bulgaria, Greece, Brazil, China, India and several African countries. There's even a file for HN Holdings. Could it be the same company that is building the shopping mall in Nairobi? This one is registered in the British Virgin Islands, not Kenya. Strangely, it appears to be a subsidiary of GRM. Marc Bonnier is named as company secretary on the paperwork. The firm seems to specialise not in building development but in imports. In fact they are importing large quantities of plastic buckets into Kenya. But why are they sending out repeat invoices for different amounts of money?

As she puzzles over the invoices, a pattern emerges. The buckets are purchased for $1 each in China, then sold on to the Health Department in Kenya. What is staggering is the sale price: $49 per bucket. How can a plastic bucket cost $49? There must be a mistake somewhere.

She struggles to make sense of it.

By lunchtime, her head still spinning with the impossibility of matching up the numbers, she decides to go out to a café instead of to the office cafeteria in case she runs into Marc and he asks her how she is doing. She doesn't want to appear stupid. Instead, she tries to phone Laura for advice, but her phone is switched off.

Then she remembers she has another phone call she promised to make.

*

She has to listen to a long recorded menu of selections before she finally gets through to the Council's Planning Department.

'All objections must be in writing. We can't discuss details over the phone. You can view the submitted plans at the Planning Offices,' replies a nasal voice flattened with boredom.

Still, she's made more progress than with the Nairobi Planning Department. The HN shopping mall development she's trying to insure seems no more ludicrous than chopping down trees to build more flats. The fluffy pink cherry trees look lovely in this overbuilt part of London, and besides, one of them is Pidgie's home. Yes, if she finishes early one day, she'll go over and check out the plans. Somebody has to keep a watch on these developments; otherwise the sky gets eaten up before your eyes.

'How are you getting on, Violet? Is it all beginning to make sense?'

Marc leans over her desk and places a hand on her shoulder. A shiver runs through her, but she tries to keep her voice cool.

'I can't see the point of all these invoices, Marc. Why is the invoice that comes from the British Virgin Isles so much bigger than the invoice that comes from China?'

'Re-invoicing is an essential tool for wealth preservation, Violet. We use a corporation in an offshore tax haven as an intermediary between the onshore business and the home country. That way, most of the profits accrue to the offshore corporation, with obvious tax advantages.'

'I see.' She hesitates. 'But how . . . ?'

'Look, say a company sells a million dollars' worth of goods in a particular country, that company would be liable for tax on the profits, wouldn't they? But say the goods are bought by a shell company in a low-tax jurisdiction and that company in turn sells on the goods to the first country, all the profit would accrue to the tax haven company, so no tax would be due.'

She feels a thud in her stomach, as though her little ship had struck a rock.

'But isn't that a bit – ?'

'It's what we're here for, Violet, to provide a service to our clients. It's our business.'

'But those buckets – it still doesn't explain why HN Holdings are selling buckets to the Kenyan Health Authority at $49 each which only cost one dollar to buy.'

He sighs. 'It's not up to us to judge the business practices of our clients. We just provide a technical service.'

Her heart is pounding. Her mind is racing, trying to find another possible interpretation of what she is hearing.

'But you . . . your name . . .'

'Part of the GRM service is anonymity, so the identity of the beneficial owner needn't be disclosed in the home country. We provide the nominee officers and directors for the shell company, and we issue shares to the beneficial owner, or we help them to set up a foundation. Most tax haven countries have strict laws on disclosure of confidential information.' He pauses and lowers his voice, speaking close to her ear. 'I'm hoping you'll soon be able to act as a nominee, Violet, when you've got the necessary knowledge. It's not difficult, but you have to be on the ball. I thought HN Holdings might be a good one to start with for you, because of your knowledge of Kenya.'

'I see,' she says, though she really doesn't want to see.

'Look,' says Marc, 'it can take a bit of getting used to. Why don't you take the papers home with you this evening? Get things in perspective. I have an international call to take right now, but if you're free tomorrow evening, maybe we can talk about it over dinner? Yes?'

She can hear the phone ringing in his office. He squeezes her shoulder again, his hand lingering just a moment too long, then disappears.

She slips her jacket on over her dress. In the lift going down, she changes out of her high heels into her trainers and runs to the bus stop.

'I'm not sure I can do this job, Laura.' On the top deck of the bus, she pours out her misgivings into her phone. For some reason, her eyes are wet with tears.

'I know it doesn't seem right at first, but you'll soon get used to it, Violet. Everybody in the City does it.' Laura sounds tired and harassed. In the background the baby is yelling above the noise of the news on the radio. 'I read somewhere that ninety-eight out of the hundred top London Stock Exchange companies have subsidiaries, associates, or joint ventures in tax havens. If it wasn't GRM it would be somebody else doing it, and you'd be out of a job.'

'I think I might be happier just dealing with insurance.'

'How are you finding working with Marc?'

'Fine. Actually, he asked me out for dinner. But now I'm not so sure . . .'

Laura laughs. 'Don't be such a fogey, Violet. Go. Enjoy yourself! But don't say I didn't warn you.'

BERTHOLD: *Wrest 'n' Piece*

Once in every lifetime, someone comes along with a key to open up the rusty old door of your heart. My excitement over the possibilities of romance with my new neighbour had seized my imagination, and I had come up with a seductive variation on the Gold Blend Gambit: it would be me giving the dinner party, and the next-door goddess who would be the guest. A sweet old lady, i.e. Inna, would be dispatched to her door as a decoy to invite her round for a neighbourly dinner. Then on the elected evening she would ring the bell, the door would open, and there would be Berthold Sidebottom, the distinguished actor, at his most scintillating. Da dah!

Getting to that point would take planning and preparation – a visit to the barber (one has to make the most of what one has), long-overdue laundry, maybe even a spot of shopping. Most of my clothes dated back to the time of Stephanie, who had a strong organising streak and an eye for value. Mother had always said she had the heart of a shopkeeper.

The meal itself would be Inna's domain, the menu both exotic and irresistibly seductive: globski, klobski, sloshki. But what if she was a vegetarian? So many women are sentimental and tender-hearted when it comes to furry animals. I would have to prime Inna to find out in advance and prepare a deliciously suitable alternative. It would be Inna's first serious outing in her new role. These musings gave a new focus to my daily routine, pushing the pain of my recent loss into a safe warehouse in the back of my mind.

However, before I could put the Gold Blend Gambit into

operation, I received news from the hospital. Mother's autopsy had been completed at last, she was found to have died of natural causes (what else?) and her body was now available for immediate burial or cremation. I had been so taken up with planning the Gold Blend Gambit that I had made no progress at all in planning the Burial at Sea.

I reached for the Yellow Pages that was propping up one leg of the armchair, and telephoned the undertaker's firm with the largest display advertisement: Wrest 'n' Piece. You have to wonder where they get these names from. It was a man who answered my call, a mature man with a sonorous voice, excellent diction and a funereal manner.

'I'm so sorry about your loss, sir . . . No, we don't offer burial at sea . . . Cremation is often felt to be a very satisfactory and dignified ceremony for all involved. Less expensive than burial, especially if the family themselves take responsibility for disposing of the ashes, which you could always sprinkle at sea or any other location of sentimental significance. Though of course expense would not be the principal consideration for most of our clients . . . Yes, of course we can collect from the hospital . . . If you would give me your address, I can send a written estimate. Let me take some details . . . Berthold? . . . Berthold Sidebottom?'

Through the crackle of the line, I thought I detected the faintest echo of a snigger. One becomes sensitive to that sort of thing.

But to my surprise, the funereal voice added, 'RADA, 1982?'

'Mhm?'

'Jim Knox.'

'Jimmy! Jimmy the Dog!'

Jimmy the Dog and I had been script buddies and booze buddies at RADA. I remembered him as a tall dark-haired, large-nosed type, with the air of a dejected beagle, the sort of actor that usually gets cast as a petty villain. He'd had moderate success with a number of small roles in TV crime series while I was carrying the torch for the Immortal Bard in provincial rep. In those days, before email and Facebook, it was easy to lose touch with friends.

'Ha ha. Remember that night at the Dominion? When Kate Bush's bra strap pinged?'

'I'll put him on the . . . mmm . . . list . . . mmm . . . mmmm . . .' I hummed.

Posing as roadies, we'd gatecrashed the Prince's Trust charity concert at the Dominion on Tottenham Court Road where Madness were topping the bill. The amazing thing is we managed to pull it off for almost an hour, until the real roadies turned up so stoned that they didn't realise what was going on; they just giggled while security tried to hustle them out. There was a big hoo-ha because of Prince Charles and Princess Di being there, though we never actually saw them. But we got to listen to most of the concert, and Jimmy claimed he'd groped Kate Bush on the stairs before eventually some dude fingered us as phoneys.

Later that year, Madness brought out their hit single 'Our House', sugary with nostalgia for a vision of working-class home and community that struck a chord with Lily. She used to sing it as she pushed the Hoover around the flat, which by then was already up for grabs under the newly introduced Right to Buy. Though for Jimmy and me, stretched out on the sweaty mattresses of our student digs, it was just a great sing-along-able song.

'But Jimmy, what made you – ?'

'Become an undertaker? Security. Regular income. I needed a deposit for a flat. I got tired of resting. And you'd be surprised how handy the drama training is in providing a touch of solemnity at the seediest occasions. How about you – Dirty Bertie?'

It was a long time since anyone had called me that. Dirty Bertie and Jimmy the Dog. We'd raised hell all over town. No party was cool without us, no girl awoke a virgin. That was our legend, anyway.

'Mostly stage work. A bit of resting. Quite a bit, actually. And looking after my aged mother of course.'

'Oh, yes. Really sorry to hear she died. I met her once, remember?'

I vaguely remembered that Mum had been décolletée, and had tried to ply him with sherry. That was not unusual.

'We'll give her a magnificent send-off, Bertie. Let's fix a date, and you can start contacting people.'

Alarm bells rang. 'I don't think Mum would have wanted a big fuss made,' I muttered. Though it was probably just what she would have wanted.

'Are you sure? She was quite a lady, Lily. Quite a goer. I'd like to do my bit to carry the flame of her memory.'

Oh God. Had it gone beyond décolletage and sherry? 'Look, Jimmy . . .'

'Don't worry about the expense, Bert. I'll cut you a special deal. For old times' sake. For Kate Bush's bra strap.'

A wave of nostalgia rocked my voyager heart – not exactly nostalgia for Jimmy the Dog, but for friendship and that uncomplicated time when the tide of my life was at its flood, with all the currents of fortune still for the taking.

BERTHOLD: *Jimmy the Dog*

Jimmy the Dog was a surprising source of comfort and support during this time. Although I knew he'd learned it at
drama school, the sonorous patrician voice with its perfect
consonants was reassuring. He guided me through the whole
post-life process, the death certificate, the probate forms. He
explained the intestacy rules, for as far as I could tell Lily had
died without making a will – not that there was much to
inherit, apart from the tenancy of the flat.

It was Jimmy who suggested a woodland burial. Wrest 'n'
Piece had recently acquired a piece of woodland moments
away from Finsbury Park with its superb transport connec-
tions, he told me, which they were planning to develop as a
natural burial site with the long-term goal of offering woodland burial alongside their other professional post-life services.
Lily's funeral would be, as it were, a dry run – and as such the
fee would be a fraction of the normal cost. Jimmy would be
the celebrant, I would be the chief mourner, he and I would
design the service on secular socialist lines, as a celebration
and a reunion for all who had loved her. My job was to assem-
ble the story of her life, and a small select band to join in the
solemnities.

There was a dog-eared, leather-bound address book among
Mother's papers, which she kept in the cardboard box under
her bed. Most of the names in it were unfamiliar to me, I had
no idea whether they were current or not. Ted Madeley's
address was still there, though he was long dead. There was
even an address for Berthold Lubetkin in Gloucestershire,

though he had died in 1990. Her lovers Jack Blast and Jim Wrench were listed – were they still alive? Jenny and Margaret, Ted Madeley's twin daughters, Mum's stepdaughters, were listed under their old addresses. Should I invite them to the funeral? I wondered. According to Mother, Jenny and Margaret, who would have been about ten years old when their father remarried, had hated twenty-year-old Lily with a passion. 'Little witches,' she used to call them. I don't recall meeting them until I was around nine years old and they must have been thirty. By then they'd evidently mellowed, because I have a distinct memory of them coming round to the flat on Mum's fortieth birthday with a bunch of flowers. They made friends with Howard, my older half-brother, who had shaggy blond sideburns and the carefully cultivated mien of a ladykiller. He bragged to me that he had bedded both of them together, which I frankly didn't believe. Why would anyone want to cuddle up with those two? Even then, they were a scary pair.

There is a photo of me with all three of my half-siblings on Hampstead Heath. I'd no recollection of the occasion, but it must have been shortly before Howard left home. In the photo we are all grinning in that stupid 'say cheese' way, and I am holding an ice cream. I had hazy memories of nocturnal activities involving a rope with Howard and his friend Nige, a schoolboy tearaway who lived for a while in Madeley Court, and the beatings from my father that inevitably followed.

Howard, I remembered, used to show me his dirty postcards and fill me in with a wink on the activities in the marital bed, which I also didn't believe. Why would my adored mother want to do *that* with any man, let alone with my horrible father?

My father's address was in the book, even though he had died back in 1983. Poor Dad. I can feel for him now, fleeing the ossified certainties of Ossett and arriving, a widower with a small child, in huge, humming London. No wonder soft-hearted Mum with her penchant for improvement was moved to rescue them. But it hadn't turned out well. I'm not bitter now, but the first nine years of my life were scarred by his volatile personality and his explosive temper, which Mum spent the remaining forty-three trying to heal.

Another recollection flashed in unbidden from the dark edges of my mind: the black, still water of a canal; a cold, late afternoon of tricky crepuscular light; Howard, Nige and I walking along the towpath, each of them holding one of my hands. A rope tied around my waist. I couldn't recall exactly what had happened next: darkness and terror were what I remembered. When I got home I was soaking wet, and Dad took his belt to me. I crawled through a thirty-minute tunnel of fear, pain and shame. According to Mother, that's when my stammer first started. B-b-bridge.

The address book had a new entry for my half-brother, Howard Sidebottom, in Kilburn – new in the sense that one address had been crossed out and another written in, though how long ago I have no idea. Mum had tried to keep in touch with Howard, for whom she still had hopes even after she had given up on Sid. When I lived at home, after our dad had left, he sometimes came over for dinner in the evening. I penned Howard a quick note to the address in Kilburn, thinking that in spite of everything it would be good to see him again.

Mother's latest ex-husband, Lev Lukashenko, only had an address listed in Lviv, Ukraine, and as far as I knew, Mother hadn't seen or heard from him in years. I had already left home by the time she married him, and I wondered guiltily whether it was maybe my leaving home that had rushed her into this unsuitable marriage – she liked having a man about the house, and Lev liked having a woman or two in his life. But I wrote to him anyway. I wrote to them all, on the bright pink Basildon Bond notepaper that Mother favoured: this isn't the sort of area where you can buy black-edged notelets.

I took twelve letters to the post office and was horrified to discover the cost of postage. 'It's a bloody rip-off,' I groused at the sullen woman behind the bullet-proof screen, in honour of Mother, who had never missed a chance to fulminate against the evils of our time including privatisation, Jeremy Clarkson, and pay-day loans.

'Spivs and speculators poncing off the people of Britain! Of course we had plenty of that in wartime, but in them days we sent them to jail! Now they're running the country! Poor Ted! If he was still alive he'd be spinning in his grave.'

Flossie, not cognisant of the issues but excited by her mistress's anger, would do her best to join in. 'Ding dong! Ding dong!'

'Ding bloody dong, Flossie!' Mother railed.

Maybe too much rage had taken its toll on her poor heart. The old world which had nurtured her throughout her life, the world of public provision and municipal housing created for her by men like Harold Riley and Berthold Lubetkin, had given place to a new world of offshore wealth and public austerity, of Buy to Let and bedroom taxes. The buildings still stood but their heart, like hers, had slipped away.

VIOLET: La Maison Suger

At seven o'clock Marc is waiting for her in the vast glass-and-steel atrium of the GRM building. She is wearing her dove-grey outfit and high-heeled shoes. Her trainers are in a carrier bag under her desk. As the lift doors open she sees him standing there and her heart thumps; even though she's been working with Marc for two whole days, it still comes as a shock to realise just how attractive he is. He smiles when he sees her and strolls across the marble floor as elegantly as a cheetah, one hand in his pocket, the other holding a laptop bag.

'I booked a quiet table for us at La Maison Suger. I hope you like traditional French cuisine.'

She nods. Her stomach is performing strange side-flips. She isn't sure she will be able to eat anything at all.

The Maison Suger is all candlelight and white linen, behind a discreet façade. The waiter leads them through to a quiet side-room where they are the only diners and hands them glasses of champagne. Jazz is playing softly in the background.

Marc clinks his glass against hers. 'To your new job, Violet! To our work together!'

Although her French was quite good at school, the menu printed on stiff cream paper is incomprehensible, with ingredients she has never heard of, or familiar tastes in new combinations. *Suprême de poule faisane à la citronnelle, condiment tamarin, raviolis de foie gras, langoustines rôties au beurre d'agrumes, saveurs marron-clémentine.* The words swim before her eyes with promises of delight. He interprets for her. His English is perfect, but with a French accent that purrs cosmopolitan sophistication. It's funny, she hadn't noticed his accent so much in the context of GRM, but here it seems more pronounced. He tells her his father was an art dealer in Paris, his mother was an English art historian; she tells him about her family in Bakewell, who seem embarrassingly ordinary by comparison.

The waiter hands him the wine list, which he reads with a frown of concentration. The wine he chooses is subtle and mellow. It leeches into every fibre in her body, filling her with sweet lassitude. The food is beyond delicious, flooding all her senses. Everything is as perfect as she could have imagined. So what little nagging demon possesses her to return to the topic of re-invoicing?

'I've been wondering about those shell companies, Marc. I can't understand the point.'

She has an inkling by now, but she hopes she's wrong and maybe he'll have an innocent explanation.

'It's just the way global business works. It oils the wheels.' He takes a slow sip of wine and leans back in his chair.

She leans forward, her heart thudding. 'But doesn't it oil corruption? It seems like HN Holdings are siphoning billions of dollars out of one of the poorest countries in the world. They're stealing from the wretched of the earth. I've seen –'

She stops. She can hear her voice getting shrill. She wants to tell him about the Kibera slum, but it is a memory that pre-dates words, a memory embedded in the sights and smells of childhood: the mud streets with their ramshackle tin huts, garbage rotting in the gutter, the ragged children with no school to go to, kicking a ball aimlessly in the dust.

'The way for these developing countries to stop corruption is to tighten up their own law enforcement, Violet.' He looks bored, as if he's rehearsed this argument many times. 'They have to get their own house in order. It's too easy just to blame the West all the time.'

'But shouldn't we be helping them to stop it, instead of helping the bad guys?'

He sighs exaggeratedly. 'What our clients do with their money is their own business. We don't preach. We don't ask questions. We just smooth the progress of their investment goals.' He reaches a hand across the table and lays it on hers. 'It's our business. It's what we do. This is a good break for you at GRM. Don't be naive, Violet.'

'Maybe I am naive. If so, I'd rather be naive than a crook.'

As soon as she blurts it out, she knows it's the wrong thing to say, but the wine has loosened her tongue. It isn't even as if Global Resource Management takes the lion's share of the 10,000 buckets at $49 each – it's Mr Horace Nzangu, whoever he is. His British Virgin Isles-based shell company is simply set up and managed by GRM, who deduct their 2% commission. The buckets which Mr Nzangu resells to the Health Department in Nairobi come from a factory in China, at a cost of $1 each. Probably their actual makers received less than 1p a bucket.

'Don't get so emotional, *chérie*. It's not personal, it's just business. This is the system we work within. Look at it this way – wealth-makers need incentives. If they aren't allowed to keep the wealth they generate, we'll all be poorer in the end.' He squeezes her hand. 'Is it because of your family?'

'It's not my family. It's not even the corruption in Kenya – everybody knows about that. But I didn't realise that we over here . . . that you . . . ! You've just helped someone to steal four million pounds from the poorest of the poor and taken your commission. And you seem to think it's okay! Just business!'

'It's not my job to solve the world's problems, Violet. Believe me, corruption in Kenya doesn't depend on companies like GRM.' He leans forward and forks a mouthful of meat. She watches his teeth chomping up and down as he chews.

'You mean they're corrupt but we're so-o-o civilised?' She takes another gulp of wine and waves her hands in the air.

'Oh, for God's sake, Violet! You're making yourself look ridiculous. Drop the preaching and welcome to the real world!'

There's something about the glint of the candlelight that hardens his features instead of softening them, a mean and hungry flash in his eyes, a cruel downward slant at the corners of his mouth she hadn't noticed before. Sensitive chin-dimple men are not supposed to behave like this. For the first time, she wonders how old he is. He must be almost forty – way too old for her. What was she thinking of, accepting this date?

'I don't think God's on your side this time.' The wine has emboldened her. *Fight the good fight!* is ringing in her brain. 'Didn't anyone tell you, the meek will inherit the earth?' She stands up, ready to leave.

'Fine. Good luck to them. I'm all for it. In the meantime, let's enjoy what life brings.'

He gets up from his seat abruptly, pushing his chair over. Then he strides round to her side of the table and pulls her into his arms, holding her close to him. She can feel the beating of his heart, and her own, beating harder and faster, against his.

'Violet, lovely Violet, I've been thinking about you, wanting you, ever since your interview.' His voice rumbles darkly, urgently in her ear. 'We could be so great together. Don't spoil it.'

Nick, with his floppy-puppy fumbles, never spoke in that voice. Now is the time to surrender, to let the shrillness melt away. As she wavers, he grips her tight and presses a kiss on her mouth. His lips are hard with an edge of sharp bristle. Something explodes in her head. She pushes him away, and as she does so catches a glass of red wine with her elbow. The red liquid flowers on his suit like blood from a gunshot.

She kicks off her high heels, shoves them in her bag, and runs out barefoot into the night.

BERTHOLD: *What a piece of work is a man*

Night is the time for ghosts and memories, when the usual reference points of day are put to sleep, like Flossie under her tablecloth and Inna snoring lightly in Mother's bedroom, while things that lurk in the shadows creep out. When I'd cleared out her room for Inna, I'd scooped together all Mother's papers and photos into a large cardboard box and shoved it underneath the boiler. Now I got them out and spread them under the muted light of the table lamp, as I tried to prepare my funeral speech. I stared at the blank page in front of me, waiting for the light bulb of inspiration to click on in my brain.

There was a fat brown envelope stuffed with leaflets, half-signed petitions, gestetnered flyers, crumpled posters. All through my childhood, Mother was the one to make a stand, start a campaign, mount a protest, organise a picket, lead a march. As a kid, I had found it all horribly embarrassing.

Another envelope contained essential financial information – on Jimmy's instructions I'd already applied for probate and cancelled her pensions, but I'd left the bank account with her standing order for the rent in place for the time being, though the money in it would run out pretty soon. More envelopes were stuffed with household bills, receipts, and guarantees for long-defunct appliances. All that claggy paperwork that sticks to us as we pass through nature to eternity.

Sucking the end of my pen for inspiration, I mulled over my speech, searching for clues to the essence of this woman I'd lived with for so many years, yet whose inner life I'd hardly known. According to the pre-war school reports, she had been a bright girl but inattentive. Postcards from windy East Coast seaside resorts showed her smiling unconvincingly. There were Girl Guide badges – she'd baked buns to fund-raise for the war effort. I made a note of that. Here in a thick cream envelope were her three marriage certificates, to Ted Madeley, the councillor who had fixed the flat for her and died soon after, to my strap-happy dad, Wicked Sidney Sidebottom, and to Lev Lukashenko, who had run off with what remained of her money. I had dreaded an existential revelation – for example, that I was not her son at all but a stray kid she had adopted, like my half-brother Howard. But here was my own birth certificate – I had been her only child.

There was nothing to shed light on her claim to a love affair with Berthold Lubetkin, nor to nourish my secret hope that the genius architect had been my true father, and not the swindler Sid Sidebottom. If I had hoped to find love letters or personal diaries, I was disappointed. She had kept her love affairs, like her smoking, secret. Once I had left home I would sometimes find, on my occasional visits, an overflowing ash-tray or a stranger lurking in her bedroom, but if they ever wrote letters, she had either burned them or returned them.

Wrapped between the pages of a newspaper dated 1967 was a childish hand-drawn card. It was a picture of a house with a blue door and a pointed roof, and a wisp of smoke coming out of the chimney and a blonde woman with matchstick legs standing as tall as the house itself. Inside the card a greeting – my eyes misted up as I read: *To the best Mum in the wurld*. She had treasured it all these years.

On a parchment scroll inside a cardboard tube was her Speech Therapy Diploma. After her success with my stammer, she found her vocation and undertook the training which allowed her to practise in the NHS. 'Which became her lasting passion,' I wrote.

And there, right at the bottom, was the tenancy agreement for the flat in the names of Mr and Mrs Ted Madeley. Soon to be in the name of Mr Berthold Sidebottom, if all went to plan.

Mother had often talked with admiration about reformers like Aneurin Bevan, the post-war Health Minister who created the NHS, Alderman Harold Riley the Labour council leader in Finsbury, Berthold Lubetkin the architect, Dr Chuni Lal Katial, the public health campaigner and the first elected South Asian mayor in Britain, who commissioned Lubetkin's Finsbury Health Centre, and short-lived Ted Madeley who briefly led the Housing Committee. But the actual men who haunted her bedroom were generally of a different ilk. It was as if her reforming zeal spilled over from social improvement and attracted her to men who needed improvement; flaky, unreliable types like Wicked Sid Sidebottom and Lev Lukashenko, who sponged off her and made her life a misery. As the Bard put it, 'overmastered with a piece of valiant dust'.

It's normal, I suppose, for a boy to resent his father and want his mother all to himself, Mr Freud had a word for it, but in my case it was more than just a subconscious feeling of sexual rivalry. I was a scared little kid, bullied by Howard and strapped by my dad, with only Mum to stick up for me. 'Sensitive' was the word she used to describe me, as though I was a troublesome tooth.

Handsome Howard was my role model as well as my tormentor. Mum used to say it was from Howard that I got the yen to be a performer. He was working by then at the Shoreditch branch of Dolcis but he fancied himself as a rock star and practised air guitar in the evenings at home, while I crooned squeakily into a hairbrush, 'Don't be cruel to a heart so true.' If I made a mistake he grabbed the hairbrush out of my hand and whacked me, probably a response he'd learned from Sid.

Then one day when he was in his late teens, he came home with an electric guitar, a sleek shiny little devil, which he said he'd bought with the money from his shoe-shop job. I stared open-mouthed. This was not pretending – this was the real thing. He struck a chord and growled in a voice I had not heard before, 'Hey, Bert, take a walk on the wild side.' I was electrified.

Sid reached for the belt. 'You're not playing that in this house!'

Howard gave him the finger and walked away, taking the guitar. Next day, while Dad was out, he came back for a hold-all of clothes. Mum pleaded with him to stay, but he wouldn't listen.

Mum missed Howard and continued to talk about him for a long while as though he was still part of our lives. From time to time he came back for a meal when he was sure that Dad was out. After he left, Mum took my side more determinedly in my run-ins with Dad, until the day came when she told him to clear out too. I didn't hear their final row, but when I asked where he was that evening, she said, 'It's just you and me now, Bertie. He's not coming back.' We were sitting on the sofa with a book – I think it was Lamb's *Tales from Shakespeare* but I may have imagined that. 'We'll be all right together,' she said. I can still remember the rush of triumph spiked with panic that took my breath away.

After my parents divorced I didn't see my father again for a few years. Mum said he'd been bringing us down and we were better off without him. She removed his photo from the wall and launched us on an all-out programme of personal improvement and social betterment. Education and culture were to be my gateway to social mobility, and every weekend she dragged me around all the free resources of the libraries, art galleries and museums in London. I guess some of it rubbed off.

Ted Madeley, her first husband, had once been a teacher and had argued that the revolution would come about without bloodshed through education, she said. 'See, Bertie, it's the post-war consensus. The welfare state will sweep away class differences by advancing the working classes.'

I quite liked the thought of being advanced without all the bother of an actual revolution, so I worked hard at it. Highbury Grove School, which I attended from the age of eleven, was not the nearest school, but the nearest one that Mum judged would bring me into the right sort of milieu for advancement.

I can still remember the shock of seeing my first live performance at the theatre. It was a schools matinee performance at the Young Vic of *The Merchant of Venice* which we were 'doing' for O-levels. I remember the blanket of stillness settling over us as the lights went down, and the tiny spotlit figures on the faraway stage commandeering my senses, my intellect, my breathing, my emotions, taking me on such a journey through madness to wisdom that when we came out on to the pavement in broad daylight three hours later and I saw the next audience already queuing to enter, I thought it must be some trick; I could not believe that same whole experience could be repeated again and again.

I joined the drama club at school, with a head already full of the Shakespeare soliloquies I had practised with Mum. By the time I was sixteen I knew I wanted to be an actor. Mum didn't discourage me, but urged me to get a qualification I could fall back on. I promised her that if I didn't get into drama school I would train to be a teacher like Ted Madeley, which satisfied her yearning for financial security and for a better social standing than I had inherited from my dad.

Nevertheless, she and Sid must have kept in touch because out of the blue he turned up at my school's Sixth Form performance of *Hamlet*. I didn't spot him until Act II Scene 2, sitting in the third row, his eyebrows bunched in a frown. *What a p-p-piece of work is a man. The b-b-beauty of the world.* I almost lost it. But Mum, sitting in the front row with the other parents, caught my eye and rescued me with a discreet forefinger placed between her lips. My guardian angels, Mum and the Immortal Bard.

Dad came up in the interval, stylishly turned out as always, and handsome in a way that caused a stir among the mums in the audience. I thought he was going to berate me for being a pansy or something, but he said, 'That was beautiful. I'm really proud of you, son.' I saw tears were shining in his eyes, but it was too late by then.

While I was getting changed out of my costume, I caught an oblique glimpse out of a side window that overlooked the school car park. Under a tree in the far corner, I saw my parents standing close in conversation. Then Dad tried to put his arm around Mum, she shoved him away, and he strolled across and got into a car that was parked alongside the teachers' cars. And what a car. It was a shiny midnight-blue Jaguar with a personalised number plate SID 123. I watched him get in, reverse slowly out, and drive away. Mum came back inside to look for me, and we walked together to the bus stop. I didn't tell my mother I'd seen Dad's car, I somehow felt that would be disloyal, and she never mentioned it.

Funerals are a time for celebration not for blame, but if I was to blame Mother for anything, it would be for the absence of positive male role models in my life. This was turning out to be a more complicated and nuanced story than the simple triumph over adversity that is the usual stuff of memorial tributes.

'Ding dong! God is dead!' called Flossie.

'Yes, I know. I'm just trying to summarise the story of her life.'

'First of March, 1932!'

'To thirteenth of April, 2014. Beloved mother. Brave spirit. Rest in peace.'

VIOLET: *Planning*

Next day, Violet telephones Laura for a post-mortem of her faux-fab date.

Laura laughs. 'Ha ha! I warned you! Let me guess – French restaurant, French accent, father an art dealer in Paris . . .'

'How did you know?'

'He's already tried that on with half the women at GRM. Actually, he's just a jumped-up real-estate salesman from Quebec. Don't beat yourself up over it, Violet. Once you get to know him, he's good to work for. He's fun, he knows his stuff, and it's a growing field – wealth preservation.'

'I can't ever go back there.'

'Don't be an idiot, Violet. Don't give up your job just because of a grope. It's a rite of passage that all the women at GRM go through.'

'You . . . ?'

'Mm-hm. I was already married, so I didn't go on the restaurant date. But sure, there was a quick fumble in the lift. He doesn't mind the occasional slap, you know.' Laura chuckles. 'In fact he'll respect you for it.'

They agree to meet for lunch in town next week at a baby-friendly venue, and buoyed by Laura's encouragement, she gets ready to go into work. The lilac outfit, to show courage. The high heels to make her feel tall inside. Now, sitting on the top deck of the bus, she suddenly gets cold feet. Though she knows now that Marc is just a jerk, and she was naive to fall for his patter, strangely that doesn't seem to cancel out the effect of the chin dimple and twinkling smile. Laura is right to laugh. She was an idiot. How will she ever be able to face him again?

By the time the bus has passed through two stops, she's decided to leave, to find something different. But how will she explain to her parents and friends, who were so supportive of her brilliant City career, that her dream job is no longer a dream?

'Next stop Town Hall.'

The recorded announcement on the bus startles her out of her reverie. She looks out of the window. They have stopped beside an imposing grey building with stone steps at the front. On impulse she jumps up and races down the stairs.

It appears that the Planning Department offices are not in this Town Hall at all, which is now an arts centre, but in another building miles away. She catches another bus back and pings the bell at reception.

A young planning officer ambles out in his shirtsleeves. He looks her up and down and says very politely, 'I can show you the plans, miss. Come this way.'

He leads her to a long echoing room with a huge square table where plans are spread out under a blinking fluorescent light. There is a smell of polish and dust.

'It's this parcel of land here, in front of the council estate,' he points. The lines, hatches and numbers seem incomprehensible at first, but the young man is doing his best to be helpful.

'In front of Madeley Court?'

'That's it, miss.'

'Isn't it a bit close?'

'It's within planning guidelines.'

He seems incredibly young for the job he's doing, more like a sixth-former than a real planner, with rosy cheeks, a fluff of downy hair on his upper lip that is struggling to be a moustache, and a pair of heavy black-rimmed spectacles, as though he wants to make himself look older. It is a known fact that people who wear spectacles are usually brainy, but this does not seem to apply in his case.

'But there are lovely cherry trees growing there.'

He glances down at her high heels and his tone becomes more respectful.

'Public open space is expensive to maintain, miss. We've had to make cuts in our environmental budget. But we're demanding additional planting as part of the scheme, which the developer will be responsible for maintaining.'

'So you've already agreed it?'

'Hm.' He looks shifty. 'There have been preliminary discussions with the parties involved. It's still got to go before the Council.'

'But what do *you* think about it, Mr . . .' She peers forward to read his name badge, '. . . Mr Rowland.'

'It's not up to me, miss. I just follow the guidelines.' He looks surreptitiously at her shoes again.

'But you must have your own opinion. Isn't that what you've been trained for? Does it seem reasonable, to build a new block of flats on the garden of an existing one? Or are they pushing their luck a teensy bit, do you think?'

'Well, there is a severe shortage of building land in the borough,' he ventures, trying to keep the words tucked in under his little moustache. 'We're facing a housing crisis. The Council urgently needs the money, and we need to build more one-bedroom flats for tenants displaced by the removal of the spare-bedroom subsidy.'

Despite his schoolboy looks he's already learning to put on that weary middle-aged air of officialdom. Maybe it goes with the job, she thinks, and wonders whether the Nairobi town planners are like that too.

'You mean there's a subsidy for spare bedrooms?' This is good news, as she has two. Maybe there will be an extra subsidy for the six unslept-in beds.

He soon puts her right. 'It's really just clawing back of housing benefit if people are living in a property deemed to be too big for their needs. We don't at present have enough one-bedroom flats and studios to rehouse them into, so if they can't afford the extra rent, they may end up homeless.'

'Homeless?' That doesn't sound good. 'But these new flats they're planning to build are two-bedroom flats. And they're not aimed at people on housing benefit, are they? With en suites and wrap-around balconies and all that?'

'The rents are classed as affordable. That means up to eighty per cent of the market rent.' The flickering light bounces off his spectacles, so she can't read the expression in his eyes. 'It's not me that makes the policies, miss.'

He must be just out of school, she guesses. If any official is profiting from this development, as might be the case in the Nairobi shopping mall project, it probably isn't Mr Rowland.

Suddenly he blurts out, 'And the cherry grove is just the start of it. They've got their eyes on the whole estate. They'll let it go downhill until it can't be repaired any more, then sell it off for redevelopment. A shame, really, because it's one of the Lubetkin originals.'

'Lubetkin – what's that?'

'He was the people's architect. One of the great architects of the post-war consensus. We learned about him in college. Those guys weren't just into building flats, they were building a whole new society. You've heard of Le Corbusier?'

'Isn't that a kind of French liqueur?'

'M-m.' He shook his head. 'He was a French architect who believed in simple functional design. He inspired a whole generation of architects, including Lubetkin.'

'I don't know much about modern architecture. But I've been to the Lloyd's Building.'

'Quite special, isn't it? If you ask me, it's totally insane what they're doing here. But don't quote me on that.'

'Thank you. That's very helpful,' she says.

'In fact the whole housing scene's insane,' he rattles on, as if buoyed by his small act of rebellion. 'Everything is high-end, high-spec Buy to Let for overseas investors. I can't buy a flat in the borough on my salary. I've been engaged for eighteen months but I can't afford to get married, let alone start a family. I'm still living in Walthamstow with my parents.'

'That's awful!' She sighs, though in her opinion he looks far too young for marriage.

'You need to get your letter of objection to us by the end of the month. Quote the number of the planning application. And if more people write in, it'll carry more weight.'

He speaks very quickly and quietly, looking around to make sure no one is listening in. Then he points out the planning number and she writes it down on the back of her bus ticket.

It is 10.15 a.m. now, too late for work. She catches the bus home and phones in sick to GRM, claiming a painful wisdom-tooth treatment which she hopes will make Marc feel guilty.

VIOLET: A patch of grass and a few cherry trees

Knowing something is wrong is easy, but knowing what to do about it – that's the hard bit. She'd never thought the flats were anything special, but now she tries to picture the tall narrow building whose plans she's just seen filling the front garden. Fourteen storeys would completely block out the view and the sun, even from the top floor of Madeley Court. And unfortunately the cherry trees would have to go. No spare-tree subsidies are on offer.

She phones Jessie, who is a bit of a green freak.

'You can't let them get away with it, Vi.'

'I know. But what can I do?'

'Listen to the voice of the trees and you'll think of something.'

That's so typical of Jessie. She listens, but apart from a bit of rustling, the trees aren't saying anything at all.

The only thing she can think of is to start knocking on the doors of the flats. But the response of the residents is discouraging. No one has read the planning notices; some people reassure her that the notices are not about building flats at all, they are about a lost cat, a notorious pisser called Wonder Boy, hopefully run away or run over. Some people agree to sign a petition if one is drawn up, but nobody feels inspired to write a letter of protest.

Madeley Court seems to be home to many newcomers like herself, in transit from somewhere to somewhere else. 'Thank you, but we're not staying long,' they say. 'It doesn't affect us.'

There are several groups of young people – students, maybe – who open the door and tell her politely, 'This flat is private. It's nothing to do with the Council.'

She is amazed by the variety of people who live here. Behind each door, it seems there's someone from a different continent. Two Chinese girls stand at the door and giggle uncontrollably as she talks. An old man with an Eastern European accent and broken spectacles held together with parcel tape invites her to come inside and see his tractor gearbox. A small wiry woman, evidently an artist, comes to the door covered in paint, a dab of mauve on her nose. There are people from Europe, Latin America, India, Pakistan, China, and some she has no idea where they come from. She's pleased to find several households from Africa; a young musician from Malawi, a couple of sad-eyed refugees from Eritrea, a large jolly Zambian family who invite her in for cassava pancakes, though there is no one, as far as she can tell, from Kenya.

There's a range of ages too. The grumbly older people are mostly white; the young families teeming with toddlers are from a mix of ethnicities. Some old people come to the door timorously, open it on the safety chain, look at her fearfully and back away as if they think she's going to mug them. How pathetic. Some have problems of their own they want to grouse about – repairs that need doing, complaints about their neighbours.

What do all these people have in common to bind them together? Yes, it's a bit different to Bakewell around here. In fact it reminds her more of Nairobi – dynamic and precarious, as if it could all fall apart at any minute. A gloomy mood settles over her as she realises that nobody seems to care much about a patch of grass and a few cherry trees.

BERTHOLD: *A coffee jar*

How to sum up a person's full life in a ten-minute speech – especially somebody as complicated and contradictory as Mother? I had still not finished writing my funeral oration on the morning of the funeral. A gloomy mood settled over me as I tried to take up where I had left off two days ago. The Immortal Bard, usually good for a quotation or two, had abandoned me. I put my pen down and turned my melancholy gaze out of the window at the cherry grove. A quick movement down below caught my eye. It was the next-door goddess flitting between the trees like a lovely bright-plumed bird. Alas, our amorous encounter would just have to wait until after the funeral. However, a closer glimpse would surely be inspiring. I gathered up my notes and scuttled off to Luigi's.

I was out of luck. By the time I got downstairs, it was spotting with rain and she had vanished. The coffee seemed worse than usual too, and Luigi had swapped the *Guardian* for the *Daily Mail*. I'd have to talk with him about that, but not today. I sipped the sub-standard latte and concentrated on fitting my random notes into a fine uplifting narrative of Mother's life, using omission and invention as necessary. The Lily that emerged on the page was a finer and more laudable person than Mother, but she also seemed bland, slightly dead. That's what death does for you, I guess.

When I got back to the flat an hour later, buzzing with caffeine, Inna was hoovering noisily, and Flossie was having another outbreak of atheism, so I hardly heard the sound of the doorbell above the racket. Then it rang again. *Ding dong!* Who could it be?

My first thought was that it must be Mrs Penny, dropping in for a snap inspection. It was no good pretending we were out because the sound of the Hoover was clearly audible. Would Inna remember to play her part? Would she remember not to let slip that we were this very afternoon due to go to Finsbury Park to celebrate the funeral of the woman whom she was impersonating? *Ding dong!* It rang again. I braced myself and answered the door.

'I'm sorry to bother you . . .'

There she stood; not Mrs Penny but the next-door goddess. Though close up she looked much younger than I had imagined, too young for a goddess, more like an angel, a trainee angel maybe: radiant, beautiful, her hair pulled back in a frisky ponytail, her teeth gleaming and her cheeks dimpling as she smiled – at me!

'I know. I know. You're having a dinner party. You've run out of coffee!' I blurted.

She looked at me strangely and recited her introduction. 'I'm sorry to bother you. My name's Violet. I live next door. I'm just . . .'

Violet. A shy wayside flower with a heavenly perfume.

'Violet. Ah! Do come in. I have a jar waiting for you. All things are ready, if our minds be so.'

I disappeared into the kitchen and rummaged in the cupboards. Where had I put it? It should be on the shelf with the tea. Then I spotted it on the counter beside the kettle. It was almost empty. Bloody Inna must have been helping herself. Damn her! There was hardly any left. I returned to the hallway with the near-empty jar. Inna was there – she'd turned off the Hoover and was introducing herself.

'Hello, Blackie. I am Inna Alfandari. I am mother, or mebbe I am sister of mother. Berthold? I am mother or sister?'

'Inna, have you been drinking the coffee?' I cut her short.

'Of course I drink him. You buy him for drinking, no?'

'Yes. No. I mean, there's hardly any left.' I smiled apologetically at my lovely neighbour. 'But you're very welcome . . .'

She furrowed her delectable brow. 'I'm just trying to inform the residents about the planning application.'

'. . . to what little I have. Planning?'

'Yes. The notices are on the lamp posts. Or they were, until the kids ripped them off.'

'Notices? Yes, they're for Wonder Boy, the lost cat. Don't grieve. I'm sure he has found another home.' I had to stop myself from saying, 'Don't grieve, my lovely.'

'No, not those. These were for a planning application to build a block of flats on the garden. Where the cherry trees are.'

I gazed at her lovely features, the earnest pleading in her eyes. Maybe she was a touch crazed. Like Ophelia. It would add poignancy to my passion. 'O, you must wear your rue with a difference! There's a Violet. I would give you some violets, but they withered all when my father died.'

Withered. Died. That last line brought me to my senses with a shock. My mother. I glanced at the clock. Less than an hour to go until the woodland burial, and I still had no idea where it would take place. *Green Glade.* Jimmy had sent a map, with artistically hand-drawn clumps of trees, a wildflower meadow and meandering footpaths, but no actual street names.

'I'm sorry. I'm afraid we're in a bit of a hurry just now. Got to get to a funeral. Maybe we could continue our discussion another time. Planning. Yes, very interesting. A lot of it around.'

I thrust the near-empty jar of coffee into her hands, 'Your guests I hope will like it,' and ushered her towards the door, my hand resting lightly on her shoulder.

VIOLET: *Towel*

Violet wonders whether it's worth persevering with her door-knocking campaign. Truly there are some weird people in these flats, including one who pushed her out of the door with an empty coffee jar.

The heavy rain makes it even more dismal. The walkways between the flats, although undercover, are awash. Some downpipes must be blocked because the water has brought to the surface all the nasty things that are usually hidden out of sight in gulleys: dead cigarettes, dead insects, dead fast-food wrappers, even a dead pigeon. She steps past it quickly, noting that it has two feet, so it's not Pidgie. In the rainy season in Kenya water poured out of the sky for an hour or so and every-thing was washed clean, then the sun came out. But here in England it seems to be rainy season all the time.

She's finished all her side of the block, and rings the door-bell of the first flat on the west side, waits a moment, then rings again. There is someone at home, she can hear a radio playing inside, and soon the door opens. The man who stands there is wearing nothing but a towel wrapped around his middle.

'Yes?' he says belligerently. Then he looks her up and down and adds in a friendlier tone, 'What can I do for you?'

She knows that look of appraisal, when a guy is trying to suss out whether to make a move on you; she would normally make her excuses and leave. But she hears a child's voice call-ing from inside the flat, 'Who is it, Dad?'

She launches into her patter. 'I'm sorry to bother you. My

name's Violet. I live upstairs. I'm just letting people know about a planning application that will affect the residents of these flats.'

'I'm not staying here long.' He sounds bored.

'There's a proposal to build a fourteen-storey block of flats just in front of here, where the cherry trees are.'

'Really?' He sounds less bored.

'Really. The notices went up on the lamp posts last week, inviting comments or objections.'

'So you're getting the tenants agitated?'

'I hope so. Would you be agitated enough to write a letter to the Council?'

He smiles. Nice teeth. 'Sure. It's bound to affect property values.' Actually, he has quite a nice torso too. 'Would you like to come in? I'll get some clothes on. I've just come out of the shower.'

The warning bells ring: it is not a good idea to be alone with this half-naked man in his flat. But the appearance of a boy at the door makes her relax. It's the same boy she saw getting out of the limo.

'Arthur,' the man says, 'make Violet a cup of tea, will you, while I get dressed.' He turns to her. 'Is tea all right? Or would you prefer coffee? I'm not sure about Arthur's barista skills.'

'Da-a-ad?' whines the boy, kicking the door frame with his socked foot.

'Tea's fine,' she says, and steps inside out of the rain.

BERTHOLD: *Mud*

Just as Inna and I left the flat for the funeral, the heavens opened. Inna ran back to fetch her umbrella, a jolly leopard-skin-print number, which she flicked open as we raced towards the waiting minicab. Through the blur of rain, I noticed a small red car pulling up at the kerb behind us. Mrs Penny was at the wheel, staring in our direction.

'Quick! Let's go!' I yelled at the driver, handing him the piece of paper with the hand-drawn map.

'Green Glade? Never heard of it. Have you got a postcode?'

'Um . . . not exactly. N4 it says. Just go!'

The minicab driver pulled away slowly. The red car didn't follow. Phew!

'Go where? N4's a big area, mate.'

A steady rain was falling, drumming on the roof of the minicab. Inna was perched on the back seat next to me like a bird of ill omen, dressed all in black with a jet necklace and matching jet earrings, a dab of pink lipstick, and clutching her wet umbrella, unaware of the lucky escape we had just had.

'Head north,' I told the minicab driver, 'and I'll phone the funeral director.'

But Jimmy the Dog was doggedly not answering.

We passed up Kingsland Road, and Inna, peering through the misted-up window, started jumping up and down, 'Oy! Stop here! Stop! My friend will know. He come from Georgia, but been in London long time.'

The cab driver pulled up outside a shabby shop which appeared to sell mainly international phonecards and 'herbal

Viagra'. Hm. That was something I might need to look into, should matters with my beautiful neighbour approach a consummation devoutly to be wished. It was a long time since I had put the beast through his paces.

'Ali! Ali!' Inna shouted from the pavement outside the shop under her leopard-skin umbrella, and moments later a huge man with a black beard, a gold front tooth and an embroidered skullcap opened the door. He looked at her, laughed, and hugged her in a giant embrace. She showed him the piece of paper. He frowned and turned it this way and that, muttering something I could not hear. She stood on tiptoes and kissed him on the chin – she could not reach his cheek – and hurried back to the cab.

'He not very sure. Mebbe Finsbury Park next-door railway.'

As the minicab driver got on the road again, the mobile in my pocket rang.

'Jimmy? Thank God! Listen, I don't know exactly where we're going . . . have you got an address? Or a postcode?'

His voice sounded faraway and scratchy. 'Calm down, Bertie. Meet us under the railway bridge at Finsbury Park Station. You can follow the hearse.'

Follow the hearse – that sounded like the first sensible thing I had heard all day. The cab driver put his foot down and off we went, ploughing through a tropical-style downpour; the windscreen wipers dancing their crazy hand-jive barely managed to maintain visibility. I would have asked him to pull over and wait it out, but we were now pushed for time.

As we ducked under the shelter of a wide flat bridge, the drumming on the roof ceased instantly. And there in front of us, with its sidelights still on, was the hearse. I jumped out, and went over to where Jimmy was standing on the pavement. He looked superbly funereal, dressed in black tails with a black top hat and a black silk handkerchief in his breast pocket.

He shook my hand solemnly, and patted my shoulder. 'Well done, Bertie. You made it. It is a little difficult to find. Nuisance about the rain. Of course *she* is beyond reach of all that now,' he nodded solemnly towards the coffin in the back of the hearse with a single white lily laid on top of it. 'Safe from tempest, storm and wind.'

'Death lies on her like an untimely frost upon the sweetest flower.' A tear sprang into my eye, but something about the coffin bothered me. 'The coffin – it seems a bit cheap, Jimmy.'

'Cardboard, old pal. Biodegradable. More environmentally friendly. We've all got to do our bit on climate change, haven't we?'

I didn't like the look of it at all; it reminded me of those big supermarket boxes they pack loo rolls in. But I supposed it was too late to do anything about it now. At that moment, two elderly women, dressed alike – all in black, with black hats, white frizzy hair and bright red lipstick – rushed up to us.

'Where is Green Glade cemetery?' they gabbled. 'Is this Lily Sidebottom's funeral?'

I was so taken aback it took me a few moments to recognise Ted Madeley's twin daughters.

'Bertie?' The first twin looked me up and down.

'Jenny? Margaret?'

'Jenny. That's Margaret.' She pointed at the other twin, who was standing at the back of the hearse, trying to peep inside. At first sight, she seemed identical, but as I got used to their likeness I also noticed differences; Margaret appeared older, more frail and stooped, though of course they were exactly the same age. 'Thanks for getting in touch, Bertie. It's good to have a chance to pay our respects. She was a fine lady, Lily, even though we didn't always see eye to eye.'

'Fine. Yes, indeed,' I murmured.

When I had last seen them, they were in their thirties. The

cruel hand of time had indeed scrawled his ugly mark over their once pretty features. Then again, I had been just a boy, so it was a miracle that they remembered me at all. Mum had kept in touch for a while, but I hadn't seen them since I left home. I heard they had both married in their thirties, and both lost their husbands in their sixties. That's one of the strange things about twins, the way their lives mirror each other.

'Why is the coffin made out of cardboard?' asked Margaret.

'It's ecological,' I said. 'This is going to be a woodland burial.'

'But won't it go soggy in all this rain?' From the edge of the railway bridge, water was sloshing down on to the traffic like an overflowing bathtub.

'Lily was a great campaigner on climate change. It's what she would have wanted.' That shut her up. 'This is Lily's friend, Inna Alfandari.' Inna had been prowling around the hearse, examining the coffin. I introduced Jenny and Margaret as Lily's stepdaughters.

'I am mother? I am sister?' Inna whispered, glancing at them with a nervous smile.

'Friend. Just a friend, Inna. A confused friend.' I did a quick Lear's Fool roll of the eyes.

She winked beadily, 'Hey ho! Rain it rain it every day!' Then she flicked out her umbrella as if for an approaching storm, and they all gathered under it, even though it was quite dry under the bridge.

'We'd better drive up as close to Green Glade as we can,' said Jimmy, who was wearing fancy grey trousers and leather-soled shoes. 'Just follow us in the cab. You and I can carry the coffin between us when we get there. It's not heavy.'

He introduced the driver of the hearse as Miss Wrest, the owner's daughter, a lugubrious mousy-haired young woman wearing a top hat and a black suit, her face blanked out with panstick make-up which also covered her lips. I have never slept with a female undertaker, but this may be one life experience that passes me by.

As soon as we left the shelter of the bridge, the rain sheeted down. The minicab followed close behind the hearse. Miss Wrest was a nervous driver, heavy on the brakes. Once we almost slammed into the back of her when she braked sharply to avoid a drunk who lurched out into the road, and after that the cab driver held back a bit. As the hearse sailed past a parade of shops, a bus pulled out, getting in between us and the hearse. It had the smirking George Clooney poster on the back, which I took as a bad omen.

We only just managed to keep behind the hearse as it turned right – our driver's view was blocked by the bus. After that we wended our way down some anonymous residential roads and soon came to a halt in a cul-de-sac, at the bottom of which a footpath led towards a bank of trees. Here we got out, and opened our umbrellas. I noticed a not-very-prominent sign stuck into the ground that said *Green Glade*, with an arrow pointing towards the footpath. Beside it stood a couple of guys waiting under a green and white striped umbrella, whom Jimmy introduced as the gravediggers. They were wearing smart but soggy black tracksuits with a Wrest 'n' Piece logo on the breast pocket, and both had pencil moustaches, presumably because they thought it was part of the gravedigger look. A third man – a thin elderly guy wearing a damp black suit, a bit short in the leg, and a bowler hat – stood beside them under his own black umbrella. I wondered who he was. I shook his hand and introduced myself, and he mumbled something I didn't catch, his words mashed by the booze I could smell on his breath.

Jimmy was right – the coffin bearing my mother's body was not heavy at all. So many years of life and love reduced to this puny parcel of cardboard and dust. I held back my tears as we hoisted it on to our shoulders, him on the right side, in front, me at the back on the left, leaving his right arm and my left arm free to hold umbrellas. This awkward equilibrium was like the balance of gladness and sadness in my heart as I bore my dear mother's mortal remains towards their resting place. Although frankly, the rain was annoying.

Mousy Miss Wrest, who was wearing knee-high black boots, the only one of us with sensible footwear, strode out in front, holding a black umbrella. Inna and the Madeley twins huddled behind us under Inna's leopard-print umbrella, and the gravediggers, sheltering under the green and white, brought up the rear, with the thin bowler-hatted man tagging along beside them. With downcast eyes we set off up the muddy path. The trees dripped all around us. My mind was so caught up with the solemnity of the occasion that I hardly noticed the slipperiness underfoot, but Jimmy was slithering about in his leather-soled shoes.

The footpath from the cul-de-sac joined another larger track through woodland, which was gravelled and raised, about the width of a railway track. Here under the trees the rain was gentler and the ground less treacherous. We followed this for some two hundred metres, until another *Green Glade* arrow pointed up a grassy rise towards a grove of trees through which I caught a glimpse of a wide green glade. It would indeed have been an idyllic spot, had it not been for the rain.

Even in her sensible boots Miss Wrest struggled to keep upright on the wet grassy slope, now partly trodden into mud. I cunningly pointed my umbrella downwards, and used the spike to stick in the ground to give myself a bit of leverage. I daren't look over my shoulder to see how the old ladies behind were doing. In front of me, Jimmy was skidding dangerously, flailing with his umbrella arm. We had made it about halfway up the incline, when his phone rang. Balancing the coffin on one shoulder, he fumbled in his pocket.

'Yes, Phil, yes, okay, I get what you're saying . . . parting of the ways . . . sorry, I can't speak now . . . Green Glade . . . sorry it had to end like this . . .'

Suddenly a roar like a low-flying jet reverberated through the trees, making the ground shake beneath our feet. In the moment that I lost concentration, Jimmy slipped. The coffin slid off his shoulder and bounced down the steep path on to the track below. I turned, lost my footing, and slid after it, my opened umbrella acting as a sort of parachute. Jimmy did a sideways skid and managed to bring down the three old ladies and the bowler-hatted gent, before landing beside the dented coffin, his phone still pressed against his ear in one hand and his umbrella aloft in the other. Only the gravediggers were upright, and they were still on the main track, standing by being elegantly unhelpful.

Amidst all the confusion, I was aware that there was a terrific amount of noise – the low-flying aeroplane now sounded more like a high-speed train roaring past quite close by behind the trees, Jimmy was still jabbering into his phone and the three women were screaming their heads off. The screaming seemed a bit excessive, I thought, but in a moment I could see the reason for it. The wet cardboard coffin had burst open, and the corpse had tumbled out, stiffer than its container, to join the melee. Inna was screaming and crossing herself. Margaret had fainted. Jenny, who was underneath it, was trying to push its shoulder out of her face. I looked, and looked again. Even beneath its muddy coating, the corpse didn't seem quite right.

I screamed too. 'There's been a mistake! This isn't my mother!'

'Don't distress yourself, Mr Sidebottom.' Miss Wrest laid a soothing hand on my arm. 'Appearances of a post-life loved one can often be deceptive. Death is a great counterfeiter, you know.' She patted me with her fingertips; her nails were painted scarlet, the only touch of colour about her.

'She was probably done by one of the trainees,' added Jimmy, replacing his phone in his pocket. 'We've had some new jobseeker placements in the funeral parlour. Lily would have been in favour of that, you know, helping to prepare the long-term unemployed for useful jobs. We've all got to do our bit on the economy, haven't we?'

'But . . .' I looked again. It looked distinctly unlike Mother. '. . . it's a man. An old man. An ex-old-man, I should say.'

'It not my Lily! It fake!' cried Inna.

The dead man's false teeth had popped out and were grinning up at her from the mud. His face looked partly shaven with some ghastly cuts in the skin.

'Nonsense! Look, we've got the death certificate!' Miss Wrest flourished a soggy piece of paper, which did indeed bear my mother's name.

The thin bowler-hatted man looked about him in surprise. 'Is thish not Mrs O'Reilly's funeral?'

'No,' replied Miss Wrest. 'She's with the Council up at St Pancras. They undercut us.' She glanced at her watch. 'It'll all be over by now.'

'Could you tell me, will there be a wake after thish funeral?'

'No,' I snapped. 'Now piss off.'

'I'm very shorry,' he slurred, 'I think I made a mishtake.' He crawled towards the solid ground of the path and staggered off on his muddy way.

Inna was struggling to get up, but couldn't find her footing. Her glasses were down in the mud beside the false teeth. I reached down to offer her a hand, lost my balance, slipped, and crashed. A piercing pain shot through my left eye. When I put my hand to my face, it was covered in blood.

Then I blacked out.

When I came round I was in the back of an ambulance woo-wooing through the streets of London. A male paramedic was pressing a blood-soaked pad to my face and the world was half dark. Miss Wrest was sitting beside me holding my hand. She had lost her top hat, and her long mousy hair was damp and tangled over her face. Most of the panstick make-up had washed off too, so that I could see her features, which were pudgy and babyish but not unattractive – as far as I could tell with my remaining eye.

'What happened?' I asked.

'You stabbed yourself in the eye with the spoke of your umbrella,' Miss Wrest answered calmly. 'You were extremely distressed.'

The memory of the ghastly scene flooded back to me and I struggled to sit up, but the paramedic pushed me back gently but firmly on to the stretcher.

'Lie still.'

'Mother! What happened to my mother?'

Miss Wrest squeezed my hand reassuringly. 'Don't worry.'

BERTHOLD: *Gauze and ashes*

By one of those weird backflips of fate to which life is prone, I found myself lying in a hospital bed with a cardboard bowl beside me while Inna perched next to me with a bunch of grapes in a paper bag. My head was throbbing horribly and I felt nauseous from the after-effects of the anaesthetic. The cardboard bowl was full of soggy and bloodstained bits of gauze.

'Oy! You all right, Mister Bertie?' She gazed down into my injured face with a look of undisguised horror in her beady eyes. Of course I could not see what she saw, but it must have included a dramatic gauze bandage over one eye, and maybe a bit of dry blood. 'You going to be one-eye blind?'

'Could be,' I shrugged, not wishing to put an end to the flow of sympathy, though the pretty young doctor had reassured me that the injury had been superficial, the emergency treatment had been successful and my sight would be unaffected.

Inna crossed herself and sighed. 'When you come home I make golabki kobaski slatki. We drink vodka.'

'Lovely. Can't wait.' Though I had resolved to go easy on the slatki. Just in case. 'It's my birthday on the sixth of May. And we can invite our new next-door neighbour.'

'Blackie?'

'Violet. You'd better check that she's not vegetarian.'

I wondered whether she would be filled with revulsion at the sight of my eyepatch, or whether tender-hearted sympathy would prevail. Women are so unpredictable.

★

After Inna had gone, I managed to snooze for a while. I was awoken by a voice calling my name. Carefully I opened my good eye. I can't have been asleep for long, for it was still light, and the ward was full of clatter and voices. An elderly woman with white hair and red lipstick was leaning over me, but the image was somehow split, like in a mirror, so she appeared to be on both sides of my bed at once.

'Hello? Bertie?' said the one on my left.

'Hello? Bertie?' echoed the one on my right.

My headache had intensified and everything around me seemed fragmented and unreal. Can one have double vision, I wondered, with only one eye?

'Jenny,' said the one on my left. 'Margaret,' said the one on my right.

'Oh. Hello.' I tried to move my head to look from one to the other, but my neck had seized up. 'Thank you for coming.'

'We got these for you,' said Margaret.

Jenny slapped down a box of chocolates on the bedside table. 'The nurse said you were doing well. They'll be sending you home soon.'

'I hope so. I can't wait to get back to my flat.'

They exchanged glances.

'The thing is, Bertie . . .' said Margaret.

'There's something we need to talk about,' added Jenny. 'You see, it's not really your flat.'

'Not mine? What d'you mean? Who else's could it be?'

'Actually, it's ours. Our dad left the tenancy to us in his will.'

' "To my darling daughters, Jenny and Margaret, the tenancy of my flat." That's what he said,' Margaret added in an irritating faux-naive bleat.

While she was talking, Jenny had reached for the box of chocolates and stripped off the cellophane film.

136

'Aren't you going to eat these, Bertie? They were quite expensive.'

'Oh, by all means. Help yourselves.'

'But no rush,' said Margaret, selecting a chocolate, popping it in her mouth and licking her fingers. 'Stay until you find somewhere that suits you.'

'But now we're widows, we've been looking for a nice two-bedroom flat where we could live together.' Jenny took the box and mirrored her sister's action. 'We don't want to chuck you out, Bertie, but with house prices in London the way they are, there's not much in our price range.'

'But I'm not planning on moving anywhere. The tenancy was my mum's and now it's mine.' Mother's death-bed words echoed in my brain. I had assumed she was talking about the Council, or one of her exes, but maybe it was the twins she had been warning me against. 'She succeeded to the tenancy automatically when your dad, Ted Madeley, died. That's the rule. And she passed it on to me.' I could feel my face going red. My bad eye began to throb. The twin faces started to spin, frizzy white hair framing vampire-red lips. I wished they would just go away.

'The thing is, Bertie,' Jenny pursued, 'we didn't want to tell you this, but you'd have to find out eventually. Ted, our dad, and your mother weren't actually married. They never tied the knot legally, so your mother never actually inherited the tenancy. They were going to get married, but after Lily lost the baby –'

'What baby?'

'Your mother was three months gone when they moved into the flat. He promised to marry her.'

'It broke our mother's heart.' If there was a hard-cop, soft-cop act, Jenny was the hard one.

'But she lost the baby at twenty-two weeks.'

'They must have got married. I've got the wedding certificate. I can show you,' I said.

They exchanged significant glances.

Jenny spoke first. 'You see, our mum and dad were never actually divorced. He may have married Lily, but it wasn't . . .'

'. . . legal.'

'And once they moved in together Ted's health went downhill. He was forty years older than her, remember. He . . .'

'. . . wasn't up to it.' She lowered her eyes and whispered, 'Sex!'

'His heart attack happened while they were . . .' Margaret offered me the box of chocolates but I shook my head. I was beginning to feel sick.

'I still don't see how that makes it your flat,' I said.

'The tenancy was our mother's by law, and we have the right to inherit it,' Jenny snapped.

'Dad promised it to us,' said Margaret. 'But he said Lily could stay there until she died, and we respected his wishes.' She crammed two more chocolates into her mouth. One of them must have been caramel, for it stuck to her teeth as she said, 'Glbut now she's tragbiclly passed away . . . glb . . . it's time . . . glb.'

'Anyway,' Jenny's eyes hovered between the two chocolates left in the nearly empty chocolate box. She made her selection and pounced, 'The Council won't transfer it to you now because you're on your own, and it's a two-bedroom flat.'

Margaret added in a little-girl bleat, 'It's our childhood home, Bertie. It's where we grew up.' Her watery blue eyes seemed to have filled up with tears. 'Don't turn us out on the street!'

I knew this was nonsense; they had stayed with their mother when Ted moved in with Lily, and could hardly have set foot in the place. For all I knew, they had made the whole thing up, even down to the dead baby.

'But Berthold Lubetkin promised . . . !' I tried to sit up, but a searing pain in my eye forced me to fall back on to the pillows again.

'Lubetkin?' snorted Jenny. 'He had some funny ideas, according to our dad, but it was nothing to do with him. He was just the architect. And anyway, he's been dead for years.'

Pain is exhausting, as well as being unpleasant in other ways. I must have let out a groan between my clenched teeth, for Margaret laid a hand on my arm, 'Don't stress yourself, Bertie.'

'Nurse! Nurse!' I called in a feeble voice, 'Please can I have some more painkillers?'

'I think he needs to rest,' ordered the nurse, the same almond-eyed beauty who had given my mum her final catheter. She flapped my visitors away with slender hands and handed me two white caplets and a cup of water.

As I surrendered to sweet oblivion, the twins merged into one, dwindled as though caught in the wrong end of a telescope, turned into a speck, and disappeared.

Later, after the dinner trolley with its remnants of reheated beef and congealing custard had rattled away, I wondered whether this visit had really taken place or whether those images were an effect of imagination combined with medication.

Next morning, before I was declared fit to return home, I had two more bedside visitors: Jimmy the Dog and Mousy Miss Wrest. Although they were wearing their day clothes, not their funereals, they came into the ward solemnly side by side, with downcast eyes – anyone could spot they were undertakers. Jimmy was holding a large parcel wrapped in black tissue paper. Miss Wrest was holding a wreath of white flowers, which looked as though they might have been lifted from a hearse.

'How are you, old pal? How's the eye?' asked Jimmy, peering into my bandaged face with more dramatic solicitude than Inna had been able to muster.

'They think I've lost it,' I said, thinking I might as well milk it for all it was worth. 'They're going to try and operate again later. They've got a top-notch Egyptian eye surgeon, but they're not holding out much hope.'

'Oh God!' said Miss Wrest. 'How awful! We brought these for you.'

She laid down the wreath reverentially on my lap as though I was a coffin, and muttered something in a low voice to Jimmy. I couldn't hear what she said, but I thought I caught the word 'insurance'.

'And these.' Jimmy handed me the tissue-wrapped parcel, which was surprisingly heavy.

'What . . . ?'

I unwrapped it. Beneath the tissue was a white cardboard box with the Wrest 'n' Piece insignia embossed in gold. Inside it was a chunky brass casket.

'Your late mother's ashes,' said Jimmy, with a respectful nod of the head.

'We offer our sincere apologies for the confusion,' added Miss Wrest.

'Unfortunate mix-up,' murmured Jimmy. 'They cremmed the wrong coffin.'

'But the guy . . . the stiff . . . ?'

'It was supposed to be him that got cremmed.'

As the fog of incomprehension from the painkillers started to lift, the pain in my injured eye became more intense, but even I could see that there was something odd about this story.

'But why was her body at the crematorium in the first place? I mean, did someone put the wrong body in the coffin?'

Jimmy looked shifty. 'Mix-up at the funeral parlour.' His eye fell on the one remaining chocolate in the box the twins had brought, and he wolfed it down like a wolfhound.

'Unfortunately we had to let our regular mortician go,' murmured Miss Wrest. 'He'd been with us for forty years. Knew the trade inside out. But he was getting too demanding.'

'Shame, though. These work experience placements – we try to help the unemployed of course, but they're unpaid, so what can you expect? Sometimes they lack . . . motivation,' he added.

'Philip thought he was indispensable. We had to show him,' she said.

'We all have to do our bit for austerity, Bertie.' Jimmy's voice was grave.

'Still, cremation is usually regarded as a very desirable post-life option,' Miss Wrest asserted. 'It can be more expensive than burial.'

'Yes, but . . .' My brain still wasn't working properly.

'You can still scatter the ashes at Green Glade, old pal,' said Jimmy.

'At no additional cost,' added Miss Wrest.

VIOLET: Dralon

In quiet moments at work Violet finds herself scanning employment ads and job-search sites. There's plenty of unpaid work experience out there, but the actual jobs now are mainly in tech start-ups or property development, which don't interest her.

Marc treats her with formal politeness, and makes no reference to their dinner date. Remembering the look in his eyes as he dabbed at the wine on his groin with a napkin now brings a small smile of satisfaction to her face. But the truth is that her flame of enthusiasm for her job has fizzled out. She wants something different – but what? She doesn't know. The only two jobs for which she applies both require references – of course they would. She can't name Marc Bonnier or Gillian Chalmers as referees without explaining why she wants to leave GRM, so she bangs in the applications just giving her academic references, knowing she doesn't stand much chance.

Meanwhile, the campaign to save the cherry trees has taken off. On Sunday evening she finds herself sitting squeezed thigh-to-thigh between Greg Smith – that is the towel-man's name – and Mrs Cracey on the maroon Dralon couch in Mrs Cracey's sitting room that smells faintly of cat pee. A couple of thin multicoloured cats are hanging around looking for an inviting knee to jump on to. The wheelchair man, whose name is Len, is parked in one corner. Mrs Tyldesley, the artist lady who lives next to Mrs Cracey, sits opposite them on a matching Dralon armchair sketching away. Greg's son Arthur is perched on a kitchen stool, sucking his biro with concentration and scribbling on a notepad. They are drafting a petition to the Council to save the cherry trees.

The room reminds her of her grandmother's sitting room in Nairobi, with the same heavy Dralon furniture, a crucifix on each wall, and frilly net drapes obscuring the windows, even down to the same print of Jesus holding a lantern and knocking on a closed door, which her grandmother used to tell her represented the door of her heart. The sad look on Jesus' face always made her feel a twinge of guilt, and she pays her penance now by volunteering to type up the petition and email it to Greg who will run some copies off at work.

BERTHOLD: *Gobby Gladys*

The look of alarm on Inna's face when I came in through the door after my discharge from hospital made me feel a twinge of guilt that I had exaggerated the seriousness of my injury. I slumped on the sofa, moaning from time to time, and let her ply me with tea and vodka. I had hoped the hospital would issue me with a pirate-style black eyepatch when they discharged me, but the one at the dispensary turned out to be confectionery-pink and rubbery. On my face, it looked like a misplaced cupcake.

'Oy, you look like crazy, Bertie! One-eye blind crazy!'

'The doctor said I've a fifty-fifty chance of losing my eye, Inna,' I said. Which was not entirely true – the doctor had said my eyesight was not at risk – but why waste all that goodwill that people seem to summon up for the blind?

'Better you not lose it too soon. You ev birthday on Tuesday. I will invite Blackie coming for dinner. I will make golabki kobaski slatki.'

'Lovely. But remember her name is Violet, not Blackie.'

'Blackie, Violet, all same – innit, Indunky Smeet?'

The parrot looked mardy and did not respond. It must be tough for a creature of limited intelligence to handle so many name changes. I was brimming with excitement but I put on a display of nonchalance for Inna's benefit.

'I was thinking, Inna, should I invest in one of those George Clooney-type coffee machines?'

You never know what will please a woman.

'Too expensive,' Inna declared. 'Waste of money. Dovik got one. Coffee in Lidl is better.'

Due to factors beyond my control, for which I largely blamed Jimmy, I had never managed to deliver the oration I had so painstakingly prepared for Mother's funeral. But now, lying on the sofa in the sitting room, I turned my melancholy one-eyed gaze on the casket of ashes which Jimmy had given me in hospital and which I had placed on the mantelpiece. All that energy and complexity compacted into a box of dust. I tried to recall what she had told me of her life. What I did not know would now remain a mystery.

Mum had been wont to brag of her humble origins. She had been born in a flat above a pie shop on Sutton Street, Shadwell, she claimed; not even a real flat. Just two rooms on the first floor, sharing the hall, staircase and mezzanine kitchen with another family. There was no bathroom, only a communal toilet in the back yard. Nevertheless, Mum said, they were better off than many families, who lived in just one room, or in a lightless basement. Her father, my Grandad Robert, born in 1890, had survived the horrors of the Great War and worked as a tally clerk in the Port of London. He had witnessed at first hand the humiliating scramble of unemployed dockers fighting each other for a brass tally, which was the promise of a day's work, tossed by a foreman into the hungry crowd. Once he saw a man killed in the crush. It affected him deeply, and Mum told me in a hushed voice that her father, before he died, had made her promise never to cross a picket fence. I puzzled over the mystery of the fence, but I did not question it, so powerful was the mystique of my grandfather. I snuggled beside Mother on the sofa and let her voice lead me through the gallery of the sepia-tinted past.

Her mother Gladys, she told me, was born into a Yorkshire mining family in 1900, and had moved down to London during the Depression to work as a maid in the household of a Chelsea dentist. Never one to hold her tongue, Gladys, nicknamed Gobby Gladys, had stormed out after an argument over wages, and found a job in a rag factory in Whitechapel. Within two years she'd set up a trade union branch there. Gladys and Robert met at a rally in Bow at which George Lansbury was talking about his vision of a better society. Gladys, pint-sized and pugnacious, wearing high heels and a red felt hat with a flower on the side, jumped up and yelled that all this talk about ethics and aesthetics was highfalutin claptrap and we must fight the fascists in the streets. Robert, giant-sized and peaceable, looked on in awe and asked her out for a drink afterwards. There was a photo of them at their wedding, he tall and handsome in a double-breasted suit, she barely reaching to his shoulder even in high heels, wearing white silk, and flowers in her hair. If you looked closely, you could just detect the bump under the silk that was baby Lily, who was born in the year that George Lansbury became the leader of the Labour Party, and trundled around to Labour Party meetings and rallies all over the East End, her pram stuffed with leaflets.

I never met my Grandad Bob, he died before I was born, but I was once taken to meet Granny Gladys in her old people's home in Poplar. She was a tiny shrunken figure hunched over her Zimmer frame in a small overheated room that smelled of disinfectant and pee. There was a sampler on the wall embroidered in cross stitch, with the motto 'Fellowship is Life'.

'Kiss your granny, Bertie.' Mother gave me a little push, and I stumbled forward.

Her cheek felt dry and soft like crumpled tissue paper. She was still gobby; she railed in a shrill quavering voice against

Stanley Baldman, and Mum whispered that she meant the pre-war Prime Minister Stanley Baldwin who had been dead for twenty years. At tea, when I reached for a chocolate biscuit before it was offered, she rapped my fingers with a spoon.

When Granny Gladys died, Mother was inconsolable for weeks, but I was secretly glad, because I didn't like her much, and after the funeral I got Grandad's walking stick with a carved dog's head for the handle. Mother inherited the sampler, which she hung on the wall in the sitting room. She also inherited both Granny Gladys's gobby spirit and Grandad Bob's steadfastness. Even now, remembering the way her voice choked as she spoke about him brought a tear to my eye.

'What does it mean, "fellowship is life"?' I had once asked, poking at the sampler with Grandad's walking stick.

She turned on me, her eyes shining with tears, and said, 'They were only in power six years, and they gave us the NHS, unemployment benefit, pensions, proper education and thousands of new homes, including this one, Bert. That's what fellowship is.'

VIOLET: *Seven dwarves*

Greg comes back to Mrs Cracey's flat on Monday evening and presents a bundle of papers and some clipboards with a flourish. Len and Mrs Tyldesley are there too. Mrs Cracey pours five glasses of whisky, and declares that the garden of the Lord always blooms better with a little irrigation. Violet cheers and clinks glasses. Getting involved with the cherry tree campaign seems much more worthwhile than helping HN Holdings siphon money out of Kenya into Horace Nzangu's British Virgin Isles company.

Armed with the clipboards and petitions, they go out knocking on doors. Everyone signs, and some people even agree to write individual letters. Afterwards she goes back to Greg's flat for a coffee. He has one of those hi-tech coffee-making machines like Marc's that hisses and makes a lot of noise then produces a fragrant black dribble of coffee. It must be a man thing.

'Where's Arthur?' she asks.

'He's with his mother,' says Greg. 'He stays with her half the week.'

Her stomach flutters a brief warning. She felt comfortable in the flat when Arthur was there, but being alone with Greg is not on her agenda. He is a lot older than her, with a complicated marital history and an appraising eye. This is not a man she wants to get involved with.

'That must be tough. For both of you.' She glances towards the door just in case she needs to make a quick exit.

'It takes a bit of getting used to,' he says.

They perch on stools in the kitchen; she stirs half a teaspoon of sugar into her coffee, which is a bit too strong and makes her pulses race. He doesn't talk about his marital problems or his work: he talks about his passion for sailing, and his ambition to sail around Cape Horn.

'Does Arthur like sailing too?' she asks, as if saying Arthur's name will bring him into the room with them.

He laughs. 'I'm working on him, but he prefers Minecraft.'

She remembers the forlorn look on the kid's face as he stepped out into the road, hunched over his screen.

'What made you take up the cause of the cherry trees, Violet?' he asks.

She tells him about the eruption of new building in Nairobi. 'The sheer arrogance of it. They think they can get away with it, because nobody will object. Or because they've paid somebody off. How about you? How did you end up living here?'

It seems odd that someone who seems to have money is living in a place like this. But Greg, like her, had only recently arrived in the flats, and, like her, he isn't planning to stay long.

'I'm having some building work done on my house. It ran into problems and I had to move out in a hurry.'

'That sounds bad.'

'It is. Structural. You?'

'Mm. I was staying with a friend before. In Croydon. I can't really afford it here unless I find some flatmates,' she adds with an embarrassed giggle.

Apart from the coffee machine, his flat is even barer than her own. It does have curtains, but no beds. Greg and his son had been sleeping on inflatable mattresses on the floor.

'You can borrow some of mine,' says Violet. 'I've got seven of everything.'

'Seven?'

'The previous occupants were dwarves.'

He laughs. His teeth are even and white, with pointed canines. His sleek dark hair is greying at the temples, his cheeks and chin perfectly chiselled, handsome in a George Clooney sort of way.

But way too old for her.

Between them they heave and manoeuvre two beds, two desks and three chairs out of her flat, into the lift, and across the walkway to his flat. The move takes them the best part of an hour. At the end of it they are breathless and exhausted.

'Let me take you out for dinner,' he says.

She hesitates. The thought of good food in a proper restaurant with attentive male company is tempting, but she mustn't get herself into a situation she can't get out of. There is something quick and hungry about him which reminds her of Marc. She's learned her lesson.

'Thanks. But I've promised to skype my grandma in Nairobi.'

She closes the door of her flat and sets the latch and the chain. She still doesn't feel quite safe here at night; the strange noises from the flat next door and the shouting in the street after the pubs close always put her on edge. She lowers the blue sari curtain and whisks up two eggs for an omelette, planning to skype her grandma after dinner. Then the doorbell buzzes.

She jumps up, her heart pounding, and listens. It buzzes again. Lucky the chain is on. Probably it is just Greg with a spare bundle of petitions, but you can't be too careful. She opens the door on the chain and peers through the crack out on to the concrete walkway where dusk is already drawing in. The shadowy figure standing there is almost invisible, dressed all in black; a stray beam of light from her kitchen window glints on a pair of diamanté-framed spectacles. It takes her a moment to recognise the old lady from next door.

'Allo, Blackie, I am next-door Inna,' the old lady croaks. 'You vegetable?'

Calling her Blackie is one thing – she guessed from the old lady's tone that it was meant more descriptively than offensively. But no one has called her a vegetable before. What does it mean?

She opens the door. 'Vegetable?'

'You it it? I cook golabki kobaski slatki. Tomorrow half of seven.' The old lady's face crinkles up into a smile.

'Oh, I see.' Though she doesn't see at all.

'I am mother-sister from Lily.' Behind the sparkly spectacles, her dark eyes dance bright and merry.

'Mhm?'

'I cook. You no vegetable, okay?'

'Okay?'

The old lady chortles and disappears into the dusk rubbing her hands. Seriously weird.

She closes the door and slices a tomato and toasts some slightly stale bread to go with her omelette, half regretting that she had turned down a proper meal in a restaurant. Then she skypes her Grandma Njoki in Nairobi.

'Violet! Violet *mpenzi!*' A blurred and pixelated image of a wrinkled brown face with rubbery pink gums and pearly-white false teeth fills the screen of her laptop. 'When you coming to visit us in Nairobi?'

'As soon as possible, Nyanya Njoki! I'm saving up.' Which is not entirely true, but suddenly seems like a good idea.

BERTHOLD: May 6th

The day of my birthday dawned, and I gingerly removed the rubbery pink cupcake from my eye. Everything seemed normal. So far so good. I was getting bored with lying around, and my anticipation of the evening ahead was making me restless. I needed a blast of coffee, and maybe Luigi would know where I could buy one of those Clooney-type coffee machines. Just as I hauled myself out of bed, Legless Len appeared at the door.

'What yer gonna do about them flats?' he demanded, wheeling himself over the threshold and into the living room, looking puffy and red in the face. His forehead and his cap looked like one continuous blob of angry red.

I'd known Len for years. He was a former taxi driver – a protégé of Mother's, who had pulled out all the stops to get him moved into a ground-floor flat and have it adapted for a wheelchair after his legs were amputated. He had repaid her by backing Mrs Crazy in the Tenants Association election. Yet somehow they had remained friends, probably united by their love of talking birds.

'What flats?'

'Them they're building aht front.'

'I'm sorry, Len, you're going to have to explain.'

Len had an annoying habit of assuming everyone could read his mind. If indeed he had one.

'You've not read the notices, Bert. You should always read the notices.'

'What notices?'

'Them the Council put up. The Local Authority. Them that has authority over us.'

He liked the word 'authority'. Now I vaguely remembered someone else had mentioned those notices recently. So much had happened in the last few days, I could not be expected to remember everything, let alone something as trivial as lamp-post notices.

'It's nothing to do with flats, Len. It's a lost cat.'

'That's where you're wrong, Bert. People like you, intellectuals, you think you know everything already, so you never bother to find out.'

It was gratifying to be called an intellectual, even by someone so ill equipped to judge as Len. But his voice was uncharacteristically aggressive.

'You follow ideas that come into your head, Bert, but you've got nothing to guide you, no values.'

What had got into him? He was sweating slightly, with a ghastly pallor. Maybe he too had fallen in love with the goddess from next door. I had noticed them talking in the grove once or twice. Poor fool, what chance did he stand?

'Your problem, Bert, is that you've got no team that you support. See, friends come and go, your family passes away, politicians let you down, but your team is for life.' His voice quivered with emotion.

'Look, I'm sorry, Len, I have to go out. Can we discuss this another time?'

He had now planted himself in the middle of the room like a poisonous red toadstool in his Arsenal cap. He looked as though he was going nowhere.

'By the time you come back it could be too late. Look!'

He gestured towards the window. I drew back the net curtain and looked out over the grove. At first nothing much seemed to be going on. Then I observed two men in hard hats strolling around among the cherry trees, looking this way and that, consulting a large sheet of paper. A van was parked at the kerb, too far away to read the name of the firm. I wheeled Len out on to the balcony. One of the hard-hat men was zapping a laser measuring tape at the trunks of the trees. The other one was making notes on a clipboard.

As we watched, another figure ran into the grove – a small fierce woman wearing a purple military-style coat with a generous sprinkling of brass buttons and a polythene shower cap. She darted up to the man with the laser measurer and grabbed it out of his hand. Next she ran up to the man with the clipboard, tore off the sheets of paper, ripped them up and scattered them in the air. Then she produced a fold-up umbrella from her carrier bag, extended it to its full length, and started hitting them over their backs and shoulders. The men didn't hang around for more. They legged it through the grove, climbed into their van, and a moment later, it roared off down the road. The purple-coat lady – it was Mrs Crazy of course – looked around her to make sure they had all gone, then tossed the laser measurer into the bushes and struggled to re-telescope her umbrella, which seemed to be jammed, probably because it was now bent.

'She got big crazy!' exclaimed Inna, who had joined us on the balcony, with a tremor of respect in her voice.

The drama over, we were just about to go back into the flat when a further movement down in the grove caught my eye. A slim young woman, lithe, mahogany-skinned, a vision of pure beauty, sprinted lightly like a dryad along the curved path between the trees. She ran right up to Mrs Crazy, embraced her in her lovely arms and clasped her in a hug. I have never before felt a twinge of envy for Mrs Crazy, but she didn't seem as ecstatic as I would have been. She disentangled herself from the embrace, shook the dryad by the hand, and disappeared like a witch into the wooden shed beside the community garden.

'See what I mean?' Len's voice brought me to my senses. 'We need to get our act together, Bert. We can't have women taking all the glory. Action is the man's role, innit?'

'What many people do not realise, Len, is that innit is an expression derived from the Ancient Greek "enai" meaning "it is".'

'Yeah?' He looked pleased at his own brilliance. 'Greek! Well, blow me down! There's a petition going around, Bert, for everybody to sign. But in my humble opinion, your mum Lily would have called for direct action. We've gotter get organised.'

'Don't mourn, organise!' cried Flossie, displaying a level of political consciousness unusual in a bird.

'That's it, Flossie. You tell him.'

Len, who bred budgerigars himself, had a soft spot for Flossie – maybe the reason his friendship with Mother had endured despite their political differences.

'What kind of action do you have in mind, Len?'

'Well, we could occupy the Town Hall. Chain us-selves to the trees and what 'ave you. Take a leaf out of Lily's book, God rest her soul. A lovely lady and a real positive thinker, for a communist.'

I could see now that going out for the Clooney-style coffee machine would be a futile gesture and might even backfire on me. Clooney, after all, was just a shallow cappuccino-sipping celeb, whereas I was a man of principles with more to offer an angel than mere coffee. I'd better go out and buy a padlock and chain, like the one that had been on my stolen bike. If chaining myself to a tree was what it took, so be it.

VIOLET: *Niha*

It's surprising how many people from the flats witnessed the scene with Mrs Cracey and the hard-hats in the cherry grove; Mr Rowland from the Council Planning Department has already received several phone calls when Violet phones him.

'No, planning permission hasn't been approved yet,' he tells her. 'It's on the agenda for June. It's not against the law, you know, to go around measuring trees.'

'Well, they obviously assume it's in the bag,' she retorts in her high-heels voice, even though she's already standing at the sink in her trainers.

'They can assume what they like. But it still has to go to committee.' He sounds defensive. 'The problem with most of the letters is that objections have to be based on planning grounds – not just because people don't like it.'

'What exactly are planning grounds?'

'It's got to fit in with the Council's own strategy on things like access, transport, amenities, etcetera.'

'Why didn't you tell me this before?'

The line goes quiet for a moment. 'Look,' he says, 'I'll do my best with the letters I've received. And the petition. But I can't promise anything.'

'Has any money changed hands?' she demands. 'Is anyone making a quick buck out of this?'

'I'll pretend I didn't hear you say that.'

If she hadn't been so upset, she might have made some excuse when Greg rings her doorbell that evening shortly after six.

He's still wearing his work suit and carrying a big leather briefcase.

'I heard about your act of heroism,' he says with a grin.

'Ha! You heard wrong. It wasn't me, it was the old lady. My only act of heroism was to shout at some poor guy in the planning department.'

'Whatever. I think you deserve a treat. I've got a table booked at the Niha. Will you let me take you out for an early supper?'

She would have said no, but she too feels she deserves a treat. They agree to meet downstairs in half an hour. While he goes to fetch his car, she changes into a dress and high heels, which boost her morale as well as her height.

The Niha is a small Lebanese restaurant near the Barbican, quite close to the GRM building. She's actually been here once at lunchtime with Laura. In the evening it's cosy, low-lit and intimate. Without asking her, Greg orders sayadieh for both of them, assuming she will approve of his choice, which of course she does, and a Lebanese red wine called Château Musar which costs twice as much as their entire meal. While they wait for it to arrive, she tells him about her conversation with Mr Rowland.

'Planning grounds! Why didn't they say so? They seem to make up the rules as they go along!'

'Local government is full of self-serving jobsworths,' he says, 'wasting our money on red tape and vanity projects. I'm having a bit of trouble with local planners myself. I won't bore you with the details.'

Over dessert, their conversation becomes more personal. He talks about sailing in the Solent. She tells him the difference between Bakewell tart and Bakewell pudding. When she describes, giggling, how the original cook at the White Horse Inn accidentally spread egg and almond mixture across the jam, he reaches out his hand and places it over hers.

Quietly, without a word, she draws hers away.

At nine o'clock he drops her back at Madeley Court and goes to park his car in his rented garage. No kiss, no invitation for a nightcap, not even a stray grope. So far so good, she thinks.

She locks the door, kicks off her high heels, and pads to the kitchen in bare feet to put the kettle on. While it's boiling she changes into her pyjamas – rather frayed hand-embroidered silk which her former Singaporean room-mate left behind in place of the new M&S teddy-bear print she stole, along with Nick. Rummaging in the tin for a peppermint tea bag, she mulls over the evening with Greg. Should she let their relationship go further? He's good-looking, more of a gentleman than Marc, and the father of a very cute kid. But much too old for her, and she's enjoying her freedom too much.

The kettle boils. She goes into the kitchen and pours hot water over the tea bag in a yellow mug, and is just about to take it to bed with her, when her doorbell buzzes. Once. Twice. Three times.

BERTHOLD: *L'Heure Bleue*

Inna, bless her, spent two hours in the kitchen with her pinny on labouring over the menu for my birthday, while I took myself off to the bathroom for a fragrant relaxing soak, taking care to keep my injured eye dry. Without its pink cupcake cover, the wound and surrounding bruise looked ghoulish – but ghoulish is sexier than comical, I surmised. Though of course you can never tell with women.

I splashed myself with Eau Sauvage and put on my cream M&S 100% cotton shirt, freshly washed and pressed (by Inna) after its last outing at Mother's funeral, but the suit wasn't back from the dry cleaner's yet, so I wore my black jeans. Inna wore her black skirt and silk blouse, with her pearl earrings and her hair pinned up with a tortoiseshell comb for the occasion. She had put on lipstick and sprayed on some of Mother's perfume to cover up the smell of cooking. The moody musky fragrance of L'Heure Bleue awoke in me a sentiment of nostalgia and longing akin to love, and I poured us a little aperitif of sweet sherry from Lidl in memory. Then we sat down at the table to await the arrival of the woman who, I felt in my bones, would change my life. As the minutes ticked by, my eyes strayed more than once to the brass casket on the mantelpiece containing Mother's mortal remains and I even imagined I heard her whisper a tender admonishment to get married again, and to keep always to the sunny side. I felt her presence in the room, certain that she was glad and excited for me on this important evening as I waited.

And waited.

And waited.

At half past eight I said to Inna, 'Are you sure you invited her? Are you sure she said she'll come?'

'Definitely I ev invited. Half of seven. She said no vegetable okay.'

'God is dead! Shut up, Indunky Smeet!' Flossie was anxious too, and sounding off randomly.

At nine o'clock I said, 'Hadn't you better go and find out what happened?'

VIOLET: Cholera big leak

Violet feels both relieved and annoyed. Relieved because it's only that dotty old lady from next door standing there buzzing the bell, not some sinister killer or mugger, nor even Greg with his disconcerting stare. Annoyed because it's after nine o'clock, and she wants to tell her to go away, but finds herself politely inviting her to come in.

'You come it golabki kobaski slatki wit us?' The old lady peers around the hallway with undisguised curiosity.

How long has this old lady managed to survive in the UK with such appalling English? Those people who bang on about compulsory English lessons for foreigners may have a point. Her Grandma Njoki has never even been to England, but even she can speak better.

'I make for you is get cold, you come it.'

'That's very kind of you. Maybe another time.'

'Not other, come now, Berthold waiting.'

Berthold: that's the name of that funny old guy next door who gave her an empty coffee jar.

'Please give my apologies to Berthold, but I've already had my supper.'

'You no worry, Berthold make no problem – he homosexy, no ladies.'

She hadn't guessed he's gay, but that's definitely a plus: she can relax and have fun without worrying about giving out the wrong signals or attracting unwanted advances.

'You Africa?' The old lady studies her with frank curiosity. 'Which country you from?'

'I was born in Kenya but I've lived –'

'Aha, Kenya! My husband, Dovik, been there for bacteriophage research. Cholera. Big leak.'

What on earth is she on about? Maybe she should go and say hello out of friendliness, so he doesn't think she's homophobic. But it is getting late.

'It's really a bit too late. I'm just on my way to bed.'

'No worry. He got birthday. New chain special for you.'

'Chain?' What does this signify? The guy is a weirdo, but he seems harmless enough.

'I'd love to. But as you can see, I'm already in my pyjamas.'

'Pyjama no problem.'

The old lady seizes her hand and pulls her out through the door into the night.

BERTHOLD: *Silk pyjamas*

Like it says in the song, she was wearing pink pyjamas when she came. Not that pale girly shade of pink but a deep rose colour made of heavy silk with an embroidered pattern at the ankles and cuffs. Sort of harem meets M&S. Her hair was loose and tumbled over her shoulders. She looked divine. I was touched that she had gone to so much trouble for my birthday.

'Violet!' I pulled out a chair for her at the table. 'Can I get you a drink?'

'I'm sorry I'm late,' she murmured. 'I hope you haven't been waiting too long.'

'No matter,' I said. 'How poor are they that have not patience! What wound did ever heal but by degrees?'

An expression of sweet puzzlement glimmered on her face. Then Inna bustled in with a steaming plate of golabski covered in thick juicy gravy she calls yuksha – one of her specialities and not nearly as bad as it sounds.

'Pliss. Ittit!' she growled.

A look of panic flitted across the angelic features. 'I'm so sorry, I've already had supper. I couldn't manage another thing.'

'Oy! You no like my golabki?' Thunderclouds gathered on Inna's brow.

I intervened. 'It's okay, Inna. She needs to preserve her figure.' To my surprise a thundercloud also gathered on the heavenly brow, so I quickly added, 'Which in form and moving is express and admirable.'

Inna grumpily lifted the golabki and slapped them down in front of me. That was good as I was starving by now. Then she fetched a plate of kobaski – sausages covered in the same juicy gravy – and slapped them down in front of Violet, who raised her delicate pale palms in a gesture of refusal.

'Oy! Oy! You no eat kobasa. You Jew?'

Violet silently cut off an inch of the kobaski and raised it to her lips. As she bit, a fat gob of gravy slithered off and landed on the knee of her silk pyjamas making a dark oily stain. She looked down, and burst into tears.

To my surprise, Inna also burst into tears. 'My good Jew husband never eat kobaski!' she wailed. 'Oy, he was good man! He said I do anything for you, Inna, but I not eat kobasa! Now he dead! Murdered by olihark! I missing him too bad!'

The two of them were at it, blubbing like a burst water main. Should I join in like a new man? What would George Clooney have done? Soon they had their arms around each other and were blubbing on to each other's shoulders. This was definitely not in the script.

'Okay. Tell us what happened to your husband, Inna,' I said, sceptical of the tale about the oligarch, which she had mentioned before.

'Killed by biznessmyen. Arkady Kukuruza. You know it?'

'I can't say I do.'

'He want buy secret of bacteriophage, mekka big profit. Dovik say, my friend you cannot mek profit from this. It come out of toilet. Kukuruza say, "Alfandari, I can mek profit from anythink. You look out, you next time dead."'

The gist of her tale was that this gangster-oligarch tracked down the hapless Dovik in London and made him an offer he didn't realise he couldn't refuse.

'What a farrago of bollocks, Inna, if you'll pardon the mixed metaphor.'

'He invite him in restoran for biznyess talk, and mek him to eat poison slatki!'

Poison slatki! I felt the blood drain out of my head. Is that where she got the idea? Is this practice common in her neck of the woods? While I was reviewing my options, she started her sinister keening once more.

'*Povee vitre na Ukrainou!* Blow wind into Ukraina. Beautiful song. Beautiful country. People has beautiful heart. Only problem is oliharki. They make all money blow away out of my country. Money flies into Vest, but people cannot follow! Oy-oy-oy!'

'Shut up, Inna!' I commanded. Let's face it, there's only so much bollocks that a man can be expected to put up with on his birthday, especially when he's just on the point of making it with the woman of his dreams. But to my dismay instead of listening to me, my lovely neighbour too was getting bewitched by this bullshit.

'It's exactly the same in my country, Inna!' she cried. 'They rob the people and spirit the money away into secret bank accounts! And we facilitate them! The money flies away but the people have to stay behind in poverty. Thousands of Africans drown in the sea trying to follow where their money has gone!'

'Oy, Blackie, world is same everywhere! Better we eat, drink, sing, forget all this sad story!'

Then Inna disappeared into the kitchen again and came back with a small bottle of vodka and a plate of freshly baked slatki, filling the air with their almond and honey scent. Violet stopped crying and her face lit up. Panic seized me. As she reached to take one, I grabbed the plate from Inna and crammed all six of them into my mouth. Would George Clooney have been man enough to sacrifice himself for the woman he loved?

Violet stared, and her round brown eyes filled up with tears again.

Inna took her in her arms. 'Oy! Oy! You no cry, Blackie! This man no good for you. He lady-man, too much like sweetie slatki. You will find better one.'

'No, Inna, I'm not gay . . .' I spluttered out a mouthful of crumbs, feeling suddenly wheezy and tight-chested.

'Poor Bertie, you still feeling sad for you mama. I understand.'

To deny being gay is incredibly uncool, according to George Clooney, and I didn't want to sound like a homophobe, so I shut up. Anyway, it seemed like Violet hadn't heard, for she started to moan, 'I just messed up on a perfect job and I spilled wine all over my boss! I've ruined my life!'

I wanted to hold her close in a comforting embrace and explain the sacrifice I had made to save her from possible poisoning, but Inna had already got her arms around her, so I had to content myself with pouring another round of vodka.

We raised our glasses.

'To absent loved ones!' I said, and would you believe it, I started to blub too.

All that went on for at least an hour, then someone – I think it was Violet – started to giggle. By then the vodka bottle was empty, and so was the bottle of Pinot Noir I had bought as the perfect accompaniment for globalki, as well as a bottle of sweet sherry that Inna had discovered under her bed.

Flossie was asleep, her cage covered with a tablecloth to keep her quiet. Inna was asleep with her head on the table; stray silver hairs had escaped from her plaits and were trailing through the gravy. I fell asleep on the sofa, with the rose-silk angel snuggled up chastely in my arms.

I have no idea how George Clooney celebrated his birthday.

BERTHOLD: *Candlewick dressing gown*

I woke up next morning to the sound of rain drumming on the rusting lid of the barbecue on the balcony. I was a year older. Violet in her silk pyjamas was gone and Inna was standing over me in her ghastly sea-green candlewick dressing gown with a cup of weak instant coffee and a grumpy expression on her face. There were still traces of gravy in her hair.

'Oy, she no eat nothing!' she moaned. 'No golabki no kobaski no slatki! Skinny little blackie bird!'

I was still in the sitting room, still fully clothed. My neck was cricked from the too-short sofa, my mouth tasted of wet dog and my gut was smouldering like a volcano, probably from the slatki, but mercifully I was still alive. There was nothing but a mess of dirty plates and glasses on the table to remind me of the night before, which I hoped Inna would soon tackle.

'Put it down there, Inna,' I gestured her to put the cup on the coffee table beside me, while I shrank back into the glooming peace of my thoughts.

The instant coffee was lukewarm by the time I drank it; then I staggered into the bathroom for a pee. I vaguely remembered that I had already been once or twice in the night. I should really talk to Dr Brandeskievich about my prostate. Does George Clooney have these problems? I wondered. It would be good to have a man-to-man on the topic, to share mutual misgivings about the onset of mortality. I seemed to remember that on one of those bathroom trips I had glanced out of the window and seen a ghostly figure – or a figure and its ghost – standing in the grove, staring up at the flats, the light from the street lamp lighting up a double blur of white hair like a halo, but maybe it was just a hallucination brought on by the toxic slatki.

Inna interrupted my reverie with a typically crude allegation. 'You no make love on to nice-looking girl because you love man. I understand. No problem wit me.'

'Look, Inna, how many times do I have to repeat . . .'

She pursed her lips and stared out of the window at the relentless rain. I followed the line of her gaze and caught sight of something that set my sluggish heart pounding. There at the kerb behind the cherry trees, a little red car was parked and a woman wearing green was getting out of it, unfurling an umbrella. She made her way along the winding path through the cherry grove towards the flats.

'Inna! We have a visitor!' I yelled.

'Wait!' Inna said. 'I quick quick dressing!'

'No need. You're fine as you are.' The sea-green candlewick dressing gown and gravy-crusted hair could only add to the impression of senile dementia. 'This time you are my mother, Okay? Not sister. Mother. A bit confused.' I flapped my hands and rolled my eyes.

She nodded and mimicked.

'Remember your birthday?'

'First of March, 1932!'

'First of March, 1932!' echoed Flossie, understandably irritable at being woken up by having the tablecloth yanked off her cage.

There was not even time to dash into my bedroom and put some fresh clothes on. I smoothed the crumpled front of my shirt, where the rose-silk angel had so recently laid her lovely head. On the cream M&S 100% cotton I found a long curly black hair, which I removed and folded into the breast pocket close to my heart.

Then the doorbell rang. *Ding dong!*

Mrs Penny was wearing the same green dress she had been trying on in Oxfam when we last met, the buttons straining a bit over her breasts. Her plump bare ankles, made shapely by the high heels, bore the same ghoulish flea-bite stigmata as before.

'Come in, Mrs Penny!' I shook her lettuce-limp hand. 'Please meet my mother, Lily!'

Inna scuttled up in her sea-green dressing gown, flapping her hands and rolling her eyes.

'Hey ho! First of March, 1932!' she cried.

So far so good.

'It's so lovely to meet you,' gushed Mrs Penny, shaking out her wet umbrella and propping it by the door. 'I've heard so much about you from your son. Actually, I think we nearly met the other day, when you were getting into a taxi in the rain. You seemed in a bit of a rush.'

'We were going to a friend's funeral.'

'Hey ho! Rain it! Rain it! Every day!' added Inna with gusto.

'I hope you don't mind me dropping in like this. I was just passing, and I thought we could resolve the transfer of the tenancy now. It's a good idea to change the tenancy over while you're still . . . er . . . with us in mind as well as body, Mrs Lukashenko? Not that you won't be with us for years to come. But you never know what is waiting around the corner.'

Inna peered around the corner into the hall and shook her head. 'Nobody there.'

'Quite.' Mrs Penny smiled and produced a clear plastic

file-envelope from her shoulder bag. 'I've brought the paper-work with me, Mr Lukashenko. We've got it registered as a joint tenancy all the way back in 1953. Mr and Mrs Ted Madeley.'

'Look, my name's not Lukashenko, it's Sidebottom. She remarried twice. My father was Sidney Sidebottom,' I said.

'Sidebottom? That's a nice name,' she said without a trace of irony. I looked at her closely. She wasn't even smiling. 'When was that? Do we have certificates with dates?'

'First of March, 1932!' said Inna.

'It was 1960. I have the paperwork somewhere. She gets confused,' I murmured to Mrs Penny, at the same time doing a quick eye roll in Inna's direction.

She flapped her hands, rolled her eyes and chortled, 'Hey ho! Rain it, rain it!'

'Ding dong!' squawked Flossie, making Mrs Penny jump.

'Oh, I'd forgotten the parrot,' she giggled. 'Have you had her long?'

'Twenty years,' I replied. 'She was a gift from Mother's last husband, Mr Lev Lukashenko. Isn't that right, Mother?'

'Hey ho! Lucky Lily.' Inna flapped her hand and rolled her eyes.

Mrs Penny made a note. 'That explains it,' she said. 'We've had a letter in the housing office from a Mr Lukashenko, claiming the tenancy of the flat. Would you believe it – he said you'd passed away!'

Inna shrieked involuntarily, and rolled manic eyes in my direction.

'Totally nuts,' I said with a discreet hand-flap in her direction. 'He was only after her money, you know. And the flat. Mother divorced him. Isn't that so, Mum?'

'First of March, 1932!' Inna flapped her hands.

Mrs Penny made another note. 'So he's not living here?'

'Absolutely not! I've been here for eight years, and he's never been near the place. He went back to Ukraine, I think.'

'That's funny. Mr Lukashenko's letter was posted in London,' said Mrs Penny. 'He gave this as his address.'

My heart skipped a beat. The bastard! He must have got someone over here to write it for him as soon as he received my invitation to the funeral.

'Who this Lucky Skunky?' asked Inna.

'Your ex-husband, Mother. You've forgotten him already. No wonder. She hasn't seen hide nor hair of him in years. Have you, Mother?'

I caught Mrs Penny's eye and tapped my temple with my finger, though Inna was doing such a good job my gesture was superfluous.

'Husband dead,' she sighed. 'Oy! Good man, good hair, good whisker, all dead.'

'Three husbands! No wonder she gets confused,' Mrs Penny looked from me to Inna curiously.

'That's why we wanted to change the tenancy agreement sooner rather than later, Mrs P-Penny. She's not going to get any *less* confused. It can only get worse.'

Under her scrutiny, I could feel my stress level getting stratospheric. My pulse was pounding; my brain had become a compost heap of rotting recollections in which truths and untruths copulated promiscuously.

'Hm. Quite.' She chewed her biro. 'Are there other family members who might have an interest in the flat? Siblings? Grandchildren?'

You don't know the half of it, I thought, but I didn't mention the twins. Why complicate things? Their tearful claim that the flat had been their childhood home was obviously a lie, since it wasn't built until 1952 or 1953. At most they could have lived there for a few months before their mother dumped philandering Ted Madeley and moved on. As for the story that his marriage with Mother was bigamous, I doubted it was true. But even if it was – who could prove it?

'I don't think so. What do you think, Mother?' I said.

'First of March, 1932!' she affirmed.

'With the current housing shortage in London, you'd be amazed the lengths people go to. We have to be so careful.' Mrs Penny narrowed her eyes. 'There have even been cases of people pretending a dead relative was still alive.'

'Unb-believable!' My heart skipped a beat. 'B-but surely, as her only child, I have rights?' My old stutter was knocking at my jaw, threatening to undo all Mother's careful therapy.

'Usually the spouse is the successor, if there is one. According to our guidelines, there can only be one succession per tenancy, apart from by marriage, where it's automatic. In your mother's case, with all the divorces and name changes, we'll have to line up all the ducks.'

'Ducks? Two divorces. The first husband died.'

'Oh, I'm sorry.'

'Of natural causes,' I added, to preclude any doubt.

'That helps. What about utility bills? Whose name are they in?'

'Only Mother's. I can't lay my hands on them right now, but I can forward them.'

I'd cleared out all that old stuff when I prepared Mother's room for Inna, but more would inexorably arrive, as is the way with bills.

'And do you have evidence of relationship and residence, Mr . . . er . . . Lukashenko?' She bit her biro so sharply I heard it crack.

'Berthold Sidebottom. My father was Sidney Sidebottom, her second husband. I've got my b-birth certificate somewhere.

My name's not on the b-b-bills, but I do have corresp-pondence at this address going b-back years.'

'Lovely!' said Mrs Penny. 'May we see?' Suddenly, with largesse to dispense, she had become royal.

I dashed into my bedroom and riffled through the shoe box where I kept my papers. There was library membership, dental appointments, invitations to auditions, the hire purchase agreement for my bicycle, even my pitiful bank statements. I could have found more, but I didn't want to leave Inna alone with Mrs Penny for a moment longer than was necessary.

When I rejoined them in the sitting room, Inna was saying, 'First of March, 1932,' and Mrs Penny was shaking her head, 'Would you believe it!'

I wondered what the question was.

'That's pretty.' Mrs Penny pointed to the shiny brass casket on the mantelpiece. 'Is it antique? Your mother was just explaining it contains ashes, but I didn't get her drift.'

'Yes, it's . . .' My mind went blank.

'God is dead!' Flossie prompted.

'. . . it's a p-parrot. A deceased parrot. Flinna was her name. Originally, we had two, but one died.'

'Shut up, Inna!' squawked Flossie.

'Take no notice,' I chuckled, 'she gets confused. Here, here are some p-papers showing my address.'

I fanned out a handful and held them in front of her. All those official-looking bits of paper brought a smile to her bureaucrat face at last.

'May I?' She pulled out a chair, sat herself down at the table, and went through them one by one, ticking boxes on the green printed form headed Tenancy Transfer, making notes in her file. I could feel my chest tighten as I watched. It's at times like this that I would normally get the sherry bottle out, but we'd polished it all off last night.

'We can complete the procedure later, if you could drop by my office one day next week with your birth certificate and your mother's marriage certificate to your father. Originals, please – we can't accept photocopies.' She handed me a card. 'Are you happy to hand over the tenancy of this flat to your son, Mrs Lukashenko?'

Inna glanced from her to me. 'Is council flat. I like him privat.'

I felt like leaning across and slapping her. It would be just like her to bugger it up at the last minute.

Fortunately, Mrs Penny took that as a yes. 'If you could just sign here, Mrs Lukashenko.'

She pushed the green form, and her blue biro, across to Inna, who picked them up and signed her name: *Inna Alfandari*.

VIOLET: *Placards*

It has been raining all night, but at the last minute a patch of blue sky appears. Violet has already forewarned Human Resources at GRM about a follow-up dental appointment, and meets up with the other residents under the cherry trees at 10 a.m. to march to the Town Hall with their petition. A good forty people have turned out. Mrs Tyldesley, the artist lady, has painted a lovely banner with swirls of pink and green around a rather idealised image of the flats. Len leads the procession with a placard tied to the back of his wheelchair: 'Sod Off Specalators'. He would never have got away with that at Lady Manners, her old school in Bakewell. Despite the tough-talking placard, Len looks a bit pale and puffy. According to Mrs Cracey he has diabetes. Isn't that what Elvis died of? And her Grandma Alison. He should take care. Several grumpy pensioners start squabbling over whose turn it is to push him. Mrs Cracey, steaming up inside her polythene shower cap, with her eyebrows pencilled on in a look of surprise that borders on horror, shoves them aside with her umbrella and grabs the handle. She has a home-made poster with a cut-out image of a crucifixion covered with real stuck-on cherry blossoms, Jesus dying in a sea of pink petals. The slogan, in red felt pen, reads: *He died that we might live.*

The African contingent is led by the young man from Malawi in a too-tight coloured shirt, tapping out a beat on a hand-drum. Some of the Zambians are drumming and dancing too, and a troupe of young people in shorts or ra-ra skirts, wearing face paint, are whooping, blowing whistles and banging tambourines like a carnival. Three white-blonde Polish girls from the second floor are jigging in high heels – why don't they wear trainers or pumps? A couple of shy Indians are carrying a placard that reads *We ♥ Trees*, and Berthold is carrying the parrot in its cage, God knows why, and trying to teach it to say, *'Save our trees!'* though all it can manage is, *'Save our dead!'*

Greg's not there, he's at work, to her relief. Having him there, staring at her in that way, would make her feel self-conscious. She's wearing a black, green and red T-shirt in the colours of the Kenyan flag, with a Maasai warrior shield in the middle, and she's in a combative mood.

Greg's son, Arthur, has bunked off from school and is walking beside her in his grey school shorts, skipping up and down in time to the tambourines.

'What's that on your T-shirt?' he asks.

'It's a Maasai shield. They're a warrior tribe in Kenya.'

'No kidding! Warrior Queen! So why are you called Violet? Violets are supposed to be shy. Like that poem we did at school. Do they have violets in Kenya?'

No one has asked her that before. 'They have African violets, I guess. They're bigger and tougher.' She flexes her arms, showing two tight bulges of muscle.

'Are you going to have sex with my dad?' No one has asked her that before either.

'I don't think so. Why do you ask?'

'I think he fancies you. He likes girls like you.'

'What do you mean, like me?'

'You know, sort of . . .' he looks embarrassed, '. . . sort of . . . brown?'

One of the pensioners turns and stares.

'Oh.' She feels a stab of annoyance, but there's no point in taking it out on the kid, who probably doesn't know what he's talking about. She wants to ask him why they are living in this crummy flat in Madeley Court when Greg clearly has money.

But while she tries to work out a polite way to phrase the question the kid blurts out, 'We're moving soon? As soon as their divorce goes through, and Dad gets his money back? We're moving to a better place? This flat just happened to come empty when Mum chucked him out?'

'Why did your mum chuck him out?'

'She caught him sleeping with the maid?' he mumbles, his hair flopping into his eyes. 'Now she's having sex with this creep called Julian, who wears cords? It's gross? They do it in the living room or in the kitchen, and they make me go upstairs to my bedroom?'

He talks in an awkward hesitant lilt, making every statement into a question.

She feels sorry for him. 'Was the maid . . . sort of brown?'

'Mmm. I guess so.'

Behind them, a girl with blonde plaits and green face paint is tooting a rhythm on her whistle. The parrot squawks, 'Save our dead!'

'What happened to his money?'

'Mum's got it? She says if he tries to get it back she'll tell the police what he done?'

She pricks her ears up. This is interesting. 'Why, what did he do?'

Arthur shrugs. 'Dunno. They won't tell me. Dad says nobody understands that rich people have problems too?'

'I'm sure.' She tries to keep the sarcasm out of her voice. It's not the kid's fault.

He flicks his hair from his eyes. 'When we move, you can come with us if you like. Dad says there's gonna be a massive swimming pool? Underneath the house? In the basement?'

'Thanks, I'll consider it. But I might go to Nairobi.'

'Why?'

'My grandma's there.'

'Wow! Can I come?' He does another little hop.

'Wouldn't you miss your parents?'

'Not really. I don't think they're that bothered about me? Like they mostly ignore me? Except if I'm in the way?' His eyes are pale grey, like his father's, but with a watery glint. 'Have *you* still got a mum and dad?'

'Yes. They live in Derbyshire. I suppose if I went to Kenya, I'd miss them. Life's complicated, isn't it?'

As they straggle across the main road at the traffic lights, cars honk and flash their lights; the boy steps off the kerb without looking – his road sense isn't good – and she grabs his hand to pull him out of the path of a white van that whizzes up out of nowhere. Then they turn left past a parade of shops and head up towards the Town Hall.

At the Town Hall steps they are greeted by an overweight, sweaty middle-aged man with his hair in a ponytail and a silver nose-stud.

'Welcome, people of Madeley Court! My name is Councillor Desmond Dunster,' he yells into a megaphone. 'I'm the elected representative for your area, and I'd like to take this opportunity to thank each and every one of you who voted for me at the last election. And even if you didn't vote for me I hope you will vote for me next time. I want to assure each and every one of you that I am working hard on your behalf, and I totally support your petition about . . . about the important matter which you have brought to my attention. I am a firm believer in closing the loop between the people and their elected representatives and I promise each and every one of you that I will strive my utmost . . .'

What a trog. He goes on like that for ten minutes in a voice like a dentist's drill.

'Gerr on with it!' shouts Len.

'Amen!' shouts Mrs Cracey.

Berthold rests the parrot cage on a low stone wall, and sits beside it staring at the sky with his usual glum expression. Arthur sneaks up and pokes a twig through the bars of the cage. 'God is trees! Trees is dead! Ding dong!' The parrot goes mad, flapping its wings against the cage.

The tambourine girls, fed up with listening to the speech, start up again.

Bored, she strolls away from the crowd, along the pavement and around the side of the Town Hall, attracted by a patch of green that looks like a small park. Beside an entrance to the grey building that houses the Planning Department, a couple of guys are hunched over cigarettes, puffing away furtively, trying to maximise their nicotine intake in the shortest possible time. One of them is Mr Rowland.

'Hi!' She approaches.

They look up like guilty schoolboys; one of them stamps out the stub of his cigarette and vanishes through a door. Mr Rowland, who still has two inches of nicotine to inhale, smiles sheepishly and says, 'He goes on a bit, Councillor Dunster, doesn't he?'

She laughs. 'But will he *do* anything?'

Mr Rowland shakes his head. 'M-m. He'll kick it into the long grass. Of which there's no shortage around here.'

'How can you be so sure?'

'Because he's just been on the MIPIM jolly at Cannes. That's an international property conference where the big global property developers pour cheap champagne down the gullets of local authority worthies and persuade them to sell off old municipal housing estates for redevelopment into luxury housing. He'll take the petitions and stick them in the bin, then come election time he'll tell you how he did his best, but the other parties were all against him. And I'll tell you something for nothing – it won't stop at the cherry grove. They're after the whole site.'

She catches her breath. The brazenness of it.

'And can't *you* do anything, Mr Rowland?'

'Me? I'm out of here next month. I'm sick of kowtowing to clowns like that. I've got another job lined up.'

'With another Council?'

'With Shire Land. One of the biggest developers in London. Qatari owned. As a matter of fact, they're the ones that have got the application in on Madeley Court.' He takes a long last draw on his cigarette.

'You? You'll be working for them?' She stares, and his boyish looks seem to flicker and fade into something familiar and sleazy. All the cheerful high spirits she set out with this morning evaporate in that final puff of cigarette smoke.

'I'm getting married soon. I've put a deposit down on a flat. If you can't beat 'em, join 'em.' He grinds out the end of his cigarette under his shoe, and disappears into the building.

The meeting has already broken up and people are straggling home, so to cheer herself up she decides to run back along the canal.

She gets home an hour later, quite out of breath, with a warm glow in her limbs and a film of sweat on her face, ready for a shower.

BERTHOLD: *Birdcage*

Violet had disappeared. Though we'd barely exchanged a word, I'd walked behind her all the way to the Town Hall, carrying Flossie in her cage, which was bloody heavy I'll have you know. I don't really know why I brought her, but she's good on slogans, and women I've noticed are often drawn to fluffy things. However, Violet was stuck in conversation with that weird kid, of whom more later. I planned to approach her when it was over and walk back together, stopping at Luigi's for a coffee and neighbourly conversation. After our sweet, romantically chaste night of the rose-silk pyjamas, I knew I must take things slowly if I wasn't to scare her off. A lovely girl like that is always surrounded by men wanting to get her into bed. Not me. I was different. I was caring, sensitive, a big soul, a good conversationalist, a good listener, a good neighbour and friend, a good . . . whatever it took.

But then I had a crisis with Flossie. I was sitting on the wall waiting for that donkey, Councillor Desmond Dunster, to plod to a halt. The rank insincerity of his speech reeked of all that is wrong with politics today, all the scurvy self-flattering, gut-grinding, media-mouthed crap they peddle in the belief that we, the people, are too stupid or irresponsible to be trusted with the truth. I wished Mother was there and we could have lobbed a few heckles together. My injured eye was bothering me, and Flossie was stressed by all the whistling and banging of the tambourines. Suddenly the kid who'd been walking beside Violet came up and poked her with a stick and sent her flapping around, beating her poor wings against the bars of the cage. I could have strangled the little sod, but all I did was clip him around the ear. Like Sid used to clip me. Never did me any harm. But the kid made such an outcry – don't they teach them self-control nowadays? – and said he was going to report me for child cruelty. Everyone joined in: Mrs Crazy said the parrot needed its neck wrung; Inna called the kid a hooligan element; Legless Len called me a child abuser. By the time the kid and Flossie had both calmed down – he apologised to Flossie, and I had to apologise to him – Violet had vanished. And so had Inna.

I walked back to the flat alone lugging the cage, which seemed to have doubled in weight. It was almost supper time and I was getting hungry. Why did Inna choose the most inconvenient bloody time to disappear on one of her walk-abouts? Where had she got to?

Flossie had recovered from her earlier trauma and was snoozing on the perch in her cage. Rather than waiting for Inna to come back, I decided to take this opportunity to nip down to Luigi's, have a decent cup of coffee, and meditate on the ghastliness of life. I'd just slipped my jacket on when the doorbell rang. *Ding dong!*

My heart thumped. Violet? The postman? Inna who had forgotten her key? Mrs Penny?

I steeled myself and opened the door.

BERTHOLD: *Slapski*

'Bertie? Bertie! You haven't changed a bit!' A stench of alcohol and urine hit my nostrils. I couldn't immediately identify the scrawny, raddled old geezer with a boozer's nose, silver curls straggling on to his dandruffy collar, and a peaked cap pulled down over one eye who was standing on my doorstep with an empty bottle in his hand.

'Howard! Your brother!' He reached in, hooked an arm around my neck and pulled me towards him to smack a wet whisky-flavoured kiss on my lips.

'Oh. Hi, Howard.' I backed away from the blast-furnace of his breath. It was hard to recognise in this shrivelled sozzled figure the handsome, louche shoe salesman and air guitarist who had once been both my idol and my scourge. He must have been not much more than sixty, but time had not been good to him. 'It's great to see you. It's been a while. What brings you back home?'

'I tried to come to Lily's funeral, honest I did, but I couldn't find the damn place. Green something. Ended up at the burial of a lady called Mrs O'Reilly. Great wake. Beef sandwiches and whisky . . .' He paused. 'Was it a good send-off, Lily's?'

'Yes. Yes indeed,' I lied. 'Apart from the rain, of course. Someone turned up at the wrong funeral. And those twins were there – Ted Madeley's daughters. I hadn't seen them for some forty years. They seemed to think their dad had left the flat to them.'

'Heh heh heh! What a pair of chancers! They were just trying their luck. Lily once told me that Ted Madeley and their mother were never officially married. Apparently, they were planning to marry when she got pregnant again, but she lost the baby.'

'Oh, they told me . . .' What had they told me? The story had become confused in a fog of morphine and double vision, but I seemed to remember that a dead baby had also been involved. Either they were lying, or Lily was. Probably I would never know.

Howard cleared his throat. 'We need to talk, Bertie. Did Lily leave me something in her will?'

'She didn't leave a will.'

'She must have done. She promised.' His grey-red eyes watered, and he brushed them with his sleeve, then he fumbled in his jacket pocket and produced a small orange cigarette lighter. More fumbling yielded a battered ten-pack of cigarettes, emblazoned with their deadly warning. 'D'you mind if I smoke?'

I shrugged and went to find an ashtray. Suddenly his legs buckled and he fell into an armchair, his eyes scanning the cabinet where Mum used to keep her booze. 'Have you got any . . . ?'

I felt both pity and revulsion. 'No. We drank it all at the wake,' I lied. The only wake had been around my hospital bedside.

'Be a good kid – nip round to Baz's Bazaar for a bottle of Old Grouse. Here's the money.' He fumbled in his jacket pockets again and held out a tenner in a shaking hand.

I laughed. 'I'm not a kid, Howard. I'm fifty-three. And Baz's Bazaar closed down twenty years ago.'

'Heh heh. It was probably our fault, me and Nige, the amount of stuff we nicked from there. And you, Bertie. You were the villain of the piece. Remember how we lowered you into the coal hole on a rope? You were a skinny little kid. And you climbed up the inside stairs and opened the window for us?'

A formless horror welled up out of my nightmares: I dangle like a newborn spider in a black void. The rope around my waist much too tight. Something massive and formless pressing on my chest. Eyes and nose covered with black-gloved hands. Mouth full of coal dust. Try to scream. No sound comes out – only a suffocating velvety cough, cough, cough. 'Shut up! Keep quiet!' Howard's voice hissing through the grating.

'I remember trying to explain to Dad how I got coal dust on my pyjamas. And the belt.'

'The belt. Yeah. Dad and his belt. I got it too. But you know what, Bertie, I was always jealous of the way Mum used to stick up for you? Like you were her special little lamb. She used to rock you in her arms when you were crying. *Meh-eh-eh! Hush, hush, my lamb. He doesn't mean it.*' He squeaked in a mock-Lily voice.

'But she loved you too, Howard. She talked about you for years after you'd gone.'

'Nah. I was just this stray kid she'd took pity on. She lost interest in me after you came along. She didn't even leave me anything in her will, though she must have got a fair bit from Dad. Did Mum ever tell you, after they split up, he made over a million on Buy to Let? He found the tax breaks were more reliable than crime.' He chuckled glumly. 'Heh heh heh. She never told you that, eh?'

I felt exhausted and a bit sick. I wished he would go away, but at the same time I wanted him to keep on talking, throwing his bitter light into the secret places of the past.

'Do you remember when we drove up to Ossett to visit your real mother's grave?'

In the summer of 1983 Howard and I had travelled up to Ossett together, his hometown and the birthplace of my father,

Sidney Sidebottom, aka Wicked Sid, swindler, child abuser, Buy to Let millionaire. Howard had inherited our dad's good looks and his mother's musical talent, and at that time he was having some local success with a band called the Blue Maggots, loosely modelled on UB40. I was a star-struck nineteen year old with time on my hands, and although I had no great fondness for my dad, I did have a certain familial curiosity.

The Sidebottom clan, I discovered, despite the Cheshire origins of the name, had been living for generations in this dismal little industrial town halfway between Dewsbury and Wakefield. Ossett had once been a spa, but by the time we Sidebottoms came along it was known mainly for the big Ward's 'shoddy and mungo' mill where both my grandparents worked recycling rags, like Gobby Gladys, who had once recycled rags in Whitechapel. So you could say rags were in my blood on both sides of the family, and in moments of introspection I have sometimes wondered whether that might account for my somewhat shredded outlook on life. But Sid felt he was destined for greater things. Charming and good-looking, with golden curls and a silver tongue, he found a day job in a newsagent's shop and studied bookkeeping at night school.

Once qualified, he started doing the books for the newsagent and other local businesses. His popularity grew as word got around that he was rather good at minimising payments to the Inland Revenue, all perfectly legally. No one, apart from Sid himself, could say exactly when some of the money that passed through the books started sticking to his fingers. By the time he was twenty-five he had stashed away enough money to put down a deposit on a terraced house in Ossett and to marry Howard's mother, Yvonne Lupset, the beautiful and musically gifted (said Howard) only daughter of prosperous local farmers. She was six months pregnant when he took her to the altar.

Sid had an inventive mind, and over the next few years he borrowed from his in-laws and floated a number of get-rich-quick schemes: land in Madagascar, gold in Peru, chickens in Bulgaria, ostrich farming in Kenya. All colourful and fascinating ways of quickly losing other people's money.

The Lupsets let their son-in-law know in many not-so-subtle ways that they thought their daughter had married beneath her. This stirred Sid to fury. She started to come home with unexplained bruises. They had a quiet word with the newsagent, his former employer, who happened to belong to the same Masonic lodge. Irregularities in the books were discovered. Yvonne's parents persuaded the newsagent not to prosecute, but they threatened Sid with exposure should he ever lay a hand on their daughter again. Sid, who had always been quick-tempered, was now eaten up with uncontrollable rage which he could not vent on Yvonne. Besides, she had taken to drinking gin and tonic at the wrong times of day and was doing enough damage to herself already. She was thirty-three when she died. Fortunately Howard, aged eight, was big enough and tough enough to withstand a belting.

As his tale unfolded on that long-ago road trip, Howard's sombre profile flickered in the headlights of the oncoming cars; like Sid, he was quite a performer. That was all well and good, I said, and I could understand why Sid was drawn south by the great magnet of London, seeking opportunity and anonymity in the age-old tradition of fortune-seekers and ne'er-do-wells. But I couldn't understand why lovely widowed Lily Madeley had fallen for this scoundrel when he showed up in the Widow's Son looking for digs.

Howard turned towards me, and the car drifted into the

fast lane. I clutched the sides of my seat and prepared to die, but there was nothing behind us, or if there was, its brakes were good.

'She wanted a child, Bert. Ted was dead, and she was getting on a bit. It wasn't him she fell for, it was me.'

I'd been smitten by the image of the beautiful Yorkshireman with brooding eyes and the silent waif-like child at his side, and I could understand how they had pierced Lily's tender heart. I had been conceived soon after . . .

'Heh heh heh!' Fast forward thirty-plus years. Howard took a deep drag on his cigarette and swung one leg over the arm of his chair, chuckling, 'Then I decided I'd had enough belting, and it was your turn. I'm sorry, little Bertie.' He didn't look sorry at all.

'And there was something else I've been trying to remember. The rope. A canal. A bridge . . .'

'Ah yes . . . !'

At that moment, the sound of a key in the lock made us both turn. The door opened and Inna appeared in the hall, looking flushed and windswept. There was something different about her appearance, she looked somehow younger and livelier, but I couldn't put my finger on it.

'Hello, Bertie. Hello . . .' She looked from me to Howard.

He looked from her to me.

'Howard, let me introduce Inna, a friend of Mother's. She's living here now.'

A knowing smile spread over his face. 'Onshontay, madame.'

He kissed her hand and winked at me. I could tell what he was thinking. Her cheeks were pink from the wind and her eyes were bright, but for godssake, she must be in her seventies.

'Inna, this is Howard, my –'

'Aha! I know. I understand. No problem wit me.' She winked

theatrically at me and did a little bow to him. 'You like it slatki, Mister Howvord?'

'No,' I interrupted. 'No, thanks, Inna. We're fine.'

I still didn't trust her.

'You want I go out?' she asked.

'No . . .'

'What are slapki?' asked Howard, nursing a lewd smile.

'Aha! I think you will very like it, Mister Howvord!' She pursed her mouth kissily. 'Very sweety sweet.'

'Oh yeah?' Despite her age, he looked genuinely interested, the old rake.

'No, thanks, Inna. Really.'

'Nuh, you no like you no ittit, Mister Bertie.'

With a huff, she disappeared into the kitchen. Howard did gross finger-pointing gestures behind her back. I shook my head. He wiggled his fingers lustfully. I could see where this was going and I reckoned alcohol was needed.

'Look, I think I'll go and get that whisky after all. It goes well with slatki. Have you still got that tenner, Howard?'

All was quiet as I crossed the twilit grove, and the lights were on in Luigi's. There was something I needed more than whisky: calm, coffee and common sense. The temptation was too great. Luigi greeted me like a long-lost friend, although it was barely a week since I'd been in. I leaned my elbows on the counter and inhaled. Soon the heavenly aroma of coffee banished the sour smell of whisky breath and the dangerous scent of slapski, as the present banishes the past.

'The usual? Latte with?' He wielded the tamper. 'Where you been, boss? I been missing you.'

'My mother died. I had my bike nicked. I sustained an injury at the funeral.' I hadn't intended to get emotional, but once I'd started, it just poured out of me. 'And, to be frank, the coffee's gone downhill in here. You're taking this austerity thing too literally, Lu.'

'Okay. Sorry about your mum, boss. I got some of that old blend left, I make it special for you.' He reached under the counter.

'Thanks, Lu.' I felt better after I'd got it off my chest. 'And I don't like this new newspaper you've signed up for either. A tale told by an idiot, full of sound and fury, signifying nothing. I preferred the *Guardian*.'

'I know, boss, but is cheaper, and other customers like it.'

An unwelcome thought butted into my mind. Could my lovely neighbour be a covert *Daily Mail* reader? Surely she was too sweet and guileless for that poisonous brew? I picked it up just out of curiosity and positioned myself with my coffee by the window where I could see the comings and goings in the street. The coffee was barely acceptable, but the newspaper was utterly engrossing, full of tax avoidance scams and celebrities' boob jobs gone wrong. And Kardashians, whatever they are. You don't get that in the *Guardian*.

I'd almost finished the coffee when a swift black shadow in the street outside the window caught my eye. It was her. She was running in the direction of the flats, like a darling deer fleeing the hunter's arrows. I thought of springing up to follow, but I didn't act on my impulse because she would already be halfway through the grove – and besides, I was halfway through a fascinating article in the *Daily Mail* speculating that George Clooney had had cosmetic treatment on his wedding tackle – testicle smoothing, apparently – which filled me with an agreeable Schadenfreude.

When I had finished reading, I took the change from Howard's tenner and strolled up the road to Lidl to get the whisky.

★

Twenty minutes later I opened the door to the flat to be greeted by the pleasant steamy smell of kobaski in yushka, beneath which a faint whiff of whisky was still noticeable, and a slight taint of burning in the air. Inna was bustling about in her pinny, laying the table with a clatter. Howard was slumped in the same armchair holding a bloodstained handkerchief to his nose. There were some small spots of blood on the carpet.

'Hi, Inna,' I greeted her with a peck on the cheek. 'Every-thing okay?'

She pushed me away. 'Oy! You tell me he homosexy!'

Howard moaned, dabbing his nose, 'I like a bit of slapski, but I didn't think she'd get quite so rough.' I noticed some pieces of broken china on the floor. 'Did you get the whisky? Blimey, you don't get much for a tenner these days.'

Just then, the doorbell rang. *Ding dong!* Inna scuttled over to open it, still holding a fistful of cutlery in her hand.

A woman's voice, as sweet as a harp. 'I'm sorry to trouble you. I've run out of coffee . . .'

Violet! I jumped up. My heart was beating madly.

'Sorry. We got no coffee.' Inna slammed the door.

When his nose had stopped bleeding and he had finished most of the whisky, Howard wandered out into the night with an air of disappointment. I accompanied him to the lift.

'Come back and see me again, won't you?'

'I don't think so, Bertie, not while *she's* here. Don't know what you see in her.'

'It's not what you think.'

'It never is.'

With a sigh, the pissy lift carried him away.

Inna was equally adamant. 'I told him go boil his kobaska. He nearly set fire on flat. Look!'

There was indeed an ugly burn-mark on the upholstery. I

extracted the orange Bic lighter from down the back of the armchair, where it had lodged itself, and put it in my pocket. It was still half full. We'd had a lucky escape.

'Calm down, Inna.' I put my hand on her arm, and then I realised what had changed about her appearance.

Instead of a neat silver coil at the back of her head, there was a coil of glossy black. She had dyed her hair. But why?

VIOLET: *Horace Nzangu*

Violet washes and oils her hair in the shower and wraps it in a warm towel. While it's drying, she picks up the phone and dials her parents' number in Bakewell.

Handling your parents can be tricky, steering that fine course between their protectiveness and her need to live her own life. She'd intended to wait until she had a new job lined up or some good news to share before phoning her mum – easier to keep up a cheerful tone with texts and emails than to hide the unhappiness in your voice – but after her run-in with Marc and her conversation with Mr Rowland, something has snapped inside her. She's lost the confidence, drummed into her for twenty-three years by her parents and her schools, that here in Britain it doesn't matter who you are or where you come from, that hard work pays off, the good guy always triumphs, and integrity wins through in the end.

'Violet, that big city is depressing you, why don't you come back home for a while?' Her mother, as always, can tell when she's upset. 'It's so nice up here in summer.'

It's a tempting thought, to pack in her job and have her mother look after her while she chills in her bedroom, listens to music, and applies for new jobs. But she knows she would be fed up in less than a week – especially as all the kids she was at school with have moved away, apart from the drop-outs who hang around the square with spliffs and hard-luck stories. After London, the smallness of Bakewell depresses her.

'Thanks, Mum. I'll think about it. But it's cool here,

honestly. I've met loads of interesting people, and I'm campaigning to save a grove of cherry trees. Don't worry about me.'

Saying the words out loud makes her feel more positive.

'So you have become a tree-hugger, *mpenzi*?'

'Sort of. I guess.'

Her mother laughs. 'Like Wangari Maathai. She was a great Kenyan fighter for trees and for human rights. Whenever Wangari had something to celebrate, she planted a Nandi Flame tree.'

She has heard this story about Wangari Maathai several times, but never taken much notice before.

'Yeah, I remember those trees. Beautiful. Like cherry blossom.'

'Wangari said trees and people both have rights, and they need each other.'

'It's true. I wish she was here in London! The trees have brought the people together.'

She's noticed that in the face of their common enemy, the community spirit at Madeley Court has come alive. Neighbours now greet each other and stop to talk, and all the bitching is about the Council, not about each other. There are always little knots of people down in the grove, and the tambourine girls, who apparently are mostly sixth-formers at the local school, have started putting on regular noisy shows, which, if she's to be perfectly truthful, can get a bit annoying. It's like Langata, both the friendliness and the racket.

'Wangari linked the deforestation of Kenya to the despoilment of the country's wealth. But even she couldn't stop it. There is a new corruption scandal every day,' her mother says.

'Talking of corruption, Mum, when you were in Kenya, did you ever hear of someone called Horace Nzangu? A businessman?'

'Nzangu. It's quite a common name . . .' Her mother pauses. 'I think there was someone called Nzangu in our hospital many years ago, who was involved in a scandal about reusing syringes.'

'Hm. Grandma once mentioned that while Babu Josaphat was working in the hospital administration he discovered some wrongdoing relating to supplies and went to the police. Then she clammed up. She wouldn't say any more.' She still remembers Njoki's tight angry mouth and frightened eyes. 'Could that be the same man?'

'Could be. Your Babu's body was found by the roadside soon after he went to the police. No one was sure whether it was an accident or a deliberate killing. In those days there was much talk of witchcraft, and everyone was afraid. People who spoke out died mysteriously, so Njoki never talked about it.' Her mother lowers her voice. 'Be careful, Violet. These people are more powerful and ruthless than you can imagine.'

The sad resignation in her mum's tone makes her feel irritated. Why do people just accept all that crap without doing anything about it?

'But that's all old history and folk tales. If we know there's a crime, we should speak up, right?'

'Of course we must speak the truth, even if it means taking a risk. But who will listen to us if we don't have any evidence?'

'I think I may have the evidence.'

BERTHOLD: *Money troubles*

My dismal existence, already thrown into crisis by the death of my mother, imminent homelessness, unrequited love and the revelations about my criminal past, was now under attack on a new front. I had long been in avoidance about my financial situation, but the irrefutable evidence came out one day when my debit card was declined in Lidl. To my utter humiliation, in front of a whole queue of lunchtime shoppers, I was outed as a pauper.

'Look, there must have been a mistake. I'm a regular customer in here. Don't you recognise me? I spend hundreds of pounds . . . well, *lots* of pounds, on your crap products. I could switch my loyalty to Waitrose, you know. You're not the only supermarket around here,' I blustered.

'Cash or card?' the pretty check-out girl repeated. Her name-tag was full of *z*s and *ch*s. Polish, perhaps.

I knew in my heart that I was doomed and the pound of flesh would eventually be carved from me, but you have to protest, don't you, at the sheer pettifogging meanness of life? I took a breath, stabbed the air and bellowed, 'Therefore, Jew, though justice be thy plea, consider this! That, in the course of justice, none of us should see salvation! WE DO PRAY FOR MERCY AND THAT SAME PRAYER DOTH TEACH US ALL TO RENDER THE DEEDS OF MERCY!!!'

Why was I shouting? Surely Portia hadn't shouted at Shylock? The girl pressed the buzzer for the manager who arrived, harassed and sweaty, in a polyester shirt with a pile of nappy boxes under his arm.

'This gentleman is refuse to pay,' said the girl. 'He make anti-Semitic speech.'

The people in the lengthening queue behind were stabbing me with their eyes.

In the end, I returned the bottle of sherry and a jar of coffee to the shelves. Fortunately, I had enough cash in my pockets for a tin of tuna, a loaf of sliced bread and an iceberg lettuce. Still, it was a wake-up call. There would be no more lattes at Luigi's for the foreseeable future.

I stumbled back to the flat with my pitiful bag of retail therapy, where another outrage awaited me, in the form of a small blue letter that had been slipped under the door while I was out.

Dear Berthold,

We've been watching you and we think there is something fishy going on, you are trying to rob us of our birthright. We need to resolve the flat, and we would like to come to an arrangement with you without having to involve solicitors. We are getting desparate with waiting.

Your loving sister,
Jenny

PS: Our pet bunny is buried under a cherry tree in the garden so you can see why we are despirate to come home to be near his grave.
Margaret

I crumpled the letter and threw it into the recycling bin, annoyed but not alarmed. Howard had alerted me to their wiles. No wonder they wanted to avoid the law. Ha! Their bloody pet bunny of fifty years ago! And they call that despirate (sic). I could bloody show them what desperation is.

While Mother was alive, she had enjoyed three pensions – her DSS 'old age' pension, her NHS pension from her speech therapist years, and a widow's pension from Ted Madeley. In other words, she was comfortably provided for, if not quite in the oligarch league, and we'd lived sheltered from the cold winds of austerity. Her pensions, plus whatever money she had received from my dad, had been enough for us both to manage on comfortably, covering the rent, living expenses, evenings out at the Curzon, and even the occasional little holiday. I felt tempted to leave the pensions in place just for a while, until my finances were on a more secure footing, but Jimmy had warned me against it.

'You'll get done. Besides, your finances are never going to be secure, are they?'

He was probably right. My own income was the pittance I got from Jobseeker's Allowance augmented occasionally by short-run, ill-paid roles in small grant-funded theatres where the stage set was inevitably a table and a wooden chair and the actors could sometimes outnumber the audience – a commitment to Art which I doubt George Clooney has ever experienced.

Like many actors, I was no stranger to the dole office, but I always regarded the dole as a stopgap, not a solution. I mean, no one can really live on £72.40 a week, can they? My case worker was a handsome young black guy called Justin, with a gold front tooth and a degree in media studies. He took my case seriously, as though my appearance in a series of deadbeat fringe shows was his personal contribution to the arts. He persuaded the local Job Centre to subscribe to *The Stage*, and for his sake I read it regularly, and attended auditions whenever something promising came up.

My last such foray had been to audition for the part of Lucky in *Waiting for Godot* at The Bridge, a fortnight before Mother died. Fortunately, I didn't get it. Who wants to spend their evenings dragged around by a rope on a draughty stage under a railway bridge in Poplar? Justin had been curious when I gave him my edited feedback.

'So what's it about, this *Waiting for Godot*? I've heard the name.'

'It's about two guys under a tree waiting for someone who doesn't turn up.'

'Really? That's it?'

'Well, it's philosophical. About the meaninglessness of life.'

'In my opinion you're best off out of it, Mr Sidebottom.'

Meaninglessness notwithstanding, my situation was now so desperate I told Justin I would be glad of anything. He was sad to see my status slip from art to survival, but he informed me there were currently openings for actors dressed as Mickey Mouse to hand out leaflets at the Brent Cross shopping centre.

'Or there's one here that might suit you,' he said, scrolling down his screen. 'A funeral parlour in North London is looking for an actor with a good voice for burials and cremation ceremonies. Zero-hours contract but possibility of overtime.'

'Zero hours? What's that mean?'

'It's like that play you said, *Waiting for Whatsit*. Like you're permanently on call, but they only pay you if they call you up?'

It reminded me of Mother's story of Grandad Bob and the dockers waiting for the brass tallies to be handed out. A strong reluctance tugged at my soul. 'I'll look into it,' I said.

Maybe Inna could contribute to the rent, but when I suggested this, she looked aghast, crossed herself, and told me to apply for Housing Benefit. I was reluctant to go down this road because of what Mrs Penny had said. It would open me up to a whole new level of official nose-pokery. But it did add to the urgency of transferring the tenancy agreement to me. Which brought us back to the question of her signature.

Inna tossed her glossy, newly black plaits and flatly denied my accusation. 'Oy! You think I got crazy, Mister Bertie? Why you think I sign Inna Alfandari?'

The question of the wrong signature preyed on my mind. Was Inna really as stupid as she pretended, or did she have a different agenda? Was there a malign plan at the back of her gobabki-addled mind to register the tenancy of the flat in her own name?

I recalled that when she had signed that Tenancy Transfer form *Inna Alfandari* instead of *Lily Lukashenko*, Mrs Penny had folded it without a glance and slipped it back into the file. Where I hoped it would stay un-looked-at for another fifty years. But what if Mrs Penny noticed the wrong name when she opened the file?

I could invent another marriage/death/divorce which Inna, aka Lily, had forgotten about in her confusion. Maybe Jimmy the Dog would help with a forged death certificate – he owed me one. I could say that my mother had forgotten who she was and had inadvertently written down a friend's name. Surely demented old people do that sort of thing all the time? Or I could simply steal the mis-signed document and destroy it. With all these possibilities roiling in my mind, I put on a clean shirt, attended to a call of nature, gathered together my birth certificate and Mother's marriage certificate to Wicked Sid, and prepared to brazen it out with Mrs Penny.

BERTHOLD: *Eustachia*

Although there was no actual evidence of Mother's love affair with Lubetkin, there were tantalising clues hidden about the flat. For example, there was a book about modern architecture that Mother kept in the loo on the shelf above the loo roll, which featured the work of Berthold Lubetkin, with torn strips of newspaper between the Lubetkin pages for book-marks. It had nice pictures, including one of Madeley Court, and small snatches of text, just long enough for an average bowel movement. As it happened, I had been reading it on the very morning I had arranged to meet Mrs Penny.

Her office was on the eighth floor of a grim concrete build-ing around the back of the Town Hall. Lubetkin himself, according to this book, had worked with Ove Arup, the mas-ter of concrete; but his concrete swirled and flowed into playful patterns or uncluttered lines. 'Nothing is too good for ordi-nary people,' he had said. The council offices, I surmised, were an example of the 'new brutalist' school of architecture, a bracing offspring of Lubetkin's modernism that made no con-cessions to bourgeois notions like 'beauty', which was strictly for wimps. This council building no longer housed the benign supportive state that Lubetkin and his post-war colleagues had tried to engineer, but a bossy, intrusive, policing 'Them' whose role was to keep the undeserving poor in their place. In fact it was the perfect backdrop for nosy Mrs Penny and her flea-bitten ankles.

I took the lift (even in here, someone had pissed) up to floor eight and walked along a corridor lit with blinking neon and floored with carpet tiles in a jarring mosaic of camouflage green and battleship grey. If, as Lubetkin proposed, the surroundings in which we live help to mould our souls, then this environment did not bode well for my meeting with Mrs Penny.

Her name, with four others, was on the door. They sounded more like a crew of international deadbeats than public servants. Mr Matt Longweil, Mr En Nuy Yeux, Mr Fred Treg, Miss Ignacia Noiosa, Mrs Eustachia Penny.

Eustachia! Blimey!

It was a large office with five desks, but none of the other officers was there; presumably they were all out terrorising innocent tenants in their homes. Mrs Penny's desk was neat and tidy, with orderly papers, a spotted mug full of sharpened pencils, and a fluffy teddy bear with a spotted ribbon. By contrast the desk next to hers, presumably Miss Ignacia Noiosa's, was strewn with papers, dead teacups, a sickly cactus and an ashtray overflowing with scarlet-lipstick-tipped cigarette butts. Which was odd, I thought, because smoking is usually prohibited in offices, especially in shared offices.

'Come in! Good to see you. Please, take a seat, Mr Lukashenko.' Mrs Penny indicated a hard wooden chair with splintery edges.

'Sidebottom,' I said.

'Sidebottom?'

'My mother remarried. Remember we talked about it? I've brought the marriage certificate and my birth certificate.'

'Ah, yes, I remember now. Dear old lady. Three husbands. A little confused. No wonder.'

As I sat down, I felt a heavy clink in the pocket of my jacket. With my left hand I explored my jacket pocket: two coins – probably a 50p and a £1 – and something smooth and long. I peeped surreptitiously. Howard's Bic lighter.

Mrs Penny scrutinised my documents, nodded and reached for the clear plastic file she had brought to our flat. There, right at the top, was the green printed Tenancy Transfer form that Inna had signed with her own name. She opened it out and started to skim through it. Just at that moment, a telephone started to ring on one of the other desks. At first, she ignored it, and carried on scanning the form. The phone continued ringing: seven, eight . . . twelve, thirteen . . . nineteen, twenty . . .

'Excuse me.' She stomped over to the desk in the far corner, and picked up the receiver. Her back was towards me.

'Yes? . . . Sorry, Mr Treg's out of the office at the moment, can I help? . . . Urgent? . . . Emergency? . . . A fire? Oh dear . . . !'

I pricked up my ears. A fire? What a good idea! I clicked Howard's Bic and held it to the corner of a crumpled document in the waste-paper basket of the cigarette-butts desk. It smouldered for a moment, then a small flame took hold.

'. . . Nobody hurt, I hope . . . Thank heavens . . . !'

I whisked the Tenancy Transfer and a few other papers towards the flame, taking care to safeguard my precious certificates.

She smelled the smoke, turned around and screamed. I grabbed a half-full cup of tea off the desk and threw it at the bin. The fire fizzled, faltered, then picked up again. Mrs Penny tried to douse the flames with water from a kettle, but by now it was all burning briskly.

'Oh, hell!' She hit a glass-fronted alarm on the wall.

Sirens sounded. Soon there was a drumming of running feet outside in the corridor.

'You'd better get out!' I shouted, grabbing a fire extinguisher from the wall and directing it at the waste-paper basket, which immediately filled up with foam. 'Don't wait for me!'

The green Tenancy Transfer floated up on the foam, mangled and scorched, but with the signature still visible. *Inna Alfandari*. I added it to the flames. Then I raced down eight flights of new-brutalist stairs to the exit.

There was a carnival atmosphere down in the courtyard below the stairwell. Like birds freed from a cage, the council staff fluttered around and around, flapping and chattering, but only a few picked up the courage to take flight. Two fire engines arrived. Yellow-helmeted hunks played hoses on the windows, while others ventured inside.

Mrs Penny spotted me through the crowd, rushed up and threw her arms around me. 'Oh, Berthold! I hope you're okay! I kept telling Ignacia she shouldn't smoke in the office, but . . .'

She held me tight for just a moment longer than was strictly warranted by the occasion. I could smell her flowery perfume and feel her pneumatic breasts pressing on me through the fabric of my foam-spattered jacket. Down below the belt, the beast stirred. Which was strange, because he hadn't stirred like that when I had held lovely Violet in my arms.

'Fine. All's well that ends well,' murmured the beast's cerebral master.

'Thank you for trying to save my paperwork. Some of those old paper files go back years! The new ones are all on the computer, of course, but the old ones, like your mum's, are a piece of history.' She sighed. 'You were so heroic!'

Heroic! Put that in your pipe and smoke it, George Clooney.

'Don't mention it, Mrs Penny.' As I said her name, I wondered for the first time whether there was a Mr Penny.

'Please, call me Eustachia. Stacey for short.'

'Eustachia. What a pretty name. Isn't that something to do with tubes?'

'Yes. In the ears. Actually, I was born with a hearing problem. My mum liked the name.'

'It's quite unusual. But you're okay now?'

'I've grown out of it now. But as a kid I really struggled to keep up at school. I went through a phase of feeling hopeless and depressed.'

Depressed. I'd been in that bear pit myself. 'People don't realise –' I began.

'They don't know what it's like.' She raced on in full confessional flow, her voice soft and confiding. 'I felt so embarrassed about the way I talked, I hardly said a word all through my childhood. I just stayed in my room and talked to my teddies.'

This had suddenly become very personal. Her breasts, as if inflated by some intense private emotion, were still rising and falling directly below my nose.

'Then my parents split up. But I got sent to this wonderful speech therapist. She taught me how to speak clearly. She told me to go out and do something useful instead of sitting around feeling sorry for myself. "Always keep on the sunny side, Stacey," she used to say. After I took my A-levels, I went into local government. I reckoned there were a lot of people out there among our clients who were worse off than me.'

I glanced down at her ankles. They seemed shapelier, but the ugly scars were still there.

'That sounds a bit like me.'

'You, Berthold?' Her sweet face and direct manner, her own admission of vulnerability, invited confidence.

It was a long time since I had spoken to anyone about my breakdown. 'I got depressed when my daughter died. Meredith, she was called. My wife blamed me. Our marriage broke up. My stutter started up again because of the stress. Not the best thing for an actor.'

'You're an actor?'

'All the world's a stage.'

'Isn't that a quote by Shakespeare?'

'Absolutely. Shall we go and have a coffee? I know a nice p-place just up the road.'

VIOLET: Luigi's

Violet feels she deserves a treat. She's sat through an hour-long meeting with Marc this afternoon, avoiding his eyes and maintaining an air of utter cool throughout. Now she feels inexplicably sad, like she's mourning for something inside her that has died. Though she's still wearing the expensive uniform that goes with her job, her heart's no longer in it. It's not just Marc, it's the whole idea of wealth preservation that once seemed so glamorous, and now just seems sleazy. She takes her laptop into Luigi's to enjoy a real cappuccino while she checks her personal email and hunts for jobs online. There must be more worthwhile jobs out there.

She notices her eccentric neighbour Berthold is there too, sitting at a corner table deep in conversation with a pretty middle-aged woman with auburn hair. They both look a bit flushed. M-mm, she thinks. Something's going on there.

'Hi!' she greets him, but he just smiles mysteriously. He is strange, but not half as weird as the old lady he lives with – who, according to Len the wheelchair man, is not his mother at all, but just pretends to be. His new love-interest looks nice though, despite her funny hairstyle.

She logs on. There are emails from Jessie and Laura asking how she's getting on, and an invitation to a party at Billy's tonight. And – her pulse quickens – here's a response from a job she'd applied for, inviting her for an interview. It's a junior position with an investment company based at Canary Wharf, a household name, at least in some kinds of households. Good pay; terrific prospects. It's exactly what she'd been hoping for. But now she hesitates.

There's also an email from an NGO promoting women's enterprise in sub-Saharan Africa, inviting her for an interview. The pay is pitiful compared with the other, but the job is interesting and carries a lot of responsibility, and its African base is in Nairobi, so she'd be able to stay with her grandma. She can apply for both and make up her mind later.

Both jobs are asking for references, which is kind of awkward at the moment, but instead of just naming her professors at uni she writes an email to Gillian Chalmers, asking her to be a referee. She gets an automated 'Out of Office' response. Gillian Chalmers is in Bucharest but will attend to her message on her return; there is no indication when that will be. The closing date for both of the jobs is tomorrow. She takes her courage in both hands and fills in the forms online, naming Gillian Chalmers as her first referee.

BERTHOLD: *The Scottish play*

Mrs Penny phoned me next morning at nine o'clock. She said she had gathered together the singed and sodden forms from her office floor and wanted to express her gratitude. She didn't refer to our moment of body contact, and I didn't bring it up, but she did mention the coffee (Luigi had done us proud, with a double latte for me, and an extra-frothy cappuccino for her topped with chocolate, cinnamon *and* ground nutmeg), suggesting we might repeat the experience another day.

'Absolutely,' I said with faux enthusiasm, for I was beginning to regret my moment of weakness in the council courtyard. I'd detected a whiff of neediness in the way she had clung to me. There's no bigger turn-on for a man than sexual desire in a woman. But if you surrender to the beast and sleep with them, you're trapped. They suffocate you with their niceness, and next thing you know you're sitting in the back row of the multiplex every Saturday, eating popcorn and watching George Clooney. No thank you. Add to this that she was a hostile agent of 'Them', on whose whim I could be ousted from my home if I put a foot wrong, and you can see why I was holding back.

Besides, I was now bracing myself for another bureaucratic hassle. In the words of the Immortal Bard, 'When sorrows come, they come not single spies, but in battalions.' I had just received a letter from the Department of Work and Pensions, another outrider of 'Them', which winked at me evilly from its brown-envelope window.

We are conducting a radical overhaul of the system, which will put the needs of you the jobseeker first, it sneered, inviting me for a preliminary interview at Job Centre Plus to review my continuing entitlement to benefit.

I bumped into Legless Len in the ground-floor lobby, and learned that he had received one too. He was bristling with positivity.

'I reckon they've found me a job, Bert. They reassessed my capabilities!'

'That's brilliant, Len.'

'Let's hope you're in luck too, Bert.'

'As the Immortal Bard would say, the miserable have no other medicine but only hope.'

'That's truly profound. I'll add it to my collection of positive sayings.' He wheeled away, humming cheerfully.

When I arrived at the Job Centre for my appointment, I found to my dismay that gorgeous Justin had gone, and the new representative of 'Them' was George McReady, a lean foxy gingery man with a goatee beard and a Dundee accent.

'What happened to Justin?' I asked.

'He wasn't meeting his tarrgets, Mr Sideboatum,' he burred. 'And you're one of them. I see you were last employed four months ago, and that was only for two weeks.'

'Two weeks is bloody good, in my line of b-business.'

'Well, in my line of business it's pathetic. How many jobs have you actually applied forr?'

'Since then?' I racked my brain. It all seemed to blur into one long haze of failure. 'About ten. And f-four auditions.' Possibly I was exaggerating a bit.

He perused a dog-eared document covered in Justin's scribbles and ticks, and tutted.

'According to your agreement, your tarrget is six applications per week. Of which two in six should lead to an interview.'

'Six per week? That's absurd. Six p-p-per month would be p-pushing it.'

'Is this, or is it not, your signature, Mr Sideboatum?' He pushed the paper towards me.

My chest tightened. My head started to spin. His name and the vague hint of menace in his Dundee accent brought up a strange bubble in my memory of a long-ago performance of the Scottish play at Newcastle in which I'd played the porter. To great critical acclaim, I might add.

'Faith, sirr, it is.' I could hear the tense hush in the theatre, the audience breathless in their seats.

'When you signed, you committed yourself to six applications perr week. You're bound by the agrreement, and you've not perrforrmed.' He leaned across the desk with a leer, and I could feel the bones of my resolution snapping between his foxy jaws. 'Do you have any excuse to offer?'

'Faith sir, I was carousing till the second cock: and drink, sir, is a great p-provoker of nose-painting, sleep and urine.' There was a murmur of laughter in the audience.

McReady looked at me coldly. His eyes were very light grey, with hard points of black at the centre. 'Are you takin' the piss, Mr Sideboatum? If so, I dinna advise it.'

'Lechery, sirr, it provokes, and unprovokes; it provokes the desire, but takes away the p-perrforrmance.' More laughter.

'I've no idea what you're on about. But here's a couple of jobs to get you started. Come back same time next week. Let's see how you've got on. If not, it will give me great perrsonal pleasure to sanction your JSA, and send you for retraining.'

He clicked the print button, and handed me two sheets containing details of the Mickey Mouse job and the funeral parlour job.

'Sanction?' This wasn't in the script.

'In your case it means cut it off.' He flicked his fingers across his throat. 'Next!'

An aged hunched man, unshaved, uncombed, and reeking of alcohol, shuffled over and slumped in the chair I had vacated, while I shuffled over to the side-room where the computers and printers were chained to desks under the steely eye of a chignoned matron with a cruel mouth and ultra-clean hands who could have been a central-casting Scottish Lady.

I started to draft an application for the funeral parlour – it was indeed Wrest 'n' Piece – but an image floated into my mind of Jimmy the Dog at my mother's funeral, floundering in the mud with an unknown corpse, declaring, 'We're helping to prepare the unemployed for useful jobs.' Not me, Jimmy, not me. I put the sheet aside and reached for the Mickey Mouse application. 'Drama students or similar sought for retail promotion opportunity.'

The aged alcoholic who had followed me into the interview was now slumped in front of the computer next to mine, stinking heavily and snoring lightly. His screen read: *Retraining opportunities in retail*.

The Scottish Lady approached, rubbing her hands and muttering, 'Who'd have thought an old man to have so much booze in him.'

She kicked the back of his chair. He jumped up with a start and stared around him with bloodshot eyes, his glance falling on the paper I had just discarded.

'Aaargh! The graveyard ghouls!' He leaned towards me and laid a hand on my arm. 'Don't touch it without a bunch of garlic, mate!'

'You know the firm?'

'Wrest 'n' Piece. Worked for them for forty years. Know

everything there is to know about laying out a corpse. It was a good firm while old Mr Wrest was in charge.' He tossed his grizzled locks. 'Then he died and his daughter took over – with her big-nose boyfriend, James. Decided to expand the business. Privately managed cems and crems, bidding for local authority contracts. Tried to cut their costs. Laid off anybody that knew anything about bodies. Brought in a bunch of young uns off the dole to do it for free.'

'For free?'

'Unpaid work experience. Thirty hours a week.' He gripped my arm. 'They wanted me to train them up before I left. Sod that, I said. You've got to show a bit of respect for the dead. Mind you, I never got as much lip from a corpse as I did from them young uns.'

'Are you . . . ?' Through a horror of mud and pain a memory crawled into my mind, '. . . Philip?'

'Phil Gatsnug. That's me. Master mortician. Artist of the dead.'

'My mother –'

'Yeah, the old lady. Your mum, was it? Awful shame. I did my best, but the young uns messed her up. We had to send her straight to cremation. But you should ask for her ashes. They always give you the ashes.'

'Thanks, Phil. I got the ashes. But how can I be sure they're the right ones? Given the cock-ups we've had so far.'

'Sometimes they do mix 'em up.' He fixed me with a blood-shot gaze. 'Whoever they belong to, my friend, treat 'em with respect. It's somebody's mum or dad. Say a prayer and sprinkle them in a nice place. Not on your porridge, ha ha!'

His words struck a chord in me. I resolved forthwith to honour the ashes of the unknown crematee in the hope that someone would do the same for Mother; I would sprinkle them at the heart of the cherry grove that she had loved. Of course, if anyone asked I would have to pretend it was a dead parrot.

'So you resigned from your job?' I asked.

'Yes, and according to this austerity Nazi,' he waved his arms in the direction of foxy McReady, 'it makes me voluntarily unemployed, so I'm not entitled to any money for three months. I've been living off tinned beans from the charity food bank for the past fortnight, but it runs out tomorrow. I'll have to go and scrounge some bread off the pigeons in the park.'

'But with your skills, surely you'd find another job easily? People are dying all the time. Thou know'st 'tis common; all that lives must die.'

'Not enough, mate. Besides, all the big money is in weddings: funerals they want to do on the cheap. I won't compromise, see? I like to do a good job.'

I felt a sudden bond of kinship with this wounded man, this fellow soldier injured in life's battle against the mean, the slick, the self-serving, the 'it'll have to do' mentality. Despite the odds stacked against him, he had tried to do the right thing by my mother. I was glad that he'd been the last person to handle her mortal remains.

'Mmm. Thanks for trying, pal. Maybe you should set up on your own.'

'Good idea, mate.'

With a heavy heart I completed the application form for the Mickey Mouse job, signed it, and gave it to 'Them' to process.

When I tiptoed out of the Job Centre, Phil Gatsnug was asleep again, his head resting on the keyboard.

I got back to Madeley Court around five o'clock of a sultry afternoon; I had wasted most of the sweet day in the airless Job

Centre. Legless Len was hanging around in the grove enjoying the last of the sunshine that dappled through the cherry leaves.

'How did it go, pal?' I asked him.

'Great.' He tipped up his Arsenal cap so I could see his shining face. 'Telephone sales. Well-known legal firm. My job will be informing the public of their right to redress for wrongful mis-selling of financial services. Not bad, eh? I'll be glad to be off benefit and earning again. Like the man at the Job Centre said, it'll build my self-esteem and boost my aspirations.' His face glowed. 'He said he's incredibly passionate about aspiration.'

Had I been wrong to sneer at Len's dreams? There were jobs out there, even for the legless. If double amputation was no impediment to employment, why should a slight stress-stutter hold me back? Maybe Nazi George truly had my best interests at heart and all I really needed was a kick up the backside. My eyes watered with gratitude and resolve. Mickey Mouse, here I come!

'Well done, Len! Great! When d'you start?'

'Straight away. Self-employed. Flexible working. Zero-hours contract. How about yourself, Bert?'

'Yeah, I sent off an application too.'

Inna was in the kitchen, slapping minced pork for kobabski about on a chopping board, mixing in crushed garlic and finely chopped herbs, ready to force through a wide funnel into a skin made from the gut of some unknown animal. Her neat, newly black plait was coiled at the back of her head, and a frown of concentration sat between her stern black brows. In the weeks that she had lived with me, her cuisine had become more sophisticated, though using the same basic ingredients.

I told her the good news concerning the flat, and she laughed and wiped her hands on her apron before giving me a hug. Then we tipped back a glass of vodka to celebrate.

I didn't have the heart to tell her that the tenancy transfer was all but complete and I soon wouldn't be needing her services any more.

VIOLET: Chainsaw

Violet is woken earlier than usual on Monday morning by a strange sound, a persistent whining rather like a dentist's drill; only it isn't inside her head, it's definitely coming from outside. She lies in the semi-dark and listens, trying to work out what it could be but feeling too lazy to get up and find out. Then a nearer, more familiar sound startles her. It's Pidgie tapping on her window, not the usual friendly 'Hey, let's have breakfast' kind of tapping, but an urgent, wild hammering with his beak, beating with his wings against the glass. She draws back the blue sari and looks out.

There he is on the balcony. She throws a bit of bread down for him, but he ignores it, and hops on and off the parapet with his one foot, flapping his wings dementedly. Then the whining sound starts up again and she sees to her horror that a man with a chainsaw is sitting in the cradle of a cherry-picker truck backed up close to Pidgie's tree.

'Stop! Stop!' she screams, but her voice doesn't carry, or the man ignores it.

Still in her pyjamas, she runs to the next-door flat and hammers on the door. The old lady, Inna, opens it, and behind her, peering over her shoulder and wearing only the bottom half of a pair of paisley pyjamas, stands Berthold. He looks startled.

'Come in. Please.'

'The cherry trees! They're cutting them down! We've got to get everyone out there!'

He runs back into the flat to look out of the front window.

She follows. Down there in the cherry grove two men in hard hats are waving chainsaws; a bulldozer with a raised platform on the front is positioned directly under Pidgie's tree. But what are those three large mushroomy-looking things that seem to have sprouted up overnight on the grass between the trees? They look a bit like tents.

'Excuse me; I'd better get some clothes on.' She races back next door and pulls on her jeans and T-shirt.

By the time she gets down to the grove, Berthold is already there. He is still wearing just the bottom half of his pyjamas, and around his bare waist is a bicycle chain, locked securely on to the trunk of Pidgie's tree. The sawing has stopped.

'Oh, Berthold!' She flings her arms around him. 'You're a hero!'

By now it's eight o'clock and half the population of Madeley Court has gathered in the garden. They are jeering and shouting and banging tambourines, and Mrs Cracey is waving her umbrella. A half-naked man from one of the tents is shouting at the chainsaw men in some foreign language.

Suddenly everyone stops and stares as a girl emerges from the tent wearing a skimpy shift that is open to the waist, with a plump naked baby clamped to her breast covered only by a veil of dark hair. She sits down on a bench under a tree, cradling the baby in her arms. It is a moment of pure magic amidst the pandemonium: the baby's eyes are shut, his jaws are moving rhythmically, a milky leak dribbles down her breast and the baby stretches out tiny fingers to stroke his mother while she gazes down at him with a faraway look in her eyes. Then the baby stirs, whimpers and burps up a big gob of curds; the spell is broken.

At about eight fifteen she catches sight of Greg Smith

striding towards them in his suit, his mobile phone pressed to his ear and a peeved expression on his face.

'Hi!' He breaks into a smile when he sees her. 'What's going on here?'

'They've started cutting down the cherry trees! Can't you do anything to stop them, Greg?'

'Probably.' He puts his phone back into his pocket, and marches up to the workmen. 'Where's your permit?' he barks.

'We don't need a permit,' says the one driving the bulldozer.

'Of course we have a permit, don't we, Dez? We're not cowboys,' says the younger one, who has taken off his hard hat to reveal an auburn pigtail.

'Not cowboys, not gyppos,' adds Dez, looking pointedly at Berthold.

She knows 'gyppos' is a racist term for travellers, but she cannot see why it would apply to Berthold in his paisley-pattern, M&S-style pyjamas.

The two men rummage through their pockets for a permit. 'I'll have a look in the van.' The one with the pigtail sprints across the grass and comes back a moment later with a printed form.

Greg takes it out of the man's hands and unfolds it. She cranes over his shoulder.

'I think the date's wrong,' she says. 'The council meeting isn't until next week.'

'Well spotted, Violet. I'll take a copy and check whether this is valid. Thanks.' Greg folds it into his breast pocket. 'If it's not valid, you realise you'll be personally liable for any damage to council property. That includes parks and gardens. Sorry – must rush!' he winks at her, and strides off.

The workmen look put out. They pack up their tools and amble away towards their van.

She feels a bit sorry for them. She glances across at Berthold, still chained to the tree in his pyjama bottoms, and feels a bit sorry for him too.

'Why don't you get your clothes on and come for a coffee, Berthold?'

'I can't. I left the key upstairs. Can you go and get it off Inna?'

BERTHOLD: *Chainsaw*

'Oh, Berthold!' She flung her arms around me. 'You're a hero!'

Twice in one week. Things were looking up. First the plump Eustachia (I couldn't bring myself to call her Stacey) and now the slender Violet. It was a triumph of Clooneyesque proportions. Yes, it was almost worth the discomfort of the bark of the cherry tree grating against my naked back, and the particularly annoying twig digging in just beneath my left shoulder blade.

Then Mrs Crazy had arrived on the scene wearing a shower cap over her stiff faux-blonde bouffant, purple-coated, fully bejewelled, and armed with two umbrellas. She immediately set about the chainsaw man, who dropped the saw on the ground, where it whirled and whined until the other hard-hat risked his fingers to catch it and turn it off.

While they were arguing between themselves, a flap opened at the side of one of the tents, and a man emerged, a tall overweight man with shoulder-length hair, wearing nothing but a pair of saggy, baggy Y-fronts.

He yawned, scratched his head, and exclaimed, *'Ce fucking este acest fucking zgomot? Du te fucking de aici!'*

His language was incomprehensible but his meaning was not. The second hard-hat, the one who now had the saw in his hands, raised it in a threatening way and said, 'You'd better get those tents moved. We're clearing all these trees, and you're in the way.'

The Y-fronts man said, *'Nu am nici o fucking idee despre ce este*

fucking vorba. Du te fucking de aici! Am incercat sa fucking dorm!'
He fished a box of matches and a bent cigarette from the pouch
of his grisly Y-fronts, straightened it out and lit it.

'Did you hear what I said, mate? You no speekee English?
Fuckee offee back to your own countree.' The hard-hat
switched the chainsaw on and waved it about some more.

The Y-fronts man puffed meditatively.

'Chill, Dez.' The second hard-hat removed his yellow helmet and shook his head. A thin plait of hair secured with a
rubber band tumbled on to his shoulder. 'We don't want to get
into no fights.'

Mrs Crazy, not persuaded by his pacific rhetoric, thumped
him on his un-helmeted head with an umbrella. He staggered
and fell against the tent. The tent flap opened again and a
young woman crawled out on her hands and knees.

'Ce se intampla? Cine sunt acesti oameni?'

She looked about the same age as Violet, with dark eyes and
long, glossy black hair cascading Magdalene-like down her
shoulders, which was just as well because she seemed to be
wearing nothing at all apart from a pair of red polka-dot
panties.

'Du te inapoi in cort, Ramona! Nu ai nici o fucking modestie!' the
man yelled at her.

The young woman threw him a look and withdrew into the
tent, only to re-emerge a few minutes later with a baby.

It was at this point that Violet lost the plot. She rushed up to
some sharp-suited, up-himself creep who was taking a short
cut through the grove on his way to the City while talking
loudly in an Eton drawl on his mobile phone, and asked him to
help. He ordered the hard-hats to stop, and they backed off in
the deferential way of the working classes confronted by their
natural superiors. Violet gave him one of those sweet girly
looks, and I thought she was going to throw her arms around

him too, but fortunately she didn't, and off he went on his indomitable way.

'*Costum fucking grozav*,' said the underpants man admiringly to his departing back.

Then the workmen zoomed off in their van, and there was now no conceivable reason for me still to be chained up here almost an hour later. It had been a mistake to trust Inna with the key. She had said she would follow in a few minutes with some coffee and toast, and bring the key to unchain me at the right moment. What in God's name had happened to her?

While not wishing in any way to make light of Jesus' suffering on the cross, there were certain parallels in our situation, which put me in a meditative frame of mind while I awaited my release. I thought of my dear mother embarked on her fearsome journey to the undiscovered country, her ashes mixed with those of strangers and scattered to the winds by unknown hands. Yet there was a kind of consolation in the mixing: she was what you'd nowadays call 'a people person'; she wouldn't have wanted to travel that way alone.

The years she had lived at Madeley Court had been rich with love, friendship and mutuality – years of believing that a better world was possible if we would only give it a try. Years of pre-school playgroups and after-school crèches, allotment gardens and tenants committees, tombolas for Africa and India, fasts to free Mandela, anti-nuclear coffee mornings and solidarity barbecues. When the first Jamaican family had moved into the block in 1968 and Enoch Powell had warned of 'rivers of blood', Mum had plied them with rivers of tea. My childhood had been lived in a world designed by Berthold Lubetkin and charmed into being by Aneurin Bevan – paternalistic maybe, but untainted by cynicism and self-interest. An uncynical tear sprang to my eye. Chained with my back to the road, my eyes feasted on the fine proportions of Lubetkin's building, the private spaces and the communal spaces interlinked, the winding line of the walkway through the gardens uniting his vision.

If only Mother had been here to defend her domain and the ideals it embodied, wielding her umbrella alongside Mrs Crazy! But what would she have made of the long-haired tent-dwellers messily encamped in her cherry orchard? Would she have admired them as free spirits and adventurers, or abjured them as lazy ne'er-do-wells? You could never tell with Mother. She was vehemently critical of idleness, drunkenness and bad language. On the other hand, since her retirement, she had seldom been out of her dressing gown before noon, her sherry habit was legendary, and she had tried to teach Flossie to swear at the television. She deplored promiscuity, but she adored babies, whatever their parentage. Women are soft that way. Even bloody Inna – damn her, where the hell had she got to with that key? – never missed a chance to gawp into a stranger's pram.

On the wall in my room I have a photo of Stephanie and Meredith in that same pose, taken in our old flat in Clapham: Stephanie is smiling, not at me, not at the camera, but at her own inner pleasure; Meredith is a fat greedy blob of sensuality with a wisp of dark hair on her crown. If she had lived, she would be twenty-three now. If she had lived, perhaps Stephanie and I would still be together, and I would have a string of acting credits and an almost-paid-off mortgage.

Chained as I was, unable to move, my mind was wandering off down the hazardous trails of the past. I pictured Meredith as she might be now, and the image that skipped into my mind was Violet with her swept-up hair and her dimpling smile, so beautiful and so vulnerable, though at the time of the accident she had seemed as sturdy as a pony on her little legs. Here she was at long last, trotting through the dappled shade of the cherry grove, holding a cup with a lid, and Inna overtaking her in her characteristic high-speed hobble, bringing two slices of toast on a plate, which she thrust into my hands.

'It, it.'

'But where's the key?' I asked.

Inna looked shifty. Her diamanté glasses had slipped to the bottom of her nose. 'Oy! Lost it!'

She turned to consult Violet over her shoulder; they exchanged a few muttered words.

'I'm afraid Inna's lost the key.' Violet smiled and surreptitiously tapped her temple.

'For God's sake, woman! You only had it for two minutes! How can you have lost it?'

Inna did her confused act, flapping her hands and rolling her eyes the way I had taught her. I wanted to slap her. The twig dug deeper under my left shoulder blade. Above me in the cherry tree there was a sudden rustling of leaves and a large gob of something warm and moist landed on my head.

'Naughty Pidgie!' Violet chided, and leaned forward with a tissue to wipe it away.

For a moment I felt the pressure of her firm young breast on my naked chest. Confusion overcame me.

'Have you looked down the side of the sofa, Inna? Have you looked in the rubbish bin? This is getting bloody uncomfortable,' I shouted.

Not only was it uncomfortable, it was also embarrassing. The eleven occupants of the three tents, including the Y-fronts man, the lady with the baby, a couple of colourfully dressed oldies and assorted children, had all gathered in a semicircle around my tree, and were whispering among themselves.

'Go away! Piss off! Bloody foreigners!' I shouted at them, which I know was wrong, but I was annoyed because the glory of the day – i.e. the saving of the cherry trees – which should have been mine alone, had to be shared with this scruffy-looking crew and the smarmy businessman-type, who seemed to be on far too friendly terms with Violet. After all, it was I who had raced down here half naked at seven o'clock and suffered the discomfort of quasi-martyrdom, while he swanned off to his office and they hung around smoking and gibbering.

They fell silent when I shouted, then an old guy in an embroidered shirt and baggy trousers stepped forward, grabbed my hand, pumped it up and down, and made an incomprehensible speech that went on for several minutes. The semicircle of onlookers clapped politely. Next, the young woman with the magnificent tits, the one who had been breastfeeding her baby, stepped forward and handed me a long, stiff pinkish object, partly wrapped in a white cloth. To my horror, it looked like a wizened dead baby, but on closer inspection turned out to be a large salami. The woman handed it over with a little bow and said a few words. The audience clapped.

Inna, who was still standing beside me, whispered in my ear, 'She say thank you for save our home and baby.'

The young woman then embraced me, pressing her magnificent tits against my bare chest, which was quite nice, though unfortunately she was now fully clothed. Having become accustomed to these female gestures of affection, I was beginning to realise what George Clooney has to put up with.

'He say you big hero, chain yourself on tree, stop workmen knocking down tent,' whispered Inna.

'Oh, tell them it was worth the suffering,' I said nobly, gulping down the now-tepid coffee which Violet had brought.

'Is it okay?' she asked.

'Perfect,' I said, though it was weak and too sweet, and I had to stop myself from saying 'like you'. But here was the puzzle – even when she brushed against me with her breast, when she stood so close to me that I could smell the soap on her skin, even when she touched me with her ethereal hands and wiped the bird shit from my brow, even when my love blazed up through all my being, the beast below did not stir.

Inna had approached the semicircle of campers and was talking very fast, with fulsome hand gestures; they responded in kind.

'What language are they talking, Inna?'

'Romanian,' she replied. 'They from Turda. But they come to London for fruit picking.'

'Turda?' I couldn't resist a snigger, though I know it's infantile. 'Not much fruit around here.'

'Aha! I tell them this cherry is only for nice flower, not for ittit.'

'Tell them the best place for fruit picking is Kent. Apples, pears, strawberries, the lot. But how come you speak Romanian, Inna? I thought you came from Odessa, in Ukraine.'

'I born in Moldova.' She coughed and crossed herself. 'In between Ukraina and Romania, one time belong Russia, another time Hungary, another time Romania. After war Soviet Republic. Everything mixit up.'

Two bright pink spots of emotion coloured her cheeks. She looked uncannily different from the withered crone I had met at my mother's deathbed.

'Moldovan language speak like Romanian language, but write in Russian-type writing,' she rattled on. 'In my school, people speaking Romanian, Russian, Ukrainian, Moldovan. Four languages plenty for one brain, English too much for me.'

'You've been at the feast of languages, Inna.' And she had indeed stolen the scraps.

'Aha! One day, I will tell you my story! But now we must break chain!'

Even as she spoke, the Y-fronts guy, now fully clothed, came up to me and grinned. His teeth flashed gold. His gone-to-fat muscles bulged under his T-shirt. Then he gripped the bicycle chain in two places and pulled. *Pthatt!* In one tug I was free.

VIOLET: *Len*

While Violet is standing in the semicircle of onlookers in the cherry grove watching Berthold's liberation, she feels a tug at her sleeve. It's Arthur; he's wearing his school uniform but he's not going to school. He seems agitated.

'Len's gone all funny. Come and see!'

She's already late for work, but she follows the kid to Len's ground-floor flat where the front door is wedged open with a chair. The flat is untidy, with stuff scattered everywhere, and a bad smell. There are the posters of football players in dynamic goal-scoring poses pinned on the walls, but Len is slumped in his wheelchair in a starkly different pose in front of the switched-off television. His crutches are on the floor, his cap is askew, his eyes are glazed, and his breathing is coming in quick gasps like a drowning man.

'Len, what's the matter? Shall I call an ambulance?'

'Nah. I'll be all right. No fuss.' His voice is faint and slurred, so that she has to bend right down to make out what he is saying; as she puts her ear to his lips she notices a strange smell on his breath, sweet and synthetic, like pear drops.

'I think there's a bottle of Diet Coke in the back of the fridge. That should do it. I just couldn't find it,' he says.

She opens the fridge. There is nothing in there but an opened tin of baked beans, green with mould, a half-empty plastic bottle of gone-off milk and a white carton with a chemist's label on. The fridge's power is off.

'There's nothing in here. Only some mouldy beans.'

'No Coke?'

'I can't find any. Shall I make you a cup of tea?' She hands Arthur the key to her flat. 'Quick, nip up and get some milk from my fridge.'

Arthur disappears, half running half skipping.

'How long has your fridge been off?' she asks Len.

He looks confused. 'My leccy got cut off last week. I should be all right when I start my job.'

The flat is hot and stuffy, with the sun beating in through the south-facing windows.

'Are you sure?'

'They cut my benefit because of my spare bedroom. But I've got an appeal lodged. And I'm registered with an agency for tele-sales, so I should be all right soon. Just pass me my crutches, love.'

She helps him lever himself out of the wheelchair with his crutches, and he flops into an armchair.

'Will you just check on the budgies, love? They're in the next room.' He nods his head towards an open door, from where there's a chorus of chirping and a disgusting smell a bit like the parrot cage next door where Berthold and the mad old lady live.

There are three cages in the little room, with four brightly coloured birds in each, all hopping about and twittering. It's enough to drive anybody mad. Their water bottles are dry and the seed dispensers are almost empty. She takes them over to the kitchen to fill them up.

Just then the door opens and the boy comes back with a bottle of milk. He's not alone. A young woman is with him – she recognises the girl who cleaned her flat the day she moved in, but she's not wearing her Homeshine uniform or carrying her brushes. She feels a rush of annoyance. Why is this slum girl following her around? She doesn't want to be reminded about poverty in Kenya right now. She's done her bit by refusing to work for HN Holdings. Isn't that enough? Now she just wants to get on with her life.

'She was waiting for you outside your flat,' says the boy. 'Shall I put the kettle on?'

'Yes. Find out where Len keeps his tea bags.' She turns to the girl, whose name she remembers is Mary Atiemo, and says in a firm voice, 'Look, Mary, in England you can't just turn up on somebody's doorstep. You have to ring and make an appointment first. As John Lennon said, an Englishman's home is his castle.' John Lennon? That doesn't sound right. Maybe it was Oscar Wilde. Or Shakespeare. Or one of those guys who go around making up quotations.

'Please, ma'am, I need your help.' The girl lowers her eyes and places her hands together in an imploring gesture, which, for some reason, Violet finds intensely irritating. Len and Arthur are staring at her open-mouthed, so she softens her tone a bit. 'Anyway, I can't afford a cleaner right now.'

'I will clean for you for nothing,' says Mary. 'I just need somewhere to stay.'

The kettle boils and she makes four cups of tea. Len adds a saccharine tablet and sips slowly, which seems to perk him up a bit, though he still looks pale. She doesn't know whether it's safe to leave him, but she promised Berthold she'd join him for a coffee, and she has an appointment with Gillian Chalmers in an hour.

'Look, you've chosen a very inconvenient time,' she tells the girl. 'Besides, I'm moving out soon.'

'I will not stay for long.'

'I'm sorry. Whatever sort of trouble you've got yourself into, it's not my responsibility. You've got to learn to stand on your own two feet. Look, Len here stands on his own two feet, and he hasn't even got any feet!' Nobody smiles at her joke.

'I will do so, ma'am. My feet are good. But I can no longer stay in my room. I will not work for Homeshine Sanitary.'

'Have you got fed up with cleaning?' Her Grandma Njoki had told her that slum people were usually lazy, as well as dishonest.

'Cleaning okay. But now he wants I do other things for clients. Things I will not do. Even though I am poor, I still have my life.' She lowers her eyes and stares stubbornly at the floor.

Violet doesn't ask what things, because it suddenly seems horribly clear. 'Tell me, who is this "he" who tells you this?'

'Mr Nzangu. The boss.'

So that's where she heard the name before. Her head spins.

'Mr Horace Nzangu? But he's a businessman in Nairobi.'

'Mr Lionel Nzangu. It is his son. They run a business to help people come to London. But I thought it was for cleaning work. He didn't say . . .'

Violet's heart thuds and she sees now that she has no choice, she has to let the slum girl stay in her flat. But before she can get the words out of her mouth, Arthur pipes up, 'You can come and stay with us. We've got a spare room.'

The girl beams, flashing her chipped tooth. 'That is very kind. I will clean your flat. God will reward you.'

Violet is left with the guilty feeling that she has not been kind. She wonders how Mary Atiemo will get on with Greg. Should she warn her? But what could she say?

'I've got to go. I'm supposed to be at work.'

She hates being late – punctuality, her Grandma Njoki used to tell her, was among the benefits brought by Britain to backward people. But now she'll be leaving soon it doesn't seem to matter so much.

She runs up the stairs two at a time and knocks on Berthold's door.

BERTHOLD: *My crappy jokes*

I didn't have the means to take Violet out to Luigi's to cele-brate the temporary reprieve of the cherry trees, so I invited her to come up to the flat for a coffee instead. Not coffee from the Clooney coffee machine, not even Gold Blend, but Lidl own-brand. That's what we were reduced to.

'I can't stay long,' she said. 'I'm supposed to be at work.'

'Work?'

'I work in International Wealth Preservation.'

'Blimey, I could do with a bit of that.'

She giggled as if I'd said something hilarious, and I thought, if Meredith had still been alive, she would have been roughly the same age as Violet, giggling at my crappy jokes.

'I think the cherry trees'll be all right for the time being. Thanks to you, Berthold. But you need to keep an eye on Len. He's had a funny turn.' She flashed a smile, finished her coffee quickly and was gone.

A few minutes later, I saw her crossing the grove wearing a rather fetching little lilac outfit, stopping briefly to chat with the colourfully dressed elders from the tent, who were sitting out on the bench in the sunshine.

'Nice girl, but skinny.' Inna was putting Flossie's cage out on to the balcony so she could enjoy the sunshine. 'Too young. Need more fat. Other one, fatty council lady, look better for you.' She fixed me with a shrewd eye. 'You still homosexy, Mister Bertie?'

I shrugged, not dignifying her absurd obsession with a reply. To me Violet seemed not skinny but perfectly formed.

However, Inna had identified something that was puzzling me too. Although Violet had seized my heart, strangely my lust had been stirred not by her but by plump, ageing Mrs Penny. There was something urgent in her desire that roused a response in me. Likewise the Immortal Bard's passion was torn between the dark lady of his lust and the blond angel of his spirit. Sometimes the male beast is a mystery, even to men. I sighed.

'It's time for lunch. Let's open a tin of tuna.' I buttered some bread, and chopped up a lettuce. 'You were going to tell me about your murky past in Moldova, Inna.'

VIOLET: *Print*

'So you're going to tell me why you're looking for a new job, Violet?' Gillian Chalmers perches like a tiny blonde bird behind her vast polished desk on which are two porcelain cups, both empty, and a pile of slip cases in different colours. The monitor shows a picture of the Lloyd's Building at night, the windows blazing with light. 'It seems like a very sudden decision. Why didn't you come and talk to me first?'

Gillian's eyes are sharp like pencil leads. A mesh of fine wrinkles is etched on her skin and deeper lines around her mouth. She read somewhere that women who spend too long in front of a computer develop wrinkles.

'I just . . .' she starts apologetically. Gillian's grey gaze confuses her. 'I know I should have . . .'

From across the desk, she can smell Gillian's subtle perfume and a faint horsey whiff of ashwagandha. The light slanting through the blinds throws a criss-cross of shadows across her face like a cage. This remote, trapped, ageing woman seems a million miles away from the tigerish go-getter she saw in action in the Lloyd's Building.

'The thing is, Violet, you should have asked me first, before putting my name down for a reference. It puts me in a difficult position.'

'I know. I'm sorry. You were away in Bucharest, and I didn't want to miss the deadline.'

'Mmm. Well, I wish you every success finding a new job, Violet. But I need to know why you want to leave GRM.'

'It's hard to explain,' Violet mumbles. 'It's a matter of principle.'

'Oh? Principle? That sounds interesting. Tell me more.' Gillian leans forward on her elbows. She looks tired and irritable. Her mascara has run into the creases of skin under her eyes. The office is cold but she has the air con on full blast, and is warming herself up with a cup of ashwagandha that looks like faintly tinted hot water.

'So. Wealth Preservation turned out to be . . . not what I expected. I didn't agree with the practice of setting up shell companies in tax havens. In poor countries like Kenya, you see, when rich people take money out, there's less to go around for schools and hospitals, and . . . it just didn't seem right.'

'Ah. It didn't seem right.' Gillian's expression is blank, apart from the pencil-point eyes, fixed on her face. 'And what about Marc Bonnier? Did you have a disagreement with him?'

She shivers. Surely Gillian knows of Marc's reputation, like everybody else at GRM. He probably told her himself, smiling his twinkling smile, not exactly bragging, but giving the impression that he was a bit of a lad.

'It's not a personal disagreement, if that's what you mean.' She takes a breath. 'I told him I didn't think it was ethical, facilitating tax evasion in poor countries. I'm not criticising Marc. I just don't want to be part of it.'

'But it is personal, isn't it?' The pencil-point eyes seem to bore into her. 'You can tell me the truth, Violet.'

Her mind searches for neutral words which don't sound accusing or vengeful: that would be cheap. She doesn't want to get back at him – she just wants to learn her lesson and move on. But Gillian isn't making it easy for her. Keeping her tone even, she describes how she found the inflated invoices for the buckets.

'Marc said it was the way business is done here. I decided it wasn't for me.'

'That's interesting.' Gillian sits back, and tilts her head. Her expression doesn't alter. 'As it happens, I agree with you, Violet. It's unethical, and it's not the way we do things at GRM. Can you forward me the invoices?'

'Yes. I'll try.'

'Thank you. If you prefer, you can come back to International Insurance?'

She considers the possibility, but only for a moment. The world outside of GRM, even with all its chaos and hardship, has more attraction. 'I think I'd like to try something different.'

'Well, please give me the details of this job you're applying for.'

She takes a gulp of breath and makes a split-second decision. 'It's with an NGO based in Nairobi that encourages women's enterprise across southern Africa. You see, women are often the family breadwinners, and a small input of capital and training can make a massive difference to –' She stops.

Gillian is staring out of the window, expressionless.

'I'll be pleased to give you a reference, Violet.' The lines around her mouth have softened, but her eyes still look sad.

By the time she leaves Gillian's office it is almost one o'clock, and people are starting to stream towards the elevators for lunch. On impulse, she takes the lift up to the fourth floor, and walks along the corridor past Marc's office. The door is closed, but she can see through the peephole in the frosted glass that he's not in. She still remembers the key code. Her heart is beating hard, but she knows this is her only chance; another time, she won't get past security into the building without an appointment. If he returns, she'll make up some excuse. She taps in the code and opens the door.

The room feels musty and still, as if no one has been in for a while. The sun is beating in through the open blinds of the south-facing window. Whereas Gillian's office was cold, his is hot. The faintest trace of his musky aftershave lingers in the air, and there's a wilted bunch of red roses in a glass vase on his desk. Who gave him those? He hasn't wasted any time, has he? A burst of anger drives her courage. She turns on the computer and logs on – it still recognises her password – finds the HN Invoice file and presses PRINT. On Marc's cabinet next to the coffee machine a small printer-copier whirrs into life.

'Violet?' His voice startles her.

She turns. Her heart thumps. There he is, standing in the doorway, watching her. How long has he been there? How much has he seen?

'Marc . . .'

'Violet, I'm glad you've come. Look, we need to talk. Will you have lunch?' A new frown has gathered between his eyebrows, and the line of his mouth is hard, but he is still formidably good-looking. She'd almost forgotten.

'I'm sorry, Marc. I was just looking for something. I can't come for lunch.'

'Come on, Violet, I owe you an apology. Just a little lunch won't hurt.' His smile twinkles. 'I promise not to bite.'

'No . . . I . . . I'm busy.'

'Busy?' He frowns. 'What are you doing in here, Violet?'

'Oh, just . . . printing something off. Some personal stuff.' He's still staring in that disconcerting way. She can feel the blood rushing through her head. 'I uploaded it on here because I haven't got a printer at home. I know I shouldn't, but . . . !' She shrugs and performs a little hopeless giggle.

'Personal stuff?' He sounds incredulous.

'Am I interrupting something?' A woman's voice.

Gillian is standing there watching them with cool eyes.

Violet winces. It must look as though she went straight from their meeting to find Marc in his office. In other words, it looks bad.

'Not at all, Gillian! Are we still on for lunch?' Marc steps forward, smiling; his expression has switched instantly.

Watching their exchange of looks, Violet realises how little she knows about them. Marc and Gillian were an item for years. Does Gillian still have feelings for him? Was she foolish to trust her when she blabbed on about Marc and the invoices?

While Marc turns towards Gillian, she quickly gathers the four invoices from the printer and slips them into her bag.

'Of course. We need to catch up.' Gillian's eyes are now resting on her. 'And you, Violet, will you join us too?'

'I'm sorry. I'd love to, Gillian, but I have to . . . prepare for a job interview.'

So those two had already planned to have lunch together! She sees in their faces that they have secrets going way back. In a flash it dawns on her that she doesn't belong here: not in this triangle, not in this environment.

As she leaves Marc's office, she feels their eyes following her as she walks back to the lift. Outside on the pavement, she hurries away from the GRM building, gulping in lungfuls of cool fresh traffic fumes.

On the corner near the traffic lights is a newsagent, where she makes a copy of the GRM re-invoices she has just printed off. She puts the originals in an envelope and posts them to Gillian Chalmers at GRM. The copies she folds into another envelope to take with her to Nairobi.

Then she catches the 55 bus to join Laura for lunch.

BERTHOLD: Odessa

In spite of her execrable command of English, the story Inna told me over lunch was not without interest. She was born, she said, mournfully munching her tuna and lettuce sandwich, in a part of Moldova that bordered on to Ukraine, and while she was still a baby – she was coyly unspecific about her age – in the spring of 1941, when the Romanian army joined the Axis pact and invaded, her mother had fled south with her to Odessa, where she had been left in the care of her grandmother, who lived in a vast decaying mansion divided into apartments. At the end of their road the Black Sea glimmered between the trees, and a tall statue looked down over a magnificent flight of steps that connected the town to the port. According to Inna, this was a statue of the Duck of Richard Lee, which surprised me somewhat as Richard Lee is the Brentford FC goalkeeper, but some judicious googling threw light on the confusion.

'Do you mean the Duc de Richelieu?' I asked, wondering how a Frenchie had ended up with a statue in this iconic Black Sea port.

'Aha! Duck of Richard Lee! Governor of city. Odessa was full up with foreigners and Jews!'

Her grandmother, whom she described as a small lady with a coil of silver hair wound around her head, informed her that the German Empress Catherine the Great had founded Odessa a century and a half ago, when the glorious Imperial Russian Army captured Crimea and the surrounding coastal areas from the barbarous non-believer Turks, and added, jabbing with a stern finger, that if she did not go to bed immediately the Turks would come back and cut off her fingers with a scimitar. At other times, the threat came from the empire-building British or the false-hearted French, who had bombarded the city during the Crimean War.

The fear of these wicked foreigners kept little Inna awake at night. Despite its high ceilings and tall windows, the apartment in Odessa was gloomy and dimly lit, with semi-defunct chandeliers, mouldy brocade drapes, long corridors and fearsome dark closets. Her grandparents had once had the whole apartment to themselves; her grandfather had been an ophthalmologist at the Filatov Institute, but after his death her grandmother had shared it with a reserved middle-aged couple called the Schapniks, who occupied two rooms at the back from which they seldom emerged except for their interminable morning expeditions to the shared WC.

Then, in August 1941, the invading Romanian army swept south and besieged Odessa. Despite the assistance of the glorious Black Sea Fleet harboured nearby in Crimea, the city surrendered to the Axis forces. Inna learned all this later at school. At the time, the main thing she noticed was the noise, which she thought was summer thunder, and the disappearance of the Schapniks. When she asked her grandmother where they had gone, her grandmother muttered something about Jews being taken away. At that time Inna did not know what a Jew was; nor did she find out until much later about the massacre of some thirty thousand Jews in Odessa, who were rounded up and shot or burned alive in two October days in 1941.

One day, a boy appeared in their flat – a lean, shaven-headed boy with dull grey eyes and trousers several sizes too big. It seemed that he had been hiding in the school, and had followed her home. He sat silently at their big mahogany dining table and wolfed down two bowls of cabbage soup, moving his spoon so fast that Inna's eyes only took in a blur of green and silver, and the quick movement of his pink tongue around his lips when he had finished.

'What's your name?' she asked in Ukrainian.

He looked at her blankly. She tried in Russian, and received the same empty stare. What a rude person, she thought; and then she had the idea of asking in Moldovan, which was now tucked away in a back drawer of her mind where childhood things were stored. At once his face brightened into a smile. He told her his name was Dovik Alfandari, he was nine years old, and he had come with his family from Romania to Odessa. A tear trickled out of the corner of his eye, leaving a pale trail in the patina of grime on his cheek.

Dovik told her that his apartment in Odessa had been raided by Romanian soldiers a few days ago and all his family had been taken away. By chance Dovik had stayed late in school that day. When he returned home to find the door broken down and the apartment looted, a neighbour told him to go back to the school. He had hidden for two days in the store cupboard of the gymnasium.

'What did you eat?' she asked.

'Nothing,' he spluttered, shovelling more cabbage soup into his mouth.

For three years Dovik never left the apartment. If anyone came to the door, he ran and hid among the fur coats in Grandmother's wardrobe and came out smelling of mothballs after the visitors had left. He and Inna played hide-and-seek in the gloomy corridors, jumping out on each other with blood-curdling shrieks, while outside Romanian soldiers stood at the ends of the street smoking and pointing their guns at everyone who passed, and neighbours were led away in twos and threes at gunpoint. If there was fighting they didn't see it, but at night they heard shelling from the port and Grand-mother told them that the glorious Black Sea Fleet would soon liberate them from these Nazis.

'Glory to Ukraine! Glory to the heroes!' yelled Inna in Dovik's ear one day, jumping out from behind the sofa.

Dovik almost leaped out of his skin. 'Don't say that, you stupid girl!'

'Why not? Don't call me stupid!'

'It's what they shout when they take the Jews away.'

'What's a Jew?'

'I'm a Jew.'

She stared at him. 'You can't be a Jew. You look normal. Well, nearly normal. Ha ha. You can't catch me!' She disappeared behind the curtain.

'Jews *are* normal.' He yanked back the curtain angrily. 'But ignorant people think we drink blood. So they want to kill us.'

'Huh! You drink cabbage soup like everybody else. But I don't see what it's got to do with glory to Ukraine.'

'It's complicated.' He frowned. 'Too complicated for girls to understand.'

'Stupid boy!'

Inna chuckled now, recalling how she had batted him on the head with a thick ophthalmology book. Dovik told her that his family had come to Bucharest in Romania when the Sephardi Jews were expelled from Spain in 1942.

'1942?' I said, puzzled. 'Are you sure, Inna?' Something didn't seem quite right about this.

'Definitely 1942.'

'First of March, 1932!' Flossie joined in from the balcony.

'Turkey murder. Two hundred dead.'

'Save our dead!'

'Shut up, devil-bird!' Inna slammed the door to the balcony and went to put the kettle on.

While she did this, I did a quick google. The expulsion of 200,000 Sephardic Jews from Spain took place in 1492, not 1942. How ever did we get on, I wondered, before we had Wikipedia? 'Turkey murder' was a bit more of a challenge until I lighted on Torquemada, the head of the Spanish Inquisition. I learned to my surprise that many Jews from Spain had fled to the Ottoman Empire, which at that time included provinces of what is now Romania. Here they prospered under the tolerant Muslim rulers, who afforded them some protection from the hostility of their bloodthirsty Christian neighbours. This gave me food for thought. Although I had long since stopped regarding myself as a Christian, I still thought of Christians as being basically decent, tolerant easy-going types like myself, while Muslims I'd always thought of as, well, let's say a bit prone to fundamentalism.

I celebrated my discovery with a mug of coffee and another round of tuna and lettuce sandwiches for both of us.

Although Inna's grasp of the history was patchy, she embellished and dramatised it colourfully. Hopping lightly over half a millennium, she described how Good King Carol of Romania with his amusing moustaches was overthrown by the evil 'Ion Guard Antonescu'. When Antonescu joined Hitler's Axis alliance, many Jews packed up and left Romania. Dovik's family had fled eastwards through Western Ukraine, where they were harassed both by German soldiers and by Bandera's Ukrainian Nationalist militias. At last they made their way down into Odessa, where they had relatives – almost a third of the population was Jewish – only to face further catastrophe when the Romanian army arrived.

'Oy!' She sighed, and dabbed a tissue to her eyes. 'Only Dovik got away.'

After the siege ended, Inna's mother returned to Odessa and her father came home in his Red Army uniform covered with medals, but with only one leg. She turned her head and gazed out of the window, where in a moment of synchronicity Legless Len was trundling through the grove in his wheelchair.

'How did your father lose his leg?'

'Same like Len. Gangrena. On ice road to Leningrad.'

I stared at Len's stumps. 'But I don't think Len has been to Leningrad. Despite his name.'

'No, Len is deeyabet. My father was war hero got frozen in feet in Lake Ladoga . . .'

Len waved up to her from the grove, and she waved back.

'Siege of Leningrad,' she ploughed on. 'They took him in hospital for cut it off but doctor said we try new medicine. Bacteriophage. Bacteria-eating virus. Soviet antibiotic. One leg saved. Not like poor Len,' she said.

As we watched, Len rolled his wheelchair up to the encampment of tents under the cherry trees. Despite what Violet had said, he looked pretty much the same as always to me.

'Nuh, Dovik seen miracle of father's leg, and he want study this new Soviet-type medicine at Eliava Institute of Bacteriophages in Tbilisi. They find it in toilet water. I stay in Odessa and train for nurse. But all time thinking about Dovik in Tbilisi.'

While Inna was still droning on, my attention wandered to the scene below. A number of people were milling around there, but it was hard to make out what was happening.

'Did you know, Inna, that Berthold Lubetkin, the man who designed these flats, also came from Tbilisi? And his family was Jewish too?'

I thought the coincidence would please her, but she just muttered, 'Council flat,' and wrinkled her nose. 'Oy! Oy! I regret my parents. I regret my Dovik. I regret my country! England is good, but not same like home! Sandwich is good, but not same like golabki.'

While Inna paused her narrative to dab her eyes with a tissue, my thoughts drifted on the mysterious tides of history that had brought Lubetkin through the battlefields of Europe to my mother's bedroom, and had delivered Inna here from Moldova by a different route. I tried to conjure up the optimism of those post-war years, the hopes of a future free from squalor, want and disease, which had set Lubetkin on his journey towards housing good enough for ordinary people, had drawn Mother into the NHS, and had sent Dovik chasing around the world searching for a dirt-cheap cure-all medicine. Big dreams they had, in those days.

Down below in the grove, there seemed to be a lot of shouting and arm waving going on. The colourful elders had disappeared, but the beefy Y-fronts guy who had liberated me was arguing with a short man in a suit. Then a slender woman dressed in lilac approached from the direction of the bus stop. It was her.

'There's something going on down there,' I interrupted Inna's mournful munching. 'Let's go and take a look.'

A milky afternoon sun was still throwing blurred shadows through the cherry leaves in the grove. As we drew close I recognised the voice of the short man in the crumpled suit whining into a megaphone.

'. . . and I'm the elected representative for your area, so I'd like to take this opportunity to thank each and every one of you who voted for me at the last election and to reassure each and every one of you that I will strive my utmost to have this eyesore removed . . .'

'Why for he remove eyesight?' whispered Inna beside me.

But Violet, standing in the crowd, had understood what he was saying. 'These people are saving our cherry grove, Councillor Dunster, which is more than you're doing!' she yelled.

A few people cheered. Mrs Crazy waved her umbrella. 'Save our trees! Save our trees!' The ra-ra girls had arrived on the scene and started up their routine. Inside one of the tents, a baby began howling. A scrawny youth I had not seen before emerged from a tent with an even scrawnier dog on a string, which peed against the councillor's leg.

Desmond Dunster carried on. 'The Council is in the process of drawing up comprehensible development plans which will see the area greatly improved, with hundreds of new homes built, and –'

'But they won't be for the likes of us,' I heckled at the top of my voice. 'It'll be separate entrances for the private owners and floor spikes for the dossers!' I think Mother would have approved.

Violet clapped, though if I had hoped for another embrace I was disappointed.

Len turned on me. 'Why d'you always have to be so bloody negative, Bert? We might all get rehoused in new flats like they're building up Old Street.'

'I don't want to be rehoused. I like it here.'

'Well, I've put myself down for a nice little one-bed flat, the sooner the better. I can't afford the rent in here no more because of the spare-room subsidence.'

'What are you talking about, Len? You do talk some crap.' I struck out pre-emptively, to deflect attention from my own irregular situation regarding the spare bedroom.

'It's costing me twenty quid a week off of my benefit because I've got two bedrooms from when our Joey was at home.'

'Isn't that where you breed your budgies now?'

'I know, but like the man from the Council said, budgies are a luxury if you're on benefit. I agree with the policy, like, but I just can't afford the money, and there's nowhere cheaper I can go because of the wheelchair.'

I quipped, 'You could always eat the budgies.' I realise it was an ill-judged remark, but Len's dogged defence of the indefensible can be irritating.

'Bert, why are you always so down on everything? Some good may come out of it,' he said.

He was right. I, who had grown up untainted by worldliness and cynicism, had become both worldly and cynical.

'Grow up, Len,' I said.

At that moment a small red car drew up in the parking area at the side of the grove, the door opened and a dainty high-heeled shoe reached for the ground. A flea-bitten ankle followed. My heart thudded a warning. Inna, Mrs Crazy and Mrs Penny all in one place could be a deadly combination.

'Aha, is fatty Madame Penny!' Inna waved her arms.

Mrs Penny approached. She was wearing an interesting above-the-knee Campbell tartan outfit with a matching tam-o'-shanter-style pompom hat. It's amazing what people give to Oxfam these days.

'Mrs Lukashenko! How lovely to see you!' She shook Inna's hand, then she turned to me. 'Do you know what's going on here, Berthold? I was called out for an emergency accommodation crisis following eviction.'

Out of the corner of my eye I noticed Mrs Crazy watching us with a curious frown. She began to edge towards us. We were saved by the councillor who, spotting Mrs Penny's council ID tag, came bustling up, his face gleaming with official sweat.

'Mrs . . . er . . . Penny,' he bent and peered at the name. 'I'm trying to get these . . . er . . . people moved. The bailiffs have been called but there's been some delay. Have we got somewhere to put them? Do any of the hostels have vacancies?'

A bead of moisture trickled down his nose, and disappeared

into the hole made by his nose-stud. Several more of the tent-dwellers had crawled out and stood muttering among themselves. The woman with the baby sat on the bench to feed it again.

'I've just run a check, Councillor Dunster. There's nothing closer than Cleethorpes.'

'Cleethorpes is a very nice place. Get them booked in before some other bloody borough nicks it.'

'But it's all single homeless up there. Nothing for families.'

He turned towards them and spoke loudly and slowly. 'Do you understand? We're going to put you in a very nice B&B in Cleethorpes.'

'*Ce se fucking intampla?*' said Mr Y-fronts.

Inna hurried over to translate, her hands and eyes animated. I have no idea what she said, but as she spoke I observed expressions of dismay cover their faces. The man with a dog on a string let out a torrent of expletives and spat on the ground. The old lady uttered a low moan. The woman with the baby shrieked and clutched her child closer to her bosom. The big Y-fronts man staggered and keeled over in a dead faint.

Mrs Penny, clearly shaken by this display of emotion, cautioned, 'We could be penalised for not providing suitable –'

The councillor threw up his hands. 'So what can we do?' He had turned a deep, dangerous red.

'We might be safer leaving them where they are for the time being.'

Inna translated and the tent-dwellers cheered. Violet clapped.

The councillor raised his palms in surrender. Mrs Crazy hit him with her umbrella. His knees crumpled and he banged his head against a tree trunk on his way down.

Mrs Penny whipped out her mobile phone and called for an ambulance.

★

A while after the ambulance had woo-wooed away, and the bailiffs had arrived and been sent packing, Mrs Penny kicked off her shoes, threw off her pompom hat, and reclined like an exhausted flea-bitten, tartan-clad odalisque on the sofa in our sitting room, wiggling her mauve-tipped toes while Inna brought us cups of mint tea.

'You're a lucky man, Berthold, having a mother who looks after you so well.'

'Yes. We look after each other.'

Although she did indeed look after me well, Inna would often disappear to her old haunts in Hampstead for the whole afternoon. But today, for some annoying reason, she chose to hang around the flat, leaving the kitchen door open as if to keep an eye on our visitor. Maybe she'd cottoned on that I wasn't gay, after all, and thought if she weren't there I might be tempted to inflict my lust on her. As if.

'It's funny, a woman I spoke to down there just now was saying Mrs Lukashenko isn't really your mother.'

My heart thumped in my chest. Despite her odalisque pose, she was still a representative of 'Them', trying to catch us off guard.

'Lily's got a sister, and she gets them confused. They do look a bit alike. That woman's quite crazy. Early-onset dementia. A sad case.' I tried to cast Inna a warning look, but she had disappeared into the kitchen again, and soon I could smell the heavenly aroma of roasting almonds and honey wafting in above Mrs Penny's flowery perfume.

'Mm. I thought so. She had a sort of fanatic gleam in her eyes. And the way she clobbered that councillor. Nobody deserves that, even someone as morally compromised as Desmond Dunster. A dangerously deluded psychopath, I would say. I come across a lot of them, in my line of work.'

'Where they put dangerous cycle path?' Inna called from the kitchen.

'And why morally compromised?' I added.

She sighed. 'You know, trips abroad, no expenses spared. Hand in glove with the developers. But don't tell anyone I said that. While us lot, the staff, we have to implement the policies.'

She scratched her ankles, and I was wondering how to ask her whether she had pets with fleas, when she added, 'The things you have to do in this job. Like making people homeless, or cutting their benefit off. Or forcing them to have their pets put down. It's not a lot of fun.'

'Indeed not.'

'I went into housing because I wanted to help people, and all I do is bring them misery.'

A look of sorrow clouded her odalisque features and I wondered whether I had misjudged her motives. Ought I to put a comforting arm around her?

While I hesitated, Inna bustled in with a plate of warm slatki. 'It, it!'

'Please,' I handed the plate to Eustachia. She looked solid enough to withstand a small dose of poison, and I succumbed too, having survived thus far.

'I don't mind if I do.' With an anguished look, she wolfed down two, while Inna watched smiling.

'Mmm. These are yummy. Did you make them yourself, Mrs Lukashenko?'

Inna nodded.

'Oh dear, I'm not supposed to eat pastries. I'm trying to lose weight. But sometimes I just need something sweet to take the bitter taste away. I'm curious, Mrs Lukashenko,' she added. 'What did you say to those Romanians, to make them react like that?'

'I remind them October 1941 in Odessa. Romanian soldiers take Jews away. Romanians tell them they go for rehousing, but they take all to central square and shoot them. Then they throw on gasoline and make it fire. Everybody burned dead.'

'My God!' Mrs Penny dabbed her forehead with a tissue. 'It makes our Government's policies seem relatively humane.'

BERTHOLD: *Smøk & Miras*

Next day I was still feeling a bit queasy, maybe from the slitki, and I decided to treat myself to breakfast in bed, which I hoped Inna would make. But despite repeated hints, at eleven o'clock she suddenly expressed a need to go out. She applied a dab of lipstick and rouge, tied a headscarf over her newly black hair, rammed a bulging brown A4-sized envelope into her bag and headed out mysteriously into the late morning.

'Where are you going, Inna?'

'Hempstead. I got business. Back soon, Mister Bertie.'

Maybe she was going to stock up on prussic acid, though Eustachia, I noted, seemed unaffected by the slatki, even though she had eaten six of them. But now I grew curious about the contents of the brown envelope.

'What sort of business?'

'Mind it own business,' she snapped.

I got up and made my own breakfast, wondering what she was up to. Business. I wished I too had some business, somewhere I needed to go to, or a script to be working on. It was at least four months since I had trod the boards. I had had no response to the Brent Cross Mickey Mouse application. The need to be usefully employed itched like a skin disease of the soul. For all his nastiness, Nazi George had stirred a hunger in me for meaningful activity, a role in the great drama of our national life. Maybe I should write my own part in my own play; but what would I write about? I stared out of the window at the cherry grove with its winding path between the trees, now gloriously heavy-leaved, pregnant with summer, timeless yet vulnerable. The hero would be a middle-aged man seeking a renewed meaning in life who chains himself to a tree in defiance of the cataclysm of post-modernity. It was a great subject; but hadn't it been done already? As I was sketching out a dramatic structure in my mind, the doorbell rang: *Ding dong! Ding dong! Ding dong!*

It was Legless Len, in his wheelchair, his thumb still jabbing aggressively at the bell.

'Whoa, Len. One ring is enough. You'll waken the dead!'

An unfortunate slip of the tongue for one recently bereaved, but Len didn't notice.

'Listen, pal, I'm having a bit of trouble. Can you lend me a tenner?' Before I could answer, he grasped the wheels of his chair and rolled himself into the flat.

'I'm a bit strapped for cash myself, Len.' This was embarrassing. 'I thought you were working in tele-sales.'

'Nah! Got sanctioned off, didn't I? Benefit stopped. Just like that.'

'What happened?'

'Zero-hours contract. Got to be on call twenty-four-seven. Didn't go out for four days. Waited by the phone, but the call never came. Then yesterday, when it all kicked off down in the grove, I went to see what was going on, and, would you believe it, that's when the buggers phoned from the Job Centre. To make sure I was still available for work.' He took off his Arsenal cap and combed his fingers through his hair, which seemed thinner and greyer since I had last seen it. 'Do you reckon one of them Romanians grassed me up?'

'I think that's unlikely, Len. You'd need to speak a bit of English for that.'

'Well, someone must've done. Why d'they pick just that moment to phone?'

'It's a mystery. Sorry I can't help, pal. I haven't got any work myself.'

'I've heard it's the immigrants that's undercutting us.' He lowered his voice as though he was imparting confidential information, though I had read the same sentiment recently in the newspaper at Luigi's. 'If you don't give a foreigner a job, next thing you know the PC brigade's got you up against the Court of European Rights.'

'Yes, Len. The country's going to the dogs. I blame the foreigners and the budgies.'

He rubbed his forehead. 'Why the budgies, Bert?'

'Why the foreigners, Len?' I smirked. 'They can't be benefit scroungers one minute and undercutting our wages the next.'

As I unleashed this devastating repartee, an unpleasant thought popped into my head. I was due for another visit to the Job Centre soon. Would I now be dragooned into the Wrest 'n' Piece back-to-work Training Programme? I wondered how Phil Gatsnug had got on since my last visit.

'But can't you bank on the food bank at times like this, Len? Apparently there's plenty of baked beans out there for the taking. I've got a spare tin of tuna, if that's any help.'

'Thanks for the thought. It's not food I need, Bert, it's electricity. My bill's overdue. They've cut me off. I need to keep my insulin chilled. I had a funny turn yesterday.'

'I'll ask Inna when she comes back.'

'Thanks. I'd appreciate it.'

Len wheeled himself back over the threshold and down the walkway towards the lift. Thank God he had not accepted the tin of tuna. Far from being 'spare' it was, in fact, all that stood between me and starvation, at least until Inna got back.

I closed the door behind him, and that's when I noticed a slim purple envelope lurking on the doormat. How long had it been there? The postman used to come first thing in the morning, but now, thanks to the collapse of civilisation as we know it, he can come at any time during the day. Soon, no doubt, it will all be delivered by drones and even postmen will be a thing of the past.

I bent to retrieve it. It was a letter from Smøk & Miras Promotions informing me that all the promotional vacancies at the Brent Cross Shopping Centre had been filled, but inviting me to an interview at 12.30 p.m. today for a similar opportunity to promote a new brand of coffee at major railway stations. Coffee – that was my thing! It could be my first step to Clooneydom! I glanced at my watch. It was 12.30. The address was near King's Cross. Normally, I would have hopped on my bike, but as fate had cruelly unwheeled me, I grabbed my jacket and raced down the stairs to the bus stop.

It was 1.15 when I arrived at the fourth-floor (no lift – puff puff) office of Smøk & Miras Promotions in a slim Georgian house on a cobbled side street overlooking a building site behind King's Cross. A lean young man in his mid-twenties with a shaved head and a strangely tattooed scalp was sitting on a high swivelling chair behind an enormous computer screen in a box-sized office with bare walls, a skylight and a black canvas folding chair. There was a not-unpleasant smell of coffee and musky aftershave.

'Hi! Come in, Berthold! Cool name! I'm Darius. Have a seat.' He shook my hand and indicated the black chair, which was low like a deck chair, so my face came up to his knees.

'Sorry I'm late. I only just got your letter.'

'No problem. The other guys didn't show either. What it is – right – we've got totally a new concept in coffee, which is that it comes from beans!' He swivelled to face me with a radiant expression.

'Cool!' I feigned surprised enthusiasm.

'What you have to do – right – is hang out in the station forecourt at the rush hour between seven and ten a.m. and four and seven p.m., wearing a Bertie Bean outfit, and handing out free samples. Like these . . .' He passed me a small cotton bag, which looked as though it contained six coffee beans.

'Cool!' My heart froze. Bertie Bean. Oh, horror, horror, horror!

'We pay twenty quid for the day, cash in hand. No deductions.'

'Isn't the minimum wage – ?'

'That's the apprentice rate, man.' His voice was slightly high-pitched, as though the stress of lying had contracted his vocal chords.

'But I'm –'

'You may as well start at King's Cross. Come here just before seven on Monday and pick up your costume. How tall are you?'

'Er, six foot, actually.' (For your information, that's an inch taller than George Clooney.)

'Cool.'

He jotted it down on a Post-it note.

'See you on Monday, right. Seven o'clock.'

'Cool.'

As I descended the stairs after my cursory interview, I heard him locking the door of the office.

Seven o'clock. That meant getting up at six. It was several years since I had been out of bed so early. It would be a challenge.

VIOLET: Decisions

It's funny, sometimes you make the big decisions in life, and sometimes they just make themselves for you. The NGO interview was at nine o'clock, but by seven o'clock she was already up, and trying on different outfits. Something told her the lilac and dove grey that fitted in at GRM would look out of place here. She chose a straight skirt and black tights. At the last minute, she swapped the high heels for a pair of flat pumps.

The three interviewers in the tiny meeting room of the Action for Women in Africa headquarters in Bloomsbury conferred for a moment.

'Would you accept the job if we offered it to you?' asked Maria Allinda, the youngest of the three.

'For sure,' said Violet. 'I like a challenge.'

And the die was cast.

After the interview she leans against the railings of the Georgian terraced building and feels the world spin beneath her feet like a roulette wheel. All that is familiar about London will become unfamiliar with time, and she will grow in a new direction like a plant exposed to a different sunlight.

Before the job starts she'll have to say goodbye to her friends, return the duvet and kitchenware to Jessie and spend some time with her parents in Bakewell.

Pidgie is waiting for her back on her balcony, coo-cooing his heart out, not knowing that tomorrow she won't be here. She watches him hop across to the balcony next door to forage for stray seeds from the parrot's cage. 'Goodbye, Pidgie.' He'll miss the toast but he won't miss her.

Taking down the pictures from her wall she stows them one by one in her life-sized suitcase, and unpins the night-blue sari which she wraps around the yellow mugs. She's excited, of course, and her mind has already started racing ahead to the dusty streets of Nairobi; but she feels a prick of sadness too. This funny flat has been the first home of her own; she did some growing up here. There are people she must say goodbye to.

Her next-door neighbours, Berthold and Inna, are both out when she rings on their doorbell. She hopes she will get a chance to say goodbye to them before she goes. Mrs Cracey makes her a brew of strong tea, and shoos a scrawny white cat off the sofa to make a space for her to sit. He lopes away on black-socked paws, throwing a glare of resentment over his shoulder.

'Africa, did you say, poppet? Never mind. The late Pastor Cracey always used to say a prayer for the little black babies, you know.'

Violet smiles, remembering how her Grandma Njoki would always add a prayer for all the white people who had strayed from the Lord's path.

'Did you hear about poor Len? He collapsed yesterday. I had to call the ambulance.'

'Oh no!' She feels a stab of bad conscience. If she hadn't been in such a hurry for her meeting with Gillian Chalmers, she should have taken him to the doctor. She wonders how Mary Atiemo has got on with Arthur and Greg.

When she rings on the door of their flat, half an hour later, it's Mary who answers, wearing a pinafore over a baggy T-shirt and a pair of leggings which emphasise the thinness of her legs. 'Come on in, ma'am!' Her smile is still wide, but already she has taken on a slightly smug, proprietorial air that reminds Violet of the stray cat on Mrs Cracey's sofa. 'Arthur just got back from school. I'm making him some toast. Will you have some?'

'No, thanks. I can't stay long. I just came to say goodbye. I'm leaving soon.'

The flat already looks cleaner and tidier than before, and there's a delicious smell of something spicy cooking. Arthur is sitting at one of the desks, his head bowed over a page that reads: *She dwelt among untrodden ways*. Homework, no doubt.

'Hey, Violet, Warrior Queen.' He looks up. 'Good to see you. Everything okay?'

'Fine. I just got a job in Nairobi. I came to say goodbye.'

'Oh. Goodbye, then.' He looks dejected. 'Dad's not back yet, but I'll tell him you came. Hey, did you hear about Len?'

'Mrs Cracey just told me. What happened?'

'I reckon it's the Curse of Rameses?' The kid looks grave. 'Len told me about it. It's this ancient mummy that emerges from the tomb every time Arsenal scores?'

'Really?' This seems implausible. 'Well, when you see him, will you say goodbye from me?'

'Yeah, course I will. But we're moving too, in a few days? Our house is ready, only the swimming pool had to be filled in? The council surveyor said it was undermining the foundations of the next-door house? Dad says that's utter crap and he's going to sue them.'

'Mmm.' She remembers Mr Rowland and his flexible attitude to developers. 'Won't you be sorry to leave your flat?'

'Nah, it's a dump. Dad usually rents it out? It's part of his portfolio? He owns yours, too? Thanks, Mary.' Mary sets down the plate of toast beside him, and a cup of tea. 'Mary's coming with us when we move, aren't you?'

Mary shrugs and glances over her skinny shoulder as if she's afraid her good fortune will escape. 'If God grants it.' Then she looks up and meets Violet's eyes. Her eyes are shiny and brown like coffee beans. A cheeky smile tweaks the edges of her lips. 'You see, ma'am, I am already standing on my own legs.'

'Be careful. One day you may need them for running away.'

BERTHOLD: Bertie Bean

Darius was just unlocking the office as I arrived at seven o'clock, and he handed me my Bertie Bean costume.

'Sorry it's a bit short in the leg. It's the only one we had left.'

The best thing to be said about the outfit was that it provided total anonymity. Rather like a pointy burqa made of brown shiny material, and gathered at the ankles, it covered me from head to toe, with round eyeholes, a breathing hole somewhere between my mouth and my nose, and two hand holes. Well, not quite head to toe. The costume was about six inches too short, revealing my socks and trainers.

Darius eyed me critically. 'You're wearing odd socks.'

'Am I? One must have got lost in the wash.' I smiled disarmingly. 'Heaven must be full of angels wearing odd socks.'

He failed to be disarmed. 'Wear black socks this afternoon. And black shoes, right?'

'Sure.' A random memory from my childhood snuck up on me. I started to sing. 'Black socks, they never get dirty, the longer you wear them . . .'

'Cool,' said Darius coolly. 'But now you need to memorise the Bertie Bean script.'

'. . . the blacker they get. Sometimes . . .'

'It's very simple. You approach the punters with a smile.'

'. . . I think I should change them, but . . .'

'Well, you don't need to smile, because it's actually painted on the costume. But you'll find . . .'

'. . . something keeps telling me . . .'

'. . . smiling actually makes your voice sound friendlier. So what you say is . . .'

'. . . don't wash them yet.'

Mother had taught me the song in the stuttering days. We sang it together as a round.

'. . . Hi! I'm Bertie Bean, and I want to introduce you to a totally new coffee experience . . .'

'Hi! I'm B-B-Bertie B-B-Bean.' It was no good – my cortisol levels were all over the place. So I started to sing. The words didn't fit the tune, but I got them out anyway. Darius looked impressed.

'Cool! Awesome! You can sing it!' He thrust a basket of samples into my hands, and pushed me towards the stairs. 'Take care.'

The bottom of the costume was gathered tight at the hem, so getting down the stairs was tricky, and even on the pavement I could only walk in small mincing steps. I suppose women get used to walking like this, but for a bloke it's disempowering. There was no mirror in the office, so it wasn't until I saw my reflection in a plate-glass window that I realised how absurd I looked. I tried to distance myself, Berthold Sidebottom, the distinguished Shakespearean actor, from the weird figure scuttling like an upright cockroach among the busy commuters. It's a tribute to the broad-mindedness of Londoners that no one gave me a second glance.

The morning was bright with a hint of warmth as I positioned myself on the wide, newly renovated forecourt of the station where people converged from all directions and I could eye up my quarry from a few feet away, estimate their trajectory, and intercept.

'Hi! I'm Bertie Bean . . . !'

When I was a kid Mother had taken me out leafleting, so I was not surprised by the responses. What surprised me was how long it took to give away my basket of beans. You would have thought I was handing out narcotics. Most passers-by were in a hurry and dodged out of my way; some who couldn't dodge grabbed the free samples and put them into the nearest bin or dropped them on the ground; a few listened to the whole script, then politely said, 'No, thank you.' Those were the nice ones, but they were few. After an hour of this, I was filled with loathing for my fellow humans. After two hours, I was filled with self-loathing, an outcast from humanity metamorphosed into a despised sub-species, an insect on legs – a bare, forked animal. After three hours, I was beyond thinking, sweating inside my costume and desperate for a drink.

At the other end of the precinct four young people wearing red T-shirts with the logo of an animal charity were trying to sign up punters to a direct debit. As the morning wore on, I saw their expressions and gestures gradually stiffen like puppets. At 10 a.m., the hour of my liberation, I went up and persuaded them to take the remaining eight bags of beans in my basket.

'Yeah, mate, sure. Can we sign you up for a donation to save rhinos?'

'I haven't got any money,' I said. 'Else I wouldn't be doing this, would I?'

Darius was on the phone when I got back to the Smøk & Miras office. Still talking, he watched me as I disengaged myself from my costume and put on my jacket, which I'd hung on the back of the door.

Just as I was about to leave, he put the phone down. 'What took you so long?'

'I thought you said ten o'clock.'

'Yeah, but you should've been back for at least another

basket in that time. How long can it take to give away a quality product like ours?'

'Longer than you'd think.'

'You must have got the wrong technique.' He scratched the arse of a grinning demon tattooed on his scalp. 'Let's see how you get on this afternoon when they're on the home straight. Call back here just before four o'clock.'

The six hours I had to kill in the middle of the day dwindled quickly. The journey itself took almost an hour.

Inna was out when I got back. I stuck my head around the door of her room but there was no sign of her. A haze of L'Heure Bleue greeted my nostrils, and the familiar thick brown envelope, now rather dog-eared, was propped up against the mirror of the dressing table. I felt an immense urge to open it, but held back out of decency.

Instead, I had a chat with Flossie, scoffed the kobsabki that Inna had prepared for me, checked my email, had a shower and changed my shirt, which was damp with sweat.

Then it was time to run for the bus again.

When I arrived at Smøk & Miras just before four o'clock, Darius was on the phone again.

'. . . Cool. Cool. No worries. Leave it to me.' He put the phone down as I was getting into my costume.

'You forgot to change your socks.'

I glanced down at my feet, feigning surprise. 'So I did.'

'Have you any idea how ridiculous you look?' There was a nasty edge to his voice.

'As a matter of fact, I do.'

The sun had gone behind the clouds, and a cool wind was blowing empty crisp packets and discarded copies of *Metro* across the dismal granite expanse of the precinct. The rhino chuggers had been replaced by four cancer chuggers; despite the gravity of their cause their expressions were still fresh and hopeful. They each took a little bag of my coffee beans with enthusiasm, and informed me how high my chances were of contracting cancer.

'Sure,' I said. 'That's the least of my worries.'

The travellers streaming across the forecourt now were fewer and less frenetic than in the morning rush hour. I went back to my previous spot in front of a granite bench, and started singing my introduction, not so much because of the stutter, more as a way of distancing the ridiculous Bertie Bean from me, the human hiding inside the bean. As I sang Bertie's words, he became no longer me but a character in a pantomime. The churning sense of humiliation I had felt that morning had given way to a dull ache of acceptance; these were not people but punters crawling across the station forecourt, just a different species of insect. On the whole, the women were pleasanter than the men, but there was not much in it.

The young woman pulling an oversized suitcase in the direction of St Pancras Station didn't at first glance look any different from the hundreds of other punters who had crossed my path that day. It was her way of walking that caught my attention, an extra bouncy lightness in her step despite the weight of her case, as though she was skipping from cloud to cloud, the way angels do. It wasn't just an average case that you take for a weekend away; it was the sort of giant case in which you pack up your life before moving on.

'Violet!' I stepped out in front of her. 'Where are you going with that enormous bag?'

'I'm sorry?' Her eyes flickered over me without recognition. I guessed she hadn't heard me say her name. She glanced down at the samples in my hand and smiled briefly. 'I'm so sorry, I'm in a rush!' She dodged around me and hurried on.

I could have introduced myself, I could have offered to help with her bag, I could have persuaded her to stop for a coffee; but I didn't do any of those things. I stepped aside and let her go on her angelic way, following her with my eyes as she crossed the road and headed towards St Pancras without pausing at the traffic lights, without looking left and right. It was the spring in her step that bewitched me, releasing a memory that came crashing in on me without warning; it was the same carefree step with which Meredith had skipped out across the road that day, not waiting for the green man, not seeing the white van speeding up out of nowhere.

After she had disappeared into the underground I stood still for a long while, gazing out through the eyeholes of my disguise, letting the litter swirl around my feet as though I had become a part of the grey granite forecourt, as though my soul had turned to granite.

In the end one of the cancer chuggers came up to me. 'Are you all right, bruv?'

'Sure,' I said. 'Thanks. Just need to get home. Here, have these. Grind them up.' I gave him the rest of my beans. My hands were numb with cold.

I glanced at the clock. It was about a quarter to seven. I was not due back until seven, but when I got to the Smøk & Miras office the door was locked. There was no sign of life. I took off my Bertie Bean outfit, left it folded outside the door with the empty basket, and went back down into the street, thinking I would just kill ten minutes by mooching around the shops.

But it was cold in the street without my jacket, and a couple of raindrops splatted on my head so I went back inside, sat down at the top of the stairs, and waited. By a quarter past seven, nobody had come back. By half past seven, I realised that nobody was going to come back. Behind the door was my jacket and my twenty-quid day's wages. I could see the outline of the jacket through the frosted glass. As I watched the second hand ticking around on my wristwatch, humiliation and rage boiled up in my heart. I pulled myself up on to my feet, pounded on the door with my fists, and kicked the frame again and again.

'Darius, you fucking little devil-headed creep, just give me my money and my coat and let me go!'

On the fourth time, I yelled, 'Darius, you rotten thieving bastard, just give me my fucking coat and let me go!' I knew it was pointless, but it made me feel better.

When my voice was hoarse, and my fist sore from hammering, I shattered the glass panel, using the empty bean basket to shield my hand, and smashed away the glass. What I saw was that the office was completely empty. The computer and desk were gone. Darius's swivelling chair and the low black canvas chair I had sat in were gone. A few spilled bags of beans were scattered on the floor, and some unopened letters. A faint smell of coffee and aftershave still hung in the air.

As I reached in to take my jacket down off the hook, I caught my wrist on a shard of jagged glass and a trickle of blood seeped into the pale grey fabric of the lapel. Okay, so it wasn't the world's most expensive jacket, but it was the best one I had, with patch pockets and two buttons, a bit like the one Clooney wears for the photo call of *Burn After Reading*. I supposed I would have to get it dry-cleaned now. When I put the jacket on, a bloodstain appeared on the cuff as well.

By now it was almost eight o'clock and outside a few more heavy raindrops presaged a thunderstorm. I wrapped Bertie Bean hood-like over my head, and went in search of a real coffee and a bus home. Wanting to avoid the station, the scene of my humiliation, I turned the other way and found myself in a maze of anonymous streets, with no coffee shops, nor indeed shops of any kind, just a warren of council blocks. The rain had started to fall steadily, greying out the sky, and a rumble of thunder rolled out somewhere to the south. I pulled Bertie Bean over my head and trudged on.

At an intersection I stopped and looked around to get my bearings. Behind me was the roar of traffic climbing the Pentonville Road towards Islington. In front of me was ... I stared. It looked like home; lights were already on in some windows. A flash of lightning revealed a handsome, clean-lined block of brick and concrete, that pleasing chequer pattern of windows and inset balconies set back behind a landscaped garden with trees, shrubs and a recreation area, dignified yet playful. Lubetkin? Nothing too good for ordinary people?

Unaccommodated man – the bare, forked animal that I was – crossed the road and pressed my wet face against the railings. A young mother was opening the gate into the garden, with a small boy who tugged at her hand.

'C-c-can we go on the swings, Mummy?' his voice shrilled.

'Look, it's raining, love. Let's go home and have supper. We'll go on the swings tomorrow.'

The gate clanged shut behind them. My eyes filled with tears. I clung to the railings and let the sobs rake through my body.

VIOLET: *East Croydon*

There's a train from St Pancras to East Croydon at 5.50, and she's running a bit late. She drags her suitcase, heavy with Jessie's borrowed duvet and kitchenware, across the crowded station forecourt, dodging a couple of kids collecting for charity and some idiot dressed up as a coffee bean who tries to stand in her way. She's just in time. A guy on the train leans out and helps her heave the suitcase in behind her as the doors slide shut.

'Thanks. I almost never made it.' She laughs with relief.

'Where are you going with that great big case?'

He's young and nice-looking, with horn-rimmed glasses that make him look both cool and intelligent, and a denim jacket slung over his arm.

'Nairobi.'

'No kidding. Are you flying from Gatwick?'

'No, Manchester. But I'm going to see my friend in Croydon before I leave.'

At the station Jessie is waiting for her.

'Hey, adventurer!'

They laugh and hug. She can smell Jessie's warm familiar skin and herbal shampoo.

'I'll miss you, Jess. You'll come and visit, won't you?'

'Try and stop me. Here, give me your bag. I'm parked just around the corner.'

For some reason her eyes fill up with tears.

BERTHOLD: *Swish swish*

'Berthold? Berthold, are you all right?' It was Mrs Penny, placing an arm around my shoulder. I could smell her perfume through my tears as she brought her face close to my ear. 'Do you need a lift home, pet?'

'I'm fine. I'm just . . .' The words dried up.

'It's okay. My car's just around the corner. I'm going your way.'

Half leaning on her, I stumbled along the pavement until we came to the little red car. I caught sight of myself in the wing mirror, my dripping hair and teary eyes, my blood-stained jacket, the Bertie Bean hood. The way I looked, I would not have offered myself a lift.

She clicked a key and lights flashed. 'Get in.' She started up the engine. 'What were you doing around Priory Green, anyway?'

'Oh, I'd just b-been for a job near King's Cross. Unsuccessful, I'm afraid.' I tried to sound upbeat, but the catch in my voice must have betrayed me. 'And you? You're not still at work, are you?'

'I'm just finishing off some casework. I'm going to be off for a couple of weeks. I'm afraid your tenancy transfer will have to wait until I get back.' She sounded flustered.

'Going somewhere nice?'

'Not really.' There was a silence. 'I'm just having some time off.'

The way we were sitting, both facing forward in the front of the car, was curiously anonymous, almost like a confessional, with a lattice of politeness between us: we did not look at each other but watched the windscreen wipers flick their rhythm of blur-and-clear as we crawled bumper to bumper up the Pentonville Road.

'Oh? Nothing bad I hope?'

'No. Not really.'

I thought I heard a tremor in her voice but her profile was impassive. I couldn't help noticing the wrinkles at the corners of her eyes and the downward droop of her mouth.

'Actually, I'm going on a retreat. I'm going to rediscover my Inner Goddess, if you must know.' Another silence, then a torrent of emotion. 'You can't imagine the stress I'm under at work. I can't face having to turn up every day and implement policies that are so callous, that were never part of the job I signed up for. I bet you think I'm a heartless monster, don't you?' She didn't wait for an answer. 'I try to be professional, but inside I'm crying.' She was gripping the wheel with both hands as she spoke, leaning forward towards the steamy windscreen.

'Swish swish,' the wipers whispered.

I felt an impulse to hug her. 'Mm. I know the feeling.' I loosened Bertie Bean from around my neck. 'I've been crying inside all day.'

'I used to be a kind-hearted person . . .' Her voice was wobbling between bravura and embarrassment.

Swish swish. The droplets smeared across the windscreen. I thought I caught the glint of a tear in her eye but it might have been just a trick of the light.

'You're still . . . I mean, you're wonderful as you are, Eustachia. You're already a goddess!'

'Do you really mean it?'

'Of course. A goddess of mercy.' My voice sounded more tinny and insincere than I felt.

272

She looked at me out of the corner of her eye. There were black streaks where the mascara had run into the wrinkles. 'My doctor put me on benzos, you know,' she said.

'I was on Prozac.'

Taunting memories crowded in on me as I said the 'p' word. *You think you're over it, but you're not. Just look at you. You're a bloody mess.* Swish swish.

Red tail lights smeared and blurred in front of us. She drove nervously, her foot hovering over the brake.

'I started to put on weight. My memory started to go. The doctor wanted me to come off them, she said I was getting too dependent. She said I had to learn to control my impulses. But you see, I can't. I'm an emotional person. Those pastry things your mother makes, for example . . .'

'Mm. Slotki. By the way, how did you feel after you'd eaten them?'

'Since you ask, I felt absolutely awful!'

Oh God! I remembered the nausea and the feeling of choking the first time I tasted them. So maybe it had not just been my paranoid imagination. Maybe this was part of Inna's plan to get her hands on the flat.

'Totally suicidal!' she moaned. 'Like all my self-control melted away in one mouthful.'

'They made me feel strange too, but it was more physical. I think they don't agree with me.'

'Funny you should say that – my speech therapist had an allergy to anything with nuts in it.'

'Mm. Your speech therapist?' I let this sink in. Could an allergy be hereditary?

Once we were past Islington the traffic eased and the rain petered out. We were moving more quickly now, Mrs Penny biting her lower lip with concentration as she worked up and down through the gears, her left foot pressing hard on the clutch. In a few minutes we would be home.

I seized the opportunity to ask the question that had been nudging itself to the front of my mind. 'What happened to Mr Penny, Eustachia?'

She let out a sudden moan and, uncontrolled, the car lurched forward. I grabbed the wheel to avoid a cyclist on the near side.

'That lying, cheating, heartless bastard! He told me I'd let myself go and I wasn't the woman he'd married. Then I discovered he was having an affair behind my back all the time with a younger woman. He didn't want me to look different; he just wanted me out of the way.'

A tear drop glistened on her cheek momentarily. She wobbled as we passed another cyclist and I laid my hand over hers on the steering wheel, searching my repertoire of Bard wisdom.

'Sigh no more, lady, sigh no more, men were deceivers ever. One foot in sea, and one on shore, to one thing constant never.'

'Oh, that's so true.' A small smile lit her profile. She glanced at me sideways. 'Is it poetry?'

'Shakespeare. The best.'

'I bet you're not like that, are you, Berthold? Always chasing after what you can't have?'

'Me? No, not at all.'

After all, I had not chased after Violet. I had let her skip away with her suitcase across the station forecourt. I felt a stab of pain remembering, and also a slight twinge of relief. Whatever had possessed me to imagine that love could blossom between Violet and myself? She was young enough to be my daughter. Bertie Bean had saved me from making an utter prat of myself. I pulled him tighter around me.

'So what did you do, Eustachia?'

'What could I do? I went back to my speech therapist. She'd retired by then but she was like a fairy godmother to me, and I asked her advice. She told me to dump him. Best thing I ever did – dumping him.'

'So now you live alone?'

'Just me and Monty.'

'Monty?'

'Monty the Mongrel. He came from a client, an old lady I was rehousing whose husband had fought with Montgomery at El Alamein. Would you believe it? He was a war hero, and they wouldn't let her take the dog into the new place, told her to have him put down. Heartless, the rules we have to work by. She told them she'd sooner keep the dog and live on the street. So I took him in.'

'That was kind.' The words sounded banal, but they came from my heart, which pulsed with revelation. I was in the car of a genuinely good person, someone who went around rescuing stray dogs, and people.

'Best thing I ever did since dumping my ex. Only problem is the fleas. Well, here we are!'

She slammed on the brakes and pulled up the handbrake. We were outside Madeley Court. Through the leaves of the cherry trees I could see that the light in my flat was on, twinkling bright like a beacon. With any luck, globalki would be in the oven.

'Thank you so much, Eustachia. You saved me. You really did. I'd reached rock bottom and you rescued me. Like a stray mongrel.' I opened the car door and paused, glancing down at her ankles. The flea bites took on a new significance now; they were the stigmata of human kindness. 'Won't you come in for a minute? I'm sure my mother would love to see you.'

She locked the car and we walked side by side through the grove. Lights were on inside the Romanian tents – torches, or candles maybe. A sound of voices talking quietly. A baby murmuring in its sleep. I reached for her hand and gave it a squeeze.

We stood close together in the lift, our hands still touching in a companionable way. Her flowery perfume filled the metal cubicle, blotting out the smell of pee. As we passed along the walkway, I glanced at the next-door flat. It was in darkness. I shivered, but Eustachia was standing so close behind me I could feel the radiant warmth of her body through my jacket.

She murmured, 'Sounds like your mum's got a visitor.'

My ears pricked up. What was all that shrieking and yelling? At first I thought Flossie must have escaped and gone on the rampage, but as I fitted my key in the lock, I heard that there were two voices, a shrill soprano screech and a deeper baritone bellow. I couldn't understand what they were shouting, which, I soon realised, was because they were not shouting in English but in Romanian. Or Ukrainian. Or something. I was filled with apprehension, but Eustachia bristled with professional resolve. 'Old people are so vulnerable nowadays, even in their own homes.'

I opened the door. Inna was standing in the living room, her eyes wide, a kitchen knife in her hand. A man was facing her with his back towards me – a stocky, short-haired man with square hands and shoulders. In fact, if I had to put a name to him, I would have called him Lookerchunky. He was squeezed into a pair of too-tight, silver-grey trousers; a spare tyre bulged against the midriff of his dark grey shirt, which had darker circles of sweat under the armpits. A silver jacket to match the trousers hung over the back of a chair.

'Hello,' I said. 'Hello, Mother!' I rolled my eyes and flapped my hands discreetly to signal that she must act in mother-mode for the benefit of Eustachia standing behind me. 'What's going on?'

'Bertie!' Her voice was agitated. 'This . . . this my husband come from Ukraina.'

The chunky man turned to face me. 'Bertholt? Hello, old chep. Is very good seeink you again.'

He was handsome, in a brick shithouse sort of way, with ruddy cheeks, thick short hair greying at the temples, and a nose like a pork pie with two bites taken out of it. I had never seen him before. He extended his hand. I did not take it.

'And you are . . . ?'

'You no remember me, Berthold? Of course you were only small little boy. I am Lukashenko. Husband from your mamma, Lilya.' He smiled. Two gold molars glistened in his mouth. 'I heff received your letter with sorry newses of her death. I am so heppy to see it was folks alarum.'

I didn't know who the hell he was, but he sure as hell wasn't the Lev Lukashenko my mum had married almost thirty years before, whose wedding I had attended. Apart from anything else, he looked at least twenty years too young.

'You want make sex wit me?' Inna asked him, a dark gleam in her eye.

He hesitated, but only for a moment. 'Of course, my darlink. If you like it.' He took a step towards her. 'To me you are most beautiful woman in world.'

'You speak true?' She lowered the knife, which I noticed had fragments of cabbage on the blade, and a flirtatious smile lifted her lips.

All the while, Eustachia was hovering in the hallway, struggling to make sense of the scene she had stepped into.

I reached out my hand to her. 'Come on in, Eustachia,' I said. 'Can I offer you . . . ? What have we got, Mother?'

I half hoped Eustachia would make her excuses and leave at this point. I could see the situation had little potential for intimacy, and was rife with danger. Although I had experienced her kindness and touched her vulnerability, I still did not entirely trust her bureaucrat heart.

'Golabki we ev. I mekkit for you.' Inna edged towards the kitchen, keeping her eyes fixed on Lookerchunky. She was wearing her pinny, which also had fragments of cabbage on it. On the counter in the kitchen were some large sliced cabbage leaves.

'Thank you, Mrs Lukashenko. That's most kind. I'm absolutely ravenous.' Eustachia turned to the stranger, who had seated himself proprietorially at the head of the table. 'Was it you who wrote to us at the Town Hall, Mr Lukashenko? About the flat?'

'Yes. Flat. Very nice.' He winked at Inna, who lowered her eyes. 'I heff lost flat in Donetsk from recent bombinks. So I decide return in London to live wit my darlink Lilya.'

'Oh yes, I saw it on the news. It looked awful.' Eustachia shook her head. 'All those homeless people needing to be rehoused.'

'Criminal fascist US-backed government bombink own citizens because they speak different language. Six thousand dead. Many children.' Drops of perspiration appeared on his brow. 'They wanted Europa but they got USA. Only the Putin can save us.'

'Putin?' Eustachia and I exclaimed in simultaneous horror, then our eyes met, and we laughed.

'He is small man but clever.'

'But he's trying to take over the world!' cried Eustachia, her cheeks prettily flushed. 'It was on the BBC!'

'Your BBC are incorrect, madam. Putin not take over world, he only want control in Russia. But he afraid America want take over world by criminal fascist Netto expansionism. This make him big patriotic hero in Russia. Like your great Mrs Tetcher.'

Putin like Mrs Thatcher? The man was clearly a dupe of Russian propaganda. Did Mrs Thatcher oil her muscles? Does Putin have a handbag? Enough said.

'But hang on, Lookerchunky, Mother divorced you. You can't just come breezing back in here because you've had a real-estate misadventure.'

'What divorce? I no divorce. I love my wife.'

'You it galubki, Lev?' Inna called from the kitchen.

'I am eat everythink, my darlink.' He turned to Eustachia, and murmured in a low rumble, 'You nice fatty lady. In my country fatty lady is very popular. Why you no come in Ukraina? I will find you nice husband.'

'That's very kind of you,' she replied, 'but . . .' Flustered, she flunked the excuse.

'Look here, Lookerchunky,' I said, 'or whoever you are . . . this lady is . . .' Spoken for. Those were the words I held on my tongue but couldn't quite utter.

We eyed each other confrontationally. The cut on my wrist was throbbing and I was desperate for a drink.

Suddenly he burst out laughing. 'You think I am Lukashenko from Belarus? You think I am madman? No! Same name but not me! I am from Kharkiv! Ha ha ha!' He chuckled at his own non-joke, while Eustachia smiled weakly, relieved to be off the hook. 'East West. All same Ukrainian people. Why for fight war? Better eat galubki and drink vodka. Ha ha ha! Ha ha ha!'

It was then that I noticed the two-litre bottle of vodka on the table.

'You from Kharkiv?' Inna appeared in the doorway with four dinner plates and four sets of cutlery. 'Nice city. I been there wit my husband.'

I glanced at Eustachia, who was still smiling bemusedly and had missed Inna's slip of the tongue. So far so good.

'Kharkiv. Kiev. Krim. Even London. Wherever you like,

darlink Lilya, we can live together.' He gleamed his golden smile.

I remembered that Mother's Lev Lukashenko came from the west of Ukraine and had stainless-steel crowns on his teeth. So who was this chunky-looking impostor? Did Inna know that he was not the real Lev Lukashenko, whom Lily had married? Did he know that she was not the real Lily, ex-wife of Lev Lukashenko, but an impostor too? Watching the two phoneys shadow-boxing, I crossed my fingers and hoped that Eustachia, who knew neither the real Lev nor the real Lily, would remain none the wiser. But I had not reckoned on the intervention of Flossie.

Just as Inna emerged from the kitchen with a steaming dish of globabki she squawked, 'God is dead!'

'My God, Lilya! Where you get this bird?' cried Looker-chunky.

'Don't you remember, Lev?' I butted in quickly. 'You gave it to Lily when you got married. Have you forgotten?'

'This bird? I give Lilya this bird?'

'You even taught her to say God is dead!'

'As I recall, there were two parrots. One dead and one alive.' Eustachia looked from him to me with a canny smile.

'Two bird?'

'Yes, two, Lev,' I said firmly, avoiding Eustachia's eye. 'One is dead. It's in the box over there.'

'My God!' He blew his pork-pie nose on a crumpled handkerchief from his pocket.

'God is dead!' cried Flossie.

Eustachia gave me a slow, sexy wink.

Inna fetched four small glasses, then she spooned the galoshki on to our plates with a generous dollop of yushchenko. 'Pliss, sit and it it.'

The impostor Lookerchunky, who had already seated

himself at the head of the table, got busy with the vodka bottle and glasses, passing the first glass to Eustachia, who raised a delicate finger as she sipped.

'It's so nice of you to welcome me into your family reunion. It gets quite lonesome in the evenings, just me and Monty.'

When her glass was half empty, I reached for the bottle and topped it up to the brim.

'Oh, you shouldn't, Berthold! It doesn't mix with the medication! And it's absolutely chocker with calories!'

'Sod the medication, Eustachia. Sod the calories.' I downed my vodka in one gulp, and the room rippled like an underwater theatre. A glimmering haze of magic descended on everyone, even on Flossie, and a song from the seventies drifted into my head. 'Love is the drug!' As the warmth hit my vocal chords, I started to sing, 'Mmm mm mm mmm . . . and I need to score!'

Lookerchunky stood up waving his empty glass like a conductor's baton. When I finished the song, he took up in his chocolate-sweet baritone, *'Vistoopeela na bereg Katyusha!'* The melody drifted from major to minor, haunted by yearning, heroism and lost love, as in the black and white Soviet war films that Mother and I used to watch at the Curzon. I listened, and tears sprang to my eyes. Inna was weeping too. She dabbed her eyes with her apron and joined in the chorus in a high-pitched wail. I noticed that the vodka bottle was now two-thirds empty.

'Povee! Povee!' Flossie wailed from her perch.

In a moment of quiet, Eustachia pitched in with a warbling soprano: 'Keep on the sunny side! Always on the sunny side!'

'Bravo!' Lookerchunky clapped his hands. 'Great philosophia! You must come in Ukraina! We heff too much of pessimism at present time.'

'It's what my speech therapist used to say,' she giggled.

By now, of course, I had put two and two together, but I did not voice my suspicion that her speech therapist had been none other than my mother. There would be plenty of time for that in the future.

'You are my sunny side, Eustachia.'

BERTHOLD: *Stacey*

The night was sweet with human warmth, ample with dimpling flesh, moist with body fluids, and punctuated by trips to the bathroom. I woke late, with a jumble of songs running through my head. Occupying most of the bed, and hogging all of the duvet, Eustachia was snoring lightly. I kissed her on the nose and went in search of coffee.

In the kitchen, Lookerchunky, stark naked, was doing the same. I took a discreet look at his beast, which dangled raw-red and uncircumcised beside the cutlery drawer. It did not seem any bigger than mine.

'Berthold, old chep, we heff to talk.'

'Yes, but not now.' I was desperate for coffee. There were barely two spoonfuls left in the Lidl own-brand jar. I commandeered them both into two cups, one for Eustachia and one for me. He could go hang himself, for all I cared.

'You mother, Lilya, she very pessionette lady.'

'Mhm.' I poured in hot water.

'We heff make loff all night.'

'Mhm. I heard you.'

I opened the fridge door. As I bent down, the dull ache in my head became a sharp pain. There wasn't much milk left, either. Really, it was too bad. Inna was supposed to take care of these things.

'She want we liff together.'

'Mhm.' I stirred the beige liquid. 'Where? Where do you propose to do that?'

'She propose me liff wit her in flet. This flet.'

'Oh no. No no no. You don't get it, Lookerchunky.'

'I understand how you feelink, Bertie old chep. But you grown-up men now. You too old for livink wit Mamma.'

'Look, there's something you need to know.' A pulse in my head was beating like a hammer on a dustbin lid. 'She's not really my mother.'

'Not mother? How is possible?'

'My mother Lily is dead.'

'God is dead! Ding dong! God is dead!' No one had remembered to cover Flossie's cage for the night. She was lounging on her perch with a morbid look in her eye.

Startled by the noise, Eustachia called from the bedroom, 'Can I do anything?'

'It's all right, Stacey. I'm just coming. Do you take sugar?'

Stacey! What a ghastly name! I supposed I would get used to it.

'I'm sweet enough as I am!'

We sipped our coffee-flavoured water sitting up side by side in bed, the duvet pulled up over our nakedness, her hair loosed from its ponytail and snaking in coppery coils over her splendid breasts. Through the wall, we heard the sounds of a shrill soprano and a mellow baritone yelling at each other. Fortunately, Lubetkin's walls were thick enough that we couldn't make out what they were saying.

BERTHOLD: *Cherry cutter*

Eustachia left early in a whirl of polyester, perfume and hastily applied lipstick. I took my time, knowing there was no coffee to look forward to and not even any money to go out and get some, until Inna surfaced.

I checked my emails, nothing much there – who the hell falls for these ridiculous Ukrainian bride ads anyway? – then I put on my paisley pyjamas to pad to the bathroom, turning the radio on to blot out the sound of Inna and Lookerchunky, who were still arguing. Sticking my razor-ready chin out in front of the bathroom mirror, I brooded over a new complexion imperfection – does Clooney have these red spider veins yet? – and the ghastliness of growing old. Then I heard the front door slam. I put my head out to see what was going on.

Inna was standing in her nightdress in the hall, gazing at the back of the closed door with a look of utter desolation on her face. 'Why you do this to me, Bertie?'

'Do what, Inna? The man is a scoundrel. A rogue. An impostor. We don't know *who* he is. I've probably saved you from a fate worse than death.'

Though judging from what I had heard last night, she had already experienced a fate worse than death, and rather enjoyed it.

'I say everything you tell me – mother, sister, friend, crazy – all I pretend it like you tell me. But you – why you not pretend some little thing for me, Bertie?'

'Look, Inna, we need to get one thing clear. That man is not moving in here. No way.'

She said nothing, her mouth set in a sullen pout.

'And another thing – why are we out of coffee? You know I need coffee in the morning if I am to function at all. It's not too much to ask, is it? Look, I'm sorry . . .'

Her eyes were filling up with tears. Was I being too harsh?

'. . . but I thought we had an agreement, Inna.'

'I make agreement wit Lily, you mother. I make promise to Lily. I leave my lovely flat in Hempstead for livink in stinking council flat wit you! Oy!'

'Mother wanted you to move in here?' I had half suspected this.

'She say to me, Inna, look after my son. He good man but useless. Witout me he will be starving of hunger. When I die he will be put out on street from under-bed tax.'

'Mother said that to you?' It's nice to know that one's parents have such confidence in one.

'Lily good Soviet woman, like saint in heaven.' Tears were coursing down the runnel-grooves in her cheeks. 'She tell me you homosexy. I understand. You no marry. You need woman in house.'

'Mother told you I was homosexual?' Could this be true? I edged back to the kitchen, where the kettle was hissing and screaming for attention.

She followed, shuffling in her slippers, berating me in a mournful shriek that echoed the cadences of the kettle.

'But I see you like lady. You chase first after black one, then after fatty one. What I can do? I think soon you will marry and I will be out.'

'Ssh, Inna! There's no need to shriek. Can't we have a rational discussion?'

But she was having none of it.

'I like nice man, nice flat, nice life. I write letters in Ukraina newspaper.' She began to wail again. 'Oy, I understand! You think I too old, you think Lev too young for me!'

'The thought had crossed my mind.'

'Young, old – love got no barricade for age! Look George Clooney! He forty-year-old man marry beautiful young wife.'

'Actually, Inna, George Clooney is fifty-three.'

My correction was lost on her. 'I more younger than Lily,' she moaned.

Something dawned on me.

I said, 'But Inna, this man, this Lookerchunky, he's not the man my mother married. He wasn't her husband. For all we know, he might be married to someone else.'

'Not husband? Oy!' Inna crossed herself fervently, as if I'd accused her of adultery. 'So who he is?'

'I've no idea. Maybe a relation or an acquaintance. Maybe just someone who read a story about a nice flat in London and a woman on her own, and decided to take a chance. The world is full of chancers like that. You can't be too careful, Inna.'

She reached down two cups, filled them both with boiling water, and placed a tea bag in one of them, musing out loud, 'All night he make love like big man-horse of Queen Ekaterina.'

'Yes. All night. I heard. Look, Inna. That's all well and good. But it still doesn't give him the right to come and live in this flat.'

'When morning come he sing beautiful song from my country. *Mmm m mmm m!*' She broke into her wailing ditty. 'You know this song, Mister Bertie? Soldier depart for great patriotic war, and his beloved Katyusha walk beside riverbank sing it to him.' She flipped the single tea bag into the other cup and began wailing again. '*Veestoopila na bereg Katyusha.*'

'Yes, it's lovely. But we've run out of coffee. And milk.'

'You see, Ukrainian people now living in London, they very

nice people but all from West Ukraine. Different religion. Different history. They take down statue from Lenin and put up statue for Nazi.' She loaded two spoonfuls of sugar into her tea and sipped carefully, sucking in air to cool her mouth. 'In my country is twenty million dead from fight against Nazi in great patriotic war. *Mmm na visokiy na krutoy* . . . My father lost one leg. My Dovik lost all family.'

'Yes. Splendid. You can tell me the story later. But have you got a fiver I can borrow?'

I pulled on my jeans and T-shirt and stumbled out into the grove clutching Inna's fiver, thinking it would be imprudent to blow it all in one splendid triple-shot at Luigi's, though the temptation was there. A fine rain wetted my hair. In my befuddled state, I noticed that something had changed in the grove, but I couldn't put my finger on what it was. One of the feral moggies, a damp scrap of ginger, ran beside me, tail in the air, and rubbed herself against my legs. I bent to stroke her but she shied away then vanished into the shrubbery.

On my way back with my bulging carrier bag – it's amazing what you can get in Lidl for a fiver – I noticed among the cherry trees there was a litter of discarded food packaging, nappies, a black bin bag of unknown contents, a peed-on foam mattress, and a large finely executed turd. Canine? Human? I clicked my tongue in annoyance.

Then I realised what had changed – the tents had gone. They must have left in the night so silently that I hadn't heard them. Then again, we were making quite a racket ourselves.

Inna was out when I got back. Oh dear. Had she run off in tears to search for the impostor Lookerchunky? Sipping my first proper coffee of the day – it was almost ten o'clock, for godssake – my mood mellowed, and I began to wonder whether I had been unduly hard on Inna, who certainly deserved a mild rebuke for dereliction of coffee duty, but had, to her credit, come up with the necessary fiver. When she came back, I would apologise.

I gazed out of the window. The familiar view was tinted with the sepia of melancholy, to which the flavour of Lidl own-brand may have contributed. Yes, I had behaved badly. I'd been a jerk. I yearned for a glimpse of a forgiving angel skipping along the path between the trees. Where had she been going with that enormous suitcase yesterday? With surprising fondness I also anticipated the stately progress of a Genuinely Good Person, a saver of strays, flea-bitten in the line of duty, coming with a file folder under her arm to rescue me. Or be rescued by me. It came down to the same thing.

Suddenly a commotion at the bottom of the grove caught my eye. A white van had pulled up by the kerb – two white vans, in fact – and men were getting out with heavy-duty tools. Then one of those fork-lift trucks with a platform on the front trundled up, I think they call them cherry pickers. Or cherry cutters in this case. Within minutes, I heard the ghastly high-pitched whine of an electric saw, which was not unlike Inna's earlier singing. Should I rush down and chain myself to a tree? Without Violet to witness my heroism, the whole scenario seemed a lot less appealing.

The same tree I had been chained to was now under attack, amid a crash of branches and a flurry of pigeon's wings. Did I owe it to Violet to continue the struggle which she had started, even though she was no longer here? Or was that merely quixotic? While heroism and inertia battled it out in my brain, a wiry figure in a purple coat had no such doubts. Mrs Crazy appeared in the cherry grove with her two umbrellas, and started beating the hapless tree cutters about head and shoulders. One of them went down with a crash. The other got on his mobile phone.

Moments later a police car pulled up behind the white vans. Two coppers strolled down the path towards the scene of tree carnage, and had words with Mrs Crazy. I couldn't hear what they said, but I could guess. Mrs Crazy listened, started to argue back, then took a swing with her umbrella. In a flash, one of them got her in an armlock. The other whipped out a pair of handcuffs, and between them they bundled her into the back of their car. The whole scene had lasted no more than ten minutes.

Then the chainsaws whined on.

BERTHOLD: *Priory Green*

I put Flossie out on the balcony to bear witness, and withdrew into the quiet seclusion of my flat to lick my existential wounds. Mother was dead. Violet was gone. Inna was still out. Eustachia had work to do. All the women who had buoyed me up in the last few months were floating other boats, and I was on my own, my life drifting aimlessly until something or someone took command. The relentless whine of the chainsaws in the grove chorused my impotence, while a rodent of self-hatred gnawed at my guts. I had taken Mother for granted, I had behaved badly towards Inna, I had let Violet down, I had taken advantage of Eustachia's neediness. I was the rat.

I had not fixed a definite date with Eustachia when we parted. Should I give her a ring now, or would that upset the balance of power in our relationship? Loneliness and male pride warred briefly in my chest. I picked up the phone, and found that some idiot – Inna, no doubt – had left it off the hook. How long had I been incommunicado? What if Violet had called for a last-ditch rescue? What if the police had found my bike? What if someone had been trying to contact me with a fabulous stage role?

Tutting, I dialled Eustachia's office number and got an answering machine. 'Would you like to see a film, Stacey?' The message I left was studiedly neutral in tone.

Meanwhile, at a lower level, life rumbled on. Unbuckling my belt, I went and settled myself in the loo with my jeans around my ankles, pulled the Lubetkin book off the shelf, and looked in the index for Priory Green.

The Priory Green Estate, where Eustachia had found me clinging to the railings, was one of Lubetkin's largest projects of social housing in London. To the modernist architects, the bombed cities of post-war Europe seemed like so many blank canvases on which to erect their dreams. Priory Green was conceived before the war but not completed until 1958. The plans had been drawn up to generous Tecton proportions and constructed out of top-class Ove Arup reinforced concrete; all the flats had a private balcony, habitable rooms faced south, east or west, and communal facilities included a circular laundry with a tall chimney, which I hadn't noticed yesterday. But during the war, building work was suspended and Harold Riley, the alderman who had commissioned the work from Tecton, was ousted and disgraced following a disagreement about two deep concrete air-raid shelters he'd had built under the Town Hall in defiance of the party line.

By the time work restarted on the estate after the war, the housing need was much greater, the political climate had changed, and Harold Riley was surcharged and personally bankrupted by his political rivals. Lubetkin himself had retreated from London; he supervised the project at arm's length from his farmhouse in Gloucestershire, a disillusioned and embittered old man.

Reading this filled me with a deep melancholy that was only partially alleviated by a particularly satisfying bowel movement. Above the noise of the water rushing into the cistern as I flushed, I heard another mournful call: *Ding dong!* Hoiking up my jeans, I went to answer the door.

It was the postman, with an envelope in his hand. Why hadn't he just put it through the letter box?

'Outstanding postage due. One pound and eleven pence. That's eleven pence owing because the postage now costs fifty-three pence. And one pound administration charge.'

'Blimey. Let me see the letter.' I didn't want to be paying out all that for junk mail. Besides, I wasn't sure I had one pound and eleven pence. He handed it over. It was a small white envelope, handwritten to Mr Berthold Sidebottom. The postmark gave nothing away. 'Hang on a minute.'

I could have just stepped back into the flat with it in my hand and slammed the door, but looking down I noticed a solid black chukka boot resting on the threshold. He had obviously been in this situation before. I had ten pence left over from my shopping, there were three twenty pences in the loose change jar and I found a fifty-pence coin in the pocket of Inna's black cardigan hanging in the hall. The postman took it all, gave me change, and made me sign something.

'Thanks, mate. By the way, your zip's undone.'

The letter was from someone called Bronwyn at The Bridge Theatre in Poplar, asking me whether I was available immediately to take up the role of Lucky in their production of *Waiting for Godot*, for which I had recently auditioned. Apparently the actor who had been playing Lucky had unluckily tripped over the rope, slipped off the stage and broken his leg, and the understudy was re-sitting his finals. She apologised for writing, but said that they had tried to phone and got a 'number out of service' message. They didn't have my mobile number. She added a PS on a personal note, saying that she'd been at the audition, had loved the way I delivered Lucky's speech with a stammer, and hoped I would integrate it into my performance.

The stammer. Yes. I recalled that it was the rope that had brought on the stammer, and I had stammered helplessly all through the audition. One of the panel had had the bright idea of tethering me with Lucky's rope while I spoke to see how I looked, and I had come out in a cold sweat. Unfortunately,

Beckett's broken lines did not work the same flowing magic as Shakespeare's; in fact they made it worse. 'God with white b-b-beard . . . since the death of b-b-Bishop b-b-Berkeley . . . it is estab-b-blished b-b-beyond all doubt . . . that man . . . for reasons unknown . . . lab-b-bours ab-b-bandoned . . .'

The letter was dated two days ago. I phoned straight away. Bronwyn was ecstatic. She would email over a copy of the script right away, she said. What was my email address? Could I start tonight?

'Tonight?'

'Would that be okay, Mr Sidebottom? You're familiar with the play, aren't you? Our bar manager has been standing in, but he's been struggling, even with the text in his hands.'

'I'm not sure I could memorise it in a couple of hours. It's quite complicated.'

'Just do your best. It doesn't matter if you get the odd word wrong. In fact it might enhance the audience experience, if you see what I mean. If you could get here for six thirty, we could just walk it through.'

Bronwyn had quite a sexy voice, deep and smooth with a slight regional burr, so I replied, 'No problem, Bronwyn. See you later.'

Ha! That would be one in the eye for Nazi McReady and his tarrgets. But how the fuck would I get to Poplar with no credit on my Oyster card? The problem was solved when Eustachia called back to say she would love to go out to see a film.

'There's that new George Clooney on release.'

'I've got a better idea. Wouldn't you prefer a night at the theatre?'

BERTHOLD: *Lucky*

Bronwyn turned out to be not nearly as sexy as her voice – tall and toothy, sporting long beige dreadlocks with coloured beads on the ends and rainbow-patched dungarees – in fact my stereotype of a lesbian. Was she or wasn't she? I studied her carefully, but it is hard to tell nowadays. Anyway, I decided not to pursue matters. But she was nice. She gave me a £20 advance on my stipend, ordered a double espresso and a cup of tea for Eustachia from the relieved bar manager, and led me backstage to meet the rest of the cast.

Then the ten-minute bell rang. Soon that hush of expectation settled on the audience, which hit my blood like a drug. My pulse quickened. My senses were alert. My breath was controlled. I was ready.

When you're onstage with the lights on you, it's hard to make out the faces of the audience, even in a space as small as The Bridge. Squinting, I scanned the dark, steeply tiered benches, which were about half full, mainly with young people funkily dressed like arts students. There was a smell of damp socks and patchouli, and you could hear in the background the hiss of the espresso machine, a hum of conversation from the bar, and the rumble of trains passing overhead. It all added to the atmosphere. Then I spotted Eustachia in the front row, smiling with a bemused expression as she watched me shuffling on with the rope around my neck.

I wondered what she made of the play, and of my performance. It isn't easy to stammer on command, but when I declaimed, 'P-p-plunged into torment . . . stark naked in the stockinged feet in Connem-mara,' I fancied I caught the glint of a tear in her eye. She had never heard me stammer seriously before, but the funny thing is, this time it wasn't real. I was acting. Even when Pozzo tugged on the rope, I felt a professional calm run through me. I took control of Lucky's lucklessness and made it my own. I didn't need anyone to tell me: I knew I was good.

She waited for me as I came out of the dressing room, and threw her arms around me. 'You were wonderful, Berthold! I'm so glad you brought me to see that, instead of wasting an evening on some George Clooney trivia. It was so profound – a scathing indictment of local government bureaucracy. People hanging around endlessly waiting for something that never appears. Actually – what *was* it about?'

'PhDs have been written about it.' I brushed aside her question as if I knew the answer but couldn't be bothered with it. 'Did you really mean that about George Clooney?'

'Oh, absolutely. Give me Berthold Sidebottom any day.'

I pulled her towards me and kissed her long and hard on her lips. She gasped with surprise, then melted like a warm marshmallow in my arms.

The actors who were Estragon and Pozzo passed us on their way out and gave us a little round of applause.

I settled like a habitué into the passenger seat of Eustachia's car and we glided swiftly through the near-empty streets of the old East End, close to where Grandad Bob had worked on the docks and Gobby Granny Gladys had ended her days. Even Poplar had become trendy enough to boast its own theatre. This creep of culture can only be a good thing, I thought, spreading enlightenment to the de-industrialised wastelands.

As we approached Madeley Court, Eustachia slowed down. 'Would you like to come back to my place and meet Monty?'

'Who's Monty?' I imagined some aged relative or lurking lover.

'Monty the Mongrel. Have you forgotten?'

Indeed I had. 'There's nothing I'd like more.'

Actually, there were several things I would like more, including another exchange of body fluids, but you can't say that to a woman, can you?

Eustachia lived in a one-bedroom flat in the basement of a four-storey house in the almost trendy area north of the Pentonville Road, not far from where my repossessed flat had been. When she had picked me up at the Priory Green Estate and driven me to Madeley Court, she had said it was on her way home; in fact I realised she must have driven well past her destination. Out of fancy, or out of pity? I might ask her one day.

The door to her flat was down a flight of stone steps. You could smell the whiff of damp as you walked in, despite the scented candles and bowls of potpourri dotted about. As soon as she opened the inner door, a scrap of brown fur hurled itself against our legs, yapping hysterically. It was a creature of exceptional ugliness, with short legs, a blunt nose, one eye bigger than the other and a coat the texture of a toilet brush. I felt an urge to kick it, but I controlled myself.

'Say hello to Berthold, Monty,' said Eustachia.

'Yah! Yah! Yah!' said the dog.

I continued to control myself. 'He's adorable,' I said.

'Oh, I'm glad you think so, Berthold. I was afraid you wouldn't like him. You can see why I couldn't bear the thought of having him put down.'

'Mmm. You're a goddess of salvation.'

I felt a sharp pricking in my ankles. Monty's teeth? Monty's fleas? Or my imagination?

'Would you like a cup of tea?' she asked.

My heart sank. What I had in mind was a shot of whisky, or at least a glass of wine – even Lidl sweet sherry would do. Despite the earlier promise of the George Clooney moment, I had a sudden fear that this relationship was doomed.

'Have you got any . . . ?'

'I don't usually keep alcohol in the flat, because of my diet. Not having it means I'm not tempted. Not by that, anyway.'

Temptation. My heart did a little fish-flip. 'I get it. A cup of tea would be great.'

'I've got redbush, if you prefer?'

'No, please! Nothing healthy!'

Despite the lack of alcohol, we somehow made it to the bedroom. I guess she had to be more proactive, to make up for the all-round sobriety. Monty, shut outside, whimpered and scratched piteously at the door. His distress brought back a sudden terrible flash of memory of my first day at school, the closing clunk of the heavy safety-glass door; Mother out of reach on the other side. Love, comfort, kindness, protection – all on the other side. I cried and banged my little fists on the door, but by the time someone came to open it, she had gone. The teacher took my hand and led me to meet my new classmates. 'Don't be a crybaby. That's enough blubbing. You're a big boy now.' At that moment, I had been cast out from Eden.

Such a desolate flashback would be enough to put anyone off his stride, and I'm sorry to say it put me off mine. That and the baleful stare of the row of teddies lined up on the bookshelf by her bed. The beast had become a mouse. Oh dear. As George Clooney must surely know, performing onstage is not the same as performing in bed. Quick as a flash, Eustachia ducked down under the duvet and popped him in her mouth. He cheered up a bit, but then the mousiness crept back.

'Look, I'm sorry,' I said. 'It's been a stressful day.'

'Just a cuddle would be fine,' she said.

I pressed her against me, and so she fell asleep in my arms with her coppery hair, loosed from its inane ponytail, spreading like autumn across my chest; but I lay awake for a long time listening to the unfamiliar sounds of people and cars passing close to our basement window and the occasional growling of Monty outside the bedroom door, wondering where the current of life was bearing my drifting boat.

Sometime in the small hours, when I made my nocturnal visit to the bathroom, Monty was lying in wait for me, with a strategic sense worthy of his namesake, the hero of El Alamein.

'Grrr!' I heard his snarl in the darkness, but before I could locate him he pounced at my bare ankles. His teeth, though small, were very sharp. Thus I too acquired purple stigmata, though in my case human kindness had nothing to do with it.

Worse, I'd somehow managed to leave the door slightly open and the mongrel, smelling his mistress's bouquet, leaped on to the bed and started to hump her slumbering form through the bedclothes. At this point my self-control snapped, and I'm ashamed to admit I kicked my rival out into the hall.

He yelped, and Eustachia moaned in her sleep.

'Don't worry, Stacey,' I murmured. 'Everything's all right. I'm here to protect you.' My sense of manhood restored, I drew her close. And in a while, groping for trouts in a peculiar river, we made the beast with two backs. My ship entered her harbour. I found out countries in her. I spent my manly marrow, pouring my treasure into her lap. At last, Cupid's fiery shaft was quenched.

I drifted off into a rounded sleep.

BERTHOLD: *Teddies*

'*Brrrrrr!*' A ghastly clamour of siren bells ripped my slumber asunder. It seemed as though I had only been asleep for a moment.

Eustachia jumped up, banged her fist on the alarm clock, then hurtled out of bed and gathered her scattered clothing from the floor. 'My! I'm going to be late for work!'

After a night like that, what one needs most in the morning is a strong cup of coffee. But I was out of luck.

'Would you like a cup of tea?' she called from the kitchen.

'Have you any . . . ?' I started to croak weakly, but I already knew what the answer would be.

'Help yourself to toast! Just pull the door behind you when you leave! Don't worry about Monty – his walker will pick him up later!'

She placed a cup of weak tea down on the bedside table and touched my bare shoulder with her hand.

'Berthold . . . !' Whatever it was she meant to say, she didn't say it.

'Stacey . . . !' I didn't say it either.

I squeezed her hand and let her go, and fished out the tea bag with my fingers.

The teddies at the side of the bed watched me jealously, as they must have watched over her and loved her through her unhappy childhood; as nobody had loved her since. Until now. An unfamiliar tremor quickened in my chest. I was the man who would cherish and protect her, whose love would oust the teddies. I leaped out of bed to share my insight with her, but I could already hear the sound of her car firing up, and I could see from the desolate look in Monty's eyes as the car puttered away down the street that he was in love with her too. I felt tempted to kick him again, but I controlled myself.

I arrived back at Madeley Court to a scene of unspeakable desolation. Six mature trees had been felled, their leaves spilled like green blood over the pavement. Immature cherries hung in green clusters that would never ripen into scarlet. The cherry grove was now a cherry grave. The two chainsaw guys were busily chopping up the limbs and stacking them in neat piles. Little groups of people came by to watch, and others watched from the balconies of their flats. The kid who had attacked Flossie was taking pictures on his mobile. I wondered where Violet was, who had blazed like a comet briefly across my path and had now curved off on a different trajectory.

In a way, I was glad she wasn't here. It would have broken her heart.

VIOLET: *Karibu*

The Nairobi night is warm, perfumed and full of stars so bright and close you almost feel you can reach up your hand and pluck them out of the sky. You only have to walk a few metres away from the low airport buildings to feel its immensity pressing down on you. Violet waits in the taxi queue, letting the smells and sounds of home flood in on her.

'Langata,' she tells the driver. 'Kalobot Road.'

At her grandmother's house there is a whole reception party waiting for her with hugs, tears and fizzy drinks.

'*Karibu! Karibu mpenzi! Ilikuwaje safari?*'

All seven cousins are there and nine children, including three gorgeous babies she hasn't seen before. The din of adults chattering, babies yelling, kids demanding attention, singing, clapping and the television on full blast in the background is overwhelming. She sits on a wooden chair and gulps down the 7 Up Lynette pours for her, though what she really wants is a cup of milky coffee and her bed.

After they have all gone, she follows her grandmother upstairs to the small mauve-painted bedroom which was once her mother's. She is already missing her parents and the airy calm of their house in Bakewell. Her Grandma Njoki sits down on the edge of her bed and asks for news about her family. Through the waves of tiredness, Violet assures her that they are well and send their love.

'When you getting married, *mpenzi*?' Her grandmother always asks this. 'Soon you be over the hill. How old you are?'

'Only twenty-three. Plenty of time yet. And you, Nyanya, when are you going to find yourself a new man?'

Her grandmother laughs, the big white false teeth flashing in the pink cave of her mouth. 'You're a naughty girl even thinking on it. You think God will let me forget Josaphat so soon?'

She asks her grandmother whether she knows of someone called Horace Nzangu.

But Njoki looks blank. 'He knew Josaphat?'

'I think Babu Josaphat knew him.'

During her stay in Bakewell she'd shown her parents the copies of the Nzangu GRM re-invoices. They were shocked, angry and alarmed. But their attempts to dissuade her from following up this old story had only fired her sense of adventure.

'Daddy told me Nzangu used to be a junior administrator in the Mbagathi District Hospital when Babu worked there. He left under a cloud, accused of rinsing and reselling used syringes and surgical instruments back to the hospital.'

'Why you talking about this *jinai*, Violet?'

'Nyanya, you used to say that Babu Josaphat was killed because he stumbled upon some corruption in the hospital, and went to the police.'

But Njoki shakes her head and says she can't remember a thing, and Violet realises sadly that she probably isn't saying this from fear, that she really is losing her memory. Her hair is completely white now and her skin wrinkled like Cadaga-tree bark, but her teeth still gleam like piano keys, she wears a flower-patterned pinafore over her dress and she still smells of coconut oil.

'*Mpenzi!*' Njoki holds her tight in her skinny arms. 'You got so thin! Thanks be to God you have come home. Go to sleep now.'

BERTHOLD: *Pigeon fancy*

'Cooo-cooo-cooo.'

I was gazing down from my window and sipping a melancholy cup of Lidl own-brand while pondering arboricide, impotence in all its dismal aspects, the fickleness of fame, and other depressing themes, when I noticed there was a bird perched up on the balcony edge close to Flossie's cage – a feral pigeon, no doubt displaced from its nest by the tree carnage below.

'Shut up, Flossie,' Flossie replied.

'Cooo-cooo-cooo,' it warbled, puffing out its iridescent throat-feathers, cocking its head on one side and eyeing her seductively with a round unblinking eye.

'God is Coo. Cooo-cooo.'

The pigeon hopped closer to Flossie's cage. I noticed it only had one leg and a scarred stump where the other should be. Maybe it was the same one I had rescued from the wheels of the white van on the weekend that Mother had died. It seemed to be on intimate terms with Flossie. Cooo-coo, cooo-coo. Maybe it had found love – like me.

Then I heard the sounds of Inna scuffling and banging in her bedroom. I thought at first she had got Lookerchunky in there, but it seemed to be going on for an incredibly long time, even by his standards. And there was no singing. Eventually I knocked on the door to see what was going on, and found her sitting by the dressing table, surrounded by heaps of belongings which she was cramming into cases, bags and boxes. Her loose black hair that rippled down her shoulders now had a broad silver channel at the parting.

'Hey, Inna, what are you doing?'

'I leaving here, Bertie! I going back in Ukraina, wit Lev!'

'Is that a good idea, Inna? You know there's a war on.'

'Oy, this war will soon finish. She is only for crazies. East, west, we all Ukrainian. Good Ukrainian soldiers don't want fight good Ukrainian people, they want beetroot soup, kvass, eppy life. Only foreign want war. Europevski, Russki, Americanski, all crazy. Better make love, drink vodka, sing beautiful song of my country. *Oy ty pyesnya! Pyesenka dyevicha . . . Mm-m-mmm . . .*'

'It's a matter of democracy, Inna,' I sighed, for by now I was only half convinced myself. 'Surely everybody wants that. Good governance, the fight against corruption . . .'

'No democracy. Only oliharki fighting against each other. Some oliharki got friend wit Mister Putin, some oliharki got friend wit Mister Cameron. But every olihark got same big house in London, inside wife blonde wit big titties, gangster wit big gun by door, and outside good British policeman for protection. *Mmm-m-mmm . . .*' She started to wail her song again as she carried on packing.

'Look, we have to stop Putin from taking over the world!'

However self-evident this was, Inna doggedly pursued her own batty agenda. 'No, no! Putin got popular because he stop Netto in knickers of time. Same like Mister Jeff Kennedy got popular because he stop Russia in Cuba wit Bay of Pork . . .' She paused for a moment, and sat back with a smile of reminiscence. 'Ah! That was good time for Dovik and me!'

'Look, Inna . . .' It was hard to know where to begin to correct her addled perspective. 'History tells us a slightly different story –'

'Pah! What use history? History got us Great Patriotic War

305

against Nazi. Twenty million Soviet citizen dead. In history everybody slightly dead. *Mmm-m-mmm . . .*' She looked at me as though I was a Nazi, and carried on with her packing.

'You never finished your story, Inna, how your father's leg was amputated, and Dovik went to Tbilisi to study medicine that came from sewerage. Improbable though that may seem to most normal people. And then?'

'Aha! Soviet bacteriophage medicine was big success! Dovik got medal of gonner. Then in 1962 big creases. American President Jeff Kennedy put rocket inside Turkey for Netto expansionism. Soviet President Khrushchev try put rocket in Cuba.'

'Not Netto, Inna. NATO.'

'So what this Netto everybody talking about?'

'It's a cheap supermarket chain in the north of England.'

'Supermarket?' She looked mortified. 'I was think it military club for putting rocket all around Russia. Supermarket! *Oy bozhe moy!*'

I knew of course about the Cuban missile crisis, but for me the big event of 1962 was my first birthday, some months earlier on May 6th. According to Howard there had been a cake with one candle, which he blew out for me, while Mum and Dad got tipsy and went off to try for another baby, evidently without success. Howard told me that in October 1962 Mum had organised an embarrassing candlelit peace vigil in the cherry grove, which he had been forced to attend, and Dad had made two grand from selling foil-lined anti-radiation suits that had fallen off the back of a lorry somewhere near Huddersfield.

I remember some years later watching a TV documentary about the Cuban missile crisis with grainy footage of rocket-laden warships motionless on a grey ocean as the two world powers squared up to each other. Inna told me that in

October 1962 all across the Soviet Union, people travelled home to be with their families in what they believed might be their last days on earth. Her parents were by then living in Crimea where her father had a desk job with the Soviet Black Sea Fleet. Dovik too came home from Georgia to his adopted family. Time and distance had transformed him from an annoying older brother into a mysterious and handsome stranger. Together they watched the confrontation of warships on the communal television in the basement of the building – the same images I had seen. She described how they held their breath as the heroic Soviet submariners of the B-59 that protected their warships, running low on air deep below the Caribbean and harried by enemy destroyers, had to choose between rising to the surface in sight of their pursuers, or firing off their nuclear torpedoes and risking igniting nuclear Armageddon which, Inna said, would finish all life on earth.

Biting her lip, she confessed that she did not want to die a virgin. Dovik gallantly offered to put that right for her.

'Ha ha! Virgin!' She clapped her hands.

I don't know whether Dovik ever realised or whether she eventually confessed.

Shortly afterwards they moved to Tbilisi and got married. Dovik continued his bacteriophage research, which according to Inna was a Soviet version of antibiotics made from viruses that thrive in effluent and infect and destroy bacteria. Inna, as a nurse at the same hospital, had administered this yukky remedy to local unfortunates.

'Mm. Shakespeare said something along the lines that one pain is cured by another.' It was from *Romeo and Juliet*. 'Take thou some new infection to thy eye and the rank poison of the old will die.'

'Aha! Very clever man! He was Soviet citizen?'

'It seems unlikely, Inna, but it's an intriguing thought.'

Could anyone really be as stupid as that, or was she having me on?

Inna and Dovik lived in a two-roomed flat on the ground floor of a low-rise 'Khrushchyovka'.

'Council house like this, but made from good Soviet concrete.'

Despite her outspoken distaste for public housing, the young couple were happy in their new flat which, although small, was a home of their own at a time when many families were still living crammed into a couple of rooms with parents and in-laws. They made it nice with flowers, pictures and traditional embroidery, and here they had their two children. 'Two boys grown up now. Both doctor. One live Peterburg, one live Hamburg. Everybody normal.'

According to Inna, the Ukrainian Nikita Khrushchev was a popular leader, spirited and jovial, who denounced Stalin and enjoyed a glass of Ukrainian shampanskoye best-in-world. It seemed as though the Soviet Union was at last crawling out of its grim past of famine, war and repression into a progressive and dynamic world power stretching all the way from Czechoslovakia to Kamchatka. Khrushchev's diplomacy even saved the world from nuclear destruction while letting Mister President Jeff Kennedy take the credit.

'No, Inna, it was the other way around. John F. Kennedy saved the world from nuclear annihilation and Khrushchev had to back down. Everybody knows that.'

'Aha! Same like Dovik know I virgin!' she chuckled.

I began to feel a bit sorry for this Dovik, who seemed like a decent sort of guy who had obviously drawn a few short straws in life, Inna being one of them.

In 1964, when Inna was pregnant with her first son, Khrushchev was ousted and replaced by Brezhnev.

'Oy! Such primitive man!' She threw up her hands. 'Primitive eyebrow! Primitive politic! Like black bear cover wit medals. Also Ukrainian! What we can do?'

They resolved to emigrate, but had to wait until the break-up of the Soviet Union in 1991 before their dream could become a reality. As the country went into meltdown, Western advisers poured in and shady people grabbed publicly owned assets in a wild spree of shoot-from-the-hip privatisation. Dovik was approached by the gangster-cum-businessman Kukuruza, who was sniffing around for ways of making money out of creaking Soviet research institutions with business potential. Bacteriophage medicine, with its low-cost effluent ingredients and unlimited upside, seemed an ideal prospect. Dovik demurred. He was not ready to hand over his baby to the mobsters, and he had other escape plans. He was already in touch with scientists at the Wellcome Institute in London who were also studying bacteriophages. He wrote a friendly letter from Tbilisi and was offered a research fellowship.

'So we come in London. Very nice place. Everybody happy. Then one day this gangster Kukuruza come back for Dovik, but now he big olihark.'

Dovik's refusal to sell his secrets cost him his life. A plate of poisoned slatki in a Soho restaurant did for him – or so Inna said.

'Oy-oy-oy! Olihark got him dead. Now I all alonely. Time for going home!'

As Inna spoke, she crammed an obscure pink garment brutally into an already full bag. 'Ah! Ukraina! You cannot imagine, Bertie, how beautiful this country. Yellow-blue, same like our flag. Yellow fields filled wit corn. Sky blue, no cloud. River like glass. Willow tree on bank. Little white house wit cherry trees in garden. *Mmm-m-m.*' She was wailing again, hopelessly struggling with the zip of her bag. 'England is good country but too wet. Too dark. Too much brissel sprout.'

Personally I am fond of Brussels sprouts, but I can see that they are an acquired taste. 'Brussels sprouts are part of your five-a-day, Inna. Here, let me do that for you.'

I took the bag from her and found the only way I could close the zip was to remove the pink garment, which turned out to be a rubberised roll-on corset. She grabbed the bag from me, undid the zip, and shoved it in again. Then the zip broke. Tears welled up in her eyes. I put my arm around her. I was suddenly feeling quite emotional too.

'I can see why you want to go to Ukraine, Inna. But I think you're taking a bit of a gamble with this Lookerchunky guy. I mean how much do you know about him?'

'I know love. That is enough.' Tears fluttered on her eyelashes.

'But love is a bit . . . you know . . . unreliable. Wouldn't it be better if you went to live near your sons?'

'Oy, I been visit in Hamburg. Nice place but everybody speaking German. Wrong type kobasa.'

'What about St Petersburg? That's closer to home for you.'

'Also nice place, but too much gangster, winter worse than London, son too busy. No, better I go in Crimea wit Lev. Nice climate, nice people, plenty seaside, plenty nice food nice wine.'

'But Inna, Crimea is in Russia now, not in Ukraine.'

'No, no, Bertie. Before was Russia, now Ukraina. Mister Khrushchev give it over. I been there.'

'Now Russia has taken it back. Haven't you been following the news? The people voted overwhelmingly. Though of course we must assume the vote was rigged.'

'Oy! Why nobody tell me?' She clasped her hands in dismay. 'Where I will go?'

'But you don't need to leave, Inna. In fact it would be nice if you stayed. Aren't you happy here?' Maybe I had been too harsh with her over the coffee and Flossie's care. From now on I would treat her like a queen.

'Everything changing round here, Mister Bertie. Blackie gone away. Mrs Crazy gone away. Romania gone away. Today they cut down cherry tree, same like in play of Chekhov.'

The Cherry Orchard, that's what I'd been trying to remember! I'd even played Gaev in 1981, in Camberwell. Something about looking from the window and seeing Mother walking through the cherry orchard wearing a white dress. I felt a lump in my throat. She would never walk there again.

'And yesterday I hear man in wheelchair got dead.'

'What?' This was unexpected and shocking. 'You mean Len?' Maybe she was confused.

'Yes, no-leg man wit poison-mushroom hat. Deeyabet must eat to make sugar in blood, and he need electric for keeping insulin in refigorator.'

A finger of guilt poked my ribs. I'd promised to try and help, but I'd forgotten. I'd been selfishly preoccupied with my own survival, and at the back of my mind I'd assumed 'They' would look after him – someone like Mrs Penny from the Council, or the Job Centre, or the NHS would be keeping an eye on him. But nobody was. While I'd been waiting for Godot, time had run out for Len.

I bowed my head, remembering his relentless optimism and his occasional bullshit. 'Poor Len. Didn't anybody help him?'

'I give him injection but insulin kaput.'

Alas, poor Len. A black cloudbank loomed on my mind's horizon. Legless Len, Mrs Crazy, the cherry grove, even Inna Alfandari – now that Mother was gone, those were the last living links that connected a secure past to an uncertain future.

It wasn't just the bricks and concrete that made this place home, it was the web of human spirit, that funny old-fashioned word embroidered by Gobby Gladys: FELLOWSHIP.

'Coo-coo-coo,' Flossie cooed from the balcony. She fluffed out her feathers and hopped up and down on her perch, turning towards the one-legged pigeon as it flapped away in the direction of the next-door balcony. Oh yes, I'd forgotten Flossie – she was still here.

'What's up wit devil-bird?' asked Inna. 'She turning into pigeon?'

'I think she's fallen in love.'

BERTHOLD: *Benefit fraud*

With what was left of my first-night Lucky stipend, I booked a cab for Inna to Hampstead, where it turned out she still had her old flat, which she had been subletting to friends of friends. I felt quite peeved that she hadn't told me before, but relieved that she had somewhere to go.

These friends of friends were now visiting family in Zaporizhia, and until they came back Inna would be able to stay there with Lookerchunky aka Lev. When they returned, their rent would be paid into Inna's bank account and would augment her tiny widow's pension back in Ukraine. The more I learned of this set-up the less I liked it, but she had it all worked out, and as she gabbled her explanation her eyes slid from side to side in a shifty way that made me suspect that I hadn't yet got to the bottom of it.

'Bye bye, Bertie.' She stood on tiptoes and gave me a peck on the cheek, then she was gone in a high-speed hobble, leaving only the trace of her distinctive spicy smell with a hint of L'Heure Bleue lingering in the hallway.

Watching through the window as she tottered across the decimated cherry grove with her bags to where the cab was waiting, a lump rose in my throat. I would miss her potty conversation and dreadful singing. I would miss the globalki, kosabki and slutki.

Then I heard: *Ding dong. Ding dong!*

'Who the f—?'

A man and a woman were standing at the door, seedy nondescript types with flat lace-up shoes, briefcases and blank unsmiling faces like the Undead. I moved to close the door, but the man was resting one brown shoe on the threshold.

'We're looking for Mrs Inna Alfandari,' he said. His voice was flat, brown and slightly nasal.

'She's not here,' I said. Who the hell were they? Mormons? Jehovah's Witnesses?

'Can you tell us where she is?' asked the woman. Her voice was also flat, brown and slightly nasal. She did not smile.

I hesitated. If they were police, they would have shown their ID. 'Can you tell me who you are?'

'Does Mrs Alfandari live here?' he pursued.

'Look, I've no idea who you are. Why should I tell you anything?'

The woman flicked back the lapel of her jacket to show an ID tag dangling on her low-rise bosom. It had a bronze company logo on top – i4F – and her name: *Miss Anthea Crossbow, Fraud Investigator.* Blimey.

'Can we come in?'

'I'm sorry,' I said, 'I think you've got the wrong p-p-person.'

'We've been watching these premises,' said the man. 'We have reason to suspect she's been living here.'

'There's no-b-body of that name living here. There's just me and my m-mother. Lily Lukashenko.'

They exchanged quick glances.

'There must have b-b-been some mix-up.'

'We're investigating benefit fraud.' The man handed me a business card, with the same i4F logo and the name *Mr Alec Prang. Senior Fraud Investigator.* 'We believe Mrs Alfandari has wrongly been claiming Housing Benefit for a flat she no longer occupies.'

'Oh, how a-p-p-palling!'

So that's what she'd been up to – the old scamp! Not poison but fraud. When you think of it, we were two of a kind and maybe that's what drew us together. Did they know that she had also been renting out the same flat, pocketing both the rent and the Housing Benefit? No wonder she could afford to be generous with the vodka. Should I tell them? No. A plague upon it when thieves cannot be true one to another!

'B-but there must b-be a mistake, Mr P-p-prang? She definitely doesn't live here.'

'Maybe we'd better recheck the Hampstead address,' murmured Miss Crossbow to Mr Prang.

'That would seem like a good idea.' I smiled to myself. By the time they got there, Inna would have arrived in her taxi to confound their suspicions.

'Would you please contact us if you discover any information about the whereabouts of this individual?' Mr Prang bared his teeth in the semblance of a smile, and I assented with equal insincerity.

'Thank you for your time, Mr . . . er?' Miss Crossbow was fishing for my name.

'It's been a pleasure.' I closed the door.

I heard the clunk of the lift and waited by the window for them to emerge in the grove, but they did not appear. Where could they have got to? Panic struck me as I reflected on their visit. Were they keeping me under surveillance too? While investigating Inna, had they twigged my own irregular situation and my mother's demise? I stepped out on to the rear walkway just in time to see an unmarked white van with two figures hunched in the front seats, pulling away at speed from behind the bins. Presumably they had been staking out the back of the flats. Still, I smiled to myself, if they went back to Hampstead now, they would be just in time to realise their mistake.

Though I was miffed that Inna had pulled the wool over my eyes, I felt a sneaking admiration for her too. She had fooled everybody – even me, even Mother, who would never have guessed her friend's duplicity and might have been horrified. On the other hand, Mother was generally tolerant of human weakness, especially when accompanied with a glass of booze.

Inna had left Mother's room in quite a mess so, putting on the radio to drown out the silence in the flat, I busied myself with clearing up the debris. Here was the pink corset, which I put in a carrier bag for Inna to collect, and some tattered black stockings which I binned, along with crumpled packaging, an empty bottle of black hair dye, a hairbrush matted with long black hair, a still-unopened pack of Players No. 6, which Mother must have hidden somewhere, several plastic cups containing what seemed to be green phlegm, and a stack of women's magazines in Cyrillic script featuring plump blonde dark-eyed models and recipes that looked suspiciously like variants on kobaski, golabki and slatki.

Once tidy, the room was more than bare – it had a desolate look. From the box under the boiler I replaced Mother's photos, covering the faded squares in the wallpaper: dashing Ted Madeley, dreamy Berthold Lubetkin, Granny Gladys with her flowerpot hat and Grandad Bob with his dog-head walking stick, and the photo of me with Howard and the twins on Hampstead Heath. They settled back on to their old hooks with a comfortable sigh. I stepped back to survey my handiwork. Even the bottle of L'Heure Bleue was on the dressing table, though it was now empty.

Out on the balcony, Flossie was flirting with her scrawny new boyfriend. Frankly, I felt she could have done better for herself – an intelligent exotic bird like that – but apparently that's often the way with mature females. I put on the kettle – there was an almost-full jar of Lidl own-brand in the cupboard – and regretted the generous impulse that had led me to offer Inna my remaining fiver for a taxi fare rather than saving it up for Luigi. I was in a fretful mood, my ankles were itching, the cloudbank of depression hovered on the edge of my consciousness, and for a man who has just shagged a very nice woman, I felt irritable and on edge.

Then, as the afternoon wore on, I realised what was bothering me. The phone. It was silent. Eustachia hadn't rung.

I stared at it malevolently. Why didn't she phone? It was her turn, for godssake. I had phoned her last time. If it became a habit, she would start to take me for granted, to give me the runaround. As Jimmy the Dog used to say, 'Treat 'em mean, keep 'em keen.' But surely, a woman couldn't do that? I mean, objectively speaking, Eustachia was nice, but nothing special. Like Flossie, I could probably do better, if I put my mind to it. Now that Mother had given me the green light. Now that I'd landed a rather recherché stage role, surely my sexual capital would be boosted. Maybe Violet would come back. Maybe Bronwyn wasn't a lesbian. My mind was hopping around like a one-legged pigeon.

Suddenly the phone rang. I leaped up.

'Stacey, is that you . . . ?' (Yes, I've come to terms with the name.)

A woman's voice replied, something I didn't quite catch, '. . . in connection with your recent accident . . .' The tone was rather tinny, which I put down to a bad line.

'No, Stacey, I'm absolutely fine. I mean, I stubbed my toe running for the bus, but apart from that I'm just fine. When . . . ?'

'Please press five to speak to a representative . . .' the voice continued.

'Stacey? Is that you . . . ?' Overcome with emotion, I uttered the 'd' word, '. . . darling?'

'. . . or nine to opt out.'

317

'Nine . . . ? What did you say? Aaaargh!' Fury possessed me. 'Piss off! You shameless phone whore, you ambulance ghoul!' I hurled the phone across the room, where it bounced against the wall and fell apart. The cover flipped off and two batteries rolled out under the sofa.

Oh hell! I got down on my hands and knees to hunt for them.

It's amazing what you can find under a sofa that hasn't been moved for a while: a packet of Polo mints, half empty; a single loose Polo mint, partly sucked and covered in ancient fluff; a blue biro, leaking; a whisky miniature, empty; an old-style shilling and a new pound coin; a packet of Players No. 6, three ciggies still in it; a crumpled flyer for Shazaad's takeaway. I found one of the batteries, but the other was elusive. With my fingertips I searched right back as far as I could reach; they encountered the second battery beside one of the legs, and something stiff and papery pressed up against the wall. I pulled it out. It was a large brown envelope.

Inside was a folded sheet of tracing paper about a metre square. I opened it out curiously. It seemed to be some kind of plan – an architect's drawing, in fact, meticulously sketched in black ink with some details and notes added in pencil. It was a drawing of Madeley Court. I tried to match up the pencilled notes to the place I knew, which had become so familiar I hardly noticed its features. A tenants meeting room which would double up as a kindergarten. A communal laundry room at the back of the block, a large roof terrace for drying laundry. These details were in the plan but, to my knowledge, they had not been built. Maybe post-war austerity had put paid to those dreams. But other elements of the plan were still in place. A wide floating roof canopy above the main entrance. Ornamental tiles in glazed terracotta. A communal landscaped garden with trees, seating and a play area. Walk-ways and landings to enhance human intercourse, diagonally placed windows and internal glazing to catch and relay the light. A wide internal staircase lit from above by a skylight. The lifts, I guessed, must have been added later.

Inside this large drawing was folded a smaller one. A flat: three larger rooms and one small one; a kitchen, a balcony, a bathroom. Generous proportions. A skylight in the hall. And in the bottom right-hand corner, a handwritten note, scribbled in the same black ink: *For dear Lily, a home for life for you and your children, Yours forever, BL*.

I studied the ink outline of the familiar configuration of rooms which had been her home for more than half a century, then folded it back into the envelope. The skylight, though, had never been made.

In the end, I reinserted the batteries into the phone and dialled Stacey's number. I imagined it ringing in that crowded fire-damaged office, with her fellow bureaucrats eavesdropping jealously.

Maybe that accounted for the coolness in her voice as she answered, 'Hello? Oh, hello, Bertie, how nice to hear from you. Is everything okay?'

She said she was busy every day next week. She wouldn't say with what, and I was left with the irritating suspicion that she was giving me the runaround on purpose, to keep me keen. On Saturday I had the matinee as well as the evening show of *Godot*, so I was genuinely unavailable. Besides, I didn't want her to think that I was so besotted she could just have me at her beck and call. So it wasn't until the following Sunday that we agreed to meet up again.

As I replaced the phone on its cradle, I noticed the corner of a brown crumpled piece of paper sticking out underneath the telephone directory – not just any old piece of paper. It was a ten-pound note, with a yellow Post-it note stuck on: Лен, it said. Inna must have forgotten it there. Well, he wouldn't be needing it where he was gone. I trousered it grimly and strode out through the tree mortuary that had once been a cherry grove.

'Boss! Where you been?' Luigi greeted me with open arms. 'You become big celebrity!'

'Oh, yeah?' I perched on a high stool at the bar while he got busy with the coffee scooper. Then he reached under the counter for a dog-eared copy of the *Daily Mail*, and sure enough on page eleven there was a grainy photo of me with a rope around my neck on the stage at The Bridge, under the headline: UNKNOWN ACTOR WOWS THE HOUSE IN LUCKY ROLE.

Unknown! Still, I read the review: . . . *called Bart Side played this challenging role with a stammer that added brilliantly to the pathos of Beckett's obscure masterpiece* . . .

This seemed odd for the *Daily Mail*, but the paper obviously has moments of insight. Come to think of it, lesbian Bronwyn had mentioned something to the same effect, which I had put down to gender confusion. Either that or I had been teetering on the brink of love and was oblivious to everything else.

'Hm. Thanks, Luigi. This coffee's good.' Though after weeks of Lidl own-brand instant, my palate may have been jaded.

'Kenya AA, boss. The best. Special for you. That little black girl that come in here tell me to get it.'

VIOLET: *Kenya AA*

One thing you can say about Kenya, it's always possible to get a good cup of coffee here. Kenya AA is without a doubt the finest coffee in the world. Violet's office is just around the corner from the Bulbul Coffee Bar on Kenyatta Avenue, and she sometimes goes there with colleagues from work to enjoy the pastries as well as the coffee – the NGO employs four local staff – or sometimes she meets up with one of her cousins for a pizza. Having longed for Kenyan food during her time in England, she now finds herself missing the varied tastes of London.

Her new job is challenging, especially as she is left almost entirely to her own devices. The woman who interviewed her in London, Maria Allinda, she soon realises knows much less about Africa than she does and is happy to let her take decisions on a day-to-day basis about where the NGO's resources should be focused. She spends her first month visiting enterprises in and around Nairobi, familiarising herself with the work that is already being done.

She meets women who humble her with their energy and optimism – women like Grace Amolo and Nouma Mwangi who set up a poultry farm on the eastern outskirts, and built a school in their community; women like Scholastica Nalo, a widow who supported four children with a small tailoring business, and has now taken on two apprentices.

Another group of women in Nyanza need funds to buy coffee bushes and lease land in an area where cholera has wiped out many breadwinners. Cholera, although easily treatable now, is still endemic in Kenya because of poverty and poor infrastructure, another consequence of the relentless corruption that sucks the blood out of a country and injects poison instead. Just like mosquitoes spreading their disease, she thinks. Didn't that mad old lady who lived next door in London say something about cholera in Kenya? She smiles, remembering the crummy flat she left behind and her eccentric neighbours, and wonders: What happened to the cherry trees?

One day, her work takes her out to the coastal island of Lamu where a cooperative of local women has opened a thatch-roofed guest house near a popular resort. The long stretch of beach with its white sand and clusters of palm trees is idyllic; you can hear the swell and surge of the great Indian Ocean and the calls of the fishermen returning in their dhows at dusk with their catch. But you only have to go half a kilometre inland to encounter the poverty. Two of the women who started the cooperative are widows of fishermen lost at sea. They have deep-set wrinkled eyes from squinting against the sun, and lean muscular bodies like her Grandma Njoki. Before they received the grant to start the cooperative, they had worked as prostitutes in an Israeli-owned hotel in Mombasa that was destroyed in a bomb blast in 2002. They came back to Lamu with their savings and started their own guest house. Gradually other women from the island came to join them; there are seven of them now. Then in 2011 two British tourists were kidnapped by Somali pirates from a remote resort a few miles up the coast, and tourism in the area slumped. But the guest house was close enough to Lamu Old Town to feel safe, and gradually business picked up again.

She approves an extension to their grant for a further year, and sitting on the train from Mombasa back to Nairobi she ponders on how little she really knows about Kenya, and what a lucky and sheltered life she has led.

BERTHOLD: *A perfect day out*

You could say I was lucky with Lucky. I perfected my fake stammer while the real stammer all but disappeared. It was as if I was coming to life after a long hibernation, alert and curious about the world I had woken into.

One Sunday in autumn, with the sun bright and low in a cloudless sky, Stacey and I climbed the path at Alexandra Palace, our hearts beating slightly from the effort. At the top of the rise we turned to look back over the city spread below us, its steep terraces, leafy parks and pincushion of towers all smudged in a smoky haze: so much history, so much splendour, so much hum-drum.

This was Stacey's idea of a perfect day out. Personally I would have gone for a cosy matinee at the Curzon, but she insisted that Monty needed his exercise. She wasn't being nearly as pliant as I'd been led to expect from our earlier encounters, and I found this annoyingly arousing. She was wearing her fawn raincoat with high heels, and holding Monty on a lead. I was wearing my white trainers and linen jacket, and wishing I'd worn something warmer. I'd been recalling my visit from the fraud investigators.

'Anthea and Alec – they're quite a pair, aren't they?' She gave a sly smile. 'Were you scared, Berthold?'

'I was a bit.' I bent down and threw a stick for Monty, who was racing up and down the hill with his tongue hanging out and a manic grin on his face. 'I didn't know whether they were investigating Inna or me.'

'I did my best to get them called off, but unfortunately these investigations can gather their own momentum. It was because Inna's Housing Benefit claim came through a different department. How is she, by the way?'

'I'm not sure. I tried to persuade her to ditch that Looker-chunky bloke, but she was having none of it. Last I heard from her was a picture postcard from Crimea. Did you know Crimea was famous for its nudist beaches?'

'Isn't she a bit old for that?'

'I don't suppose that'll stop Inna. She was never one for playing by the rules. So when did you realise that she wasn't really my mother?'

'That mad woman told me – the one who delivers sermons wearing a shower cap. I tried to warn you.'

'Mrs Crazy? You believed her?'

'One of the saddest aspects of my job is how little solidarity there is – I mean, poor people don't stick together. They snitch on each other. You know, there's a dedicated phone line in the council offices for people to report their neighbours. It never stops ringing.'

I felt a stab of hatred. That stony adversary, belligerent fruit-cake, venomous God-botherer, over-coiffed old cow. I hoped she got a good long sentence for assault and battery and would be forced to let her hair dye grow out behind bars.

'So all our efforts – the dementia, the forgotten husbands, the office fire, the casket of parrot ashes – it was all for nothing?'

'It was a good laugh, wasn't it?' she giggled.

'So where does that leave us now? I mean, what happens to the flat? Will I have to move out?'

'Not necessarily. It all depends on who you live with.'

From the summit of the hill, London straggled southwards, pulsing like a living thing, vast and complex in all its grime and glory. A wave of emotion caught me off guard.

'I'd like to live with you, Stacey.' I just blurted it out without thinking, the way I had blurted out my invitation to Inna Alfandari, but as soon as I said it, a comfortable sense of certainty settled over me like a warm coat. 'If you'd have me.'

'Mm. I'd like that too.' She smiled, then her smile opened into a laugh. 'It would be great. Your flat is so spacious compared with my little shoe box. But,' her smile wavered, 'what about Monty? Pets aren't allowed in those flats.'

I stared at the little mongrel that now stood between me and perfect happiness. He yapped a few times, picked up his stick, raced madly around in a circle, then dropped it at my feet and sank his horrible little teeth into my ankle. I moved him away quite roughly with my other foot but you couldn't really call it a kick. She picked him up and held him to her chest.

Snuggled inside the fawn lapels between those magnificent breasts he turned his beastly head and surveyed me with a look of triumph. 'Yah!'

'Couldn't we pretend he belongs to someone else?'

'Berthold, you can't build a whole life on a fib.' She threw me a severe look. 'I mean – you've already tried it once.'

The mongrel smirked. 'Yah, yah, yah! Grrr!'

'There was no need to go to all that trouble to pretend Inna was your mother. Under the bedroom-tax rules, any occupant would do.'

'I didn't know that.' The wide blue sky seemed to spin for a moment, then settle with a bump on the treetops.

'Most people don't. You could have inherited the tenancy from your real mother anyway.' She giggled. 'Of course most people wouldn't just take a complete stranger into their home like you did, Bertie.'

'Well, if I'd known . . .' If I'd known, I might have chosen somebody different; somebody more normal. But then I'd have missed out on all the globalki, slotalki, klobaski, the vodka, the wailing folk songs and off-kilter history. A whole journey into a different world, in fact. 'Still, no regrets.'

Stacey replaced the dog on the ground, took my hand, squeezed it, then let it go. 'It makes me think how different the world would be, Bertie, if only people could remember to be kind to each other.'

Her cheeks were rosy from the cold. I pulled her towards me and kissed her on the lips. She surrendered with a sigh, closing her eyes and opening her warm mouth to let me in. A sharp wind lifted the corners of her coat and tousled her ponytail. I smoothed it with my hand.

'I love you, Stacey. I love your kindness and your cuddliness. I love you because you're ordinary. I love . . .' Well, actually, I didn't love the ponytail or the dog; but even those might grow on me with time.

'I love you too, Berthold. But I'm not clever with words like you.'

'Words aren't everything.'

'Yah! Yah!'

Monty had spotted another dog, a pretty white husky, on the path ahead, and off he ran for a spot of bottom sniffing. I took her in my arms and kissed her again. I can't remember how long we stood there leaning together before we heard him yapping for attention. I held her tighter, wanting to keep her for myself, but I could feel the persistent yapping was a distraction. It had acquired a breathless high-pitched note of distress.

After a few moments she pulled away and said, 'We'd better go and find Monty. Sounds as though he's in trouble.'

Following the direction of the sound, we left the footpath where Monty had disappeared into the bushes on the trail of the white husky and plunged into a thicket of shrubs. Brambles snagged at my legs, and presumably at hers, but she pushed on single-mindedly. The dog was whining pitifully now. I would have strangled the little sod, but as we came deeper into the bushes, we saw he had almost done that for himself. There he was, hanging by his collar from a metal bar that was sticking out of the laurels, wriggling to free himself. But his weight pulled him on to the metal protrusion, which I could now clearly see was the pedal of a rusting bike, wedged in the upwards position. The more he wriggled, the more he tightened the noose. I ran forward to lift him free. He yelped his appreciation and tried to lick my face with his smelly doggy tongue. I quickly passed him to Stacey, who held him close until his whimpering subsided.

'Silly boy,' she whispered into his ear.

The prick of annoyance I felt was soon overtaken by curiosity. The bike the mutt had been hanging from had a familiar look. I pulled it clear of the undergrowth. Beneath a coating of mud on the frame I could make out the letters *Cu* . . . I rubbed at the mud with my fingers revealing . . . *be*. Red with white trim and a scratched-off patch on the crossbar where I had painted my initials. Eleven gears. But only one wheel. The front wheel, by which I had chained it to the Oxfam shop sign on the pavement, was missing. Come to think of it, I recalled that when I had discovered it was missing, just after my embarrassing Oxfam encounter with Mrs Penny (as I knew her then), the shop sign was missing too.

'I think it's my bike. It was stolen outside Oxfam that day. Remember?'

She blushed, or maybe it was just the wind reddening her cheeks. 'I think we can get it in the car, if you don't mind having Monty on your lap on the way home.'

We retraced our steps to the car park. She lowered the back seats and between us we managed to heave the muddy damaged bike into the shiny little red car. Its front forks were bent, the handlebars were twisted around and its loose chain sagged pathetically on to the spick and span upholstery. It reminded me of something else that had sagged pathetically . . . well, never mind. All's well that ends well.

'There!' Stacey patted my arm. 'Let's walk down to the lake now. There's a nice little café down there. When I was a kid, I used to come here on a Sunday with Mum and Dad and my little brother.' A melancholy shadow slid over her face.

I squeezed her hand. 'Tell me.'

'That was before my parents split up. Before Dad walked out. So long ago.' She sighed. 'We used to bring a picnic, hire a pedalo, and go off into the middle of the lake. We fed the sandwich crusts to the ducks and then there were Jaffa Cakes and tea out of a Thermos. That was the last time I can remember being really happy.'

Stacey clung on to my arm as she wobbled on her heels over a bump in the path. At the edge of the lake, Monty was barking dementedly at a white swan pedalo gliding along a few yards from the shore with a bunch of kids drinking out of cans and letting off party-poppers.

Suddenly a memory came crashing in on me: the absolute darkness, the fathomless water, the rope tightening around my middle as I dangled from a bridge in Hackney or Islington – I couldn't remember exactly where – above the white swan pedalo. Nige and Howard had found or stolen it somewhere and decided to bring it closer to home and keep it hidden under the bridge to use for fishing, and to impress their friends. I remembered their reedy excited voices as they hatched their plan. I remembered the voice of the policeman on the pavement above, interrogating them about the stolen pedalo; I remembered their squeaky emphatic denial of any knowledge of it whatsoever, no sir, it wasn't us. And I remembered the splash as Howard, or maybe it was Nige, let go of the rope.

Although there was not much of a current on the canal, the white swan had drifted away so it was no longer directly beneath me when I fell. It had floated into the entrance of a tunnel where the canal went underground. Of course I couldn't swim, and as I floundered desperately towards it, it drifted away on the ripples I made with my splashing, the faint light gleaming on its puffed-out wings like a will-o'-the-wisp luring me into the darkness. I remembered the foul taste of the water gurgling through my mouth, my throat and lungs soggy with it, something slimy stuck to my tongue as I gasped for air. I remembered total blackness; whether inside me or outside I could no longer tell.

I had no recollection of how I was rescued, but I remembered throwing up wretchedly on the towpath, and Howard coaching me as we walked home, soaking wet and shivering, through the dusk.

'So when Dad asks what happened, you're going to say you fell off a bridge, right? What are you going to say?'

'I fell off a b-b-bridge.'

Stacey slipped her hand into mine. 'Oh, you poor pet! That sounds terrifying!' She frowned. 'I wonder where they got the swan. Maybe it came from here. They find them every winter, you know, abandoned in the bushes or even dumped on the River Lea.'

'But how did they get it to Islington?'

'There are secret waterways all over London. Probably full of dead bodies.' She squeezed my arm. 'Were you scared, Bertie?'

'Mm. As scared as I've ever been.' I was shivering uncontrollably now.

Stacey held me tight. 'Let's go and get a cup of tea.'

'I'd rather . . .'

I surrendered. I let her lead me to a small round table and order a pot of tea for two.

'I'll be mother.' She poured the milk in first, from a small china jug, and then added the tea. 'Say when.'

I gulped the warm tasteless liquid and as it trickled down inside me I felt the twist of cold and fear unwind.

Mother, I recalled, had offered me tea too, and interceded with Sid to let me warm up a bit before he thrashed me. Thwack! I didn't tell him about Howard and Nige and the white swan pedalo. There was no point in getting thrashed twice – first by Dad and then by them for telling tales.

'I fell off a b-b-bridge.'

Mother said that was the first time she ever heard me stammer.

VIOLET: *Bulbul*

With so much to keep her busy since she started her new job, and determined to make a success of it, Violet has put her inquiries about Horace Nzangu on to the back-burner. But today is Friday, and she has invited Lynette to join her for a coffee at the Bulbul at four o'clock. Lynette is the eldest daughter of her mother's second brother, her favourite cousin and the nearest she has to a sister. She is a teacher, a couple of years older than her, married to a civil engineer called Archie; they have three small children, and she has only just returned to work. Lynette is round-cheeked, slim and wiry, like all the cousins, and today she is wearing a white cotton dress with small pink and green candy-stripes and narrow shoulder straps.

'*Haqbari ya leo!*' They hug and laugh, pleased as always to see each other, and gossip for a while about family news.

She tells Lynette about the projects she has visited for her job, and mentions that she came across some big-time corruption in Kenya in her previous London job that could have some bearing on how their Babu Josaphat died.

'Violet, why you can't leave that dirty history alone?' Lynette wrinkles her nose. 'All that corruption belongs in the time of Baba Moi.' That is the nickname of ex-President Daniel Arap Moi. 'It is out of date. Archie says if people always think of corruption when they think of Kenya, it'll put them off investment.'

'But Lynette, sometimes it's the investment that brings the corruption.'

'Since your British have started poking their clean white noses into corruption, our Government has just cosied up more with the Chinese, who don't give a fly what anybody does. That's what everybody says.'

'Lynette, have you heard of the name Horace Nzangu?'

She takes the four GRM photocopies out of their brown envelope and spreads them on the table. Lynette glances at them.

'Nzangu? Hm. I think he's some big *bwana* in the Health Ministry, married to a cousin of Baba Moi. So what? He's corrupt? Tell me something new.' She fakes a big yawn, covering her mouth with her hand. 'No one can touch him. That man put all his relatives in positions where they could get rich. He bled the country for twenty-four years, and we're still bleeding. Nothing we can do, little cousin. All the money is in Europe now. Better to burn those papers and pretend you never seen them.'

'What are you saying, Lynette?' Her cousin's attitude shocks her.

Their coffee arrives. The waiter is tall and slim, with beautiful eyes that linger on the women's bare shoulders.

Lynette takes a slow sip of coffee. 'Shall we order some pastries? The sticky-chocolate cake here is heavenly.' She waits until the waiter has moved away and slides the copies back into their envelope. 'Who else have you shown these to?'

'Nobody. Only the people in my office.'

'Those people have ears and eyes everywhere,' she whispers. 'You don't know who is listening.'

At the next table a group of young people are celebrating somebody's birthday. 'Happy birthday to you,' they sing. A plump girl with mauve hair extensions leans forward to blow the candles out on an iced cake, while everyone cheers and claps. Then the birthday girl makes a speech thanking her mum and dad, to another round of applause. Nobody seems to be taking any notice of them.

'When it comes to bribery, Violet, there's always two parties – one to give the bribe, and one to take it. So why don't your British look into that?'

'That's what I'm doing. It's not like you to be such a pussy, Lynette. I thought you were the brave one out of us.'

The waiter arrives with their chocolate cake. Lynette attacks hers with a fork. Violet cuts her slice of cake into four chunks and forks the first one into her mouth. It is so unbelievably delicious, an explosion of sweetness and bitterness on her tongue, that for a moment she just wants to surrender to the double bliss of chocolate and gossip and forget the whole sleazy HN story that brought her here.

'Violet, *mpenzi*, take my advice, the best thing is to find yourself a nice rich husband and forget about all that history. When you have kids of your own, you'll understand what really matters.'

'Listen, Lynette, my parents told me that in the Mbagathi Hospital when they worked there someone was collecting the used syringes, rinsing them in water, and selling them back to the hospital – not the best thing during an AIDS epidemic. But the case never went to court because no one would stand up and testify. Babu Josaphat worked in accounts, and he had evidence that this was going on, but someone killed him before he could bring it to court. I think that was Horace Nzangu. He started small. Now he's got two point three million dollars in the British Virgin Isles.'

Lynette shrugs her shiny shoulders, polishes off her coffee and cake, and stands up to go, saying Archie will be waiting for her in his pickup on the corner of Kenyatta Avenue. They hug and Lynette presses her with a soft perfumed cheek to whisper in her ear, 'You're playing with fire, Violet. Leave it alone.'

She finishes her cake, pays the bill and makes for the door. The heat in the street outside is intense after the cool of the café. The air is humid with the promise of rain and heavy with the scent of earth, cumin, burned sugar, and a background stink of petrol fumes and stagnant drains. She breathes deeply as she stands in the doorway to get her bearings. A scruffy ginger mongrel is stretched out asleep in the shade. Dogs. Rabies. You have to be careful. You can't pet them, like people do in England. She remembers her dog, Mfumu, she left behind in Karen – he will be dead by now – and the friendly one-legged pigeon she adopted in London. This little dog is incredibly ugly, everything about him seems to be the wrong size or shape. He stirs and gets up to follow her, lazily slinking in the narrow strip of shade along the edge of the pavement.

She needs to call at the office to finish off some paperwork before going home. She walks quickly, so it's only by chance that she happens to look back and notice a lean shadowy figure following behind the dog, on the edge of her vision. She turns and stares. It's the waiter from the Bulbul. 'Hi,' she smiles as he gets closer, but he looks right through her. That's strange. He watches her let herself into the office building with her key, and she sees him disappear into a side street by the tobacco kiosk.

Everyone has left the office except Queenie, the administrator, a plump motherly woman with an elaborate coiffure and nail extensions, who is still jabbing at her computer keyboard, muttering to herself under her breath. While Queenie is absorbed in her work, she takes the envelope with the photocopies out of her bag and stows it in the bottom drawer of her desk, between the leaves of a computer manual.

'You're working late, Queenie. You should get yourself off home.'

Queenie laughs and says something in the Kamba language that she can't understand.

At six o'clock they leave the office together, and make their way to the bus stop. Nairobi minibuses are crowded, chaotic and buzzing with talk and laughter. She joins the queue for the Langata matatu where a noisy crew of women are coming home from market balancing baskets on their heads.

The traffic, as always, is slow and lawless, accompanied by a chorus of horns. One of the differences she has noticed between England and Kenya is the sudden nightfall; twilight fades into dusk in half an hour. By the time the minibus drops her off on Kaunda Avenue it's already dark.

VIOLET: *Kibera*

The rainy season usually comes in November, but this year it starts early. On Sunday morning she wakes to the hammering of rain on the roof and windows. Downstairs in the kitchen, Njoki is rolling up old towels to catch the puddles that leak in under the door, and singing to herself. In spite of the mess and chaos, the first big rains are always a cause for joy, a welcome relief from the dust of summer. Njoki has just switched the kettle on for tea when the phone starts to ring in the hall; she clucks with annoyance and runs to answer it, wiping her hands on her pinafore.

'It's for you.'

'Hello, Violet, is that you?' The voice at the other end sounds both familiar and strange above the racket of the rain. Maybe there's a fault with the line.

'Violet speaking. Who is this?'

'It's Queenie. Violet, I need to get back into the office. Can you come over and let me in?'

Yes, it sounds like Queenie's voice, but she is usually a chatty and relaxed person; she has never heard her sound so anxious before.

'What, now? Haven't you seen the weather, Queenie? Can't it wait until Monday?'

'It's rather urgent. Something I need. Please, Violet. Come straight away.'

Surely no work they are doing could be that urgent, but Queenie sounds desperate.

'Okay. I'll be there in half an hour.'

She grabs her raincoat and umbrella and sets off towards the bus stop.

The road is pitted and puddly, made treacherous by the heavy rain. She tries to pick her way carefully, keeping her feet dry, but soon gives up and splashes straight through the muddy water. What on earth possessed Queenie to go out on a day like this? It seems that the rain has stopped the traffic, so there are no buses or taxis coming through. Too bad. She decides to walk, and takes a left turn off the Southern Bypass, thinking to cut through the Kibera slum and cross the river bridge, which is the quickest way from here into town. This is not normally a route she would take, but she reckons it will be safe in the middle of the day – and in any case, most people will be trying to patch up their pitiful tin-roofed shacks against the rain, or crowding inside.

She is right. The narrow alleys are empty, streaming with dirty water which pours in brown rivulets down into the Nairobi River carrying bits of debris, plastic bottles, torn carrier bags, fallen jacaranda flowers, dead rats, ownerless undergarments that swirl around her shoes. Lines of soggy washing strung across the alleys flap in her face as she passes. Chickens squawk and huddle for shelter. Wet, half-naked children splash and throw mudballs, or chase the stray dogs about. '*Hujambo!*' they wave and shout as she passes, and she waves back, holding her umbrella low.

The Nairobi River has swollen into a foaming filthy torrent. At the bridge, a gaggle of little boys are yelling and running ahead of her waving sticks. Suddenly they stop dead in their tracks, shriek, and turn back to run in the opposite direction, almost pushing her into the water. Maybe this short cut isn't such a good idea. She clings on to the railings, and a moment later three sodden goats thunder across the bridge, and behind them another gaggle of grinning boys with sticks chase them into the alleys. She can hear their excited shrieks long after they have disappeared from view.

At Kambi Muru, she carries on up to Kibera Drive, hoping the matatus will be running once more. The rain has eased now, and there are a few other people at the stop. Before long, a battered yellow Toyota pulls up full of damp people on their way from church. There is little traffic, and despite having to navigate around a number of deep treacherous puddles and a flooding water main, she is soon back at the office. She fishes her keys out of her bag and looks around.

There is no sign of Queenie.

She stands at the intersection, peering impatiently in both directions. The streets are deserted. It is too annoying. Queenie seemed in such a hurry. Njoki will be waiting for her return to sit down to lunch.

As she waits, a battered white taxi-van pulls up close by. Thinking it must be Queenie arriving, she steps forward. Then a man's voice shouts her name, she spins around, and the next thing she knows, rough arms grab hold of her, her hands are tied behind her, and as she starts to scream something dark and suffocating is pulled down over her head. Then she is bundled into the back of the van. The engine revs and roars as she lies face down on the floor, seething with fear and rage, listening to the voices of her three kidnappers discussing where they should take her in a Kamba dialect she can barely follow. Her heart is beating so fast she thinks it will burst out of her chest, but all her senses are on full alert, feeling the vibration of the engine through her cheekbone, registering every bump and swerve of the road through her spine, smelling the burning diesel from the engine and the sweat of the three men.

Then the van swerves, her head hits something hard and she blacks out.

BERTHOLD: *Happiness*

When, after four weeks at The Bridge, the final curtain came down to wild applause, *Waiting for Godot* transferred to the West End. I was pleased, but not surprised. The show had an electricity that seemed to light up the audience in that small space. Transferring to a bigger theatre lost the intimacy, but was replaced by the pulse generated by a much bigger crowd.

Stacey came along once or twice out of loyalty, but I think she got bored with the play in a way you don't get bored if you're one of the players. She was pleased when I was mentioned in reviews and my face began to appear in the better class of newspaper, though admittedly not on the backs of buses. I took it all in my stride without letting it go to my head: the sudden celebrity seemed as unreal and arbitrary as my prolonged absence from the stage had been.

During that time I would often return home after midnight, pleasantly tired in my bones from the long effort of focusing on the stage-moment, flushed with the triumph of a standing ovation or slightly fuddled from a post-performance drink on an empty stomach. The flat greeted me with a welcoming hush after the clamour of the theatre. Flossie was usually asleep, and though I missed Inna's cheerful presence I no longer felt loneliness stalking me like an assassin.

Stacey was at the last West End performance of *Godot*. There were ovations, flowers, tears, farewells, and a long boozy supper afterwards, and in the small hours she guided me towards the little red car that was parked around the corner, and thence to her bed. We made love, and as I drifted into sleep I felt a pleasant warm sensation which seemed to start in my chest and emanate throughout my whole body. This, I realised, in the sweet moment before sleep whacked me out, is what they call happiness. It was so long since I had felt it, I had almost forgotten what it was like.

VIOLET: The chair

Thwack! The blow jerks her into consciousness. She can feel a bruise starting to form.

'Tell us where you put the papers. Else we kill you.'

The older man is standing over her, while the younger one is tying her to a chair from behind. The third man, the van driver, has disappeared.

'I don't know what you're talking about. My office is full of papers.' She struggles to control the wobble in her voice. Did Queenie or someone else in her office betray her? Lynette? Could Marc have alerted his client?

'We know you got papers about Nzangu. You better tell us where you put them, else we rape you then we spoil your pretty face, white bitch.'

She feels something cold and smooth like a blade against her throat. She feels it move upwards until it rests on her cheek. Her heart is thumping like a fish on a deck, but she digs her fingernails into her palms and orders herself to stay cool. Breathe deeply, she tells herself. Keep breathing, in and out, don't let the fear take over.

'We already got Queenie,' says the first man.

'We gonna kill her too, if you don't talk,' adds the other.

Have they really kidnapped Queenie, or is Queenie part of the plot? Who told Nzangu about the photocopies? Her brain is fuzzy from pain and terror.

'I . . . I can't remember. *Mtu ni utu*, be human, brothers,' she pleads, playing for time. Her voice echoes back to her against the bare walls.

'This'll help you remember!'

Thwack! A jab of pain rushes down her left temple to her jaw. If only they would stop hitting her, she would be able to think what to do.

The blow has dislodged the blindfold, and she can see that she is in a long low-ceilinged room with a square window at one end. It looks like some kind of storeroom, with things shrouded in plastic stacked up against the walls. What things? She tries to make out the shape. They look like buckets. Hundreds of buckets. The window is closed, and the air is thick and humid. She can smell the men's sweat and the sharp scent of her own fear. A warm trickle runs down the inside of her leg.

'Waga got your key. He gone search your office. If you tell us, it will go better for you.' It is the older man talking. His voice is less aggressive than the young man.

'They're not in the office. I . . . I posted them. Didn't Queenie tell you?'

She hid the copies so casually inside the computer manual that a thorough search of the office would surely uncover them, if somebody knew what they were looking for. She thinks of the re-invoices she posted to Gillian Chalmers in London. She will have got them by now, but has she read them? And even if she has, will she do anything about them? Or might she just as well have posted them to Marc himself?

'You're lying, white bitch.' The younger man is short and heavily built, with a sneering twang to his voice.

She feels his rough hand cover her breast. She shudders. No one has ever called her white before. Nor a bitch, for that matter. In different circumstances it might amuse her.

'Who you post them to?' asks the older man, who is thin with greying hair and deeply lined cheeks.

'I posted them to the office of the corruption investigator of course.' She wonders who, if anybody, occupies that precarious post at present, since the resignation of Johnny Githongo. 'On Friday. On my way home.' She hopes they don't press for details, or they will soon realise she's bluffing. 'Whatever you do to me, he will get them tomorrow. Nzangu and his hangers-on will be in prison, and nothing you can do will save him now. But if you let me go at least you will save yourselves.' Her voice doesn't sound as confident as she intends, but at least she is managing to hold back her tears.

The two men speak together in their own language. She catches the word *ofisi* – office – and the name Waga. Their talk is interrupted by the sound of a mobile phone ringing – *ping-ping-ping, ping-ping-ping* – she listens to it for a few moments before she recognises the ringtone as her own. They must have got the phone from her bag. She hears them muttering as they fumble to switch it off behind her back; the ringing stops, and her grandmother's voice, faint from a few metres away but still distinct on speakerphone, says, '*Mpenzi*, where you got to? When you coming for your lunch?'

The men listen but neither of them speaks.

'Who is it?' asks the older one in a whisper.

Without answering him, she heaves herself forward, dragging the chair on the ground in the direction of the phone and screams, 'It's Violet! Help! Help! Help!'

Thwack! Her head jolts back as it takes the blow, and darkness falls.

BERTHOLD: A flat in Hampstead

I wished I could stay with Stacey all the time, but her flat was too small for both of us, and it was impossible for her to move in with me because of Monty. As the gloomy autumn days drew in, I resigned myself to shuttling backwards and forwards on my bike. Even happiness has its downside.

One day I got back home to find the message light on my telephone blinking away. I had received recorded messages before, offering me free cruises, computer upgrades, compensation for deafness and suchlike, in hopeful voices that reminded me of Len and his dreams of self-employment. In his memory, instead of shouting abuse, I flicked on the hands-free while I went to fix myself a sandwich. Through the crackles I heard a woman's voice that somehow combined bleating with menace.

'Hello, Bertie, is that you? This is your beloved sister Margaret. We've seen your show is a hit success and you must be raking it in, but I can't sleep for thinking about our pet bunny who is buried in the garden at Madeley Court. Don't you have any conscience . . . ?' The message ended in a choked sob.

I bit into the sandwich, crunching the lettuce between my teeth. Even celebrity, I mused as I erased the message, cannot protect one from the attentions of lunatics – another experience that I could now share with George.

Another happier consequence of fame was that I had started to get offers of parts and invitations to auditions, mainly for characters experiencing some kind of trauma. I tried for *Hamlet* at the Barbican, but lost out to Benedict Cumberbatch. Maybe I overdid the stammer. 'To b-b-be . . .' However, I was delighted to be asked to audition for the part of Lear's Fool in a new production at the National. It was always a favourite of mine, and it brought back memories of the hours I had spent coaching Inna in this role. I wondered what had become of her now.

As if by serendipity, a letter arrived the same day, asking for my help. She wrote in her execrable English that the subtenants of her flat in Hampstead – she gave the address – had stopped paying the rent, and had not responded to letters and phone calls. She asked if I could go round and investigate, adding on a PS that the key was under the blue flowerpot and she had dispatched Lev to sort them out, who would arrive in a few days. I replied that I was now working and too busy to help, but I forwarded her a cutting of a review of *Godot* in *Metro*, and the contact details of a couple of property agents in Hampstead.

Then I had a mischievous idea. Inspired in part by the sinister machinations of Rosencrantz and Guildenstern, whose fate presages the bloodbath in the last scene of *Hamlet*, I wrote a note to Jenny and Margaret, suggesting that we could meet up on Friday morning at a lovely flat in Hampstead that Lily had also inherited from Ted, which had just become vacant, that might suit their needs better. For good measure, I left a voicemail message on the i4F number for Miss Crossbow and Mr Prang, the fraud investigators, alerting them to suspicious activities at the flat in Hampstead where two individuals, both impersonating Mrs Alfandari, had taken up residence and, I had reason to believe, would be there on Friday morning.

I spent the rest of the day calmly studying *Lear*, and honing my interpretation of the Fool in preparation for the audition. Some directors give the part to a boy actor, and maintain that in Shakespeare's time the same boy might also have played

345

Cordelia, but I saw him as a mature man, in his fifties, maybe, no stranger to sorrow.

All the hand flapping and eye rolling that I had drummed into Inna now seemed a bit OTT, and I decided to give him a solemn demeanour and just a little stress stammer on the 'b': *If thou wert my fool, nuncle, I'd have thee b-beaten for b-being old b-before thy time.*

Late on Thursday evening, I received a frantic phone call from Stacey.

'Monty's dog walker has had an accident. Can you look after him tomorrow, Berthold?'

'Look, I'm sorry, Stacey, I'm too . . . b-busy . . .'

'No problem. I'll drop him off just before nine on my way to work. He won't be any trouble.'

'But dogs aren't allowed –'

'I'll hide him under my coat. Nobody will know.'

At ten to nine the next morning, Stacey rang the bell, kissed me on the lips, and handed over the little dog hiding under her raincoat.

'Don't forget to take him out for his walk.' She gave me his lead.

'I might take him up to Hampstead Heath.'

'Lovely. You're a darling. Byee!'

Scarcely had she closed the door than the little beast went and deposited a turd in the kitchen.

'Now, Monty,' I said as I cleaned it up, 'we're going out. Try to behave.'

'Yah! Yah!'

It was one of those dreary autumnal days when the sky is damp with un-fallen rain. Not a perfect day for the Heath, but

I thought it might brighten up in time for Monty's walk. Inna's flat was on one of the roads skirting the Heath in the basement of a grand red-brick house that now had seven doorbells. I rang the one that said *Garden Flat*, and waited. No one answered. There was a blue flowerpot with a dead geranium by the door, but no key underneath. I tried the door. To my amazement it opened. Maybe Lookerchunky had already got here.

'Lev?' I called. My voice was swallowed up in musty silence.

There was a pile of unopened mail inside the door. Amid the bumpf of banks, bills and pizza delivery, a brightly coloured flyer caught my eye. *Funerals by Orthodox rite. P. Gatsnug and Co.*, and on the reverse side the text in Russian. I smiled. He had taken my advice. A resourceful man, and a kind one.

The flat smelled damp, unlived in, with an undertone of mould and stale cigarette smoke. Monty ran around sniffing excitedly. In the kitchen, unwashed crusty plates and pots were piled in the sink. The sitting room was a wasteland of books, bags, discarded clothing and shoes, random household items and cigarette butts, as though Inna's tenants had upped and fled, leaving their scattered possessions. A growl from Monty startled me. I looked up to see two old ladies tottering down the basement steps.

'Cooee, Bertie! Is that you? We've come to see the flat!'

One of the twins – Jenny, I suppose – advanced into the flat. Margaret, more frail and stooped, followed, leaning on a stick, clutching a grey rag against her chest.

Jenny sniffed the air and looked around. 'Dad never told us about this. It needs cleaning up, but it would suit us down to the ground. Wouldn't it, Margaret?'

'Down under the ground!' wailed Margaret, stroking the grey rag, which on closer inspection looked like a much-laundered cloth rabbit.

'She's losing her mind,' murmured Jenny to me, 'as a result

of your callousness, Bertie. You were such a lovely little boy. I never thought you would grow up to be so heartless.'

The pathetic state of the old ladies did prompt a twinge of conscience for the mean trick I had set out to play on them.

'Look here, Jenny –' I started.

Suddenly Monty stiffened, growled. Jenny gasped. Margaret screamed and dropped the rabbit.

Behind me, a deep gravelly voice said, 'Put up hands!'

I spun around. A man was standing there – a short, heavy man with a balaclava pulled down over his head. But the main thing I noticed was the gun in his hands, a black blunt menacing piece of kit which was pointing straight at my face. I guessed it must be Lookerchunky, though he looked shorter than I remembered.

'Look here, Lev, a joke's a joke, but can you point that thing away?'

The gun did not waver.

'Put up hands, Alfandari,' the man growled, and reluctantly I raised my hands, letting go of Monty's lead.

Immediately the little dog bounded forward and hurled himself at the man's ankles. 'Yah! Grrr!'

'Monty, no!' I yelled.

The man pointed his gun down at the dog which was clamped to his leg. I heard a shot, followed by a howl of pain. A fountain of blood spurted up. Monty rocketed across the room, his coat sprayed with red. The man dropped his gun and started hopping, screaming and cursing. Then I saw that the blood was not coming from Monty, but from the man's foot.

Margaret had fainted, and Jenny was trying to drag her out through the door. Monty picked up her rabbit and started racing around the room, dragging it repeatedly through the pool of blood. The wounded man was inching towards his gun. I'm sure George Clooney would have made a dive and grabbed it, like in the movies, but my head was whirring uselessly with fragments of verse. *Absent thee from felicity a while, and in this harsh world draw thy breath in pain, to . . .*

Peeyow! A bullet whizzed across the room and lodged itself in the cupboard behind the balaclava man's shoulder.

'Put up arms!' Lookerchunky appeared in the other doorway wearing his tight silver suit and pointing a chunky silver weapon at the man.

'Lev!' I yelled. 'Who is this man?'

'Oligarki gangster! Come for Alfandari!'

'Alfandari's already dead!'

'I know. He is idiot!'

In the moment that Lookerchunky spoke, the oligarki gangster took advantage of the distraction to grab his gun from the floor and level it at me.

'You no Alfandari?'

'No, absolutely not.'

'Who you are?'

'I'm Berthold Sidebottom. I'm a well-known actor . . .'

'And you?' he addressed Lookerchunky.

'Lev Lukashenko.'

'*Oy, bozhe moy!*' He slapped his forehead. 'I make mistake! And this people?'

He gestured towards the street door where Jenny and Margaret were stumbling up the steps towards the road, shouting, 'Stop! Stop!' in pursuit of Monty, who was racing ahead with the limp bloody rabbit in his jaws.

'Monty! Heel!' I yelled and threw myself forward to grab his lead, but I tripped on the top step and landed on my chin. My mouth filled with blood. As I spat it out, I felt a piece of tooth go flying before I blacked out.

'You okay, chep?' The oligarki gangster was standing over me still holding his gun as I came round.

Suddenly there was a screech of brakes and a thud. I raised my head. A small white van had come to a halt in the middle of the road. Under its wheels, tangled in his lead, Monty was twitching and squealing horribly.

'Oy-oy-oy!' The gangster shook his head.

Lookerchunky stepped forward and dispatched poor Monty with a single shot from his chunky silver pistol.

Then another commotion of voices erupted from the other side of the van.

'No! No! Let me go, you moron! It's a mistake!'

I turned my head, to see Jenny pressed up against the wall of the van with Alec Prang, the fraud investigator, trying to get her in an armlock. Anthea Crossbow was already man-handling poor bewildered Margaret into the back of the van. The van reversed, turned, and sped back up the road. I picked up the dead dog and wrapped him in my jacket, wondering what the hell I was going to say to Stacey.

She would be heartbroken.

The gangster had found some TCP in the bathroom cabinet and was bandaging his foot up in a tea towel.

'We go for drink?'

'Good idea,' said Lookerchunky.

I applied some TCP to my cut face. Fortunately, the pub was nearby.

VIOLET: *Flamboyant*

Violet awakes to absolute darkness and a smell of something cool and antiseptic close to her face. Then she moves her head and a streak of light shows at the bottom of her vision. If she tilts her chin up she can see a low section of her surroundings. She realises the darkness is only from a bandage around her forehead which partly covers her eyes. One hand is immobile, encased in plaster and fixed across her chest with a strap. With the other hand, she gingerly adjusts the bandage a centimetre upwards, giving herself another metre of perspective. She is lying under a white sheet in a small white room. A bright patch of sunlight falls on the floor at the foot of the bed. She tries to remember . . . she remembers the three men, the sack over her head, the square window, the narrow room, the buckets, the pain, the thud of the chair falling over. Then . . . it's as though her memory is on a loop that repeats those same images again and again but will not wind forward however hard she tries.

The sound of a door opening behind her makes her tense up. Are they coming back for her? Without moving her head, she watches two white shoes advance into the room. Two small white shoes on skinny brown legs, carrying with them a familiar voice.

'*Mpenzi*, my baby, who done this to you? I thought I would never see you again! I going crazy with worry.' Her grandmother's voice is strident with relief.

Behind the bandage she feels tears water her eyes and prick the back of her nose. She wants to surrender to the storm building up inside her, to be comforted in her grandmother's arms, but the bandages immobilise her.

'I'm all right, Nyanya. Shush. I'm all right now.'

The door creaks again, and this time a pair of pretty red high-heeled sandals trip across the floor to her bedside. Lynette sits on the edge of the bed, takes her good hand and gives it a squeeze.

'Thank God, Violet. Thank God we got you out. I warned you to be careful.'

'Thank God I called you for your lunch,' Njoki adds. 'When I heard you cry out, I phoned the police straight away. Then I phoned Lynette. Oh, *mpenzi*, I thought you was murdered!'

'Ssh. Not so loud.' A soft woman's voice she doesn't recognise, maybe the nurse. 'She had a shock. She only just woken up. She need to stay calm.'

'It was nothing to do with the police,' Lynette says. 'They said you was probably with your boyfriend and they couldn't do nothing. Wait another day, they said.'

'Another day and you been dead,' adds Njoki in a dramatic voice.

'On Monday morning after Njoki phoned me, I called up the anti-corruption bureau and I told them about those papers you showed me.'

'You told *me* to be careful, Lynette.'

'I was careful. I gave them a false name. At first they weren't interested. The man I talked to said they investigated Nzangu before and he was clean. I wasn't surprised they said that, but now they knew we were on his trail. So I put the phone down.'

'Then . . . ?' She tries to raise her head, sending a shooting pain through her shoulder and arm.

'Then someone else rang me back from the bureau. They

must have traced my number. He said I must come to the bureau right away, they just got some fax from England that confirmed the same things I told them. They arrested Nzangu. They wanted to know where your papers were so you could help them with their inquiry.'

'But weren't you scared it was a trick?' She remembers Queenie's strange phone call. Did they get her too?

'I was scared like a *sungura*, but Archie took me over there and he waited outside. I said you was British citizen kidnapped, and if you disappear questions will be asked in English Parliament. That put fear into them.'

'How did you find me?' She remembers the sack over her head, the long bumpy ride on the floor of the taxi-van, the echoing room full of buckets. 'I thought no one would ever rescue me and I would die in that place.'

'When they caught him, Nzangu talk-talk non-stop like a *kasuku*. He told them he got this warehouse full of gear out near Mlolongo where they could have took you. Maybe he got scared they killed you and he be done for murdering a British citizen.'

'Oh! How I started to cry when they told me they found you! Lying on the floor tied to the chair like a chicken, all covered in blood!' Njoki lets out a wail. 'My little girl! I thought I lost you same like I lost Jo.'

The nurse intervenes. 'Sshh. Quiet. Let her rest.'

'I'm her grandmother, you know!' Njoki retorts. 'I lost my dear husband to this same *mfisadi*. They left him by the road for dead. Now they try to steal my grandchild away!'

'It's okay, Nyanya Njoki. I'm still alive.' She grits her teeth and heaves herself up until she is sitting with her back against the iron frame of the bed. There is something she needs to ask. 'That fax from England, Lynette – did it have a name on it?'

'I can't remember. Gideon? Giles? Gilbert? I think it began with G.'

'Gillian?'

'Could be. Does it matter now we found you?' Lynette can't stop dimpling her shiny round cheeks.

Njoki's voice is shrill and querulous. 'Main thing is to catch the *mfisadi* over here. The ones that got Jo, and now they nearly got you! Oh God, when I saw you lying like dead and covered in blood –'

'You better go now,' the nurse interrupts. Njoki is holding her so tight she has to be prised away. 'You making her stressed. We need to change the dressings, then she can sleep.'

The nurse offers her two tablets with a glass of water and unwinds the bandage from her head. 'It's looking better. Nothing too serious. Just a big bruise on the temple. You'll be black and blue for a few days. The arm is broken in three places. That will take a bit longer. How does it feel?'

'Mmm. It hurts, but it's more the shock.' Every bone in her body jangles with pain when she moves, but beyond the pain she feels contentment that glows in her like sunlight. She's still alive, and she's done something that needed to be done, her aching body tells her. 'I feared I was going to die in there. They'd dump my body by the roadside, and nobody would find those papers.'

'Try to get some sleep now,' says the nurse. 'You want me to draw the curtains?'

'No. No, leave them open.'

She slides back down on the pillows and gazes out of the window. Her eyelids are drowsy. The nurse must have given her a sedative. Through the square of glass she can see the tops of the trees in the hospital garden. Close by the window, the gracious arch of a Nandi Flame tree heavy with blossom burns bright against the sky. A fat grey *njiwa* flutters its wings and settles among the flowers, cooing its heart out. It reminds her of . . . something . . . what does it remind her of?

Njoki and Lynette kiss her and leave arm in arm, small white shoes, pretty red sandals, tap-tapping together across the polished floor.

BERTHOLD: *Gravity*

As soon as the credits rolled, people started shuffling towards the exit of the cinema, dragging their feet on the worn carpet. Stacey and I waited and topped up our glasses with the wine we had bought at the bar ('Oh, go on then, just a drop!'). Science fiction is not my favourite genre, and I found the storyline was over-complicated and the helmets obscured George Clooney and Sandra Bullock's faces. I was more captivated by Stacey's profile as she sat beside me in the dark, the curve of her cheek and chin, the nape of her neck where the fine coppery hairs curled, her sweet perfume, and beneath the perfume the faint nutty scent of her skin. She was wearing the same tight-fitting green Oxfam dress, which no longer seemed too tight but made her look sensual and shapely like a leafy Venus. My hand had strayed down in between the top buttons and she let it rest there.

'That ending was so beautiful, didn't you think?' *Sniffle sniffle.* 'I didn't know whether it was real or whether it was a dream.'

She leaned closer to me, hunting in her bag for a tissue. A teardrop hung on her cheek, gleaming in the darkness like a rich jewel in an Ethiop's ear.

'Mm,' I replied. It had been my idea, from a perverse mixture of motives, to see this film, but the special effects had made me feel queasy in a way that brought to mind slatki with vodka.

'But I think I prefer the theatre,' she sniffed. 'It's much more *real*. I used to be quite a George Clooney fan because we were both born in 1961, but recently I've been noticing how old he looks.'

'Old? He's only . . .'

'Don't you think he's a bit overrated?'

'Actually, Stacey . . .' I took a sip of wine and paused to savour my moment of triumph, 'I think, in fact, George Clooney's quite a good actor.'

As the house lights rose and the real world came into focus around us, we stayed in our seats and drained the last few drops of lukewarm Sauvignon Blanc into our glasses. Suddenly Stacey started weeping again as though a floodgate of emotion had been opened.

'It reminds me of how I felt when Monty died. I kept hoping he wasn't really dead.'

Was there a note of accusation in her voice?

'It wasn't my fault, you know, Stacey. I tried to grab his lead, but he just dashed across the road. The van appeared out of nowhere.' I put my arm around her. 'White van of destiny meets cute little dog.'

'You took his body to the pub and got drunk.'

'We had to give him a proper send-off.'

'I'm not blaming you, Bertie. I'm just telling you how I feel.' Something in her voice told me she *was* blaming me. 'He was the cutest dog in the world.' She dabbed her eyes. 'Do you think there's an alternative universe somewhere, where he's alive?'

'I'm sure there is.' I held her hand.

I didn't tell her that thirteen years ago the same thing had happened to a cute little girl I was looking after. Was it my fault? I had tormented myself with this question ever since. Sometimes, even now, I would catch a glimpse of a girl or a young woman that took me off guard and spun me over into an alternative life, the life that might have been mine if Meredith had still been alive, if Stephanie and I had still been together.

Stephanie had never forgiven me, and I had never forgiven

myself. Our relationship eventually collapsed under the weight of her accusations: 'You were *supposed* to be responsible, Bertie. How could you have let go of her hand? You're a typical mummy's boy, irresponsible, careless, self-obsessed!'

Was I? Or was I, in fact, as Stacey suggested kindly through a sniffle, just terminally unlucky?

However, this particular cloud had a silver lining. Monty's demise opened up the way for Stacey to move into my flat. I even let her bring the teddies, which she arranged on Mother's dressing table beside the bottle of L'Heure Bleue left by Mother and finished off by Inna. It felt strange and sinful at first to make love in Mother's bed, so full of ghosts, but after a while even that became wonderfully ordinary.

Stacey took over the chair of the Tenants Association vacated by Mrs Cracey, and helped to mount a lively campaign against the proposed fourteen-storey building in the garden, insisting, as Lubetkin would have done, that it should fit harmoniously with its environment and should provide affordable homes for low-income families. When Len's ground-floor flat became available, she helped me arrange for Margaret and Jenny to get the tenancy, aided by the fact that Margaret was now in a wheelchair. So as one chapter closed, a new chapter opened in the life of Lubetkin's Mad Yurt.

From time to time the old mood would come over me, and I would launch into a morose soliloquy on canine and human mortality, the wanton destruction of urban trees, the housing crisis, the unravelling of the post-war consensus, George Clooney's love life and other evils and inequities of our time.

Stacey would watch me with a small smile. 'I'm sure you're right, Bertie,' she would say.

Acknowledgements

This book came from hours spent walking around London, discovering among the acres of new building sites bristling with cranes the remnants of a different, older London, different not just in architecture but also in the human values embedded in those buildings. These included some by Berthold Lubetkin, which exemplified not just bold experimentation with new materials, notably concrete, but an exceptional eye for grace and beauty, as well as a commitment to building a London fit for the needs of its ordinary residents.

I had many guides and interpreters on these walks, whose insights have found their way into these pages, so first of all a big thank you to those who helped me with the basic history and geography. Thanks especially to Donald Sassoon with his comments on the text, and to Joseph Rykwert, who knows a thing or two about modernist architecture. I have learned so much from their generously imparted knowledge, and any mistakes are purely my own. Thanks to Susannah Hamilton for telling me more than I thought I would ever want to know about International Insurance, to Baiju Shah from Sheffield University for checking the Kenya sections, to Glenda Pattenden for her detailed maps of Ally Pally, to Sarah White for first taking me there and for helping me through a personal challenge which almost derailed the book, and to my daughter Sonia for telling me which bits were boring, as only one's children can.

I would also like to thank my agent, Bill Hamilton, and the great team at A. M. Heath, for keeping me on course, and Juliet Annan, my editor at Fig Tree, without whom this book would have been a third longer and much duller. Thank you to Jon Gray for another inspired book jacket. And thank you to Shân Morley Jones for meticulous attention to the proofs, and for claiming, even after the seventh reading, that the book still made her laugh.